The UNDETECTABLES

COURTNEY SMYTH

TITAN BOOKS

The Undetectables
Print edition ISBN: 9781803364780
E-book edition ISBN: 9781803364797

Published by Titan Books
A division of Titan Publishing Group Ltd
144 Southwark Street, London SE1 0UP
www.titanbooks.com

First edition: September 2023
10 9 8 7 6 5 4 3 2 1

A CIP catalogue record for this title is available
from the British Library.

Printed and bound by CPI (UK) Ltd, Croydon, CR0 4YY

For Michael
You were right, you know.

ONE

Six years ago

Theodore Wyatt's greatest regret in life was dying while wearing a cat costume. Though this story is not about him, it is important to know this.

Every year on 31 October, the Broadwick family hosted a Samhain ball. It was described to Theodore as a massive celebration of both the dearly departed and of the Ternion, the three goddesses all of Occulture honoured. This was held in Broadwick Mansion, partly because the Mayoral Offices could not be used in the days surrounding Samhain – due to highly volatile spectral activity in the building – and partly because the Broadwicks liked everyone in Wrackton to be reminded of how well connected they were.

'It's a big deal to be invited to a Broadwick ball, so don't fuck it up,' the Night Mayor of Wrackton had barked at Theodore a few days prior, just as Theodore was making a break for home on the last day of his first year working in the Mayoral Offices.

'How, as a matter of interest, can one get going to a party wrong? Just so I can figure out how offended I should be,' Theodore had asked acidly. He was already very upset at the idea of having to go to a party. Theodore had hoped to spend Samhain as he always had before he'd moved to Wrackton – sitting at home with a book and letting it pass him by. He was Apparent, a non-magical being, and the festival did not mean to him what it meant to everyone else.

The Night Mayor's eye twitched. It could've been annoyance, it could've been that something had got into it at the exact moment he started speaking; Theodore weighed up asking which it was before the Night Mayor choked out, 'If you have to ask… Just remember you're representing the Mayoral Offices as much as yourself, Timothy.'

'It's Theodore.'

'Are you sure?'

Theodore decided maximum offence should be taken.

The Night Mayor had then given him vague directions to the mansion, and followed that up by shoving a *Visit Wrackton: Samhain Etiquette* leaflet into Theodore's hands before walking away while Theodore was still mid-sentence. He still had the leaflet stuffed in his pocket, just in case anyone were to ask him if he had done due diligence in preparing to party.

Now Theodore clung to the edge of the crimson-lit ballroom, looking around for any of his wide-eyed Apparent colleagues, or any Apparent at all. It was a novelty for him, being in an Occult town like Wrackton and seeing magic up close, like visiting a theme park – if theme parks were typically found exactly halfway between Bath and Bristol, should one take a sharp enough left turn towards the faerie Redwoods. Something Theodore could talk about at parties, if he were the sort of person who usually went to parties. Or spoke to anyone at them.

He sidled up to the buffet table, piling enchanting food on a plate and staring at the enchanting décor and the equally enchanting demons, trolls, vampires, faeries and witches in attendance. Some of them were even in costume. This was an important addition conspicuously missing from the leaflet and from the Night Mayor's instructions.

Faeries were the most daunting, ethereally beautiful and draped in avant-garde outfits that could have been abstract costumes, had Theodore not regularly seen faeries at the supermarket wearing something similar. There were several vampires wearing plastic fangs as a nod to Apparent folklore, and Theodore noticed how certain vampires made a big show of laughing uproariously. The folk whose skin had a blue-grey tint were trolls and they glowered from the corners of the ballroom, though Theodore had come to understand too that this was just what their resting faces looked like. He couldn't believe that a mere year ago he hadn't been able to tell the now-obvious differences between each Occulture. No amount of leaflets could've taught him what living in Wrackton had.

'You're Apparent, aren't you?' A tall demon in a bold checked suit and red plastic devil horns sauntered up to him. His angular face was bathed in red, and he raised a strong eyebrow at Theodore's outfit of choice: a black-and-grey-checked shirt, a huge purple cardigan, and wildly unkempt blond hair. It was exactly what he'd put on that morning and had just considered changing out of before he noticed it was late and ran out the door.

'*Apparent*-ly so, yes,' Theodore said weakly, and shoved what he thought was a tiny silver cake into his mouth. This demon was the most attractive individual to look at him since he'd moved to Wrackton and Theodore didn't quite know what to do.

'Isn't this food amazing?' He swallowed. 'A shiny silver cake. It's almost like magic!'

The demon ignored both of his terrible jokes and extended a hand. Theodore juggled his plate into one hand and took the demon's, realising too late that his fingers were still covered in cake crumbs.

'Grey Quinn. I knew you were Apparent, because you're not in costume. Let me help you.' He didn't seem to notice the crumbs. Grey took the plate from him, and in a swift movement jammed a pair of cat ears on Theodore's head. Theodore had not thought he required help with this particular aspect of his person.

'There. Oh, wait.' Grey Quinn produced a marker from his pocket, uncapped it with his teeth and drew onto his face what Theodore both hoped and feared were whiskers.

'*There*. Perfect. Look at us now.' He turned Theodore around to face a mirror on the wall behind them. Theodore had no choice but to see he was indeed a bewhiskered cat, which he felt contradicted Quinn's use of 'perfect'.

He didn't voice his chagrin, though there was much of it; he was not yet aware that this was a grave mistake.

'Come on, smile.' Grey Quinn shook him jovially by the shoulder. 'Get into the spirit of things. It's a party!'

Theodore felt himself smiling, and was uncertain if he'd meant to smile, or if the demon was using magic on him.

'Go on, off you go. Have fun!' Grey Quinn stumbled away.

It was only then that Theodore had three thoughts: one, that he was not going to have fun dressed like this at all; two, that he needed to figure out a way to resist the magically persuasive charm of demons before he was forced into doing something terribly untoward, like robbing a bank or compromising the scientific method; and three, that Grey Quinn was clearly intoxicated.

Theodore wondered how many steps there were between the buffet and the drinks table.

He took another bite of cake.

The lights went out.

The room clamoured with vague concern. The gathered Occult folk pulled lighters, phones and neon witchlight crystals out of their purses and pockets. Their hosts, Imogen and Ezra Broadwick, hastened to calm the crowd.

'Does anyone know where the electricity is kept? Could one of our esteemed scientifically-inclined guests assist us?' Imogen called. Her tone was calm, but her face twisted in the sort of panic one might expect of an individual who didn't know how their home functioned.

Of his own volition this time, Theodore put down his plate of enchanted appetisers and volunteered to find the trip switch.

This, too, was a grave mistake.

'Oh you're too good. And you came in costume, that's so… *darling*. Isn't it *darling*, darling?' Imogen said to her husband, who had already moved across the room to calm everyone. She directed Theodore to the basement and handed him a witchlight crystal to illuminate his way. Theodore had had to learn about witchlights quickly upon moving to Wrackton. They were magical lamps that had their own self-contained energy source – the exact nature of which he had yet to discover, though he expected they involved noble gases – that spectral activity did not affect the way it did other electricity sources. They came in a variety of colours and shapes and Theodore was very partial to the lavender ones, which is precisely what Imogen handed him. He held it up over his head so he could see a path through the ballroom.

'Excuse me. Sorry. Cat coming through. Let miaow-t.'

An older vampire glared at him. Theodore hurried on in silence.

In the darkened basement of Broadwick Mansion, Theodore successfully found the trip switch. He thought about the plate of mini iridescent sandwiches he was going to return to. The last few days of working from home due to the intensity of the spectral disturbance in the Offices meant he hadn't had access to faerie-catered food, and had missed out on numerous sandwich-and-tea opportunities as a result. As he closed the fuse box, he reasoned that he didn't mind staying in Wrackton another year, especially when things quietened down after Samhain. The town had so many things going for it that he couldn't get anywhere else. For instance, the sandwiches. There could've been an entire *Visit Wrackton* leaflet just on the sandwiches.

Theodore pressed the switch on a freestanding lamp near the doorway to check he'd been successful. It did not turn on, and he noticed the bulb was askew.

In a move perhaps even more regrettable than accepting the cat costume, he reached inside the lampshade without unplugging it.

He didn't hear someone approaching behind him. He didn't see the flex on the lamp twitch and jerk twice. He didn't hear anything again.

TWO

Also six years ago, at the same ball

Mallory Hawthorne's greatest desire was to find a dead body. She – who this story is really about – was fourteen when this wish was granted.

'Tell me then, what does an "undependable" do?' The older witch Mallory was talking to sipped her drink, which sloshed onto the floor a little as she did exaggerated air quotes.

Mallory was losing the will to live. Her father had brought her to the annual Broadwick ball, hosted by her best friend Cornelia's parents. The night was meant to honour the Ternion and to celebrate the life and death of loved ones, but Mallory often thought it was just an excuse for folk to gather enough gossip about each other to last until the next Equinox. Things had been briefly exciting when the lights went out, but now they were back on and conversation was in full swing once again.

'No, I said *Undetectables*.' Mallory fixed a smile on her face. 'The Undetectables, Private Investigators. It's an agency myself and two of my fr— colleagues are launching tonight. Here's our card.' She passed it over, hopeful butterflies forming in her stomach. Mallory had reasoned that the party was a prime opportunity to find clientele.

The witch took it and peered at it, her eyes telling Mallory that she needed her glasses and could not for the life of her read the card, which was printed on cardstock stolen from Cornelia's parents. Nonetheless, Mallory was proud of it. On one side it said *The Undetectables* below a logo featuring a pentagram, the symbol for pi in the centre. Her other best friend, Diana Cheung-Merriweather, had suggested they needed a bold Occult reference to symbolically represent their witchly rule of three. Because the Ternion – the goddesses Hexana, Blair and Elisabella – were depicted as three powerful witches, triplets and witches in groups of three were thought to be particularly powerful. Truthfully, when Mallory took the hands of her friends, she often felt a pulse of magic flowing through her and back again, so there was probably something to it. The pi symbol came from Cornelia arguing that if they were symbolising themselves, they should also symbolise private investigators in an amusing way. Mallory had eventually agreed to it all.

Underneath the logo was the phrase '*helping you detect the undetectable*' in flowing script.

'Great stuff, I'm sure. You're a great girl, very tall.' The witch patted her on the side of the face, reaching up to do so. Mallory *was* very tall for fourteen, and all of the stately Occult folk she'd approached with cards and offers of PI services over the last hour seemed determined to compliment her on her height. Her long dark hair was drawn back into a braid, and her pale skin had been dusted with glitter as part of her costume. Diana had sourced three identical lace dresses, cloaks and pointed hats for the occasion, and was resolutely immune to Mallory's hesitance at drawing such obvious attention to her appearance.

'Just give us a call any time,' Mallory said politely to the witch, and excused herself, wondering where Diana was.

She fixed her gaze on Cornelia, who was glaring at the retreating back of the Night Mayor as he stuffed an Undetectables card into his pocket.

'Cornelia?' Mallory prompted as she arrived at her elbow, mildly concerned. Cornelia was watching the Night Mayor with such an intent look on her face that Mallory suspected she had cast a listening spell and was trying to hear what he was saying to a tall, check-suited and devil-horned demon in the corner. Fair-skinned and willowy, Cornelia had a short pixie cut, hazel eyes and glasses that were forever slipping down her nose. She wore the same costume as Mallory, though hers was hidden under one of a perpetual rotation of fancy coats, and she had chosen to forgo the glitter. Mallory smiled fondly at Cornelia, who didn't notice.

'That's all mine handed out,' Diana said, appearing from the middle of the crowd, adjusting her sleeves. '*Hexana*, what's Cornelia doing?'

'Spying on the Night Mayor,' Mallory said, biting her lip.

'Did he take a card?' Diana raised an eyebrow, brushing her dark curls off her shoulder.

'He certainly put one into his pocket. Shall we get drinks?' She held out an arm.

Diana was as short as Mallory was tall, soft and rounded all over, and striking as anything, the glitter dusted on her light brown skin catching in the neon glow of the ballroom.

'Well. That's something at least. Anyone take you up on our offer?'

Mallory shook her head. Very few Occult folk had pocketed the cards or slipped them inside their impractical clutch bags; she could see them littering the floor and abandoned on the buffet table. No one had asked them to solve anything. Mallory, though mildly disappointed, was not deterred.

'Cornelia.' Diana grabbed Cornelia's other arm and tugged her away from her intent listening. 'Learn anything useful?'

Cornelia scowled, ending the listening spell. 'I don't know if he needs mysteries solved, but I bet he's committed some crimes.'

'On what basis?' Diana asked.

'The scientific basis of I really don't like him,' Cornelia said, and refused to elaborate further.

They helped themselves to drinks. There were various spells and enchantments making the food entertaining and the lights bounce strangely off the walls. Still, magic, for the most part, simply was; Mallory could magically paint a wall, though it would take the same amount of physical effort as standing with a roller. She often thought about how little the Occult as a whole cared for magical discovery. Year after year, it was the same thing.

'I really thought this party would be different to the million others we've been to.' Diana sighed into her drink.

It was true that they had all been dragged by their parents to infinite Occult parties. Cornelia's parents were important members of the Ghoul Council, which was responsible for all things relating to and benefiting ghosts, the ins and outs of which none of them were particularly interested in. As far as they were concerned, it meant that the Broadwicks threw important magical parties and did important magical things, and this meant a lot of important magical folk were around, as well as some Apparent scientists, or so Mallory had heard. An idea struck her as she took a sip of a drink bathed in the red glow of the lights above.

'The problem, clearly, is that we haven't established a client base to use in our agency elevator pitch. So I propose we now go in search of a mystery to solve. Doesn't have to be a big one, I don't think, just something concrete.' Mallory pulled a witchlight out of her pocket. 'Let's start in the basement, and work our way up.'

Mallory led the way down the basement stairs, holding her witchlight high. It was dark and eerily silent now that the hubbub of the party was behind them. She pushed open the door. Diana held up her witchlight too, illuminating the darkness in a cold blue glow.

Though they had been looking for a mystery, Mallory was not quite prepared for the sight that greeted them.

'Oh. Oh, goddess.' Diana took a step back. Cornelia made a small strangled noise and gripped Diana's arm. Mallory ignored them both and moved into the room, having locked eyes with a man wearing faux cat ears and a huge purple cardigan. He stood over the body of a man wearing faux cat ears and an equally huge purple cardigan.

'Am I...' The ghost gestured at the body. *His* body. 'Can you go get an adult for me? Please? Perhaps the Broadwicks?

I believe I've had an accident and I need medical attention,' he babbled.

'Diana?' Mallory said gently, recovering fastest. Her brain seemed to have caught on before her body that her greatest wish had come true, a thread of excitement bubbling through her. Diana, who had backed into the corner with Cornelia and was staring at both the ghost and his body with trepidation, snapped out of her cocoon of terror.

'Light?'

Mallory hummed her assent, and Diana gently wrested Cornelia's witchlight out of her hand and set it down in front of the body, placing her own to the other side of it. Mallory set hers on a high shelf, to light as much of the room as possible. She noted an extinguished witchlight was already there, though she was unsure why it wasn't lit.

'Cornelia.' Mallory turned to her friend. 'Please close the basement door. We need to secure the scene for Mr...'

'Theodore. Wyatt. No Mister, that was my father's name. Literally, that was my father's name, letters came addressed to Mr Mister Wyatt, it was all very confusing at times.' His hands were pressed to the side of his face, static sparking as he spoke rapidly.

Cornelia slammed the door shut and slid down it, her face not betraying any of her feelings. Mallory knew she was not easily scared, but meeting a fresh Samhain ghost was practically unheard of.

Mallory sat next to Theodore's body, keeping eye contact with his ghost. She spoke softly and quietly, as though to a frightened animal, calm certainty guiding her actions. She would look back on this night and recognise it as the very moment she knew exactly what path her life was meant to take. The body on the floor was largely drained of colour, the right hand blackened and the muscles and tendons raised and red around the bulb that was still clutched in it. She did not react strongly to the sight of a dead body; it was dead, and she was there, and both felt factually acceptable. Ghost-Theodore's hand was not as badly damaged, and thankfully did not contain a lightbulb.

He rubbed his hair and knocked the cat ears from his head. Both his and Mallory's eyes flicked upwards as the ears rematerialised immediately. They were to be, it seemed, a permanent fixture. He blinked rapidly in alarm.

'Before we go get anyone, we need to establish some facts. Where did you come from?' Mallory folded her hands in her lap.

'I originally came from Oughteron, I used to live in a house and now I live in an apartment here in Wrackton, which is supposedly twinned with Oughteron, but I suspect they're less twins and more deeply distant cousins, and I look at human remains and also remains of not humans ah-haha I am a forensic para-anthropologist and I was hired by the Ghoul Council to investigate the source of spectral disturbances and I was made to come to this party and a demon wearing fake devil horns, at least I think they're fake devil horns, gave me cat ears and I came down here to fix the lights and now I am still here and I don't have any sandwiches,' Theodore said in one breath. A wild giggle escaped him.

'Okay, Theodore,' Mallory said gently, knowing instinctively that she needed to keep him calm. 'Can you describe what happened when you got to the basement?'

Theodore did, repeating himself often, but he couldn't quite explain what had happened when he'd reached into the lamp.

'As I did it I remember thinking, "Is this plugged in?" and wondering why I hadn't checked. And then… then…' He looked down at his body. 'Okay. This might sound odd, but can you confirm: am I dead?'

'Oh, definitely.' Cornelia inched forward so she was now sitting beside Diana, who was carefully scanning the room, her eyes lingering on every shadow, every cobweb.

Theodore made a high-pitched sound and buried his face in his hands.

'Why haven't I passed over?'

'Weren't you working under a Ghoul Council license?'

Mallory knew what Cornelia meant, but Cornelia had a tendency towards bluntness.

'What Cornelia means is, through your work with the Ghoul Council, did you happen to learn what a Samhain ghost is?' Mallory amended kindly.

Theodore looked at her and chewed his thumb absently. A spatter of static fuzzed from his cheek.

'Yes. I think I'm in shock. Ah-haha!' He giggled again. 'Shock, bad pun. Yes. They mentioned… rules. The spectral disturbances in the Mayoral Offices – you know about those. The ones around Samhain. Though we Apparents just call that Halloween. You probably know that.'

'We go to an Apparent school in Oughteron,' Diana said, her eyes on the lamp. She beckoned Mallory over to look at it, pointing urgently at the plug socket and the lamp flex on the floor. Mallory shook her head subtly, unsure what Diana was trying to show her. Diana rolled her eyes impatiently.

'Oh, how nice for you. Education and such. Wonderful,' Theodore babbled. 'Well, of course, Samhain ghosts are a theoretical possibility, but there are a number of conditions required to qualify. Strong enough pull to remain on earth. Die on Samhain, obviously. Body rejects ghost immediately and doesn't rejoin within ten minutes of death. Something about a positive electrical charge, I think, perhaps something as simple as a static shock.' He ticked the conditions off on his hands, spraying static into the air.

Mallory had just noted that reciting facts seemed to calm him slightly, when Theodore opened his mouth again.

'It's incredibly rare and unlikely, as in you could've come in here and found a unicorn. Have you ever seen a unicorn? I feel maybe they're not that rare, I've never actually seen a bat or an owl so maybe there are just—'

'And do you think there's a possibility you yourself could be a Samhain ghost?' Mallory tilted her head towards the body, and back to Theodore.

'I don't know. I sat here for a while, when I woke up, and it took me a bit to realise I couldn't leave because I would still… be here.'

Mallory allowed a moment's silence to elapse as Theodore took in the weight of his own words.

'Mallory,' Diana said finally, 'can we speak on the stairs?'

'We'll be right back,' Mallory said. Theodore nodded fervently and wiped his eyes. The whiskers smudged onto his fingers. He rubbed at them again, a hopeful look crossing his face.

Wordlessly, Diana pulled a small mirror from her pocket and held it up so that Theodore could see in real time as the whiskers rematerialized. He sagged with resignation.

'I'm a cat. I'm going to be a cat forever. The last living thing I said was "let miaow-t." I shall meditate on this until your return.'

'Okay, so, he's been murdered,' Diana whispered as soon as they closed the door behind them.

'What?' Mallory and Cornelia said together.

'I think an important element of being electrocuted to death involves the item in question being plugged in. And the lamp is now unplugged. He's Apparent, so maybe a demon followed him down here and used persuasion magic to convince him to put his hand inside the light, or someone hexed him. It just doesn't make sense. Sure it's possible he was thinking about something else, like—'

'Sandwiches,' Cornelia said. 'He mentioned sandwiches.'

'Right. But if he thought to check if it was plugged in but didn't actually check, doesn't it sound like he *couldn't* stop himself? Plus, now that it's unplugged… who unplugged it, and why? And why *him*? I mean he seems great, just…' Diana trailed off. Admittedly, nothing else needed to be said. Theodore seemed harmless and not enough of a threat to be the target of an Occult killing, yet someone had done it anyway.

'That's our job to figure out,' Mallory said decisively. 'We find out who he spoke to tonight, who might've wanted him dead. He mentioned a demon put the cat ears on him.' Mallory rubbed her fingers together, reaching for the memory. 'Devil horns. We should investigate Theodore's body for clues, check the lamp for any evidence, and then, Cornelia, we should probably tell your parents you found a body in the basement. While they're preoccupied, we could try interviewing folk, see who saw what.'

Cornelia snorted, Mallory assumed at the idea of telling her parents there was a body in their basement, but nodded.

'I'm in.'

'Diana, are you in?'

Diana nodded too. 'I'll get started with the lamp.'

Mallory took a breath, excitement bubbling again, and opened the door. Theodore had not moved from where he sat beside his own body.

'Theodore Wyatt, congratulations. You are the first official client of the Undetectables, Private Investigators. We are going to solve your murder.'

THREE

Now: nine days to Samhain

If Mallory's life had a narrator, they would now say something along the lines of: reader, the Undetectables did *not* solve Theodore's murder.

Despite this, by the time Mallory was twenty, Theodore was a permanent fixture in her life. One she had almost no say in, though she wouldn't have it any other way. His personality had expanded over that time, burgeoning from the skittish fresh ghost she'd met in the basement to the personification of the word effervescent. As for Mallory, though she had grown taller and her hair had grown longer, she was otherwise visibly unchanged in those years.

'Hello, Mallory, here's your post. You should really consider iron-proofing the post box, literally any semi-corporeal ghost could steal whatever they wanted. Although Wrackton's ghost population would need to increase by at least 100 per cent in order for that to even begin to be an issue.' Theodore flounced into her kitchen and tossed a small bundle of letters down beside her without waiting for a response.

He also hadn't given her a chance to open the door when he'd rung the iron doorbell, or indeed a chance to put away her phone or laptop so he didn't break it. She stiffly threw a blanket filled with iron filings over her most precious electronics. Iron, when prepared with the correct spellwork, helped contain Theodore's static charge, forcing him to be more than semi-corporeal, which was the only reason he was not banned from indoor spaces.

That, and he'd have complained a lot.

He kept talking. 'You will not believe what I was given today.' He pulled a book out of his bag and brandished it at her. 'Take it, it is a most cursed object and I wish to have nothing more to do with it.'

Mallory shuffled forward to take it from him, grimacing in pain.

'I care not what you do with it,' he continued. 'Use it as a doorstopper for all I care.' Mallory could feel his warmth starting to fill the room. Contrary to popular belief about the chilling presence of an apparition, Samhain ghosts generated a lot of palpable heat, something Mallory was grateful for the comfort of on all but the hottest days of the year.

He handed over the book and stood back, looking expectantly at her over the spray of static that lifted from the pages and both their hands. Mallory sat down carefully and settled it in her lap, the light pressure sending an ache up her thighs. She closed her eyes, her fingers resting on the cover. It seemed too many steps to open the book, look inside it, read the words and comprehend their meaning.

'Can you just tell me what it is, please?' Mallory asked.

'Well. WELL. Let me set the scene. I was working in the lab today,' he started. 'I was diligently, *diligently*, filling out a new start-of-season report on the instruments the Offices need for me to investigate the spectral disturbance this year, when this Ghoul Council rep came by and all but *threw* this book at me, saying "new rules", and nothing else, like I wasn't worthy of a conversation. Or a sentence. Or an introduction!' He paced up and down, waving his arms around exaggeratedly.

Mallory picked up the letters, his words flowing over her head no matter how hard she tried to grasp them.

There were a number of reasons why the Undetectables hadn't solved Theodore's murder.

One was that there hadn't been enough evidence – or at least, none anyone was willing to share with three fourteen-year-old girls, no matter how much effort they'd expended on finding it. Theodore's death was ruled as accidental – as he had, by his own admission, not been certain he'd checked before he put his hand inside the lamp, and he had died of electrocution.

Two, Cornelia was pulled out of school a few months later to be home-schooled, where she set her sights on studying entomology. She was told she 'lacked focus' – and was 'destructively disruptive' and 'either needed to stop bringing invertebrates to school or stop bringing herself' – so she disproved everyone by focusing so hard on bugs and getting into university that anything outside of this lens was all but forgotten. Around the same time, Diana had discovered a prop-making course and poured all her spare time into latex moulds and the potential future of working in television. Meetings of the Undetectables became fewer and further between, and then, eventually, non-existent.

Reason three was by far the most difficult for Mallory to accept.

'...And then they said, they actually said to me that if I even *think* there's another ghost in the Mayoral Offices, I have to tell them about it or I could risk Isolation.' He pulled at his cardigan anxiously.

'Sorry, Theo.' Mallory scrunched her eyes shut. 'Sorry. What's Isolation again?' The word meant something to her, but the meaning of it had floated away as soon as it had arrived. This was happening to her more and more lately.

'Where they put me in a ghostlight and throw me and the light to the bottom of Bonemarrow Lake. Forever. And that's a long time, Mallory.'

Ghostlights were crystal balls used to trap powerful spectral apparitions – apparently including Samhain ghosts – for the purposes of punishment, and over the last six years the concept of them had grown to be Theodore's biggest fear.

'And they want you to do what now that's different than before?'

'Before, it was just if I thought there was another Samhain ghost nearby, I was to not initiate contact and instead inform the Ghoul Council. Now it's if I think there is another ghost, of any sort, in my vicinity, I have to inform the Ghoul Council. The same Council that hired me to look for, among other things, ghosts attached to anthropological matter now want me to tell them about any ghosts I think might exist. When that's what I'm specifically there for. It makes me think they don't read my reports. Or understand me at all.' He trailed off at the end, his face falling into a frown.

'Oh. I'm sorry, Theodore. That sounds...' Finishing the sentence was too hard.

'Ridiculous? I thought so too. I knew you'd agree with me, because you are so reasonable,' Theodore said, extending his arms triumphantly. When Mallory didn't move to agree, he suddenly seemed to run out of whatever burst of furious energy had driven him and really looked at her properly, his eyes filled with concern. 'Mallory, are you okay? I'm sorry, I should've—'

'I'm fine, Theo. I'm almost always happy to see you.' She forced a smile onto her face; it was true, but Theodore only had two modes: dramatic and more dramatic.

He visited her most days, and she was in varying states of well-being at those times, but this was a particularly bad day for her and he could – finally – clearly see it.

This was the third reason she'd never solved Theodore's murder.

What had started out as aches and pains and relentless exhaustion not long after that Samhain ball had morphed into her dragging herself through her final years of school, just trying to survive until she eventually got a diagnosis. She suffered the fear she had made it up until finally being told by an Apparent doctor that she was, in fact, actually ill. She'd had to look up the spelling of fibromyalgia when they'd told her.

He tilted his head. 'Are you sure? If I called Cornelia and Diana right now, would you tell them the same thing?'

'Not only wouldn't you, you couldn't.' Mallory felt a sting at the mention of her friends.

She hadn't seen them in eighteen months, which felt like forever and no time all at once. Thinking about them made her sad, imagining them going to bars and shopping without a second thought, working all day and still having energy to cook food or clean their living space, whole days not taken up by medical appointments and resting afterwards. Their lives were not the same, grim, choose-your-unadventure Mallory's was.

'Of course I couldn't, but it is not nice to say so.' Theodore raised an eyebrow. 'Have you called them recently? Nothing brightens your day quite like best friend banter!'

'I'm fine. Just a bad day.' She ignored the suggestion and shuffled through the letters, barely glancing at yet another cheery postcard from her parents, who were both abroad while Mallory's dad held what he referred to as a 'last hurrah' archaeological professorship. Each postcard signified how terribly guilty they both felt about leaving their disabled only child alone, no matter how many times Mallory tried to convince them she was both an adult and capable of managing. She paused on the last letter in the pile. It was a cream envelope, addressed to the Undetectables. The first letter the Undetectables had ever received. Mallory frowned and slowly ripped it open, the movement sending a stabbing ache up her forearm.

'What's that?'

'Letter.'

'Thanks, Mallory, I almost held a doctorate and failed to learn what letters were,' Theodore teased.

'If only you'd got to the end of it, you'd have learned what books were too.' Mallory smiled tiredly at him.

She unfolded a typed letter on crisp paper. A card fluttered to her lap, and Mallory's breath hitched when she saw the familiar logo embossed on it. She set it to one side and focused on the letter.

Dear the Undetectables,
Wrackton needs your help. I am writing to you as my last hope,
as no other private services wish to take this case on, such is the
delicate nature of it.

An Apparent by the name of Edward Kuster was last seen
alive in the Mayoral Offices on 2 October. He was found dead in
his bedroom in Oughteron some days ago. The Apparent police
believe this was an Occult murder, due to the specifics of the
case. As I'm sure you know, murder is in direct contravention
of the Unified Magical Liaison's Do No Harm Charter. This
must be solved.

An esteemed member of the community would like you to aid
in the investigation – your discretion is appreciated at this time.

Call the number below and the case is yours, should you
want it.

Best regards,
J. Gabbott

Mallory's eyes clouded over as she read, but she forced them
back over and over the lines. The letter was short, but her brain
could scarcely understand what it was asking of her. She read it
twice more. It didn't seem real.

'What is it?' Theodore plucked the letter from her fingers and
held it up to his face, scanning it. His face brightened. 'A murder!
Another murder case for the Undetectables to solve!' He snapped
his fingers. 'Call Cornelia and Diana, right now, they'll want
to know. What time is it in Vancouver? Though Diana doesn't
really sleep, so it probably doesn't matter.'

'I don't want to bother them,' Mallory said, unable to keep irritation from creeping into her voice. It wasn't like she was in any fit state to do the most basic tasks of living, let alone solve a murder. She took the letter back and folded it up, resisting the urge to crumple it into a ball.

'You could never bother them.'

'Just leave it, Theo,' Mallory said sharply.

'They're your best friends. And this is a murder case, addressed to your agency. I don't see how there could be any bothering.' Theodore's face was earnest.

'Cornelia's in Sheffield studying, or in London on placement or something – or maybe she got a job there, I've no idea. She doesn't talk to me much any more. And Diana has worked so hard to get into set dressing, I don't want to be any part of the reason she leaves.' A sick feeling pooled in Mallory's stomach. Theodore never pushed contacting Cornelia and Diana this hard, and she had long since learned that if something felt too good to be true, it likely was.

'But I—'

'Was this you? Did you write this?' Mallory asked, awash with shame and embarrassment at the idea she could be so easily fooled.

'It's typed, Mallory. I cannot use a computer.'

'You could easily have asked someone else to do it.'

'First of all, I did not invent a fake murder, so perhaps write that one down. Secondly, they've always supported you, why would this be any different?'

'They're not here any more.'

'But they're always here. In your heart.' Theodore placed his hands over his chest. Mallory was only slightly sure he wasn't mocking her.

'Let's just stop talking about this,' Mallory suggested, the words more biting than she'd intended.

Cornelia and Diana had been extremely supportive, but Mallory had difficulty swallowing the news that there was no known cure for her symptoms, magical or medical.

As her friends had planned to leave Wrackton, Mallory had grown more and more frustrated. They had limitless energy. They were not bound by a need for sleep. She could not travel to visit them, though they'd asked her over many times. She could not start university, which she'd wanted. She felt little pieces of herself slipping away as Diana and Cornelia grew into themselves. She was stuck in her house taking gap year after gap year until she'd realised that the number she'd taken now amounted to how long it would've taken her to finish a forensic science degree, had she been able to. They were gone now. Her friends had moved away. Her remaining old friends had stopped asking her to hang out as much, because she was never able to. The furthest Mallory had been from home in recent years had been to Oughteron to see her Apparent doctor, and that was just the next town over. All Mallory really had was Theodore. He meant the world to her, as both her best friend and her mentor, but every time she looked at him, she remembered that she had not solved his murder, and every day it made her want to cry.

'Anyway,' Theodore said, regaining control of the conversation, 'that letter seems pertinent. It being the countdown to Samhain… No. Maybe you're not well enough for this today.'

'What? I'm fine.' Mallory pulled a blanket over her. Theodore's warming the room was helping her muscles loosen a little. She was feeling better than she had all day, but a headache still crept up her spine and into the back of her skull.

'Great!'

Abruptly, some of Theodore's energy returned. He fizzed around the edges with excitement.

'It's coming up on six years since I met my untimely end. Normally the anniversary makes me desperately sad—'

This was an understatement.

'—but I decided – as of three minutes ago – that this year, we are simply going to solve the murder of Edward Kuster. I still think you should call Diana and Cornelia and let them know about it; this would be so exciting for us to take on.' He folded his arms shyly. 'And then, if there's time, we could try again at my murder? I could then face my killer and give the Speech.' He smiled broadly.

The Speech was a missive that had been written and rewritten many times over of various things Theodore wanted to say to his killer's face. He often workshopped it with Mallory, to the point that she could recite it in her sleep.

'I think this will be great for your skill set. You already know a great deal about DNA scanning and fingerprinting – to no avail in the quest to solve my murder, but still relevant information even without a database to compare to – and fibres, et cetera. Maybe this is where we've failed in the past. My hubris, destroying chances for us both.' He took a deep, unnecessary breath, as ghosts did not need to breathe, and continued, plucking the letter back up off the sofa. 'Then this letter, from – oh, I wonder who "esteemed member of the community" is? That could be anyone. We could try making a mind map, perhaps, figure out who it could be before we begin.'

Mallory shook her head, unwanted anger entering her stomach. Even if Theodore couldn't have typed the letter himself, he could've asked a colleague to do it.

Theodore continued, his fists clenched in determination. 'That's *two known* Occult murders, including me. They require a strictly magical approach, scientifically speaking. I'm thinking we could use a magical fingerprint scanner first, say on the lightbulb, then if that yields nothing we just revisit the mass spectrometer idea. And then we find out about whatever is happening with this new murder I had nothing to do with. This is a great plan, Mallory, one I am very proud to have spent four seconds thinking about before I shared it.' Theodore tapped his fists together with finality, and a spray of static ended his speech. He looked at her expectantly.

Mallory could only think about how tired she was. How many steps were involved in getting her spell fingerprinting machine plans out again. In using magic, which she didn't do so much any more.

'That's going to take a lot of magical energy...' Mallory said slowly. Energy she didn't have.

'I know, I know it takes a lot of energy out of you,' Theodore said hurriedly. 'But just think how *good* it'll feel. Both emotionally and also next year, when you'll be starting your degree. But mostly emotionally.'

He'd said 'next year' every gap year she'd taken.

'There are nine days to my anniversary, so if we started right now that'll give us—'

Mallory couldn't take it any more.

The bitterness and the anger at how stuck she was rose up her throat, where she wrestled with it for a moment, torn between not wanting to hurt Theodore, and wanting him to stop putting so much pressure on her.

She gave in.

'Stop. Theodore, just fucking stop. Please. I'm so tired.' A tear tracked down her face, followed by another, and another until she was sobbing, each breath making her head throb. 'Nobody cares about this as much as you do any more. I'm really sorry. I can't do it. I can't solve your murder. Cornelia and Diana left because they don't care about it or us, and I don't have it in me to care either!'

Theodore stared at her, the fuzz of static intensifying. He dropped papers he must've had tucked into his cardigan and charged at her door, not bothering to open it. He went through it, and was gone.

Mallory cried alone in a rapidly cooling room.

It took hours for Mallory to both wake up on the couch and realise that she was, perhaps, the worst person she knew by a clear mile.

Theodore wouldn't trick her like that. He also wouldn't have sulked for very long if he had. The fact he wasn't here, waiting for her to wake, told her all she needed to know. The letter wasn't from him. It was real.

Mallory felt another pang in her chest. She had driven him away for no good reason.

Not for no reason, though.

She did not feel worthy of Theodore, most of the time. He had been wonderful when she started getting sick, and had never given up on her. All he'd asked was that she didn't give up on him. And she still had. It was the worst thing she could've done to him.

This was as good as it got for her. Mallory had an opportunity, but she was too tired to do anything about it. Labs were not built for people with pain. Very little was. Even being in Theodore's lab had become so uncomfortable, not just because it was impractical for her body, but because she didn't like being in Cornelia's house without Cornelia there, or without Diana sharing a joke or making a ludicrous statement for them all to debate at length.

And what would she even say if she did go to university next year when she was twenty-one, miles behind her peers who would be tiny children of seventeen and eighteen? There wasn't anything that sounded good to her. *I'm sick. I've been ill. I have a chronic illness. I have a pain thing. Life is pain. Existing is harder for me than it is for other people. I've been on a physical journey.*

I'm a late bloomer.

It all felt impossible to overcome. But even if she stayed in Wrackton she didn't have a lot of options.

Magic hurt too much to do. It took the same amount of energy to cast spells as physically doing the activity by non-Occult means, but Mallory had quickly learned that not being able to break magic down into steps meant she overexerted herself without realising. She was still a witch, but with basically no functional powers.

She made herself tea and found some biscuits she just about had the energy to eat, thinking about Cornelia and Diana and how easily they'd moved on, even though they of course had to. She'd told them to. Mallory hated how much she missed them when they probably didn't think of her at all.

Her hands curled around the cup and she felt another pang of dreadfulness over Theodore. She'd go visit him tomorrow, if she could. Or maybe he'd come back over again, like nothing happened. She unfolded the letter from J. Gabbott and looked at the number enclosed, wondering what would happen if she called it and feeling ridiculous for even contemplating it. There was no way she could go to Cornelia and Diana with this; she had been telling the truth when she'd said she didn't want to bother them.

Her phone rang, the noise startling her, mostly because it never rang these days.

It was Cornelia.

She fumbled putting the tea down, slopping some of it on her coffee table and on her well-thumbed forensic science books as she answered. The phone line crackled, and she worried Theodore had managed to break it earlier.

'Mallory!' Cornelia said, sounding very far away.

'Cornelia, how are you? This is so funny, I was just thinking about—'

'Diana...' The line crackled, fading in and out. 'Diana... murdered. Come... my house. Now.'

PERIMORTEM I

Edward Kuster dreamt of eating pizza when he died.

He would tell you, were he still alive, that he could smell it. The grease and the cheese. The tomato and the peppers. That he could hear the sound of the cardboard tabs lifting free, and the sudden burst of smell as trapped steam was permitted to escape the inside of the box. The feel of the stuffed crust between his fingers as he lifted the first slice without even bothering to give it a perfunctory dip in the garlic sauce.

The perfect pizza, the perfect slice, the perfect moment.

He would tell you how it tasted as he no longer held the slice, but instead it was unceremoniously shoved down his throat by an unseen hand.

He would tell you, were he not too busy choking, that it takes the average human two minutes to reach unconsciousness and seven to die from asphyxiation. Edward was asleep and therefore not conscious enough to struggle. It was a short death. He would tell you what it felt like to realise, just before dream-unconsciousness set in, that his tongue had freed itself from its muscular tether and lodged inside his throat, amid a chewed mass of glorified open sandwich. He would tell you how much he hated the sickening metallic taste of blood forcing its way around the blockage and the remaining stump of his tongue, down into his stomach, bile rising to meet it but having nowhere to escape as air refused to enter his lungs.

What he could not tell you was when he stopped noticing anything at all. Research suggests the human brain retains awareness of death for up to ten minutes after expiry.

Edward cannot confirm.

He would not think to tell you that, before he died, a tuneless whistle snaked through his bedroom, circling the ceiling as it watched its mark, creeping along the carpet to the foot of his bed.

This tuneless noise watched him sleep.

He would not tell you this, because Edward did not know. It had been a day like any other – October drawing in, the promise of leaves crisp and dying and cold, lonely winter nights ahead of him. This particular piece of knowledge would not have impacted the outcome.

The whistling worked its way into his ear, into his head, where the sound helped fabricate something pleasant for the moment of lucidity before Edward succumbed to death. He did not know this either.

FOUR

Mallory could not run these days, but she forced her body to propel her at the fastest walk she could muster to Cornelia's house. She'd had the wherewithal to grab her satchel, shove the letter in her pocket, and to put on a coat, but it was woollen and did nothing to stop the sheeting rain pummelling her as she eventually threw herself up the steps to Cornelia's front door and hammered the side of her fist on it, pain exploding on contact, her limbs frozen and her head pounding but neither as loud or as demanding as the painful hammering of her heart. Diana could not be dead. She couldn't be. Not like this.

There was no answer. Mallory stepped back and squinted up into the rain, her hair whipping around her face as she tried to see any signs of life. The Broadwick Mansion was three interconnecting grey stone townhouses, but not one light was on in any of the visible windows.

She knocked a few more times, ringing the bell insistently, but nobody came. Her heart picked up even faster, blood rushing into her ears. Maybe Cornelia was in trouble. Maybe they were both inside the house with a killer on the loose and Mallory was the last person Cornelia had called.

Her hands shaking, she pulled her bag off her back. It took her a few tries to open the buckle, but she scrabbled around at the bottom and found what she was looking for.

Her fingers cold and stiff, she took out the lock picks she'd carried around since she was twelve and pushed them into the lock. She fumbled, trying to find the right tension, her frozen fingers and the driving rain making it impossible to get a good grip. There was a click and she held the door to straighten herself up, but it opened inwards as she leaned her weight on it and she all but fell in on top of Diana.

'I thought I heard something. We were in the basement,' Diana said, before shouting, 'Cornelia! Mallory's here and she's trying to break in!' Then 'Oh,' as Mallory grabbed her in a fierce hug, knocking the breath out of her.

'Are you real? Are you alive?' Mallory asked, her voice catching as her lungs burned for air.

'I am real. Real annoyed at how wet you are. Let's get you inside. Why didn't you call a taxi, or ask me to come get you?'

Mallory gaped at her, but Diana shook her head and led her by the arm into the warmth of the kitchen. She was dimly aware that the lights were on at the back of the house, and that, at the back of the kitchen, the door to the basement was open, voices coming from below.

'Cornelia…' Mallory said weakly, but couldn't form the rest of the sentence.

'She's downstairs with Theodore. Do you want some tea? Hold on, let me get you some warm clothes.'

Diana concentrated for a second and a pair of joggers and a jumper appeared on the table. 'These are mine, let me resize the trousers.' She concentrated again, whispering, 'Lengthen, expand,' and the clothes grew until they looked like they would fit someone eleven inches taller than Diana. It had been a while since Mallory had seen such casual magic, and she felt a pang of longing.

'They'll be wide on you, but it'll get you warm. I'll dry the ones you're wearing, too.' She ushered Mallory up the stairs, letting her take her time, and into the guest bathroom.

'Do you need help?'

Mallory nodded, and without further comment Diana started pulling her wet clothes off. Mallory's body was in shock, the cold deep inside her bones, the chill already seizing every single muscle.

'I think this is the fastest I have ever gone from hello to undressing a girl before.' Diana grinned, but turned her back as Mallory pulled off her wet bra and didn't turn around until Mallory had pulled the jumper on herself. She forced Mallory to let her help her put the trousers on, handed her a pair of socks and clicked her fingers twice. Mallory heard the distant rumble of a kettle boiling down in the kitchen.

'You're still freezing. There's only one thing for it.' Diana steered her down the hallway, past Cornelia's bedroom, to a room Mallory had spent an inordinate amount of time in over the years. 'We're going to have to warm you like a bug.'

Red light seeped through the doorjamb as Diana flicked her fingers and the door swung open, warm air curling around Mallory's limbs.

'Sorry it has to be Cornelia's bug room, this entire house is freezing. There's a fireplace in my room, I've just never lit one before. I actually don't know a single fire spell, if you'd believe it. I should fix that.' Diana tossed a blanket that smelled very much like Cornelia at Mallory and nudged her to sit on a beanbag. She rushed out a moment later, leaving Mallory to soak in her surroundings.

Red lamps and ultraviolet light lit the bug room, illuminating various terrariums containing all manner of interesting and mildly horrifying creatures, only some of which Mallory could name. A spindly-looking oversized mantis pressed its forelegs against the glass walls of its enclosure, staring at Mallory blankly with bulging green eyes until she looked away. Cornelia's insects were creatures she had either bred herself, or got from various Occult folk across the country. Diana had left Mallory sitting beside a new tank full of small orange-and-yellow beetles Mallory had never seen before.

'Those horrible little things are Cornelia's new favourites,' Diana said, as she reappeared carrying a tray. 'I'm not allowed to call them horrible little things in front of her, even if I say it in Cantonese. They're her favourite because they have a queen. She refuses to acknowledge that she has never once cared about monarchical hierarchies in any species before now. Here's a muffin. You should have a muffin.'

Once a cup of tea was in her hands and a muffin had been forced into her, Mallory was able to explain.

'Diana, I thought you were dead.'

'Did I not reply to a text?' Diana grabbed her phone and checked. 'I haven't been online much. I was putting in fourteen-hour days until the whole thing collapsed, but I thought I was doing a good job of keeping in contact with everyone, I'm sorry.'

'No,' Mallory said, her brain swirling. Until what thing collapsed? 'No, Cornelia called me and said you'd been murdered.'

Diana put her phone down. Mallory was able to take her in now – the same, but more assured than ever – and felt strange at the idea of Diana living a totally varied, busy life in another country while Mallory had simply repeated the same pain-filled day over and over.

Over the years Diana's curves had rounded though her height hadn't changed, her features becoming more refined as she'd amassed more and more skill with a make-up brush. Her hair was pulled up on top of her head, eyeliner delicately drawn, and she was wearing yellow tartan trousers with a T-shirt tucked into them, her soft arms folded across her ample chest. Her brown eyes narrowed.

'I'm confused. CORNELIA,' Diana shouted, loud enough that Mallory winced. 'Oh, for the love of Elisabella.' She lifted her hand into a loosely curled fist and pressed it against her lips. Mallory could hear Diana's voice filling the basement, only slightly louder than the volume she was producing so close to her ears. 'STAFF CALL FOR CORNELIA BROADWICK, PLEASE MAKE YOUR WAY TO THE CUSTOMER SERVICE DESK LOCATED IN THE BUG ROOM.'

Mallory heard an incomprehensible yell, and then Cornelia bounded up the stairs.

'Hi, Mallory,' she grinned. 'I'm so glad you're here. Is there tea? Did anyone make me tea?'

'You can make your own tea. Poor Mallory was frozen solid when she got here. Also, you told her I died. She was very upset.' Diana took a pointed sip of her own tea.

'What? That's not what I said. Is it?' Cornelia looked at Mallory, who was feeling very self-conscious to not be wearing her own clothes. Still tall-ish and willowy, Cornelia had shaved the sides of her head and was wearing a confusingly huge and undulating jumper, ripped jeans and a pair of unlaced boots, all in black, because that was how Cornelia always dressed. She was the same, but there was a burning brightness in her eyes that made Mallory feel like she needed to work a bit harder to gather her thoughts. It felt as though she was looking down at a different, long-lost version of herself sitting in Cornelia's bug room, though this version didn't know how to speak to Cornelia, or how to be Mallory.

'The line was cutting in and out. You said, "Diana, murdered, come, my house, now." So I did.'

'Shit. That was probably Theodore,' Cornelia said. 'Maybe no phone calls in the basement at all while he's there.'

'What *did* you call me here for? No, wait,' Mallory said. 'Why are you home? Start there.'

'I lost my job,' Diana said. 'Fourteen-hour days, complex set dressing and they had me on prop-making too, and then the show shut down before the end of the run. I was coming back here for a bit while I figured things out, but my parents are selling the house so I was at a bit of a loose end. And sort of haven't been saving, so was a tiny bit fucked on renting outside Wrackton.' She smiled. 'Worth every stupid purchase I made.'

'And I am sick of my family,' Cornelia said. 'I was staying with them in our house in Cumbria – though it looks like it'll just be "the house" for the next while, they don't seem to have any intention of coming back here soon – while I finished an internship I had to do after my dissertation hand-in. And then realised that if I was going to look for a field job in a specific area, they still expect forensic entomologists to actually work with – sorry, work *for* – the police. And we all know how I feel about that.'

Mallory did in fact know.

'It's been years of me talking about why the current justice system isn't fit for purpose. You'd think everyone would've caught on by now. Also there aren't many jobs going in general. Bug people aren't really that in demand.'

Cornelia leaned over and tugged Diana's mug of tea out of her hand, catching her off-guard and darting out of the way before Diana could land a gentle slap on her arm. 'And Diana told me she was losing her job, so I said she could come live with me for a bit while we regroup.'

'When did you decide this?' Mallory asked faintly, filing away the fact her friends hadn't bothered to tell her they were coming home for later examination.

'Only this morning. It was a whole whirlwind thing.'

'I was already about to get on a connecting flight when I thought to call,' Diana said.

'We would've called you tomorrow anyway, but Theodore said you weren't doing very well today. Or yesterday, seeing as it's after midnight now,' Cornelia said casually.

'What?' Mallory shook her head in confusion.

'It was the first thing Theodore said when we got here, that he'd been to see you and you'd got a letter about a murder and didn't want to bother us. I told him we'd have answered your call in a heartbeat,' Cornelia said.

'You never answer my calls,' Diana said accusingly.

Cornelia shrugged. 'That's because I contain multitudes. Stop sidetracking me, I'm getting story details. Tell us about it, Mallory.'

Mallory reached for her pocket before remembering that she wasn't wearing her own clothes.

'Ah,' Diana said, realising what Mallory was doing. 'One second.' She closed her eyes and muttered under her breath, and the letter and an old lip balm from Mallory's jeans pocket appeared in her hands. 'It's not too wet.' She passed it to Mallory, who flattened it on her knee.

'It arrived addressed to the Undetectables,' she said as Cornelia and Diana leaned in close to read. 'I was thinking, maybe we could call the number and find out more about it. What do you think?' She hadn't known until this moment what she wanted them to think. That she desperately wanted to get back to a place where she felt sure of herself around her friends, investigating a murder.

Cornelia picked up the paper and raised it to her face, sniffing it. Diana grabbed it from her before she could lick the edge of the paper.

'It's certainly lacking in detail. How did this J. Gabbott even find us?' Diana said, scanning the letter again. Mallory's heart beat heavy in her chest, afraid they were going to turn her down.

'Gabbott does say they tried every other PI agency,' Cornelia pointed out.

'They had one of our cards, somehow.' Mallory's tongue felt swollen in her mouth just trying to talk to Cornelia. 'I think we should call.'

Diana and Cornelia looked at her and she took a deep breath, trying to settle her pulse. 'Just to see. We don't have to take it.'

'I was expecting an elaborate tale of a hoax letter,' Cornelia said finally.

'I thought it was a hoax too, but… the simpler explanation is that it's real,' Mallory said. 'And if we meet with this J. Gabbott, find out more information, we can decide.'

'You know what? Let's do it,' Cornelia said, raising her palms. 'What's the worst that could happen?'

'Don't say shit like that, you're tempting the goddesses,' Diana said, but she tilted her head towards Mallory. 'I'm open to trying.'

Mallory dialled the number with shaking hands.

'Is this J. Gabbott?'

'Who is this?' a soft voice said.

'M– The Undetectables.'

'Are you going to help us?' There was a spike of relief in his voice, one Mallory felt unable to say no to.

'We would definitely like more information.'

There was a pause.

'I don't think it's safe to talk over the phone. I'll come to you. What's your address?'

The artists formerly known as the Undetectables sat in Theodore's front-of-basement office, watching the neon-lit stairwell in anticipation. It felt safer than inviting a stranger into Cornelia's house.

The Broadwicks had been horrified at both the nature and location of Theodore's passing. Although he was semi-corporeal, it transpired that his eternal cat costume, and the fact that Theodore unwittingly broke anything that used electricity, were considerable sources of distress to his colleagues, and he had been forced to relocate for the majority of his work week, unless the work week required analogue access to the Mayoral Offices. With the Ghoul Council's permission, the Broadwicks transformed his place of death into a lab so that he could continue his research, financially allowing his every whim as and when he needed more equipment. He had protested this on the grounds of wanting distance from his place of death, but they were so very sorry, and he was so very pressured into taking it.

'You should've asked him his first name,' Theodore said, giving Mallory a comforting pet on the arm. 'I think a name says a lot about a person. What that says is up for debate, but names do say a lot. Isn't it odd how we get one surname from two surnames and then if you create more life, they get one surname from two surnames and so on and so forth until someone's demise? Unless you're double-barrelled, like Diana. I should ask her about that. Note to self.'

He said nothing about their earlier fight. Mallory didn't have the energy to figure out what that meant. Maybe he'd forgiven her already.

Feeling was returning to her fingers and toes, and along with it a sense of shame for jumping to such a terrible conclusion about Theodore, even though nobody blamed her for thinking it. Diana had immediately returned to her usual levels of platonic affection, holding Mallory's hand and petting her hair and hugging her whenever she thought it wouldn't hurt Mallory. With Cornelia, Mallory seemed to have forgotten how she used to speak to her at all.

'Do we know what we're going to ask, besides details on the murder? Are we pretending we're an established agency?' Mallory chewed her lip.

'If I knew, I would have said by now,' Cornelia said, with a small smile.

'Of course. Obviously. I'm just... checking.' Mallory winced. Cornelia hadn't replied meanly, but Mallory couldn't help but feel she was doing it wrong. Cornelia had seemed genuinely happy to see Mallory, but there was something intangibly changed between them. Mallory was finding it very distracting.

'What kind of murder do you think it is?' Theodore asked. 'Something sexy, I hope. A real humdinger of a murder. A murdery murder. A proper, decent killing. A ginormous crime of passion. A—'

'Theodore, I've been back for five seconds and I've already heard you say more in two sentences than I would say in three days in the lab at the Internship That Shall Not Be Discussed,' Cornelia said.

Cornelia's tone suggested to Mallory that the internship would, in fact, be discussed at length and in detail, continuously.

'Just brainstorming. Getting you into the mindset needed to solve murders. You know, I am something of a murdered person myself,' he said, pulling his cardigan around him.

A booming knock startled them.

'Mallory, as the head of the Undetectables, it's for you!' Theodore threw open the door. 'And this one looks like they've just seen a ghost.' He took in the visitor and then whirled away from the door to hover near his iron table, hands braced on the metal as he turned the pages of a random book, whiskered cheeks twitching with something.

The visitor was a pale man clad in skinny trousers and a zipped hoodie over a blue shirt who stood at the doorstep, toeing a canvas shoe. He was drenched from the rain, because of course it was still raining; it was an event when the Wrackton forecast suggested anything other than grey skies and wintery showers.

'Are you the Undetectables?' The man eyed them with interest, but not in a way that made Mallory uncomfortable. He was older than they were, yet could've been cast as a teenager in an Apparent TV show. That made him approximately thirty to thirty-five years old, in Mallory's estimation.

Mallory stood stiffly and invited him in, her face breaking into a polite smile, as it always did. Mallory had lost many things to her illness, but she was determined that she would never lose her composure.

'That's us. I'm Mallory, this is Cornelia, Diana and Theodore. What can we do for you?'

The man stepped into the room, wiping his feet on the doormat. His lace loops flopped against the canvas.

'I'm Jacob Gabbott. I'm an aide to the Night Mayor. He asked me to hire your services.'

'Van Doren? What does *he* want?' Cornelia asked suspiciously. She had taken against the Night Mayor as a child when he killed a spider in front of her, and, when confronted, said he'd do it again. Her old hatred of him had not faded, it seemed.

'It's better if he explains it to you himself. The Night Mayor, I mean. He asked me to… but…' Jacob shook his head.

'What does he need? So we can evaluate if this case is worth taking.'

Diana shot her a look, but Mallory ignored her. She could feel a semblance of herself creeping back, and wanted to take charge of the situation.

'Erm. It's… well. It's an Occult murder,' Jacob whispered. 'I'm not supposed to say anything else. But I would be grateful if you'd… come and get the details? I've got a car waiting.'

'Would there be a fee allocated?' Diana asked. 'Some of us are between jobs.'

'I don't know exact details, but I do know it would be worth your time,' Jacob said.

'Jacob, if you could excuse us for just a moment.' Cornelia jerked her head to the back of the lab. Mallory shuffled after her. Theodore took this opportunity to move towards Jacob and say, 'Does the scent of rain ever compel you to dance? I couldn't help but notice that you smell very strongly like rain. It's quite nice.'

'Are you a cat?' Mallory heard Jacob respond, and she shook her head and followed her friends to the furthermost corner.

'Mallory, what are you doing?' Cornelia whispered.

'Finding us employment,' she said decisively. 'Diana, you're good at attention to detail. You can collect scene evidence.'

'I am good at attention to detail, thank you for noticing.'

'Cornelia,' Mallory continued, afraid of what she was going to say, 'you're good at spell identification and you wanted a path into forensic entomology – this could be it. I am a puzzle solver and Theo and I have been… well, we've got some scientific things figured out that we can maybe use. We have Theodore's lab here, and Theodore himself. We have knowledge, and we have the time. Let's do it. We only have to take this one case. If it's not for us, we disband the Undetectables for good. But if it is… we'll have solved a lot of our problems.'

Diana and Cornelia exchanged glances.

'I do need to learn fiscal responsibility,' Diana said, tilting her head.

Something passed between the two of them. They each reached out and took one of Mallory's hands. She felt a familiar pulse of energy pass through her.

'We're in.'

FIVE

'I'm coming too,' Theodore said, when Mallory emerged dressed once again in her own clothes. Nobody disagreed with him.

'Okay. Get in the witchlight.' Diana held one up and Theodore sighed dramatically, wariness crossing his face.

'The things I will do for science. This is slightly too close to a ghostlight for comfort, but corporeal comforts are beyond one such as me.' He sniffed.

'What's that for?' Mallory asked, pulling her hair up into a neat ponytail. Diana had dried her hair too and Mallory was anxiously trying to rearrange herself.

'It's simple physics, I can't believe we didn't think of it years ago,' Diana said. 'Theodore's static doesn't affect witchlights, and he can pass through them, so there's no reason he couldn't be contained *inside* one. Like a ghost vessel, sort of. It was a silly, tangential plot point in one of the episodes of the show I was working on – when I say things like this out loud, it makes me understand why the show was cancelled.' She frowned.

'I take offence,' Theodore said.

'Colour me shocked.' Diana poked at his cardigan, static flying. 'When I thought about it I realised there was probably merit to it. They're all over Wrackton, right up to the limits of where Theodore can go—'

'And I have range in general, just not in haunting,' Theodore said. He couldn't leave the limits of Wrackton without getting thrown back to the basement.

'—and he can travel freely within those limits without having to walk anywhere or break anyone's car.' Diana grinned. 'It'll be a case of have ghost, will travel.'

Jacob stared at Diana. Mallory had all but forgotten he was there as Cornelia gathered up her coat and her phone, ushering Theodore away from her as she transferred the latter to her bag.

'It's fascinating how much we don't know about magic still. I bet you could do so many things with a witchlight. A spell, or… something even cleverer than that,' he said earnestly, looking at Theodore from under his eyelashes. It distracted Mallory just enough from the pang of guilt that she hadn't figured out a way for Theodore to travel more quickly around Wrackton herself over the whole time it had just been the two of them.

Theodore sighed again. 'If I die… Oh, no, that's already happened.' He disappeared in a small burst of static. Diana dropped the witchlight into her bag.

'That's us ready.' Diana placed a hat on her head, adjusted the rim, and nodded to Mallory.

'Yes. Jacob, where did you say the car was?'

'It's circling. I'll go and get the driver to stop.' He hurried out the door. The Undetectables followed. Cornelia locked the basement door behind her with a wave of her hand, and her dress coat swirled around her as she turned and bounded up the stairs behind Mallory, her skin flushed with excitement. Diana clutched her bag to her chest as they waited, fingers worrying a years-old badge that said, 'Be gay, solve crimes.'

Cornelia wordlessly passed Mallory a bottle of water and a vial of painkillers she had stuffed into her coat pocket, like she always used to when Mallory first got sick. A whisper of painful nostalgia settled into Mallory's stomach; she wished she didn't need the help.

The Mayoral Offices were in Wrackton's main town square, a granite-and-concrete jungle of pillars, punctuated with neon signage and black velvet window hangings. The car pulled away, leaving them at the foot of the long staircase up to the Offices. Mallory shivered in the cold air, the movement making her muscles scream. Cornelia glanced at her and picked up both their bags.

'After you,' Cornelia said. They followed Diana's short form, who followed Jacob's much taller one, up the stone steps. Every step hurt Mallory, but Cornelia stayed right behind her, counting them off as they moved.

'Thirteen left. Imagine how long it would take a *Sonata lutumae* beetle to walk up these? Days, probably. If they didn't die half way. Eleven.' Cornelia chattered non-stop. Diana looked back and met Mallory's gaze. She didn't quite roll her eyes at Cornelia, but came close. Mallory didn't have the energy to reciprocate.

Shaking from the effort, Mallory peeled off her coat as soon as they got inside the doors, sweat dripping down her back.

Jacob waved his badge at a bored-looking receptionist, who ignored him. Faltering, he tapped the badge on the desk, violet light flaring in the dark corridor behind them as he did so. He ushered them down to Van Doren's office as witchlights blinked on lazily ahead of them as they moved, the corridor so long it seemed impossible that Van Doren didn't have to sprint up and down it between meetings.

Eventually, with Mallory feeling as though she might collapse, they reached the doors of Van Doren's office. Jacob knocked and leaned his head against the door. Practically on cue, the witchlight directly over his head went out, plunging them into near darkness. He squinted up at it, muttering a spell under his breath. Reluctantly the light flickered on, blinking once, twice, before extinguishing again.

'Just a moment,' he murmured, seeming intent on pretending he wasn't fighting with an inanimate object. 'Takes a second for him to respond...'

They waited. Jacob opened the door, an apologetic smile on his face, and disappeared inside. He returned after a few seconds.

'He'll call you in when he's ready. Sorry about this. I'll be next door if you need me.' He flashed them a chagrined look.

Three slow minutes passed, Mallory's muscles cooling and stiffening as they waited. Cornelia stepped from foot to foot and Mallory wondered if she had made a mistake to bring them here.

'Come in!' a distant voice called.

The walls and tiled floors were fully purple, and everything in the room was in varying shades of tasteless grey. Vincent Van Doren himself was sort of grey-looking, which may have come from years of working nights, but perhaps was simply down to the grisly horror of the murder at hand. He paced back and forth, but stopped dead at the sight of them.

'Who are you?'

'The Undetectables, private investigators. We're here to save your arse,' Cornelia said. Mallory wished she hadn't.

'Is this a joke? If it's a joke, let me know now. I am not an unreasonable man. I will try to find the humour in it.' His gaze danced over all three of them. He did not, Mallory noticed, seem to recognise Cornelia at all.

'I don't see the joke, personally,' Cornelia said.

'Forgive me.' Van Doren didn't sound like he wanted forgiveness. 'You just seem a little… inexperienced.' Van Doren raised a hand sporting a garish emerald ring and pointed it at them.

'Interesting how that's only a problem in certain areas of your life,' Cornelia said pointedly.

Mallory and Diana exchanged glances, unclear on her meaning, but Van Doren twitched in annoyance.

'Before we proceed, I need to see some sort of qualifications.' He held the ringed hand out, his other hand pressed against his brow.

'I think our collective expertise will show itself through the course of our work. Between us and our fourth team member – a doctor of forensic para-anthropology with a lifetime of experience, and then some – we hold degrees and specialisations that allow us a wide scope in the types of cases we can take on. I could bore you with the details, but this seems urgent.' Cornelia glided into the seat in front of Van Doren. Mallory and Diana followed suit.

'Right.' Van Doren looked between them all, searching their faces for something. Whatever it was, he didn't seem to find it, so he grunted. 'Did my aide give you any information?'

'We received a letter from Jacob Gabbott stating that an Apparent, Edward Kuster, has been killed and that a prominent Wrackton resident wanted our assistance in solving the murder. We were brought here by car as per his request,' Mallory said smoothly, following Cornelia's lead.

'Is that it?' He shook his head. 'Do I have to do everything myself? Yes, an Apparent was murdered. But it appears that it was by one of our own.' Van Doren gripped the table in front of him, shaking it aggressively to emphasise every word. A bird skull rattled in its bell jar. His office was full of strange, macabre oddments.

'How do you know this was an Occult murder?' Cornelia interrupted. Diana shot her a glance and went right back to fidgeting with the brim of her hat, her fingers worrying the velvet trim.

Van Doren fixed a gaze on Cornelia over his glasses.

'We know. I've been reliably informed it's magical. Edward Kuster's last known location was right here in the Offices. Why we hire freelancers I don't know, but he was here, doing something computery, I expect. I can't... this can't get out.' Van Doren stood and folded his arms behind his back, pacing up and down. 'This is very sensitive. I will need to speak to the whole team. The fourth – your doctor – I will need to meet this fellow, or, indeed, lady fellow, and make sure everyone… checks out.'

'Ah yes, the two genders.' Cornelia rolled her eyes.

He glared at Cornelia again.

'He will be available for future meetings, should you wish to meet with him. He can be very discreet,' Mallory said, though she was sure it was the first time anyone had ever described Theodore as such. She was not sure introducing him to this meeting, with Van Doren as wound up as he seemed, was the right move. She had to hope Theodore would forgive them for a fruitless trip in a witchlight.

Van Doren ignored her and resumed pacing. 'If we've a private team picking up the slack, nobody will question how long it took for Wrackton police to find clues. We'll have covered double the ground with a skeleton force.'

'I don't see how that helps anyone?' Diana frowned. 'Surely it makes more sense to call in more Apparent police than to hire a third party.'

He ignored Diana too.

'Of course, the papers can't know we're struggling with a small team or that I have absolutely zero belief in their abilities to get this resolved in a timely manner,' he said, though not to anyone but himself.

Diana cleared her throat.

'He knows we can hear him, right?' Cornelia whispered.

'This is the only way.' Van Doren stopped moving, wrapping his bejewelled hand around the back of his chair. 'This has to be solved quickly, and buried quickly.'

'If Oughteron police know about it already, won't it be in the papers?' Mallory asked carefully.

'Hexana, of course it will. I'm talking about avoiding an *international* scandal. A murder that is being tightly and swiftly investigated by a crack-shot police force is much, much better than the sagging incompetence I deal with, or the humiliation of hiring...' He waved his hands at them.

'Hiring *what*?' Cornelia said, a dangerous edge to her voice.

'Are you in or not?' Van Doren continued without waiting for a response. 'I've asked our mortuary to take a stab at the autopsy tomorrow – Apparents won't touch Kuster with a bargepole in case the magic is contagious.' Van Doren closed his eyes, rubbing the emerald-ringed hand over his face. 'Then of course we'd need utter discretion concerning all interactions between the Offices and the... Undetectables, you said?'

'What's in it for me?' Cornelia asked. 'I mean, for us?'

Van Doren licked his teeth. 'Money, of course.'

Cornelia snorted. The Broadwicks were the wealthiest family in a town that took financial care of its residents.

'Status, commendation letters for future job opportunities, a seat on the Council. Whatever you want.' Van Doren shook his head. 'Within reason. The focus for Wrackton henceforth is growth, prosperity and proper punitive measures.' Van Doren ticked these off on his fingers, as he no doubt had done at countless Council meetings. 'We cannot risk anyone prematurely believing there is a threat to the foundation of Occult society. And the Unified Magical Liaison cannot believe Wrackton has a municipality compliance problem. Murders do not happen here, nor are they committed by those who live here. Occulture doesn't *do* big crime.'

All Occult towns around the world answered to the Unified Magical Liaison, a large-scale governing body. It operated mostly on shame and fines to keep Occult towns in line, and it mostly worked. Its control was less efficient when it came to Occult folk living in Apparent towns, of which there was a not-insignificant number, though the UML tended to avoid acknowledging this fact, resulting in Occult towns like Wrackton being treated with a particular kind of reverence by its inhabitants that was akin to pride. 'This has to be shut down quickly,' he finished.

'But what', Mallory asked, trying to calm her desperation to know, 'do you want us to *do*?'

'Let me be clear.' He leaned forward. 'I want you to help me investigate this murder. Quietly. Find out what you can, ask questions. But you cannot be found out. I can't reasonably be seen spending Wrackton's resources on outside help. The headlines themselves would be damning enough.'

'So if I had any objection at all to any policy or law you proposed in future,' Cornelia pressed, 'I could request an audience with you to have it shut down?'

'Cornelia, some of us actually want money, not a favour,' Diana said.

'We are wasting time here.' Van Doren slapped the table. 'My aide obviously found you to his satisfaction. If you don't want to get involved, you're free to leave.'

Mallory didn't want to leave with nothing. Her eyes slid to Cornelia and Diana, who were both staring intently at Van Doren.

She had to make a choice. For herself, to keep her friends around.

'We'll take the case – with a fee for Diana and me, and a favour for Cornelia.' Mallory ignored both a sharp intake of breath from Cornelia and the anxiety at having made a decision without consultation. 'Now please, if it's not too much trouble, tell us what we need to know.'

Van Doren physically deflated and sat down heavily in his chair. He crossed a long leg over the other and rested his chin on his folded hands.

'The victim's name is Edward Kuster. All I know is that there was no sign of forced entry, no signs of physical violence or fighting. His body was still warm, though we suspect he'd been dead for some days, or weeks, perhaps. A revealing spell confirmed magic had been used in his vicinity, though I think that was hardly necessary in this case.'

Van Doren reached into his desk and produced a purple manila file, and all but threw it across the desk at them. Cornelia caught it and Diana flipped it open, passing it to Mallory.

There were police report pages inside – real ones, and an evidence bag with what looked like a single sudoku puzzle torn from a book, illegible ink scrawled along the bottom of the page.

Mallory's eyes could barely take in the report. She saw 'severed tongue, perimortem, sharp force torso carvings, algor mortis, TOD?' And they made sense to her in isolation. She knew a lot about forensic terminology and police procedure, had found comfort in learning when she couldn't move for pain. But together, the gears of her brain ground in protest at being asked to assemble a complete picture.

'I'll need these back before you leave, I borrowed them from O'Sullivan,' Van Doren said quickly. Mallory looked up just in time to see Cornelia's eyes narrow at him.

'Who's O'Sullivan?' There was a challenging edge to Cornelia's voice.

'She's… ah. She's the DI in charge of the case.'

'Since when does Wrackton have a specific homicide team?' Cornelia demanded. 'Last I checked, Wrackton police were three sad Apparent glorified park wardens in a trench coat.'

Cornelia did not like the police. The Wrackton force was a particular source of oft-voiced repugnance, as they were a small unit of Apparents on permanent loan from Oughteron who de-escalated minor public disturbances, and – as Cornelia had so eloquently put it – assisted with guarding public property. They would've worked perfectly within the community if not for their biting desire for more power, a constant push to build a for-profit prison – ostensibly to strengthen Apparent–Occult relations by solving overcrowding problems in Apparent prisons for vast sums of money – and their unbridled disgust at the mere concept of admitting Apparent science was limited in its usefulness in solving minor magical crimes. Cornelia had never liked their approach.

Mallory cracked a small smile at Cornelia's vehemence. There was no stopping her; even Cornelia at times was powerless to stop Cornelia.

'Since it became necessary.' Van Doren inhaled. 'The working theory is that he died by asphyxiation, though they aren't sure how.'

'Small question I'll repeat, as you still haven't really answered – if you have hired more police, why do you need us?' Diana discreetly held a hand out to Mallory, who passed the file back. She hadn't been able to take any of it in. 'Why not just rely on what you have?'

Mallory could feel herself blushing, feel her friends judging her impulsive choice to say they'd take a case that shouldn't have been presented to them. Jacob's letter burned hot in her pocket.

'There is a particular need to get this taken care of quickly and efficiently. There is a lot at stake here. A man is *dead*.' Van Doren paused. 'And my re-election is in February.'

'What are the conditions?' Mallory asked finally.

'If you're worth what you say you are, you'll find out the information you need yourselves—' He cut himself off, shaking his head. 'We will not speak like this again until this is solved.'

He held his hand out for the file. Diana closed it and passed it back to him, but didn't release her grip on it.

'Do not embarrass me. I can find out where you live,' he said, then winked.

A chill rolled down Mallory's back. Diana clamped an arm around Cornelia's and steered her to the door. Van Doren turned away from them, scratching at the skin beneath his ring.

Dismissed.

Mallory thought that this might be the day she died from her illness. It wasn't life-threatening, but sometimes she felt as though her body was ready to fully shut down. The prospect of having to physically walk out of the Mayoral Offices and take the stairs again was enough to make her cry but she forced herself out into the corridor.

The door closed behind them and they were alone.

'I cannot believe that prick threatened us. What an evil... ham,' Cornelia spluttered. The light above her flickered again, and she glowered at it.

'I think it was a bad attempt at a joke,' Mallory said. 'I'm sorry I made a decision for us, I thought...'

Cornelia and Diana both waved her apology off.

'It's like you said,' Diana said. 'We need something to do.'

'And this isn't just something,' Mallory said, grimacing through her pain. 'You saw those notes. The fact the Apparent police he's got on the case are so sure they can't solve it. None of this happened around Theodore's murder.' She pointed stiffly at Diana's handbag where Theodore was still nestled in the witchlight, probably furious. 'They just dismissed it. Found an alternative explanation.'

'And they were wrong,' Cornelia added.

'Of course they were. The point here is that there *isn't* an alternative suggestion. Edward Kuster dying isn't dismissible. Apparents know it, even Van Doren knows it, which is why he's flailing around asking us to get involved. This is magic. *Undetectable* magic.'

Mallory gritted her teeth in determination.

'And that's what we do best.'

SIX

Eight days to Samhain

They stepped out of the taxi into the Mayoral Square at 9:02.

'Can we class 9:02 as being late for a 9:00 sharp appointment?' Cornelia asked as they took the steps up to the mortuary. Despite the lack of sleep, Mallory felt somewhat in control of her body again. Sometimes resting reset her just enough. Other times, she could be out for days or weeks. Pain was unpredictable.

'Yes, we can. Jacob said to wait here on the steps.' The details of their visit had been quickly hashed out just before they left the Night Mayor's office, when he'd approached them and offered to get them in to view the autopsy, but that felt like a distant, painful dream. They had got a taxi to Broadwick Mansion and managed to sleep for four hours before dragging themselves back out. Cornelia had given Mallory a bedroom to sleep in and she'd gladly taken it to save her going home.

Mallory had decided that she and Cornelia would see the body, and that Diana should go to the scene of Edward Kuster's death to take photographs, and search for evidence that hadn't been collected. She had promised to send regular text updates to both of them.

> *Diana*
> I'm here. It's still sealed off. Don't seem to be cameras in the hall so should be okay

> *Diana*
> Diana isn't getting arrested today

> *Cornelia*
> I look forward to more quality updates.

Cornelia snorted and shoved her phone back into her pocket. Mallory texted a heart back. 'Where's Jacob? Maybe he's late too.'

'Guilty.' Jacob walked through the door of the mortuary, making her jump. 'Oh, I'm sorry, didn't mean to frighten you. We have clearance passes here. Now. Erm.' He coughed. 'Dr Ray asked me why she should facilitate you three – though its only two of you, I see! – being present for the autopsy, so I sort of panicked, and told her you were med students.' He looked hopeful. 'So if you could maybe pretend to be medical types, that would be great for me.'

Mallory felt a swoop of pity. 'Don't worry, we'll handle it.'

'I think Dr Broadwick has a nice ring to it, I'm sure I can make it work,' Cornelia said.

'Great. Thank you.' Relief flooded his voice. 'Anyway. Follow me, please.'

Jacob approached a hatch cut into the wall and showed their passes to the bored receptionist behind it.

> *Cornelia*
> We've to pretend to be med students. You good?

> *Diana*
> Police heree lying myArsee off

Cornelia looked at Mallory in alarm and Mallory forced herself to take a deep breath. Diana was good with folk. Diana would get herself out of the situation.

'They're in Room 2.' The receptionist went back to doing whatever she had been doing before being rudely interrupted by a man of indiscriminate age and two individuals who looked far too enthusiastic for the setting they were in.

'Have you been here before? I can't say I ever have,' Jacob said, steering them down the right corridor. 'I wouldn't know how to handle it myself. Death and such, really freaks me out. My dad wanted me to get into politics. I was an orchestral flautist before this, but I never really anticipated this…' He waved a hand around him.

'I daresay you'll get used to it.' Cornelia touched everything she passed with curiosity, fingers brushing notices and signs as though she hoped it would annoy someone. All the things that made up Cornelia were the things Mallory was so very afraid people would see when they looked at her; on Cornelia they were charming, even beautiful, but Mallory suspected she would wear them differently.

'Room 2. Here we are. Do you...' Jacob swallowed. 'Do I need to accompany you?'

'Relax, mate.' Cornelia clapped a hand to his shoulder.

'I'll wait out here, then. You can just give me the condensed version.' Jacob pressed himself back against the wall opposite the door, almost trying to push himself into it.

'Don't worry, we've got it under control.' Mallory knocked twice before entering the room.

'Recording interrupted by two unceremonious invaders with no timekeeping skills.' The pathologist stood with her arms folded as they filed in. Her elegant mouth was drawn into a thin line of disapproval, her brown eyes narrowed. Her dark hair was drawn back into a ponytail and everything about her was neat and tidy and brimming with annoyance. Cornelia planted her kit at her feet and rolled up her sleeves, casting her eye over Dr Ray's mortuary technician, whose tawny skin was flushed as she perched herself meekly in the corner of the room on a metal stool.

Mallory realised she knew her: Izna, an ex-girlfriend of Diana's. She waved subtly, hoping Izna didn't know they weren't med students. Izna's smile didn't quite reach her eyes, and Mallory remembered it had been a breakup of medium quality.

'What are we—?' Cornelia started.

'Gloves.'

Izna jumped up and grabbed a box of them, holding them out to Mallory.

'I am Dr Priyanka Ray. You may call me Dr Ray. I am about to resume my examination of the body. If you interrupt, you will leave. If you *touch* anything, you will leave. If you distract Izna,' she tilted her head at her technician, 'you will leave. If you ask me any question I deem to be inane, you will leave. There will be no warnings.'

Dr Ray resumed her preparations and Cornelia leaned into Mallory, her whispered breath tickling the hair behind her ear. 'I think I'm in love with her.'

'If any of you profess any further love for me, you will leave,' Dr Ray added, and Cornelia straightened, grinning. She was almost unflappable; Mallory blushed on her behalf, so embarrassed that she felt she had said it herself.

'As I explained to Jacob, you were to arrive here at 9 a.m. sharp. Med students surely have a better grasp on time than that.' Dr Ray raised a disapproving eyebrow. 'You remain quiet for the rest of the autopsy, you get to stay. Understood?'

Only now did Mallory allow herself to look down at what Dr Ray had been doing. She stifled a gasp at the sight of Edward Kuster laid out on the metal table. She was not sure what she expected to see, but it was not this. He had not been found for days, and yet he looked freshly deceased. There was no real smell, just the scent of disinfectant. He was waxen and greyish and real, and it made Mallory want to vomit.

The words of the police report swam back to her. His tongue was in a metal dish beside him. There was a strange, interconnecting circular symbol with embellishments carved into his stomach, fresh-looking, but no blood seemed to have been spilled.

'Don't look too closely at that,' Dr Ray said, just as Mallory felt her vision swim, her eyes unable to take in the whole picture. She felt a pang of familiarity she couldn't decipher.

Dr Ray clicked her fingers to restart the recording, speaking clearly so the microphone hanging over the table could hear her.

'The victim is male, five foot ten, white, and has been identified as Edward Kuster of 85 Bernard Close, Oughteron. Hospital records received from Oughteron General state his blood type as A-negative, no diseases present and no medical attention was sought prior to his demise.' Dr Ray moved around the body slowly, examining the spaces between Kuster's fingers. Izna checked between his toes.

Mallory watched with her lips pressed firmly together, the scent of chemicals burning her nose.

'Toxicology reports will determine the presence of drugs in his system. There are sharp-force injuries to the surface of the torso, complex symbology of magical origin, confirmed by the physiological effects that occur when the symbol is examined in full by folk of either Apparent or Occult nature. This was created with an undetermined object, though it's unclear if it happened peri- or postmortem. There are no other injuries immediately evident on the surface of the body, save for the severing of the victim's tongue, which appears to have occurred perimortem.'

Dr Ray paused next to the dish with the tongue in it.

'There is evidence the victim died of choking asphyxiation,' Dr, Ray continued. 'This is suggested by the victim's tongue, found lodged in the victim's throat at the scene by a crime scene investigator, as well as the presence of cyanosis and confirmed blood chemistry changes. The lacerations on the tongue are congruent with bite marks, and impressions will be taken from the victim's teeth to ascertain a match.'

Mallory shifted and Cornelia leaned forward to get a better look at his torso.

'Evidence found at the scene and reported to Oughteron police suggests the victim had been dead for at least a week. However, the victim was pre-rigor, with an internal body temperature of thirty-six-point-four degrees, which is inconsistent with these findings. No insects were found at the scene.'

Cornelia twitched at that mention, like something very interesting had been revealed. Mallory supposed it had; insects always arrived, that much she knew from Cornelia. It suggested the assumption he'd been dead for a while but that Occult interference had prevented decay had some merit to it. Izna pulled over a trolley full of various, violent-looking tools, and Dr Ray picked up an electric saw.

'Internal examination of the torso has begun.'

The process was gruesome; for all Mallory had read about it, she did not anticipate how horrible it would be to watch someone examine the insides of a human body. She now had more intimate knowledge of Kuster's intestinal tract than she ever would her own.

Dr Ray finished her autopsy and left Izna to clean up the body. She shed her gloves and picked up the tray containing swabs and samples and gestured to them to leave the room.

'Wait.' Cornelia pulled a box containing two beetles out of her pocket. 'Can I just…?'

Dr Ray stared at her, and Cornelia hastened to explain, her eyes lighting up at the chance to talk about her favourite topic.

'These are *Sonata lutumae*, or sound beetles.'

Cornelia held one up, rotating her palm so Dr Ray could see their shiny orange-and-yellow shells. 'I did my... first degree's dissertation on their ability to pick up magical traces. They're not native to Wrackton, but they do tend to habitate around Occulture, suggesting some sort of symbiotic benefit,' she said. 'They pull magic towards them, like pollen to a bee or a pollinating beetle, using a static charge.' She paused. 'I understand a revealing spell was completed at the scene, but the beetles can confirm physical magic on any surface. Including, say, a body. Like a luminol test. Or a litmus test of sorts.'

Dr Ray hadn't reacted. Cornelia kept talking.

'I hypothesise they can also hold magic for some time – given that it takes a number of weeks for the colour change that occurs to subside. There are so many possible applications for this – as living DNA swabs, for instance – if they were properly researched.'

Mallory and Theodore had a way of making this happen, of furthering their investigation and the future of Occult forensics, but the task felt so insurmountably daunting she pushed it away.

'So here, they'll simply change colour and make a noise if magic is present. I'll just let them walk on the deceased, and recapture them, and we'll be on our way.'

Dr Ray continued staring, and Cornelia waited.

'You may have all day, but the dead don't tend to wait around,' Dr Ray said eventually.

Cornelia dropped two beetles on Edward Kuster's stomach, and then gently recovered them, gingerly avoiding letting her fingers brush his skin. Their shells immediately changed to neon green, and they both emitted a high-pitched peeping noise.

Dr Ray's eyebrow shot up. 'I've seen many things on a body, but never… that.'

'That was fast, too,' Cornelia said.

Dr Ray looked like she wanted to ask something, then thought better of it, moving to the door.

Mallory hovered. 'One last thing. Do you have any photos of the crime scene we can see?'

Dr Ray pursed her lips. 'An interest in pathology, is it?'

'Absolutely. If we could pathologise everything, we would.' Cornelia smiled broadly.

Dr Ray's brow furrowed in amusement, but she reached into a cabinet and pulled out some of the photographs of the scene.

Edward Kuster lay on his bed as though he was sleeping. His mouth looked full – of his own severed tongue, Mallory assumed – and the carvings were even sharper, fresher, than what was on the table in front of her, though her eyes swam and she felt vaguely nauseated.

'Hexana,' Cornelia breathed. 'That's… something.'

Dr Ray shook the photographs free of Cornelia's vice-like grasp.

'I won't pretend I'm not fascinated by this case,' she said, dropping them back into the drawer. 'We don't get murders here, as you well know, but this… The markings, the magic… This is something strange.' She smiled despite herself.

Mallory realised Dr Ray was much younger than she'd originally thought, and very beautiful.

'Thanks for letting us be here,' Mallory said politely.

'If you need anything else to aid your studies, I'm sure young Jacob would be happy to make ludicrous requests of me again.' Dr Ray swept up the hall, Izna scurrying after her.

Cornelia and Mallory pulled their phones out immediately.

> **Cornelia**
> Diana are you okay??

> **Mallory**
> Please let us know you got out of there safely

> **Diana**
> I'm a motherfucking genius. Met O'Sullivan. She nice,
> but sus. Got info, share later

Cornelia practically collapsed in relief. 'She's okay. *Hexana*, I've seen lots of photos of cadavers while studying, but that was…'

'Real.'

'Very real. But we're going to figure it out. It's too interesting not to.'

'And Edward Kuster deserves justice. He deserves someone knowing what happened to him.' If nothing else, Mallory could get Kuster the justice she hadn't been able to get for Theodore.

Jacob rounded the corner just then and looked startled to see them huddled in the corridor. He clutched a coffee cup between his hands and his skin was a little green.

'Do you need anything else from me?' Jacob edged away from the room.

'Not in the slightest.' Cornelia eyed Jacob's coffee as though it were oxygen and she were unable to breathe, and Mallory slipped an arm into hers.

'We can get you coffee on the way home, Cornelia. Thank you so much for taking time out of your day to accompany us, Jacob. We'd better get going.'

'Of course. Thank you, Mallory,' he said weakly.

Mallory was relieved to breathe clean, corpse-free air when they stepped outside. She still ached all over, but she supposed she'd make it through a day in the lab, even if her brain wouldn't.

A certainty settled over her as she looked up at the cloudy, grey sky.

'There was something about that carving on his stomach that was familiar. One thing is for absolute certain: an Apparent couldn't have put that on him, there's just no plausible way,' Mallory said. 'This was an Occult killing.'

And Mallory and her friends would find the murderer.

SEVEN

'So what are you thinking?' Mallory asked, adjusting her coat in the ever-present glow of the Night Mayor's face light, which was exactly as it sounded: a light in the shape of the Night Mayor's face, lest anyone forget what Vincent Van Doren looked like for even a moment. 'And let's walk back, it's not raining.'

Cornelia hesitated, her thumb poised over the taxi app. 'You sure?'

Mallory nodded, trying to ignore the rush of anxiety at just her and Cornelia walking together, alone. 'I want to get the smell of formaldehyde out of my nose.'

Cornelia pulled down the collar of her jumper to scratch her neck, scrutinising Mallory as she did so, and Mallory saw something red and bruise-like at the base of her throat. Before she could ask what had happened, when Cornelia took her hand away, it was gone.

Cornelia shrugged and fell into step beside her, going at Mallory's pace. It was always a gamble; a walk could make her feel much better, or it could land her in bed for days with pain, but it was the first break in rain in a long stretch and she wanted to take advantage.

'So I'm thinking that the carvings are the key, probably.' Cornelia put her hands into her coat pockets, a bounce in her step. 'They're Occult, like you said. And familiar, but I'm not sure how. Yet.'

'You'd expect blood from cuts like those. Could the weapon itself have been Occult?' Mallory took slow, deep breaths, cool, fresh air hitting the back of her lungs.

'Possibly? What kind of weapon would do that? And why did he bite his tongue out?'

'Pain?' Mallory suggested, stumbling over an uneven part of the path. Cornelia caught her wrist and elbow automatically, steadying her. Her arm tingled where Cornelia had touched when she let go. 'Thanks.'

'Pain is possible. Did it seem personal to you? But then, what could Kuster have possibly done to justify that kind of death?'

Mallory shook her head. 'I've no idea.'

'The whole foundation of the Unified Magical Liaison of Magical Municipalities rests on the idea of Occulture not doing harm to anyone,' Cornelia said, meaning the Do No Harm Charter brought in at the end of the Vampire Wars. 'Which definitely means not doing a murder. This has to be something big, something worth breaking a sacred covenant. Worth facing whatever the UML thinks is a suitable punishment, on top of being exiled.'

'Maybe Diana got some information from the crime scene.' Mallory pressed the signal crossing button, watching the neon line of light that stretched across the street turn from red to yellow. Wrackton was quiet – rush-hour over, children in school, barely any cars on the road – but she took the moment to lean against the pole, trying to stretch out her quivering muscles.

Cornelia bit the inside of her lip, watching her. Mallory pretended not to notice.

'I wish we'd taken the crime scene photos from the mortuary with us, or got copies. It felt a bit risky to ask,' Mallory said. The images in her mind were already fading, twisting into grotesque caricatures of Kuster's death.

Cornelia nudged her arm gently. 'I thought about this. If only we'd been shown where the photographs were kept. And if only one of us knew a duplication spell.'

She whispered under her breath, and the crime scene photos appeared in her hands.

Mallory's face broke into a smile, wind pushing stray hairs onto her face. 'Excellent work, detective. There's no way of knowing how Kuster died—'

'Yet.' Cornelia pointed at her as they crossed the road, turning onto a long, narrow side street.

'Yet, but having all this information to hand will help. Do you remember anything from the police file? I was… tired last night, so I only retained snatches of it here and there.'

'Diana had her hands on it; I'm absolutely confident that our resident… Let me check my notes to see what she wishes to be called.' Cornelia pulled out her phone. 'Ah yes, "motherfucking genius", probably retained more than either of us.'

'Then there's the question of who could do such a thing,' Mallory said.

'If I had to pick one person in this whole town who could've killed a guy, my money would always be on Van Doren.'

'Show your workings, Cornelia.'

'Because anything dodgy that has ever happened in Wrackton, it's been Van Doren. Do you want to see my scandal collection of Van Doren newspaper clippings? I have a whole section dedicated to his work with investors buying up land on the edges of Wrackton, and not re-classifiying it, so he can build a for-profit prison here in Wrackton. A prison, Mallory. We haven't had one of those since last *century.*'

'Since when do you read the newspaper?' Mallory grinned at her. Cornelia had always taken a subject and run with it.

She could learn how to be friends with Cornelia again, with a little practice. A little bit of pushing beyond whatever it was making her feel like she was being stripped raw every time Cornelia's eyes met hers.

'I do! I used to, too, but I do! Whenever Theodore was finished with the papers I'd read them, and when I was in London I'd get nostalgic for teatime with Theodore, so I went and got his favourites.'

A witty retort was forming on Mallory's lips when a car screeched around the corner, music blaring. Mallory heard shouts and Cornelia automatically stepped in front of her, her hands raised.

'Good luck driving without any tyres, arseholes!' she shouted, then stopped. 'Oh my GODDESS.' A most un-Cornelia-like squeal escaped her as the car doors opened and two faeries jumped out, one sporting a tall, glittery mohawk, running to envelop her in a hug.

'There're my favourite witches,' the one with the mohawk said. 'Hi, Mallory.' They walked to embrace her.

'Felix!' She fell into the hug, Felix's smooth brown arms pulling her tightly to them. She didn't tell them it hurt, feeling a mix of happiness and pain stirring together.

Felix Cole had been one of Mallory's friends in the Before Times. Before she had to stop hanging out with everyone, before they forgot to invite her places. Felix had joined a band and left Wrackton as soon as they were eighteen, and had been touring ever since.

'I can't be your favourite witch,' Cornelia said. 'What about Diana?'

'Diana is my *favourite*. You are my favourite *witches*. Could I accuse you if it was not true?'

Mallory glowed at the idea of being Felix's favourite anything, though told herself it was because they only had three witch friends she knew of.

'Don't pull the faerie card. We all know the rules of faerie truthfulness are a game no mere mortal should attempt to play.'

There was no single level nor astral plane where Mallory felt confident that Cornelia could be described as a 'mere mortal'.

'The fact of faeries being unable to lie is irrelevant to the concept of me attempting to give you a compliment,' the smaller, pale faerie said.

'Something I would like to say I would never attempt again, though we know that's not true,' Felix said.

'Shut up, Ben, don't encourage them.' Cornelia laughed, as Ben wrapped his arms around her waist and dragged her around the road with enthusiasm. Mallory had heard of Ben, and was glad to put a face to the name.

'Never.'

'Scandalous outfit, Felix,' Cornelia went on, allowing herself to be enthusiastically hugged. Mallory said nothing because she did not possess the energy for it. They didn't have time for this. They needed to get to work.

'It was for Diana's benefit, not for you. I belong on the fashion pages, baby.' They grinned, glitter peppering their cheeks. Felix was unbelievably beautiful, and, like many faeries, defied all gender norms. 'Where is Diana, anyway? We heard you were back, didn't believe it until I saw you bobbing along the road here.' They turned. 'Oh, Mallory, this is Ben DeLacey.'

Ben had now let go of Cornelia and turned briefly to wave at Mallory.

'Nice to meet you.' His smile crinkled the corners of his pale eyes.

Mallory waved back limply, feeling suddenly unsure of herself.

'Are you headed home?' Felix asked Cornelia.

'We'll drop you there. Come on.' Ben opened the door for Mallory and she slid into the back seat, the overpowering scent of the seven different air fresheners hanging from the car mirror hitting the back of her throat.

Cornelia slid in beside her and gently squeezed her knee. Mallory had to stop herself from flinching at the sudden pressure. She shut her eyes for a moment. Kuster's cut-open body seared behind her eyelids and she opened them again. She wanted to be in Theodore's lab working on things, talking through the facts they'd learned, making her murder board, but standing for so long had sapped her of energy and all she could really think about was a nap.

'Corneliaaaa,' Ben sang. 'I am just, so happy to see you.' He twisted his head to grin at her again. His brown curls crackled with static against the vinyl seat covers.

Mallory thought that if an Apparent chose to draw an approximation of a faerie prince, they would draw Ben. He was pale-skinned, soft and fat in a way that was equal parts beautiful and graceful. Mallory could imagine herself falling in love with Ben very easily, were she likely to do such a thing. Which she wasn't. She had long since talked herself out of having feelings for anyone.

'I'm so happy you're back. Why are you back?' Cornelia asked, slapping the back of his headrest.

'We'll get to that. How the fuck have you been?' Ben asked.

'I was going to ask the same thing,' Felix said.

Cornelia launched into a truncated version of how the fuck she'd been as Mallory sat and tried to find a way into the conversation, but every time a sentence formed in her head, Cornelia had moved on to another topic at breakneck speed.

'And how about you, Mallory?' Felix looked at her in their mirror. She felt all eyes on her as she tried to think of something to say.

'Oh, you know. Hanging out with a ghost, the usual,' she said vaguely, then giggled. It was the worst question anyone could ask as she hated the pity, and the sympathy, that came with having to admit her life was not like theirs.

'We – as in Hemlock and Crown – are playing tomorrow night at the Larix,' Ben cut in before she had to elaborate. 'We'd like to see you there. All three of you. Bring your friends.' He winked at Mallory in the rear-view mirror. She looked away.

'We're doing some Apparent stuff, hoping to pull a big crowd in. Well, Ben is. His idea,' Felix said.

'It might be a little out there, but I think it's a solid idea. Basically, if you've seen us play before, it's that, but it's also nothing like that at all. Langdon and Cloud needed a little convincing, but it's going to be great,' Ben said.

Mallory had to admire how even with ingrained faerie eloquence and an inability to lie, Ben did not excel at making sense.

He pulled up outside Cornelia's house, the engine idling.

'I'm not sure we're going to be able to make it,' Mallory said tentatively, wondering how long was polite to remain in the car before insisting she got out. Fatigue was pulling curtains down over her brain function.

'Oh, what!' Ben said, twisting around to look at her again. 'But we haven't seen Cornelia and Diana properly in *months*.'

Mallory's gaze flicked to Cornelia, who chose to look out the window at that moment.

Months implied Cornelia and Diana had been together somewhere.

'That was London, right? Amazing show,' Felix said.

Cornelia and Diana had been together in London without Mallory and never told her.

'We've got a project on, so we probably can't make it,' Mallory said, trying to keep her tone light.

Cornelia sighed. 'Projects. The ender of fun. She's right, though.' She reached forward and patted Felix's arm. 'If we manage to make any headway with... the project, we'll let you know, but I think we'll have to sit this one out.'

'If you change your mind...' Felix said.

'Maybe we can see what we can do,' Cornelia added hopefully. 'Gotta get back to it.'

She leaned over the headrest and kissed Felix on the cheek. They reached a hand back behind their seat and flapped it around until Mallory took their fingers briefly. A peace offering.

Theodore greeted them at the basement door. He took a look at Mallory, who had paled considerably on the journey home. Diana reached up to ruffle her hair as she passed, running up the stairs to hug Felix and Ben, even though she'd seen them recently. It stung Mallory to think about and she looked away.

'You were gone a while,' Theodore said, concerned.

'We were walking, then we got a lift home.'

'You accepted a lift? It's a miracle! We all know that you'd rather desiccate on the floor than ask for help.' Theodore held the door open for her.

Anger flared at the back of Mallory's throat, but she kept it down. It bothered her when anyone pointed out her reluctance to ask for help, because it flew in the face of the confident, capable Mallory everyone used to like so much. She did not want to be someone folk had to do things for. She wanted to be someone whole. Someone nice. Someone good.

She held off the urge to go to bed until Diana was back in the basement.

'Theodore, can the Undetectables use your office as our headquarters for the time being? I have an idea.' Mallory looked around at the walls, the movement sluggish. She was running on empty.

'Of course you can! You don't even need to ask! *Mi casa es su casa*,' Theodore said. 'Quite literally, in Cornelia's case. Goddess, it's just occurred to me that Cornelia and I can't even say we *live* together.' He gripped the lapels of his cardigan and bowed his head. 'Every day I am confronted with realities I would rather deny.'

Mallory turned to her friends, her mind awash with fatigue and pain and a sense of betrayal.

'Diana, if you could assemble whatever information you got today so we can look at them in' – Mallory checked the time, not bothering to modulate the harshness of her tone – 'an hour. Could you also draw up a report of your findings and anything you noticed? And Cornelia, if you could assemble the photographs—'

'Photographs of what?' Diana asked. Cornelia handed them to her and Diana's face scrunched in dismay.

'And the brainstorming we did on the way home. Start sticking all the information up on the wall – photographs, descriptions, any information we have all in one place. And anything either of you remember from the Kuster police file.'

'I read it, therefore I retained it.' Diana tapped her forehead. She lifted a notebook. 'And then I wasn't a total fool, so I wrote it down.'

Mallory had reached the end of her mental checklist. Hurt, exhausted tears pricked the backs of her eyes. 'Did you get all that? Sorry, it's just I need to sleep. Now. But I'll be back in an hour, and we'll comb through everything.'

Diana, Cornelia and Theodore watched her with expressions that Mallory couldn't parse as she dragged herself up to her room. Every time she blinked she saw pictures of Kuster. Kuster, whose memory rested in her hands.

Apparents had many odd customs that Occult folk did not share, but Mallory respected them. She didn't know if Kuster had believed in an afterlife, or if he had anyone to protect him like the Ternion protected all of Occulture, but she knew Kuster deserved answers.

Her body forced her to do what it did best: rest.

EIGHT

'We have met all of your demands,' Cornelia greeted her. She had, in the hour Mallory had been asleep, created chaos in the basement, Diana and Theodore sitting in the middle of it. Mallory got to the bottom of the basement stairs and plucked her old lab coat from the hook, where it had hung, unused, for years. Hers was pale pink, Diana's was blue, and Cornelia's was black, because of course it was.

Half of Theodore's basement comprised an analogue laboratory with iron-plated workbenches so that his static glow did not interfere with his materials. The Broadwicks had provided vintage microscopes retrofitted with mini witchlight crystals and basic instrumentation that would not break should he come into contact with it. Some more powerful machinery sat inside an iron cupboard, should Theodore wish to direct someone else to use it for him. The chaos in this instance was contained at the front of the basement. An iron-and-glass partition wall split the laboratory from the research room; the latter contained four crammed-in desks – one iron and three not – an assortment of chairs, an armchair and sofa – for receiving guests – a side table and a cupboard labelled 'artefacts and instruments' that was open to reveal packets of crisps and other snacks. One neatly covered section of the iron partition hosted an assortment of papers and photographs, as well as a whiteboard, and a map of Wrackton. Books covered every otherwise unoccupied surface.

'A murder board!' Mallory said approvingly, surveying the pattern to the chaos. 'I've always wanted an official one.'

'I'd do anything for you,' Cornelia said, not looking away from the map.

Theodore gave Mallory a quick hug as she passed. Hugging a ghost was like hugging a human, except static-y, like hugging a glass of sparkling water. It wasn't wrong, but it didn't feel quite right, either.

'How was your nap?' Theodore wrapped his hands around a mug of tea as he settled himself cross-legged onto his iron chair. He couldn't drink it, but he could feel the warmth from it. The mug crackled with static and Mallory reached across him to grab a biscuit before carefully sitting down.

'I feel a little better, thank you. Eager to get started.'

'What was seeing the body like?'

'Challenging, but informative.'

Diana settled into her own chair, the sheaf perched on her lap.

'First, we need to ask an important question. Who is Edward Kuster?'

'An Apparent.' Cornelia grabbed a marker and started scrawling on the whiteboard. She had spread everything out neatly, not a piece of string in sight, with space above and below the photographs for writing, the photos of the carvings and the tongue prominent. It was exactly what Mallory had envisioned. Even if it was a little gross.

'Died in Oughteron, near the edge of Wrackton, on the Oughteron Forest side. Bit off his own tongue. Found with carvings in his torso that look Occult, though we aren't sure what they are. I think we're all in agreement that they're somewhat familiar, though.'

'He was twenty-six. He was not discovered for several days, perhaps a week. There were no insects found on the body,' Mallory added.

'Which suggests decomposition hadn't set in at all. Insects can arrive within twenty minutes of passing.' Cornelia pointed the marker at her.

'He was last seen in the Mayoral Offices on 2 October. According to the file we read, he had been working on data recovery for a computer containing records of items kept in the Mayoral Offices,' Diana said. 'A visitor tag was generated when he arrived, but the Offices themselves did that. Nobody actually saw him come in. He clocked out at 9:02 p.m. None of his neighbours have reported seeing him since.'

'What about friends? Did anyone find any friends?'

'He didn't seem to have any,' Diana said. 'His housemate – Apparent, according to the report and the detective I spoke to, so not a valid suspect – noticed he wasn't coming out of his room after about a week. There was no evidence he'd eaten anything, he hadn't picked up his post, and his bedroom door was locked. The housemate got concerned when Kuster didn't answer his knocks, and called it in. According to the police report, Kuster doesn't have any living relatives. He posted semi-regularly on social media and I've done a deep dive in addition to what the report said, but he rarely interacted with anyone and the last post was made on 2 October at 10:23 p.m., supporting the theory that this was roughly when he was killed. His housemate was the closest thing he had to a friend and according to him, they barely exchanged a couple of sentences a week. I can't find anyone that could be deemed a suspect. He really had no one.'

They had properly utilised the entire hour she was asleep. Mallory was both impressed and annoyed at herself for missing it.

She shook her head to clear it. 'Diana, did you learn anything from the crime scene?'

'Hexana, okay. So I got there, right, and it was all quiet. I was just snooping around the bedroom, taking some photos of the area, looking for anything useful, any clues – I assumed any physical evidence would've been taken away, but I was hoping for something that was missed,' Diana said. 'Then I heard footsteps and I was going to get inside a wardrobe, but thought hiding inside a closet was a little on the nose, even for me, so I panicked and just stood there. Then someone says, "Police!" and I turn and it's this woman, and my brain *literally* went blank like the only thought I had was, "Is this a spell?" but I realised no, it was just me being out of practice in subterfuge. It's on my resolutions list for Yule.' Diana took a breath, leaning forward. 'Anyway. I digress.'

'How unusual for you,' Cornelia said, drily.

'Shut up, Cornelia. So she's looking at me and I'm looking at her and I get a second thought in my head, which is, "What lipstick are you wearing?" And another, functioning part of me is like, don't say that. Then Mallory's face flashes in my mind and I say, "Forensic science student!" and the lies just pour like melted chocolate.'

A flash of irrational irritation crawled over Mallory's skin. She might never be a forensic science student, or a student of any kind.

'Turns out this is Detective Inspector O'Sullivan,' Diana went on. 'And, surprise to end all surprises, she's a witch – the only witch on her Apparent force in Oughteron, recently promoted to DI, and on loan to head up Wrackton's motley pseudo-homicide team. I tell her my classmates – all mean, icky folk – sent me to the crime scene as a prank. It was like her guard dropped instantly, which you would think I would think was a good thing, but there was something… *off* about it. If she got to DI rank, surely would-be criminals weren't just successfully lying to her face? And we know I'm good at making things up on the spot, but still. There was maybe some reverse psychology happening there, to get me to implicate myself or something, but I felt – and this is pure conjecture, to be clear – as though *she* was startled by *me* being there, and talking about me gave her something to focus on that wasn't whatever she was doing there on her own.'

'Are you ever going to tell us what you learned? Some of us are ageing rapidly over here,' Cornelia said.

'And some of us are not ageing at all,' Theodore added.

'Yes! Hexana, give me a minute. So THEN, I ask her about the case.'

'How did she react?'

'She seemed to be taken in by my pitiful tale of callous classmates, so she tells me Kuster was found in a locked room. They found no evidence, apart from what's on his body – the carvings, the tongue, all gross by the way – and the only things in his room were a witchlight, one of those *Visit Wrackton* touristy ones, a laundry basket, a laptop, and a stack of medium-quality books. No weapon, no knife, nothing useful like that, no sign of forced entry. It's a locked-room mystery,' she finished. 'Happy, Cornelia?'

'Very.'

'Great,' Mallory said. 'That's something. Don't know what it is yet, but it's something. Write that up.'

'Can I see that photo of the body, please?' Theodore said, his head tilted thoughtfully. Cornelia passed it over.

'This poor man.'

'It's so horrible,' Diana agreed.

'This carving, though. Don't you recognise it?'

'No,' Cornelia said. 'That's been bothering us. Tip of the tongue.'

'If I, a literal ghost, recognise where I've seen it before, I should think three witches would.' Theodore stood and pulled at a stack of books, static spraying. 'Here.' He put the book down on the desk next to Mallory.

He flipped the pages rapidly and stopped on a glossy photo of the Observatory, from which Wrackton's Occulture observed the Ternion.

'It unfolds,' Theodore prompted. Mallory leaned forward and carefully peeled back the insert, revealing a new image of a stained-glass window at the back of the Observatory, curving around the wall and extending up to the ceiling. It depicted a scene from the story of the Ternion – Hexana, Elisabella and Blair – in individual panes. The bottom of the window was yellow glass, melting into navy at the top. Constellations shone through on clear nights. There, and repeating behind the image of Blair, was the exact pattern of interconnecting circles, lines and stars carved into Kuster's torso.

'I knew this,' Mallory said, reading the description. 'Circles for Blair, lines for Elisabella, stars for Hexana.'

'Oh yeah!' Diana said. 'Looking at it makes me feel a bit sick, but I know this.'

'I should hope so. How long have you lived here? How many Ternion events have you been to?' Theodore spluttered, aghast. Diana, Cornelia and Mallory shrugged as one.

'I never really went to the Observatory after we left Occult primary,' Mallory said. 'I know the basics, of course. They emerged as the chosen daughters of Morrigan and Hecate at the end of the Vampire Wars, and they keep Occulture safe and harmonious.'

'Same here,' Diana said. 'Though I thought they were actually the daughters of Morrigan and Hecate. And I didn't think anyone really spent time in the Observatory any more, bar older folk.'

'I agree with Mallory, I thought they were chosen daughters, though I've heard the actual daughter story somewhere before,' Cornelia said. 'My family only dragged me to the Observatory when there was something important going on. It's just a part of Occulture, but we don't have to be part of it, necessarily. The Ternion will help us if we need them, regardless of if we go to a glass building to do it. That's been the way for a lot of folk for a long time.'

'Like standing in a garage doesn't make you a car,' Theodore said sagely, nodding.

'Honestly, the last time I remember hearing anything new or interesting about the Ternion I was at most six years old. And I was probably not paying attention,' Cornelia continued.

'I don't really remember it coming up much for me, either. The circles-lines-stars thing does ring a bell, but...' Mallory tried to pull up anything concrete, but couldn't.

'All I've really retained is that Samhain is an excuse for a party,' Diana said. 'The reasons why don't matter that much, unless you're super into it.'

Theodore frowned. 'I once heard a story about how the Ternion formed – the proper story, with proper details. I can tell you, if you like.'

'Sure,' Diana said. 'Not like we're doing anything important.'

'It was hundreds of years ago now, some months before the end of the Vampire Wars,' Theodore said airily, a spray of static lifting from him as he leaned an elbow on the iron table. Mallory realised he was looking at an old newspaper cutout shoved in the pocket of his cardigan. She bit back a smile. 'Elisabella, Hexana and Blair were ordinary yet powerful witches who believed that unity among Occulture was paramount. Without it, vampires and faeries and witches and trolls refused to cooperate. Why, I can't tell you.'

The article, Mallory presumed, did not say.

'They decided a change needed to be made. A unifying feature that everyone in Occulture could get behind. One that included the Do No Harm Charter, that forbade vampires from biting anyone or using magic again.'

'Why did they?' Cornelia asked suddenly. 'Stop the vampires?'

Diana and Mallory frowned at her. It was a given that vampires were forbidden from ingesting blood at all, and something Mallory had always accepted as fact.

Theodore looked up at her. 'It was thought that blood led to violence. That they would drink blood for a time and require more and more to continue having magic. It is thought that the in-fighting was a direct result of their consuming witch blood and, eventually, the blood of other vampires. The Ternion put a stop to it, though how exactly the article – the *story,* that I know off the top of my head without looking at anything' – he shoved the cutting back into his pocket – 'doesn't say. I've never been able to find out.'

'A wise and informative tale,' Cornelia said. 'Thanks, Theo. I don't think they ever explained that to us in school.'

'I mean, they probably did,' Diana said. 'You were just busy being a little delinquent.'

'The subject of my delinquency is fraught with inconsistencies and downright lies.' Cornelia threw the cap of her marker at her.

'So it's probably something to do with Ternion power, then? The murder,' Mallory said, but her friends didn't respond, bickering over the marker cap. Mallory could feel them losing interest and scrambled for what to do next. 'Cornelia, the beetles changed colour in the mortuary. I totally forgot to ask – what exactly does that mean?'

'It just means someone used magic in the vicinity of the body and the beetles were able to hold on to it. Like a litmus test, but very sensitive, and they can hold that magic for a long time.' Cornelia chewed her lip, thinking. 'Up to a month, sometimes two, depending on environment.'

'Does that mean they've physically got a sample of the magic the killer used in them?' Mallory felt out of her depth asking what she felt Cornelia would think were ignorant questions, but Cornelia's face brightened.

'It does! This sounds like you've got an idea coming. I've missed your ideas.'

'Do you think there would be a way to extract the magic from the beetles? Without hurting them, of course,' Mallory said hastily. An idea *was* forming in her head, but she wasn't sure if it was a good one.

'I haven't tried, but in theory, yes. How they pick up magic is not dissimilar to how pollinators gather, so it'd be a similar removal process. I'm pretty sure I'd just have to ask them politely,' Cornelia said nonchalantly.

'Great.' Mallory turned to Theodore. 'Theo, our plans for the spell fingerprinting machine… Do you think it would work with the beetles?'

'First of all, *love* this idea. We love to see Mallory using science,' he said emphatically. 'Secondly… yes. I think this a really good, secondary use for the spell fingerprinting machine. Unlike the primary use we've discussed before.' Theodore widened his eyes meaningfully at her.

'Which we will discuss again at a later date,' Mallory said. Today was not the day to talk about it.

'The what in the who?' Cornelia asked. 'What is this?'

'Theodore and I have come up with a spell database that we modelled on a fingerprint database,' Mallory said quickly, before Theodore could explain the real function of it. 'He talked me through the design of it, I put it together over the last couple of years.'

'I stood very far away at all times, even though nobody puts me in the corner,' Theodore added.

'So, the same way in Apparent science that a fingerprint can be matched to an existing database of fingerprints, we thought a database of spells would be helpful for identifying magical crimes. The database itself was easy – I programmed every known spell we could find into it. We just haven't found a way of introducing magic to it that wasn't directly cast at the machine. And I...' She trailed off.

'Haven't been in the position to supply much magic,' Cornelia said, nodding. Her and Diana's expressions said they understood, even though Mallory knew they couldn't possibly.

That was the crux of the matter. A spell database that stored magic would give Mallory access to spells that she hadn't used in years. It wouldn't cure her, but she wouldn't have to expend energy on producing magic, only on using it. Using her own wouldn't work, but a database filled with the spells of other witches would make magic accessible to her. She could be a witch again.

But the thought of asking for that kind of help was crushing.

'Yeah, I think the beetles would be happy to help out,' Cornelia continued. 'Is it here? This... spell fingerprinter. Sprinter. Petition to name it the Sprinter.'

'Petition granted,' Theodore said. 'I love it, it's so... zingy.'

Mallory did not agree that years of anguish and hard work should be boiled down into anything *zingy*, but said nothing. She moved to the back of the lab, pulling a laptop-sized machine and a small electronic pad from an iron-lined cupboard.

'Theodore, stand behind the iron screen, please,' Mallory called. Diana wheeled it in front of him. 'Cornelia, do you have a spare beetle?'

'Yes.' She produced one in a small box from her pocket.

'Do you just carry those around now?!' Diana shrieked, aghast.

'Obviously.'

'Do a spell, any spell,' Mallory prompted.

Cornelia whispered into the beetle and it glowed green, chirping.

Mallory set up the machine on an empty bench, and beckoned Cornelia to bring the beetle over.

'In theory, we can put the beetles here, and the machine should...' She stepped back as it lit up and started scanning through her database.

'Is it working? Mallory, you're a genius!' Theodore shouted. 'I am also a genius, but I impart my genius to you!'

It beeped quickly.

MATCH FOUND: LIFE DETECTION SPELL.

'Fuck me,' Cornelia said. 'This is awesome.'

'So now if we try with the Kuster beetles, we just wait and see,' Mallory said. 'It's incredibly unlikely it's a spell any of us would know, but maybe it's just a spell we've encountered that's been altered.' She returned to her seat, looking at the crime scene photos.

'What's that?' she pointed to six lines scrawled at the edge of the whiteboard.

Worthy i am
Who never learn
Of dross lord
Souls... find the
End near comes
more! one three

'That was in the police file, in an evidence bag,' Diana said. 'It was written on the bottom of one of those sudoku puzzle book pages. I thought it could be a clue, something left behind by the killer, but I can't figure it out. I think it's a riddle, but a very, very shitty one.'

'It looks like it's in some sort of code, maybe,' Mallory said, squinting at it. She vaguely recalled seeing it in the police file, remembering the crackle of the evidence bag under her fingers.

'I tried a few decoding spells. Basic ones, like from puzzle games, but can't figure it out. It could've been written by Kuster, for all we know. O'Sullivan didn't mention it, anyway, but I thought it was worth looking at. If it was in an evidence bag, someone thought there was a good enough reason to take it from the scene.'

Mallory frowned, trying to make it make sense, then let her gaze fall back on the photographs.

'I wish there was a way to just look at the whole scene from above, see if there was any way for the killer to get into the room,' Cornelia said.

'That's an idea,' Diana said slowly. 'Wait, Francine Leon!'

'Diana, please no,' Cornelia groaned.

'You've heard of Francine Leon, Mallory, right? I've told you about her?'

Mallory shook her head, suddenly aware of just how much time she'd spent away from her friends.

'You're about to hear more than you can imagine,' Cornelia said ominously, with the tired energy of someone who'd heard a lot about Francine Leon very recently.

Diana ignored her. 'Francine Leon was this Apparent who was, first and foremost, a noted lesbian. And same. When I die, I want "Diana Cheung-Merriweather, noted lesbian and motherfucking genius" on my gravestone. Francine had a really cool wife, who... actually I'll come back to that.' She grinned. 'But even more important than that, she is basically the founder of modern forensic science.'

'Wait, really?' Mallory was surprised. It was news to her, but she was also used to reading Apparent histories that erased some of their key players. She felt a flicker of irritation that even with the greatest of efforts, it seemed she wasn't more knowledgeable than her friends on anything.

'Her name is rarely mentioned, though she was instrumental in forensic technique developments in the last century.' Diana lit up, seemingly at the idea of a new captive audience. 'She didn't have any formal education or anything, but got heavily involved with the police, believing that they weren't solving crimes properly. Also relatable. She built these dioramas using dollhouse furniture that were scale reconstructions designed to show the *what* of a crime, to help train police to better pay attention to information found at scenes. And I've just thought… I'll be back soon. I'm going to use the kitchen, for space, Cornelia.' Diana gathered up the photos of Kuster and left in a hurry.

'Did you get any more context than that?' Mallory asked. Cornelia and Theodore shook their heads.

'Few can understand the rapturous expression upon Diana's visage. Least of all me.' Theodore sighed. 'There is much to know about the inner machinations of the minds of my young friends.'

The Sprinter beeped and Cornelia was out of her seat before Mallory had a chance to react. Theodore slunk back behind the iron screen.

'Mallory, darling, you aren't going to like this one bit.'

Cornelia held the beetles on her hand, staring at the screen.

NO MATCHES.

ERROR?// TRACE UNDETECTABLE/UNKNOWN.

'All magic leaves a trace,' Cornelia said, jabbing at the display.

This was the first thing Mallory had ever learned about magic, so she knew this.

'The trace is definitely detectable, because the beetles changed colour. There's an extensive body of research beyond my own confirming that *Sonata lutumae* react to magic. Don't you, Selene?' Cornelia stroked the back of her neon-green beetle with a finger.

Selene curled into a ball and emitted a high-pitched whistling sound, like a tuneless pan pipe. Mallory and Cornelia startled in alarm. The second beetle did the same thing. It was over in moments, the beetles moving as though nothing had happened.

'That was weird,' Mallory said, frowning.

'Can someone tell me what's going on?' Theodore called from behind the screen. 'The iron is reflecting my static back at me, it's making it hard to hear.'

'No match.' Mallory returned to the research room and pulled the screen away. She took a marker and added this to the murder board herself.

'I'm thinking something rather wonderful, Mallory, and I think you'd like to think it too.'

'What's that?' Mallory forced her attention towards him.

'What are the fundamental principles of forensic science?'

'Every touch leaves a trace,' Mallory said immediately. It was the same principle as magic.

'And we've got a lack of tangible evidence.'

'Yes.'

'So what does that tell us?'

Mallory tilted her head. 'It tells us nothing.'

'No. It doesn't. The lack of evidence *is* the evidence.' Theodore pointed flourishingly.

'I… I don't follow.'

'You see, we are looking for evidence where there isn't any, and that *is* the evidence. What sort of creature leaves no trace?'

'There are no creatures that leave no trace.' Mallory frowned.

'PRECISELY!' Theodore said.

'So you're saying the answer can't be nothing?'

'Yes.'

'So you're saying the lack of it being a known spell means that there is something hidden there? That there's nothing to find, no basic science to go on, because someone wanted it that way?'

Theodore broke into a grin. 'You get me. You always get me.'

Mallory looked at the desk, an idea forming. 'We've still got the mass spec plans, but I left them at h— Oh, of course, you've got more of them in your pocket.'

'You thought I didn't have copies of my plans? I know I dropped the originals in your house.' Theodore handed over the mass spectrometer schematics. 'Perhaps that was all part of *my* plan. And not at all that I'm clumsy.'

'Theo, I'm sorry—'

He shook his head.

'No. It is I who is the sorriest. I insist that we must not waste time tossing sorrys around our research room like wayward tennis balls at a tennis match where there is a dog playing fetch also present, but press on.' He flattened the plan so Cornelia could see it.

'What's the mass spec plan?' Cornelia said. 'Did you guys rest *at all* the last few years?'

Mallory ignored the second question.

'So, you know what a GC-mass spectrometer is?'

'Big machine,' Cornelia said immediately.

Mallory laughed. 'Yes. At its most basic explanation, it identifies the elemental or isotopic signature of a molecular sample. The "GC" part just stands for gas chromatography, which helps analyse chemical compounds. It's an all-in-one machine, so to speak. What we want to do, what we hope we will do, is use a mass spec to isolate a magic sample, one from your beetles.'

'I'm with you so far.' Cornelia nodded.

'Mallory sounds so professional.' Theodore beamed. 'She reads lots.'

'The idea is that we'll be able to identify the *type* of magic used in a spell, rather than match a specific spell, as with the Sprinter. It's expensive, so this is all theoretical. But everything on earth is made up of elements and compounds, so it's reasonable to assume magic is made up of those too.' Mallory glanced at Cornelia, worried she'd lost her, but she had her full attention.

'Being that magic is on earth,' Theodore said.

'So with a mass spectrometer, you're breaking things down to their basic components, and it should, in theory, show the specific signature of the magic molecule we introduce. Rather than trying to identify the individual spell, we just need to show it was cast by a witch, or a demon, or a troll, or a faerie, or even a vampire,' Mallory continued.

'And how does this help us?'

'We just need to show it *could've been done* by our suspect, when we have one. Like blood typing in Apparent court cases. You can use a blood type match in conjunction with other, stronger evidence, but a mismatch eliminates a suspect immediately,' Mallory said. 'So our theory is that the mass spectrometer would show that witch magic is carbon, vampire is iron, faerie is nitrogen – though actually testing this would help.' She stopped. 'Sorry, I've been talking for ages.'

'Yes you have and it's been the best age of my endless existence,' Theodore said.

'This is fascinating. Or would be, if I understood half of what you were doing,' Cornelia said, looking as impressed as Cornelia had ever looked. Mallory blushed. 'Go ahead and order one, we've got the space.'

'I'll look up rental places,' Mallory said.

Cornelia looked at her blankly. 'Rent?'

Mallory had never really been able to understand Cornelia's attitude to money. Although Occult towns operated on a universal basic income, the Broadwicks had so much more money than Cornelia seemed to appreciate.

'Cornelia, my dear friend,' Theodore said. 'My sweet summer peanut, though you were born in the depths of winter. A brand-new mass spectrometer costs as much as a small house.'

'And?'

'And you do understand that though it is the price of a small house, nobody can reside in it, and that I forever run the risk of breaking it?' Theodore said.

Cornelia shrugged. 'I'm sure there's insurance or something? Don't worry about it, not like the Broadwick coffers will feel it.'

'Allow me to take care of procuring one for us,' Theodore said grandly to Mallory, then turned to Cornelia. 'Could you order one for me? I can't use a computer. And even if I could, they won't let me sign for it. Because I am dead.'

In the kitchen, Diana was surrounded by papers, tiny furniture, and the shell of a small house.

'Are you making a dollhouse?' Cornelia picked up a tiny bedframe and squinted at it.

Diana scoffed. 'No, Cornelia. Not a "dollhouse". A to-scale, completely accurate crime-scene reconstruction *diorama*. That *happens* to be encased in a convenient and appropriately-sized shell.'

'Otherwise known as a dollhouse. Like the ones Francine Leon made,' Cornelia said.

'No. No. They're so much more than that. Francine Leon was limited by her Apparentness. I have taken the *dioramas* she made and I have made them… more. Hers showed the *what* of the crime. Mine also shows the potential *how*. Or it will, when I'm done. Look, here's a little Kuster.'

Diana handed a miniature paper Kuster to Mallory.

'This is cool. How does it work?' Mallory watched mini-Kuster walk around her palm in a circle, very much alive pre-murder.

'Rather than us acting out a reconstruction, I thought it best if we watched the scene and tried to determine how the murder happened. Kuster died in a locked room by Occult means, it's probably to do with the Ternion in some way, and it's up to us to figure out how. Or it will be. When I'm done.'

'Great work, Diana,' Mallory said. 'We were going to stop for lunch, actually.'

'This is the best idea you've ever had.'

They ordered food from the Larix, a faerie- and troll-owned dive bar by night, run-down café by day, situated on the very edge of Wrackton, next to Redwood Forest. The doorbell rang and Diana returned with three paper bags and Langdon, one of Felix and Ben's bandmates, in tow. His uncles were the Larix's co-owners, though he'd left town with Felix as soon as he could. Langdon bounced in the room with charming confidence Mallory recognised instantly. Another friend she had lost contact with in recent years. He brushed long, dark curls out of his face, his warm brown skin highlighted with just the barest blue-grey tint when he stood in the light.

'Langdon wanted to say hi.' Diana organised the table, moving her diorama away so everyone could sit down.

'Cornelia! I heard you two were back. And even if I hadn't heard, no one else would order this combination of food.' He gave Cornelia a hug, though she was busy texting someone and barely looked up at him. 'Are you coming to the gig tomorrow night?'

'Gig? What gig?' Diana asked. 'We're in!'

'We can't, we've got a lot of work on,' Mallory said firmly. 'Next time.'

Diana's face fell and Mallory felt a swoop of guilt.

'Awh. Well, if you change your mind, you know where we are. Voted the bar with the stickiest floors.' Langdon winked as he left.

'Are you sure we can't go?' Diana asked, elbowing Cornelia into distributing plates. 'I'm sure we could make it work.'

Cornelia looked to Mallory, and shook her head. Mallory's cheeks burned.

They tore into their food in companionable silence, Mallory insisting they put away the crime scene photos until they were done.

'I can spend another hour or so looking through our clues, and then I think I need to head home for the evening,' she said.

Cornelia was still texting, smiling into her phone. She noticed Diana and Mallory staring at her and hastily put it down.

'Sorry. What did you say, Mallory? Wait, I heard it. No, you don't need to go home.'

'I need clean clothes, and my meds, and I don't want to put you out,' Mallory said awkwardly.

'Don't be ridiculous. There's so much space here. It makes way more sense for you to move in, even temporarily,' Cornelia said.

'Are you sure? I wouldn't...' Mallory trailed off, not sure how to say that she wouldn't want anyone to see her on the really bad days. It was bad enough when Theodore saw her then.

'If I can't provide an official headquarters for the Undetectables, what can I do? It's decided. And if you need help moving your stuff, I can ask B— uh, a friend. I can get a friend to help,' she said, then busied herself organising the cakes they'd ordered for dessert.

B could be *Ben*. Mallory thought about how excited Ben had been to see Cornelia, and felt naïve to have not realised at the time. Even if they were just friends, she should've seen it coming; of course she would replace her with someone else. Someone better than her, someone more worth Cornelia's time.

She forced her thoughts to still, inhaling slowly. She was moving in with Cornelia and Diana. She wasn't being left behind.

Diana scowled at Cornelia. 'We don't need help with that. I can pop over if Mallory needs. She's not moving her furniture in here, like.'

'Yeah, totally, you're right,' Cornelia said vaguely, then shook her head as if to clear it. 'But yes, that's that decided. Mallory lives here now.'

Mallory felt it was almost too good to be true.

NINE

Seven days to Samhain

'I've asked my friend to help me move your stuff over,' Cornelia said, looking up at Mallory from her corner. Light had faded outside, and at some point Cornelia had turned on the witchlights. Mallory had tasked her with going through a massive book of spells, in the hopes they'd find something that used the Ternion symbol carved into Kuster's torso. Every so often Cornelia would input potential spells into the Sprinter and test them against the stored sample they'd got from her beetles, grumbling when nothing came of it. Because this was largely boring work, she had not gone long without interrupting Mallory.

'Oh yeah?' Mallory turned away from staring at the symbol, the word TERNION written in big letters on their murder board beside the terrible riddle, and photos of Kuster, as she had been doing for some hours now. She tried to keep her tone casual. 'Who is this friend?'

Cornelia shrugged, casting a sideways glance at Diana, who had taken over the seating area with her diorama, whilst Theodore was in his chair, filling in yet more documents. Mallory could see Diana was deep in her work. Whatever Cornelia was about to say, she didn't want Diana to hear. Mallory's heart picked up, unsure she wanted to know who this person, this *B*— was.

'So I recently—'

There was a knock on the door. Cornelia was on her feet in seconds.

'Hello, I hope I'm not interrupting anything,' Jacob interrupted. He bobbed into the room, looking even more rumpled than he had at the autopsy. His mass of curls stuck out from underneath a beanie and his shoes both erred on the side of untied. 'I just wanted to let you know that, erm… I made a mistake, saying you were med students. It didn't go down well with Mr Night Mayor. He said it was, quote, "messy".' Jacob made rueful air quotes. 'It's a bit embarrassing, but I won't be able to, erm… help you out with getting you into places any more. I'm sorry. Not without going through the police, anyway, but I don't have the power to do that.' He picked at a scab at the base of his index finger.

'That's okay,' Mallory said. She felt a deep ache in her legs which stopped her from standing to speak to him. 'Mistakes happen. It was a great help for us to observe the autopsy, anyway.' She gave him an encouraging look.

From the corner of her eye, Mallory noticed Theodore rubbing at his cat whiskers and she smiled sadly. They'd tried to wipe them away many times; the whiskers were part and parcel of the ghost outfit.

'Hello again,' Jacob said to Theodore.

Theodore mumbled something and fiddled with a pen.

Jacob stared at him for another moment before saying, 'I'm sorry again, for how I was, yesterday.' His eyes darted over the murder board and back to Mallory. 'I think I was so freaked out by the whole… dead body… thing. Silly of me. Are you working on the case right now?'

'Just figuring some stuff out,' Diana said, without looking up from her diorama.

'We were just wondering if you'd heard anything you could tell us about Edward Kuster? Mr Night Mayor mentioned the last known sighting of him was in the Offices,' Mallory asked suddenly.

Jacob tilted his head. 'I didn't see him, so I don't know anything, if I'm honest. I rarely see or hear anything useful. I'm always sent off into the bowels of the Mayoral Offices.'

'Would that make it the Mayoral Orifices?' Theodore asked.

Jacob blinked, continuing. 'I'm sorry, you must think me so useless, but if I hear anything worth repeating, I'll pass it on. I'd love to see you solve this murder.' He smiled earnestly.

Mallory shook her head. 'You're not useless at all. Thank you for answering.'

'Your finger is bleeding. Do you need a plaster, Jacob?' Theodore said.

Jacob looked down at his hands and groaned. 'Can't even walk into someone's house without spilling blood.'

Theodore was back in seconds and handed a plaster over. Mallory felt the urge to look away as Theodore's hand brushed Jacob's, static sparking between them.

'I can't do much, but I guess if you need anything – anything else, that is – you know where to find me. Oh, gracious.' Jacob caught sight of the big moon-shaped clock on the wall behind

Mallory's head. 'I better go, my girlfriend is waiting. See you again. Theodore.' He smiled shyly and hurried out.

There was a beat of silence. If ghosts could cry, Theodore would've been in tears by now.

'Maybe by "girlfriend" he just means friend, who is female,' Diana said facetiously, because it was the use of 'girlfriend' she hated most in the world.

'Or maybe by "girlfriend" he meant he's a heterosexual male with an exclusive interest in women. Who are alive,' Theodore snapped, uncharacteristically.

'Theo, not every man with a girlfriend is straight.' Cornelia pulled him into a hug. Diana nestled into his other side and Theodore opened his arms for Mallory to join. She did, pressed up against Cornelia. She could smell chocolate biscuits and cinnamon shampoo mixed with Theodore's slightly-burnt-toast scent.

'We do not erase bisexuals, pansexuals or queer people in this house.' Cornelia affectionately stroked one of his cat ears. Mallory could see how soft her hair looked up close, and was filled with a rush of affection for Cornelia that she pushed down as she pulled out of the hug.

'Diana, are you done with the diorama?' Mallory smoothed her hair back, her brain chanting *B, B, B* as she forced herself to accept Cornelia's confessional moment had passed them by. She tried to keep her emotions in check as she returned her attention to the murder. To Kuster.

'Almost. Follow me upstairs.'

Mallory waited a beat, hoping Cornelia would get the hint to stay and tell her who this friend was. But she gathered up a book and her notes instead.

'Need me to carry anything for you?' Cornelia held her hand out to Mallory as she passed and Mallory pushed her hands into her pockets.

That moment of honesty, whatever it could've been about, evaporated.

Mallory shook her head and followed Cornelia out, ignoring Theodore's curious look as she passed.

'Observe,' Diana said grandly.

She sat them at the kitchen table, Theodore at the furthest end so he wouldn't get static on everything, and pulled the diorama out. Contrary to Diana's assertions that it wasn't a dollhouse, the diorama was contained in one, though Diana had painted the shell black and stuck scaled crime scene tape she'd made around the outside.

She had managed to accurately recreate Kuster's bedroom. A faded striped bedspread on his double bed, the green paint on the walls, the overflowing laundry basket, the drawn curtains over his window, the desk with a still-glowing laptop and paper strewn across it, a beaten-up desk chair, a bedside table with a stack of books and a *Visit Wrackton* novelty witchlight perched on top. Occult folk had figured out a long time ago how to turn the ordinary into novelty tourist items, so most Apparents who had had any kind of involvement with Occult towns had some kind of Occult object in their possession. Though it was normally tarot cards.

Mallory had to admit, it looked exactly like the photographs.

'This is amazing.'

'If I can't dress sets, I can build crime scenes,' Diana said happily. 'Francine Leon would be so proud of how her legacy has evolved. Probably, I've no idea how clued in she was on Occulture.'

The Kuster figurine stood outside his bedroom door.

'Some of this is the educated assumption of what he did, but that might give us a clue how this worked,' Diana said. 'So we assume it's 2 October. He got ready for bed. Animate,' Diana told the scene.

Kuster reached out a paper hand and pulled open his bedroom door. He closed it behind him, and locked it.

'The door was locked from the inside, as confirmed by the housemate and police report. He now gets ready for bed – O'Sullivan said they found the clothes he'd been wearing that day in his laundry basket, and the police report recorded those as evidence. He was wearing a T-shirt and pyjama bottoms, and there were clothes left on the floor in front of the laundry basket, so again we are making educated assumptions about what he did.' Kuster stood still and his paper outfit changed. 'Now he gets into bed, pulls the blankets over himself.' The lighting changed inside the diorama as the witchlight went out, the laptop glow disappeared.

'Then it's a question of what happened next,' Diana continued. 'How did the killer get in? This was the room as it was found when his body was discovered.'

They watched paper Kuster lie in his bed. Watched him bite down on his tongue, writhing and thrashing. Watched the symbol appear on his torso.

'Someone got a knife – or a knifey spell – in, somehow. It's not like Occult folk can magically teleport into rooms, and they'd have to know the layout of Kuster's room and his precise location to make those carvings completely remotely. Could the window have unlatched?' Cornelia asked.

Diana shook her head.

'Do you know what's strange about locked-room murders?' Theodore asked, clearly about to share whether they wanted to hear it or not. 'I mean, really. You do a murder, commit a heinous crime, and then just... lock the door behind you? Or don't use the door? And then the investigators will spend all their time being foiled by a piece of wood, rather than the murder.'

'A well-formed thought, Theodore,' Cornelia said.

'Locked doors and metaphors,' Theodore said. 'That's the title of my memoir I will have to laboriously write by hand.'

'I've looked through my spellbooks, but I can't really see anything of use,' Cornelia said. 'But that's all I've done. We're missing so much context.' She dropped her head into her hands. 'This is taking up so much more of my time than I thought it would.'

'I know,' Diana said. 'I'm used to long days, but I'm exhausted already.'

Mallory swallowed. They couldn't give up now.

'We've barely started! We agreed to get justice for Kuster, and we barely know anything yet,' Mallory protested, trying to keep her face neutral. 'There is a spell – or spells – that is either a spell-knife or is used in conjunction with a literal knife, that makes its victim choke, that can enter a room without someone being there to cast it, or can allow someone to lock a door behind them, and it has something to do with the Ternion.'

'What if Kuster murdered himself?' Theodore asked.

Mallory glanced at him. 'How would that even be possible?'

'I don't think it is, I just wanted to participate.'

'Anyway. Can you play it again please?' Mallory said. Diana did. Kuster walking into his room. Kuster lying down to sleep. Kuster dying.

'There's just nothing in the room,' Mallory said. 'If this is exactly as he was found, he kept nothing around. Some books, a witchlight, a laptop, clothes. Have clothes ever killed someone?'

'Do you mean literally in an Occult sense, or would you like to learn of the horrors of Apparent consumption under late-stage capitalism? Because I can go for hours on this topic,' Diana said.

'I've heard that song before, thank you,' Cornelia said.

'Is there any indication of timing on this thing?' Mallory stared at Kuster, trying to force her thoughts, but she was hitting a wall. 'Not that it matters, if there was nobody around and we have no suspects.'

'According to the police file, the last thing he did on his laptop was make a social media post about how every day is the same,' Diana said. 'This was at 10:23 p.m. on 2 October, and seemed to be manually posted rather than scheduled, because there was nothing in the scheduled queue. I am a smidgeon impressed they thought to look. Nobody else has seen him since, there has been no further activity from the account, and that's the last day he scheduled a job or answered any emails. As the housemate noticed a week later that he hadn't taken anything from the fridge or picked up any of his post dating back to the day he was last seen, I am reasonably confident in assuming approximately 10:30 p.m. on 2 October is the time of death. Also, I think you should care a little more about fast fashion, Cornelia, but that's just my opinion.'

'*Hexana*, what happened to you?' Mallory murmured at paper Kuster.

'I thought this would be more helpful, to be honest,' Diana said, shrugging. 'But maybe when we make some headway on the Ternion spell, we'll understand. Without viable suspects – do *not* say Van Doren, Cornelia – it's sort of unsolvable.'

Fear crept into Mallory. There was a chance her friends would get bored of this case. Get bored of her. She pulled a caffeinated drink out of the fridge, took a long gulp and swallowed her meds, realising as she did that she'd forgotten to take them earlier in the day. Mistakes like that could cost her entire days in bed.

Diana stared at her diorama. She raised an eyebrow conspiratorially.

'I have a suggestion,' she said.

'Hit me with it.' Mallory rubbed her face.

'Let's go out.'

'What?'

'To the gig. Tonight, the Larix. See Ben and Felix play, come back, get some sleep, start fresh tomorrow.'

'That's a great idea,' Cornelia said. 'Finally! Let's go do something fun. I've missed this shithole of a town.'

'It's not a shithole, Cornelia.' Diana shoved her lightly.

'It is. But it's *our* shithole, and I'm very fond of it.'

'This is a murder investigation,' Mallory protested, somewhat aghast. 'We can't just go… gallivanting.'

Cornelia and Diana both laughed.

'That was very cute of you, but Diana is right,' Cornelia said. 'We've both been away for so long, I want to see… some friends, blow off some steam, come back and get going again. It's one night. Not even that! A couple of hours. You should come. If you feel up to it.' She tilted her head conspiratorially. 'Besides, I bet you haven't been going anywhere while we've been gone.'

'She hasn't,' Theodore the Betrayer said.

Mallory shot him a look.

This felt terribly irresponsible. She wanted to tell her friends that just because they could go and get another job if they messed this up didn't mean she could. That a man was lying on a slab in the mortuary and that they'd been tasked with solving his murder. She wanted to demand how they could contemplate their own fun at a time like this. She wanted to scream about how unfair it was that they could go off and live their lives and come back and have everyone they knew rally around them and vie for their attention, when Mallory had been there all along and everyone had forgotten about her.

She took a deep breath, the words on the tip of her tongue. Anger surged through her, her hands shaking from how much she wanted to say it all, to watch their faces change, watch them hear her.

She exhaled.

They maybe had a point. Go out, see people. Getting out of the house might help her think better, even if the act of going out was risking a pain flare.

It was a rebellion she hadn't dared allow herself in years.

'Fine. The Undetectables are released for the evening,' Mallory said. 'We'll go to the Larix. But we restart work tomorrow morning. Nine sharp.'

'Off for a night of frivolity and festivity!' Theodore said, clapping his hands. 'To which I am not invited, on account of the technology issue. And it's fine. I'm not even upset about it. I couldn't be less upset. Do I seem upset? As if I do, you're wrong.' He stood, pulling his cardigan around him. 'If anyone needs me – which they won't – I will be in the lab all night. In the dark. And the quiet. Alone.'

TEN

Crown and Hemlock had just finished their soundcheck by the time the Undetectables walked in, dressed up for a night out against Mallory's best judgement.

Cornelia and Diana squeezed her arms gently and shouted something she couldn't hear, before immediately scattering. Mallory hesitated at the entrance, and then tried to find somewhere to sit, frustration tugging at her throat. They'd insisted she come here with them, and then they'd left her. Mallory considered turning around and going back to the lab and to Theodore.

Cloud, Crown and Hemlock's faerie bassist, had glamoured their usually light hair a deep blood red with thorns braided through it, and they waved to Mallory as they approached the bar for a drink, leaning on their cane for support, which had also been glamoured with thorns. Faerie glamours were mostly cosmetic and were almost always breathtaking.

Mallory's heartbeat thrummed in her ears, both from the terrible bass from the Larix's sound system, and from the effort of navigating her way around people who were inclined to bump into her or press against her, all of which hurt, all the time. She slipped around and between clumps of folk, whispering a padding spell to help her clothing absorb some of the impact. It hurt her to do it, but not as much as being pushed by music enthusiasts would.

She scanned the crowd for Cornelia or Diana, and Felix or Ben. She was taller than a lot of the people in the crowd, but it was dim, made worse by dry ice and smoke from cinnamon cigarettes.

Mallory changed tack and headed to the bathroom, her boots sticking to the floor as she walked. It had got much worse since her last time here, so it was possible Langdon hadn't been joking that the Larix was award-winning for stickiness.

She met Grey Quinn as he blocked her way through a doorway, his hands in his suit pockets. Mallory remembered him well as the demon who had consigned Theodore to a feline-esque eternity. Mallory steered around him with a nod, Diana bobbing at her elbow suddenly. She pushed Diana ahead of her into a narrow hallway lined with paste posters advertising a Samhain séance, some torn and revealing posters from years gone by underneath.

'Sorry about that, Felix asked me to help with their outfit,' Diana shouted in her ear.

'It's fine,' Mallory shouted back.

'I'm going to get a drink. Did you actually need to pee?' Diana shouted, just as there was a lull in the music for a moment. Mallory winced as her ear rang. Quinn was gone from the doorway.

Diana grabbed Mallory's hand and guided her back into the crowd, making Mallory even more pleased she'd used the padding spell as elbows and hands thwacked off her from all sides. She darted forward to grab two bar stools. Mallory was already relieved to be able to sit.

'Drinks are on me, it's been too long since you've had a night out,' Diana shouted, and had got the troll bartender's attention before Mallory could disagree.

She wasn't supposed to drink on her meds. None of them should've been drinking; they were meant to be working on a murder case. Nevertheless, a vodka sherbet lemonade appeared in front of her. She popped the accompanying fizzing sweet in her mouth and Diana took a sip of her chocolate fudge rum. Faeries were very good at beverages.

Mallory looked around through the haze and spotted Grey Quinn now standing beside the door to the managers' office, just behind the bar, close enough that Mallory could hear him knocking. It was not a secret that the Larix was a front for other, less legitimate faerie and troll business, including – but not limited to – the troll mafia dynasty that spanned far beyond Wrackton, and that Van Doren looked the other way. Cornelia had on occasion insisted that Van Doren leaned into whatever they did, and that it wasn't just between the faeries and trolls. Mallory didn't think she wanted to know, especially as it implied Langdon's uncles were involved.

Grey Quinn always dressed well, using clothes to indicate intent. This was a power suit, a blue silk jacket and trousers, shiny lace-ups, a physical stance that said he was going to win. Quinn was a notorious property dealer and hotelier. Often demons went on to be lawyers, and only the most hapless among them would become salesmen, but Quinn was a prolific, ruthless and powerful investor rumoured to have the ears and wallets of the Apparent government.

'That's a very good suit on this, a night of… what did Theodore call it?' Diana said in Mallory's ear.

'Fun and frivolity. I agree.'

'I think I could pull off blue silk,' Diana said. 'And that red pocket square is perfect, a striking contrast. Someone should tell him.'

'And risk the wrath of Theodore?'

Theodore would likely never forgive Quinn for the cat costume, even if he wouldn't say it to his face.

The door opened and one of Langdon's uncles popped his head out. He scanned the club. Mallory strained to hear.

'Let me,' Diana said, noticing, and cast a listening spell. They pressed their heads together.

'Not you again,' Langdon's uncle – Mallory couldn't remember his name – growled.

'A pleasure, as always,' Quinn said smoothly. 'You know why I'm here.'

'We're busy, as you can see.'

'Investors will be swooping down on this place soon, including the big man himself.' Quinn smirked. Langdon's uncle gestured for Quinn to come in. He wasn't in the management room long; Mallory hadn't even got halfway through her drink by the time the door reopened.

'Please save yourself the trouble of asking again. It would take more than *that* for us to part with the Larix,' Mallory heard someone shout from the office as Quinn emerged, his eyebrows drawn together and angry.

'What do you think that was?' Mallory asked, straightening up carefully. Diana made a noncommittal movement.

Mallory stared after him as he slipped through the crowd, losing him when a group of witches started posing for photographs in the middle of the floor.

Something tugged at her memory.

'Cornelia said she'd heard a bunch of Wrackton investors had been buying up land with Van Doren. Her theory was in case of prison-building opportunities?' Mallory said. 'Maybe that's who he meant by "the big man".'

'Blaaahhh, boring. We're having an off night from thinking, Mallory, try to enjoy it.' Diana took another sip of her drink. She grinned around the rim.

Mallory put her straw in her mouth and chewed absently, her eyes drifting away and meeting Ben's as he jogged towards them with a big smile lighting up his beautiful face.

'Diana! And Mallory! You said you were busy! Did you tell Felix you were coming?' He enveloped Diana in a hug.

'I was just with Felix, they asked me to help with their costume,' Diana said, her voice muffled by his chest. 'Cornelia is here too, somewhere. We lost her as soon as we got in.'

Ben pulled Mallory into a hug, surprising her. 'I'm glad you came too, Mallory.' Her heart jumped a little in happiness.

Ben glanced back over his shoulder and saw Cloud and Langdon waving frantically to him from the green room, which was neither green nor a room, merely an alcove to the side of the Larix's stage. 'SHIT. I have to go. See you after!'

He ran off.

'Do you want to stay here, or move closer?' Diana asked.

'I can stand for a bit,' Mallory said, and moved into the crowd with Diana at her side. It had started filling up more now.

'Fuck, you're not even wearing heels,' someone said next to Mallory.

A pretty, dark-haired vampire boy stood next to her. Diana's face immediately settled into an angry glare.

'If he's hitting on you, I can hex him away,' Diana said in her other ear. Mallory put her hand on Diana's arm in warning. Valiant though the offer was, Mallory wanted to be sure it was necessary.

'And?' she said.

The vampire looked her up and down. 'I dunno, it's just like, tall much?' He smirked at her, turning his attention to Diana who he looked up and down with distaste before brushing past her, blending into the crowd.

'What a funny, funny guy,' Diana spat. 'I swear, just a little hex. A small one. I haven't got to hex someone since... *Hexana*, it's been ages.'

'The show's about to start,' Mallory said. 'But thank you, for never wanting to miss a genuine opportunity to hex someone.'

'I only ever hex arseholes—' Diana interrupted herself by screaming with excitement as the house lights went down.

The crowd seemed to close in around Mallory, spiking her anxiety about being jostled. She finally spotted Cornelia's hair above a group of vampires and grabbed Diana's hand. After what seemed an age of dodging and ducking, her feet sticking to the floor, and the cloying smell of old beer thick in her nose, she slotted in beside her.

Cornelia slipped an arm around her waist in greeting, squeezing Mallory to her with the sort of gentle care that could only come from knowing how much contact could hurt her. Diana immediately jumped into the crowd at the front.

Mallory's heart pounded in time to the music as Felix threw themself around the stage in an alarming fashion. They were wearing some sort of sleeveless vest and a hat that was probably only still on thanks to both sheer force of will and a spell from Diana. The songs were a kind of electropunk Mallory had never heard before, and Felix writhed about the stage, kicking the mic stand over and bouncing up and down on massive platform boots as Ben and their other bandmates threw fake blood at each other. At least Mallory hoped it was fake, as real blood seemed a little too gauche, even for Crown and Hemlock.

'This isn't so bad!' Mallory said in Cornelia's ear.

She spotted Diana up the front of the crowd in a mosh pit with some faerie folk. Two troll bouncers, who were not bouncers because they were trolls, or indeed trolls because they were bouncers, stood at the edge of the stage, just in case things got out of control. It was never really the Occult folk that did it, but overzealous Apparent folk who were completely taken in by the music. The thing that interested Mallory most about faerie glamour magic was how much of it was just putting a sheen on an existing talent. Cloud was a great bassist, Felix's voice was already powerful and versatile, and Ben was an incredible guitarist. Langdon was also in the band, though Mallory couldn't see what his particular function was other than endearingly creating chaos.

'I have definitely heard worse things,' Cornelia shouted, so close that she tickled Mallory's ear and made the hairs on her neck stand up. Mallory laughed and pulled back as an Apparent and a couple of witches started pushing each other.

The song ended and Mallory could breathe again, but Felix, after shouting something Mallory couldn't quite understand, immediately launched into the next one. Ben jumped off the stage and ran into the crowd, almost taking off the heads of some enthusiastic dancers at the front with his amp lead, and Mallory found herself heading to the bar for another drink.

By the time she'd paid, Cornelia had disappeared from view. Not because she had been swallowed up by the crowd, but because someone had attached himself to her. Not with his teeth, because that was forbidden by the Unified Magical Liaison, but with his lips, which was somehow worse.

The vampire from earlier.

Mallory gulped her drink and ordered another. She was willing to bet he was who Cornelia had been texting constantly, that he was the 'friends' she'd wanted to see tonight. He was *B*.

As Mallory tried to think happy thoughts and not look at the vampire-and-Cornelia-amorphous-blob in the middle of the dance floor, Diana re-emerged, a sheen of sweat on her face but her eyeliner still perfect.

'Excuse me, but what in the absolute Hexana-loving fuck is going on?' She pointed at Cornelia. 'That's the guy! The vampire who talked to you! Hex-boy!'

'I don't know.'

'*Did* you know?'

'I didn't know.'

'*I* didn't know.'

'I'm really glad we've established that we had no knowledge of this,' Mallory said, feeling unsteady. 'I got you another drink, though.' She pushed Diana's drink closer and took a sip of her own.

Diana took the glass furiously. 'He... he seems... awful.'

'Based on our one interaction with him, yes.' Mallory clenched her jaw.

'*Look* at him.' Diana waved a hand at his appearance. He was wearing a leather jacket and an obscure band shirt. 'No, Mallory. I refuse to be the sort of friend who doesn't tell their friend that said friend has an absolute fucking douchecanoe attached to their face, and offer to hex it away, cause I can. And I will.'

Diana blew on her fingers and his hair ruffled. He pulled away from Cornelia to fix it, looking at the ceiling as if there'd be an air vent somewhere, before immediately kissing her again.

'It's fuckboy haircuts today, breaking of sacred covenants and draining the life out of our friend tomorrow.'

'That won't happen. Vampires take the Do No Harm charter seriously. Cornelia wouldn't let anyone use her magic. *Anyone*,' Mallory said. An image of the bruise she thought she'd seen on Cornelia's neck appeared in her mind as she spoke, but she shook it away. It had been a trick of the light. Cornelia would never.

'It's still a valid concern. If he didn't look like he thinks he's the coolest fucker in cool town, I would have zero concerns. But as it stands, I am concerned.'

'Do you remember when we were fifteen and you were dating that girl,' Mallory said slowly.

'Which one? I have lost count.'

'Blonde hair, played guitar?'

'Ah! Faerie. Lina.'

'And remember you were obsessed with her within, like, a week of meeting her, and Cornelia tried to gently point out that Lina had dated every single lesbian and bisexual girl she knew of and then some, and you accused Cornelia of slut shaming, when her point was not to get too attached because it was likely you too would be part of the "and then some" and Lina was not as into you as you were into her, and you didn't talk for a month? Because I remember that, Diana. It didn't go down well.'

Diana laughed.

'Goddess, I was such a shithead. Sorry about that. I suppose you're right. It's not like she's mentioned him before, though?'

'She has.'

'You said she hadn't!'

'No.' Mallory shook her head. 'I mean, haven't you noticed how distracted she's been? Texting constantly, being vague about "seeing friends". I think she tried to tell me earlier. She's never like this, but it's reminded me of you and Lina.'

'And me and Gennie. And me and Ella. And me and Sophie. And me and Drea, and me and Miley...' Diana said dreamily, and Mallory realised she only recognised half the names on Diana's girlfriend graveyard list.

Diana sighed. 'If she's already all in we can't just... give an opinion, I guess. Even though I have one.'

'I know you do.'

Diana wrapped a gentle arm around Mallory's waist. 'You will never have to worry about an intervention for me. I will never date ever again. You need to hold me to this, Mallory. For at least a month.'

'I can't make any promises, but I believe in you,' Mallory said. Her heart was warming at how quickly Diana had slipped back into being Diana around her. It was like they'd never been apart, though it had been almost two years. She tried to let herself enjoy it.

'What about you?' Diana said. 'I heard Ben is newly single. And I heard him say he was glad you came.' She paused. 'I bet that's not the only—'

'Do. Not. Finish. That. Sentence,' Mallory said in warning.

Diana waggled her eyebrows, but busied herself with her glass.

'And no. He's… no.' Dating or even starting anything casual right now, when Mallory had barely any energy to stand here, didn't feel like an option for her.

She watched Ben continue to throw fake blood all over the stage, feeling like he deserved someone who had more to give. Felix grabbed Ben close and licked slowly up the side of his face, Ben still playing guitar right between them. The audience screamed.

'Yeah, you're right. New plan. I have the numbers of some girls and non-binary individuals looking to date in your area, should that be of interest to you? They're people I worked with, I can name at least… six,' Diana said, thinking. 'No, seven.'

'And some of these are girls you wouldn't date yourself, but are happy to pass on to me?' Mallory grinned.

'Look, Mallory. I am awash with eligible dates. I have just taken a vow of chastity I plan to uphold for *at least* a month. I need to learn who I am on my own. Your support is wanted at this time.' She paused. 'Especially when you invariably have to remind me I've made this choice in a week's time.'

'I never have to have these conversations with Theodore.'

'Obviously. I've missed you.' Diana squeezed her hand gently. Mallory kissed the top of Diana's head, her drinks making her feel freer.

Crown and Hemlock eventually finished just as Mallory was planning on going to find a seat somewhere. Cornelia and the vampire made a beeline for them, hand in hand. Diana subtly rolled her eyes so only Mallory could see.

'Guys, this is Beckett. Beckett, this is Mallory and Diana,' Cornelia said, her eyes bright.

Mallory waved. Diana pulled her shoulders back, looking up at him defiantly.

'What did you think of that set?' Mallory asked politely, not quite looking Beckett in the eye.

'We loved it,' Beckett answered before Cornelia could open her mouth. 'It was brilliant. Exactly what you need on a night like tonight, just like I told Corn she needed. She said you're working on some kind of murder case?'

Mallory took another sip of her drink. Cornelia did not like any contractions of her name, so it was not hard to notice how she flinched slightly at the easy way he dropped off the remaining syllables.

'We are, yes.' Diana took a swig from her own drink. 'Cornelia, we got you one too.' She pushed a drink at her and then bounded over to where Felix and Ben were surrounded by a group of Occult.

'I just think we really enjoy music like this. I feel like it's so transcendental, but in an experimental way,' Beckett declared, then darted a glance over her. 'We'd totally get it if you didn't agree, though. It's not everyone's *scene*, you know?'

Mallory made a non-specific noise of neither agreement nor assent. She hung on to the periphery of Cornelia and Beckett's conversation, though conversation usually involved two people communicating, and what Beckett seemed to be doing was speaking for Cornelia and daring her to disagree. As soon as the crowd around Crown and Hemlock thinned, Mallory went to join them.

'Good song choices!'

'My thanks to you, fair maiden,' Felix said, an old faerie greeting that somehow worked for them. Cloud waved at her through the crowd and Mallory waved back, feeling too awkward to do anything but give them a hopefully enthusiastic thumbs-up as Diana reached an arm around their waist and gave them a squeeze. Mallory knew Cloud as Felix's friend, but they hadn't been around long when she'd had to start skipping out on shows. She turned her attention back to Felix who was talking about why they'd made the choices they'd made, something about musical stabs and energy, which Mallory did not understand but respected, nonetheless. It was just nice to be hanging out with Felix. She caught sight of Langdon as he was enveloped by a small group of witches, and the circle of well-wishers around Ben grew larger and more impassable. She'd hoped to say bye to him before she left, feeling the possibility he could be her friend.

She was flagging, energy-wise. There would be another band on soon, and she wanted to get out of the Larix before even more people showed up.

'VERY good choices, good sir,' a voice said behind Mallory, and she cringed involuntarily. She was learning that Beckett was unnecessarily loud and obnoxious in a way that made her feel that he must be at least somewhat aware and doing it anyway.

'Thanks,' Felix said coolly, not meeting his eye, and turned back to Mallory. Beckett reached a hand over to clap Felix on the arm. It was not a friendly clap; more a warning, on the right arm, reaching across their body to do it, and Mallory could see it brewing before it happened. Felix flicked Beckett's hand away from them, and suddenly Beckett was surrounded by faerie folk, fans, the remaining members of Crown and Hemlock and the troll bouncers. Ben stood beside Felix, his grey eyes flashing.

Crossing the body of a faerie was an insult.

'What the fuck are you doing?' Felix said.

'Oh, calm down. I forgot which arm insulted your forefathers, I thought I was doing it right.' Beckett's nose wrinkled. 'I'm not sure why you're treating me like I've done something really wrong here, it was an accident.'

'Then apologise?' Felix said.

'It's not hard, a simple "I'm sorry" and it'll all be forgotten,' Ben added.

'I just said I made a mistake.' Beckett pushed his hair back, a defiant leer on his face. 'You don't see me demanding an apology for throwing blood around. It was so insulting. I wasn't even going to say anything about it, but where's the reciprocity? You apologise for that, I'll apologise for touching the wrong arm.'

Mallory backed away, Cornelia right behind her. Mallory could see her hesitating, but knew Cornelia knew the same truths Mallory did. Beckett had done this to himself; Felix could handle this. Diana's face said, 'I told you so,' and Mallory had no doubt that despite her earlier warnings, Diana's mouth was going to say it later too.

'That is ridiculous,' Ben said.

'That', Felix said, pointing to the stage, 'was art. Not an insult. Certainly not an intentional one. I can't say the same here for you.'

'Perhaps we'll just agree to disagree?' Beckett swayed a little on his feet, then slowly, deliberately, reached a hand out again to touch Felix.

Ben was in front of them in seconds, his hands raised in a warning. Diana was not far behind him, her hands flexing in what Mallory recognised as preparation for a hex.

'Woah. Woah,' Beckett said. 'Calm down. Show's over. And it wasn't even that good to begin with.'

Felix lunged for him and Ben grabbed them at the last second, holding them in place as they struggled to get to Beckett. The bouncers and other faeries, and – to Mallory's dismay – Diana, closed in. Beckett hadn't stopped smirking, but now his eyes flicked across the gathered crowd, assessing the risk.

'Beckett,' Cornelia said, her steady voice cutting across the rumbles of posturing.

He looked at her for just a moment. Mallory didn't see what passed between them, but then Beckett waved a hand at Felix, and stomped off towards the back of the Larix, running his hands through his hair.

Felix visibly deflated and Ben patted them on the shoulder, his face relaxing. 'That was fun. I'm going to get a drink,' he said, his energy returning.

'Ben, just—' Felix started, but he was already out of earshot.

The crowd recovered quickly, fans encircling the remaining band members, but the energy had changed. Felix and Cloud both looked like they were struggling to feign enthusiasm.

'I'm just gonna go find Ben, I'll see you both later,' Langdon said, offering Mallory a hug that she gladly took even though he held her ribcage too tightly, before he mussed Cornelia's hair. She scowled and punched him on the arm, but broke into a grin as she did so. He winked as he left, winding through stragglers with ease.

Cornelia looked off in the direction Beckett had disappeared in, her expression unreadable.

'I'll let him cool off,' she said, noticing Mallory's questioning gaze. 'He's just…' She caught Diana's eye and jerked her head towards the exit. Mallory wondered if she could feel the energy sagging too.

'I'll call us a taxi.' Mallory's phone was in her hand, the number already on her screen. She reached the edge of the club and was about to step outside when she heard the screaming.

PERIMORTEM II

Ben DeLacey was on a high when he walked into the basement and died.

His ears had been ringing from the moment he stepped off stage. Feedback from the amp and the fading throb of Crown and Hemlock's own music meant other sounds were somewhere his ears couldn't quite reach, placing the cheers and words of well-wishers and his fellow bandmates on a different wavelength. He briefly thought about how he should probably finally invest in in-ear monitors. He did not know these were his final moments.

As he stepped off the stage, he could practically taste ice-cold water from a pint glass dripping beads of condensation, the ice clacking gently and hurting his teeth. He had wasted a few precious minutes after greeting fans on something he'd already forgotten the specifics of, a vague irritation that drifted away as he got closer to quenching his thirst.

His hands were on a cool case in the Larix basement, ready to rip back the cardboard that was the only thing between him and sweet relief when the ringing in his ears intensified. Ben would've described it as a strange whistling, wrapping its way into his head. He did not realise that this was his last moment of awareness.

He thought about Felix.

He thought about music.

He thought about what he wanted to be when he was older.

Then he bit off his own tongue, his teeth pressing and mashing on to it, sinews snapping under the pressure until it broke free. It stayed in his mouth, blood pouring back down his throat, and he didn't feel it. He didn't notice he was choking, his tongue blocking his airway as he lay down on the ground. Nor did he feel any pain as the whistling sound bit into his stomach from the inside, carving its secrets into his torso. He arranged himself carefully, still thinking of Felix, of music, of a future, when the ringing stopped, and so did Ben's heart.

ELEVEN

'HELP! SOMEBODY HELP!' Langdon ran up the stairs at the far end of the club. The background music stopped and the house lights went up. Felix froze in mid-conversation, their head turning towards Langdon.

'It's Ben! HELP!' His face was a mask of terror.

Mallory turned, almost in slow motion. Diana's arm automatically reached into the fray and pulled out Felix, whose expression had fallen. Faerie folk ran for the stairs as Beckett emerged from the shadows. He took in the panic with interest that bordered on performative, a bounce in his step as he made a beeline for Cornelia, shaking her twice on the shoulder and failing to elicit a response. Mallory grabbed Cornelia's arm, pulling her in the direction of the stairs, her decision to ignore Beckett barely registering as she moved with the crowd, Cloud close behind her.

Mallory knew instinctively what she was going to see when she got down to the lower level, though she had hoped she wouldn't. A creeping chill across her skin told her that something terrible, something unimaginable, had happened.

The lower floors of the Larix were labyrinth-like. It felt like a dream as Mallory, Diana and Cornelia followed the sound of faerie folk crying – an eerie, inharmonious humming that made her skin crawl.

On the ground, in a tunnel piled high with boxes of drinks, laid out like he had simply gone to sleep, was Ben DeLacey. Felix's bandmate, Diana and Cornelia's friend, and the second murder victim.

There was chaos. Folk pushed and shoved, trying to see, trying to prove that he wasn't dead, and Felix and Cloud shoved people away from Ben's body, knowing he was dead, knowing he was not breathing, his eyes closed and his body unnaturally splayed, his clothes twisted underneath him. He could've been sleeping, but there was a sense of wrongness about the whole thing. The edge of his T-shirt had ridden up over his hip bones and Mallory could see the edge of something carved into his stomach. An envelope was propped up on his arm.

'His… his…' Langdon said, his shivering back pressed against the wall, his eyes wild with the horror of it all. 'He's not breathing.' His hand was on Felix's T-shirt, holding them back with white knuckles as Felix stared at Ben, tears streaming down their face.

There was impossibility in the air, suffocating them all, making the room smaller and smaller, a cave with sharp edges pressing in, cloying with realisation, truth, shock. He had been with them, alive, just minutes before.

Now he was gone.

Diana grabbed Mallory, accidentally pressing her thumb into the crease of her elbow causing her to hiss in pain.

'Sorry,' Diana whispered, but the pain snapped Mallory into focus.

Mallory looked around the space, her eyes skipping over the frightened faces of faeries and witches and the troll bouncers who were trying to strong-arm folk into staying away from Ben. They were going to trample the scene.

Thinking this made something in her brain click into place. Scene. Crime scene. Her job. She knew this procedure, had learned it, never imagining that she'd need it in a club on a night out she didn't want with friends who had just lost someone important to them.

'Cornelia,' she said. 'Look at me.'

Cornelia's eyes met hers, burning hazel into Mallory's blue.

'We have to secure the scene. We have to look at him, look at the room, before the police get here. Can you do it?'

Cornelia nodded.

'Diana.' Mallory clasped her hand. 'If you need a moment, take it, but we can't afford more than a moment.'

Diana closed her eyes. A tear rolled down her face and she angrily wiped it away.

'I don't need a moment.' She was clearly lying, but Mallory could see the determination in her eyes.

Mallory squeezed her hand again and reached out to take Cornelia's small, delicate hand with her other. The pulse of their collective magic flowed through them.

She let go and nodded to Cornelia, who had the loudest voice. 'Clear the room.'

Cornelia loosely cupped her hand over her mouth, magically amplifying her voice.

'STAND BACK. This is a crime scene. Step back!' She bowed to the nearest group of faerie folk and motioned them away.

Mallory turned to the nearest troll bouncer.

'Please get everyone else upstairs, they cannot stand on or touch anything in this room. This is a crime scene and it needs to be preserved for when the police get here.'

The bouncer gritted their teeth and moved folk away, pushing back against the rising tide. Mallory turned and grabbed another bouncer. 'Do you have a rope, anything we can do to close off the stairs?'

They brought her one and as soon as the faeries were away from the bottom of the stairs, they sealed it off. Mallory continued mentally cataloguing what she needed to do, what the scene required.

The room was emptying out, leaving the Undetectables in the space with Ben's body.

'Okay. Diana, do you have your phone? Take photos. As good a quality as you can get. We don't touch anything until you do,' Mallory said. 'We need gloves. Cornelia, can you?'

'Here.' Cornelia whispered and several pairs of latex gloves appeared in her hands. She passed them out.

'Okay.' Mallory's voice was loud in the empty space. Crying and shouting and thumping footsteps sounded overhead. 'Diana, take—'

'I've got this. I learned at Kuster's scene,' Diana said quietly.

'Okay. We have… minutes, probably, before the police arrive. We can't be here when they do. Especially not you, Diana – I don't think you'll get away with forensic science student again. Can you do this?' Mallory asked.

Cornelia and Diana nodded.

In the sudden quiet of the basement, the Undetectables got to work.

Diana took photographs of Ben's body, the envelope, the carving. Tears poured down her face as she worked.

'Goddess, Ben, I'm so sorry.' Diana stood. 'You can touch him now.'

A piece of Ben's hair lay over his face and Mallory fought the urge to smooth it back into place. Instead she carefully peeled his lips back and grimaced. His tongue had been severed, just like Kuster. She lifted his shirt up and let Diana take photographs of the carving in his torso. Just like Kuster, it had been cut with a laser-like precision. There was no blood here.

Cornelia picked up the envelope and slipped it into her pocket. Mallory didn't stop her; if it was important enough to share, they could pass it back to Van Doren for the police to see, consequences be damned.

'We need to swab his body, for the mass spec.' The words were barely out of Mallory's mouth before Cornelia handed her a beetle box.

'Is there ever going to be a time when you having insects on you *won't* somehow turn out to be appropriate?' Diana wiped her face.

'If there is, I'll let you go on about it unnecessarily,' Cornelia said.

Mallory gently tipped the beetle on to Ben's torso. It instantly turned green and peeped loudly and insistently. Cornelia scooped it back into its box.

Diana diligently combed the entire floor, photographing every square inch of the space. Nothing was excluded: a small pile of plastic wrapping, an empty beer bottle and some shattered glass. Mallory picked up some of the glass and the bottle, wrapping them in her gloves and shoving them into her bag.

Those few minutes felt like hours before Mallory heard sirens in the distance, audible even in the awkward, heavy silence of the basement. Cornelia met her gaze as they heard hurried footsteps above them as all the faeries still inside the Larix scattered. They got to the other side of the rope barrier.

'Shit.'

Mallory heard shouting up in the bar of the Larix, and Wrackton police descended the stairs.

'You need to leave this area,' said the first uniform, and Cornelia opened her mouth to say something.

'We were just leaving. We… we didn't think he should be alone,' Mallory said. 'We'll leave you to your case.'

'Our *case*?' he said, looking at the body. 'We don't even know if there is a case yet, we were just told a body was found.'

'Of course, sorry. We'll be going.'

He frowned. 'You'll need to talk to O'Sullivan before you leave, you're witnesses.'

'You mean *Detective Inspector* O'Sullivan,' the second uniform said, mockingly. 'Respect her with her full and proper title.'

'She's probably planning on making an entrance, seeing as she didn't leave with us. Maybe you'll get to see her shiny detective badge.' Uniform One snickered, and the two other uniforms with him joined in.

'Oh and maybe she'll tell you all about her time on her first homicide team, back in her *usual* job where she was very important,' Uniform Two said, and his team laughed harder, nobody caring that they were standing over a body, breaking the solemnity of the space.

'Someone just died,' Mallory said, her voice louder and clearer than she thought it would be. 'Have some respect.'

They ignored her.

'Not only will she pop up and tell us how to solve it, she'll tell you how she would've murdered him differently. I bet she'll be delighted there's been another one so soon, she seemed keen.' He jerked his head at Ben.

Mallory inhaled, trying to process both the disrespect, and the way O'Sullivan's team talked about her. A jarring contrast to the interaction Diana had described.

'If this doesn't make the case for a Wrackton prison, the Night Mayor is going to have to start lopping heads off folk himself,' Uniform One said as the Undetectables trudged up the stairs.

'Who's to say he's not doing it now?' Uniform Two said, and they all laughed. It flowed over Mallory's head as the realisation hit her squarely. She wanted to return to that place of control, but cold shock pushed its way through and she knew she was done.

Ben was dead. Murdered by the same killer as Kuster.

Upstairs, the Larix was in disarray. There were empty cups and bottles strewn everywhere, tissue and old ticker tape stuck to much of the floor. Faeries and witches who had known Ben were huddled in small groups, some crying, some staring at the stairs. All the doors were open and a crowd still gathered outside.

The bouncers had stopped trying to remove folk and were just standing around, unsure of what to do. Mallory felt she should say something to the remaining Occult folk, but couldn't find the words. She wanted someone to say something to her instead. Diana's eyeliner still hadn't budged, her eyes swollen. Cornelia sniffed repeatedly, wiping her sleeve over her face.

Van Doren strode through the doorway with Jacob in tow. He looked down at the floor in dismay, his shoes sticking to the wood. His hand caught in a séance paste poster as he skirted around a pillar and he tore it down in disgust after examining it for a moment.

'Vincent,' a voice said. Mallory turned just as a slightly dishevelled Grey Quinn emerged from a dark corner of the Larix, bearing down on Van Doren. 'I've just been speaking with—'

'Not here,' Van Doren hissed. 'Not now.'

'But—'

'The police pulled in as I got here, shut up.' He glanced over Quinn's shoulder. 'We'll talk later. I'm needed.'

Quinn held out a hand to the Night Mayor who took it, pulling Quinn close and whispering insistently in his ear. Jacob stared into space as Mallory belatedly realised she should've cast a listening spell, straining to hear anything over the quiet murmuring of the folk still in bar. Van Doren clapped Quinn on the shoulder, sharper than perhaps strictly necessary, and Quinn was gone into the night.

'Ridiculous timing,' Van Doren muttered, adjusting his coat.

Mallory pulled herself out of her shock momentarily, and approached him. 'Mr Night Mayor.' There was something immediately different about his appearance; how he'd carried himself in the office the day he'd hired them was a stark contrast to now, but there was something else too that Mallory's mind had noted, but had forgotten to make her conscious of.

'What do you want?' Van Doren snarled, turning to her.

'Sorry to bother you, I know I shouldn't,' Mallory said, aware he'd said they couldn't talk properly until the case was solved, though a second murder seemed like a good enough reason to change that.

'And?'

'It's another one.'

'Another one what?'

'Another… murder.' She looked to Jacob for help. He raised his eyebrows in confusion, his hands shoved deep in his coat pockets.

'And?'

'It's… the same as the first.'

'And why are you telling me what I already know?' Van Doren asked. 'Get out of my way, please.'

Mallory watched him turn to go.

'We knew him. Well, they knew him,' she blurted.

He turned back. His features had softened.

'He's faerie. His name is Ben DeLacey.'

'Right. May he live forever in the Fair Kingdom,' Van Doren said, then cleared his throat. 'I've always hated nightclubs.' He waved vaguely, dismissing her.

Jacob smiled awkwardly and followed the Night Mayor.

The Undetectables climbed into a taxi and the door closed just as a howl rose from Redwood Forest, indicating the beginning of the faerie death ritual, which meant Ben's family had been notified. It would last seven days and seven nights, and due to Ben being so young, a representative from the Court of the Fair Folk would arrive in the next day or so to oversee the proceedings.

'This is really, really real, isn't it?' Cornelia said. It was not often that Mallory saw Cornelia look as vulnerable as she did in that moment, but behind her glasses, her eyes looked haunted. 'We have to solve it.'

'We will. We promised we would when it was someone we didn't know, and we doubly promise now,' Mallory said softly.

It was unconscionable that someone within their community could've done this, so brazenly, in a club full of Occult folk, but they had.

'I don't know how we do that,' Diana said. 'We're so out of our depth. We have no idea how the killer is getting into spaces unseen, where the magic to do something like this comes from.' A fresh round of tears fell and she didn't bother wiping them away.

'We know absolutely nothing,' Cornelia said. 'Like bugs, but worse, because bugs still know more than we do.'

'It's just as Theodore says: magic can only be as effective as the knowledge you already have. We just need to up our knowledge.' Mallory squeezed Cornelia's arm lightly. She smelled like sugar and deodorant and home, and Mallory was glad of her friendship. Glad she had someone to sit with her when bad things happened.

As the taxi turned a corner, the Redwoods disappeared from view. She felt numb. Her logical brain tried to override the emotions building up in her chest, in her limbs, so familiar and so alien all at once. She'd never seen someone she knew, even tangentially, die before.

Diana leaned into Cornelia on her other side. They sat in silence for the rest of the drive home.

TWELVE

Six days to Samhain

'Time to get up.' Cornelia was leaning over Mallory, a sweet-scented shadow close to her head. Sunlight streamed in the window, the curtains undrawn as they had been when they'd arrived in her room, and Mallory blinked. It felt like no time at all had passed. Her body hurt as much as it had when she'd got into bed. She'd taken medication she kept for emergencies to force herself to sleep.

'What time is it?' Her voice cracked. Speaking hurt. Breathing hurt. Everything hurt.

'Just after nine.'

Mallory nodded and crawled out of bed, pausing for a moment to take her meds and look around the room as she gulped from a glass of tepid water she didn't even have the energy to chill with a spell.

Cornelia watched her with an expression Mallory couldn't read.

'Is that Felix?' she croaked, hearing faint rumbling voices down the hall.

'They turned up this morning in a mess. I got them to sleep for an hour or so, after we told them we were working on the case.' Cornelia's hair stood on end, and after a couple of attempts to finger-comb it into submission, she grabbed a beanie out of the wardrobe. There were dark shadows under her eyes, but she seemed determined to pretend she was fine. Mallory knew all too well what that felt like.

'May I?' She held it in her hands, watching Mallory attempt to stand up fully.

Mallory nodded and looked around for fresh clothes. Something to make her legs feel comfortable and supported. Something to stop the pain, even a little. When she hurt most, tight-fitting clothing helped, like compression tights, or a pair of workout leggings. Not that she was ever inclined to work out. Exercise was often touted as a cure, but Mallory couldn't fathom how that was meant to work when she could barely stand up as it was.

'I can do a binding spell,' Cornelia said, suddenly.

Mallory wondered if she'd spoken out loud. 'What?'

'For your legs. If they feel uncomfortable, I can bind them individually.'

'How did you...?' The sentence felt impossible to work through. Her tongue was heavy and her brain felt like it was underwater, and this wasn't even as bad as it could be. She needed coffee.

'It's something you always look for when you're in a lot of pain, something tight on your legs. And maybe a binding spell would work?' Cornelia smiled ruefully and Mallory took a moment to understand. She never spoke about her pain, not really, but Cornelia consistently paid attention to what was going on. Mallory didn't have the energy to protest.

'That would be amazing. Thank you. I'll be right back.' Mallory struggled into the bathroom to get changed. When she returned, Cornelia motioned for her to get onto the bed. Mallory did, feeling strange as Cornelia leaned over her again, less shadowed now, her eyelashes brushing against her cheeks as she blinked.

Cornelia gently pressed her fingers on each of Mallory's shins, and Mallory felt them grow hot where she touched her, a strange pressure starting in her toes that spread up to the tops of her femurs.

Mallory stood up experimentally.

'How's that?'

'Pretty good, actually. How long will this last for?' She tried not to feel too hopeful. There was no proven cure for her illness. A lot of programmes and supplements said 'proven', just like a lot of diets and that bomb detector hoax that was just a golf ball finder aerial said they were 'proven', and Mallory wished she could be among their 'proven' ranks, but as of yet, nothing lasted forever.

'A few hours, maybe five if you're lucky. It's not perfect, obviously, but I just thought it would help.' Cornelia adjusted her glasses and her hat and opened the bedroom door. 'Breakfast, and then we riot.'

Mallory cracked a smile. 'Research, not riots. Please. I don't have my riot body on today.' She paused. 'How did you come up with this spell?'

'It's something I thought about in the night, when I couldn't sleep. I found the binding spell in an old book, and I wondered if the reason we can't find our killer's spell is because it's not there. It's adapted magic of some sort.' Cornelia motioned vaguely. 'Magic can be anything, as long as folk understand what they're doing. The killer could be using literally anything at all, but might have understood an alternative use for the spell that we'd never be able to guess.'

'Make a spell hard to identify, call that undetectable.' Mallory sighed.

'Speaking of – the mass spectrometer, or as I like to call it, the Magic Magical Machine, arrived this morning. I asked them to set it up for you, so it's ready to go when you are.' Cornelia held open the door for her.

In the kitchen, Felix hunched over a mug of coffee. Theodore made a brief appearance, excusing himself to go to the Offices after offering a static-filled hug to Felix, who barely registered the contact. Diana had animated the salt cellar to dance for them, but Mallory knew it was futile. Grief had permeated the walls of their house. Dancing salt cellars and forced smiles would not shake away the blanket of sorrow that had settled over all of them.

Cornelia looked between them. Mallory could feel her gearing up to fill the silence.

'I know what would cheer us up,' she announced. 'Does anyone want to hear about the Empathy Cage Prison scandal?'

Nobody responded. Felix picked at the pancakes Diana had pushed in front of them.

'Of course we do, Cornelia, you're so interesting,' Cornelia said. 'Thanks, guys. So. Back in the last century, we used to have prisons in all the Occult towns.'

'Really?' Diana said. 'I thought that went out way before.'

'The last one was shut down by the only Night Mayor in Wrackton who was not a Van Doren, back in the seventies. And do you know why?'

Mallory cleared her throat. 'Are you going to tell us why?'

'Yes I am. I am going to tell you why. Essentially, the prisons were founded on the idea that a reasonable punishment for Occulture was to strip the individual of their power. This came up every year with the UML. The Ghoul Council were in favour of keeping the prison, as were some other voting members, so the prison stayed. Until the Night Mayor in the seventies petitioned for it to be permanently decommissioned.'

'Why, though?' Diana asked. Mallory couldn't help but feel she was not asking why it had been decommissioned, but rather why Cornelia was subjecting them to this discussion.

'Glad you asked!' Cornelia slapped the table. There was a forced joviality to her actions that Mallory couldn't ignore. 'Entering the prison strips away magic. If the guards were suitably protected, they were fine, but if they weren't, prisoners would drag unsuspecting guards inside their cells, stripping the guards of their magic too and rendering them unable to leave.'

'Interesting,' Mallory said.

'The last prison was in the Mayoral Offices. Van Doren's mother was the last Night Mayor before him, and she wasn't successful in getting the prisons back up and running. Van Doren's changed tack now, I think. He wants a for-profit prison for Apparent overspill, rather than wasting money on locking up Occult folk. It's a pity, really. I've often dreamed of what would happen to him if we shoved him in there.' Cornelia turned to Mallory. 'Speaking of the devil, what did he say to you when you spoke to him yesterday?'

'Not much,' Mallory said. With a bit of distance, she realised just how odd the interaction had been. 'He was very weird, actually. Really didn't want to hear anything I had to say, more dismissive than usual.'

'Van Doren? Dismissive? Shocking,' Cornelia said.

'Felix,' Mallory said, broaching the subject they'd been avoiding, 'what are your plans today?'

'Ben's parents want to see me,' Felix said eventually. Their voice was hoarse, as though they'd been screaming all night. Mallory couldn't say for certain if they hadn't. 'I can't. I should've been looking out for him.'

'Felix, I swear, there is *nothing* you could've done differently last night. Nothing.' Cornelia wrapped an arm around them.

'There is no reason to blame yourself. Whoever did this is an opportunistic monster,' Diana said. 'They had to have known the Larix, had to have known nobody would be down there. Had to have known they would have time.'

'I could've done something. He said he was going to get a drink, and I thought…' Felix shook their head, tears pouring again. 'I thought, "How can he walk away from this moment?" How selfish is that? That was my last thought about my best friend while he was alive.'

'Oh, Felix.' Mallory's heart broke again and she joined Cornelia in their hug. 'You did nothing wrong.'

'I don't think I can accept that.'

Felix was telling the absolute truth. Not a part of them was capable of exaggerating. They believed this, and they might never be swayed from the terrible, awful lie of it.

'You don't have to accept it,' Cornelia said. 'But you have to accept that we believe this. Can you do that?'

Felix nodded.

'Do you think you can call Cloud and Langdon over? It would help us to find out who did this if we could talk through what you all saw, if anything,' Mallory said. Faeries had to tell the truth; it would be a quick interview.

The faeries arrived quickly. Cloud's glamour had faded, and they leaned heavily on their cane. Langdon's face was haunted. They sat either side of Felix. Diana set mugs of coffee in front of all of them.

Mallory took a deep breath. 'Thanks for coming. I'm so sorry, all of you.'

'Do you know what happened to Ben?' Cloud asked, their voice low.

Mallory shook her head. 'That's what we're hoping to find out. We were just wondering if there was anything you could tell us about last night. Did you see anyone strange, anything weird?'

'That night feels split into two,' Langdon said. 'The show was meant to be a victory lap, returning to where Crown and Hemlock started. We've been doing so well, booking bigger and bigger venues. Ben was the brains behind all of it.'

'He was sure we were on the cusp of making it,' Cloud whispered.

'Can you tell us what you saw?' Mallory asked.

'You know what happened.' Langdon tangled his fingers in his sleeve. 'But I'll tell you. I went to get a drink from the basement – there's a fridge down there and I wanted something cold. Ben had already gone to do the same thing. We didn't bother with a rider or anything, we knew where shit was kept and my uncles didn't care. I walked in and he was…' Langdon swallowed.

Mallory waited, letting the silence stretch out as he composed himself.

'He was just lying there. I knew. I knew without checking, without touching him, he was gone. He looked like he was asleep. I ran, I think… I ran upstairs, then I realised I was screaming and shouting for help, then you were there, then the medics and the police…'

'How long after Ben do you think you went down to the basement?'

Langdon shook his head. 'I don't know. Five minutes? Ten, maybe? I can't be certain.'

Cornelia and Mallory looked at each other. If the killer had been in the basement then, there wasn't a lot of opportunity for them to get away without Langdon seeing them.

'Langdon, is there any chance you can get us a copy of the CCTV footage?'

'Of course, I'll just ask my uncles. I brought a list of who was there last night, if that helps?'

'How did you get this?' Mallory asked, taking the neatly stapled list.

'One of the bouncers started doing it a few years ago when Apparents started coming more regularly. "Never forgetting a face" doesn't mean to them what it means to us.'

Mallory and Cornelia scanned through it. 'I know the names of some of these folk,' Mallory said. 'But…'

'Here,' Langdon leaned over. 'These are Apparents, then of the Occult folk you've got faeries, trolls, a vampire, you three, Grey Quinn…'

That name again.

'We can discount the Apparents, anyway,' Mallory mumbled, mostly to herself.

'I asked the faeries that were there if they saw anything, but nobody did,' Langdon said. 'Nobody saw anything.'

'Do you think it was the same killer as the other guy?' Felix asked finally.

'Yes,' Mallory said.

'Why Ben?' Cloud asked.

'We don't know. But that's what we're hoping to find out.'

Felix bowed their head and Langdon cried silently and Mallory wanted to go back to bed and pretend none of this was happening.

'Do you want to stay here?' Diana asked the faeries. 'You can hang out in the kitchen for as long as you want.'

'Or if you want to try sleep, take any of the bedrooms on the second floor,' Cornelia said.

Felix wiped their eyes. Cloud and Langdon shook their heads.

'No. Go and solve this. I'll speak to the DeLaceys, somehow face them. Please.' Of all the folk in the room, Felix chose to look directly at Mallory when they said, 'Find Ben's killer.'

Diana took Felix's hand. 'We will. We promise.'

This was a phrase Mallory thought she never wanted to hear again.

'Felix is right. Why Ben?' Diana asked as soon as they were settled into the research room. Theodore wasn't there, so the room was colder than normal.

'And how did the killer get in and out without Langdon seeing them?' Mallory added, wrapping her arms around herself.

'Ben's a faerie, but not a Larix faerie. He keeps to himself. If you were going to go after the faeries for any reason, Langdon would be the obvious choice,' Diana said.

'Cornelia,' Mallory said, an image of Ben's body flashing in front of her eyes, 'where's that envelope?'

'What envelope? Oh fuck, the envelope from the Larix. I don't know where I've put it. Hang on, hang on…' She closed her eyes and waved her head side to side.

'Is that a spell or are you doing an impression of a bird's mating dance?' Diana asked, pinning her freshly printed crime scene photos to the murder board. Her voice had a forced jollity, but Mallory could hear that it was still raw from crying.

'Shut up, it's how I retrace my steps. Got it.' The letter appeared in Cornelia's hands. Mallory pulled on a pair of gloves and carefully opened the envelope.

'There better not be a bomb in there,' Diana said.

Mallory got the contents out without explosive incident.

'It's a letter,' she said. 'It's ciphered.' The words twisted and danced across the page, appearing to settle before picking up again.

'Should we dust for prints or something, before cracking the code?' Cornelia asked.

'We can try.' Mallory shrugged. If the killer was using specially adapted magic, she couldn't imagine them being foiled by something as amateur as leaving prints. 'Do we have a kit?'

'I ordered one the other day. It arrived with the mass spec.' Cornelia pulled out a giant, police-issue CSI kit and slapped it down on the table. Bottles clinked inside. Mallory was no longer surprised that Cornelia's impulse purchasing did not come with a side of worrying about the cost of anything, though she wondered what would happen if the Undetectables ever lost Cornelia's apparently bottomless purse. Mallory selected a small brush and dusted black powder on scrap paper experimentally.

'While I'm doing this – why Ben?' she asked.

'I don't think the killer could've known it was going to be Ben. There were so many folk there last night, anyone could've been the target.'

'He was gone what, ten minutes? The Larix basement isn't locked like Kuster's room was. Anyone could've walked in at any time,' Mallory said.

'But the space wasn't big enough for anyone to hide from Langdon,' Diana pointed out.

'So somehow, in five, ten minutes, Ben walks into the basement and is killed,' Mallory said slowly. She set the brush down. As expected, there were no prints.

'It sounds impossible. And also like the start of a really, really bad joke,' Diana said.

'What time did Crown and Hemlock finish?'

'The Larix curfew is 11:20 p.m.; they got off stage at 11:17 p.m.,' Diana said. 'I remember, because I looked at my phone just as they finished the set. Langdon found Ben between 11:30 and 11:40 p.m.'

'How do you know that about the curfew?' Mallory watched Cornelia scribble the potential time of death on the murder board.

'When I was helping Felix with their outfit, there was a poster on the wall with the curfew time underlined. Apparently local residents can hear the music and no amount of sound-absorbing spells can stop it.'

'Kuster also died at night. Is that significant? How can we even know at this stage?' Mallory mumbled. 'Okay, what else?'

'Suspects, or folk of interest at least. What do we know?'

'We saw… what's the hotel guy's name again?' Mallory asked, his name evaporating from her mind. She could just see him emerging angrily from the office.

'Grey Quinn?' Cornelia and Diana said together.

'Yes, him. Diana and I heard him talk to the Larix owners, it sounded like he had put an offer in on the Larix. He said something about other investors coming in soon too, and was very angry when they sent him packing. He mentioned "the big man". Then just before I talked to Van Doren yesterday, they were talking. I couldn't hear, but it seemed… tense, and possibly of note. But maybe that's not anything.'

'He called Van Doren the *what* now?' Cornelia's mouth scrunched in disgust.

'Then there's Van Doren behaving strangely,' Mallory continued, ignoring her.

'Get your own suspect,' Cornelia joked.

'I don't think he's a suspect, I just think it's worth noting he was very odd.'

'Then Beckett,' Diana said.

'What about Beckett?' Cornelia frowned, sounding genuinely confused. Mallory saw the flash of bruise on Cornelia's neck again. It could only be Beckett if he had magic, and he could only have magic if he borrowed it.

'You know what about Beckett,' Diana said, then ignored Cornelia's bemused expression. 'The faerie stuff. He said it was an accident, but what if it was a distraction? Plus, we watched him walk away right before Ben did, and he returned just as Langdon raised the alarm. We have to ask.'

'I mean, if you insist,' Cornelia scowled. 'But he was just drunk, I think. He's not normally like that. He's a bit… awkward.'

'I do insist,' Diana said. 'And awkward is a very kind descriptor.'

'There was something else,' Mallory said. 'Diana, what you said before about O'Sullivan. What was she like again?'

'She was helpful, readily believed I was a student and gave me a tonne of information, but there was something off about the whole interaction. I still can't put my finger on it. Relief that I wasn't questioning her about what she was doing there is the only thing I can think of.' Diana crossed her legs.

'I don't know if you were listening to what the police said last night,' Mallory said, lifting the letter. 'But they were not complimentary. They said she could've done the murders herself, that she's very eager about the case. Could be nothing, but could be something.' Mallory pointed to Diana. 'Though maybe you could call, or email O'Sullivan, see if you can get her here? Obviously we can't just tell her what we're doing, but you're clever.'

'I'm sure I can pretend I've got an urgent assignment to write. She said if I needed anything she'd help me out. Once she's here we can just wing it.' Diana took her phone out to type an email.

Mallory looked at the letter again. She knew this cipher, a basic one she'd learned as a baby witch who'd liked puzzles, and steeled herself for the spell.

'And there was another thing – they joked they wouldn't be surprised if Van Doren had done the murders, or would start committing them if it didn't result in a prison,' Mallory said. 'But then the question is—'

'How does any of that relate to the Ternion?' Diana finished.

Mallory groaned, rubbing her eyes. 'I don't know. Let me decipher this.'

She whispered a spell, not wanting to ask anyone to do it for her. Mallory felt energy drain out of her suddenly as words formed on the page, black lines spreading and curling into recognisable shapes. Cornelia and Diana leaned forward to read.

more brownie points to you,
for I have noticed your efforts and am
sorry to bear message: your time will end.
you have until I strike at midnight, Samhain.
these executions are just. you will all accede
when you understand. courage is for those
obediently following orders. Blair's bell
protects none. (more will succumb.)

A shiver ran down Mallory's spine. 'This is to us,' she said. 'Someone knew we'd be there.'

'Are you sure?'

'"I have noticed your efforts."' Mallory pointed. 'That's hardly to the police.'

'Samhain as a deadline. That's close,' Cornelia said. 'And more will die, so that's wonderful. Great. Love the smell of threatening threats in the morning.'

Diana returned to her chair, resting her face in her hands. 'I'm thinking, in case you're worried about me.'

'Nobody was worried, but thanks,' Cornelia said, still leaning on Mallory's desk.

Mallory's skin prickled.

'Does this sound a bit like the riddle from Kuster's scene?' Mallory held it up towards the whiteboard. 'I'm not a linguist, but...'

'The wording is similarly weird, but the letter was explicitly ciphered, the riddle wasn't,' Cornelia said.

Mallory hummed in response, trying to find a commonality. It was still possible the Kuster riddle was just that, a riddle he'd written.

'Maybe the riddle was a hint,' she said. 'Look at the "one three" part, maybe we were meant to reverse that and read it as thirty-one, as in 31 October? Or maybe I'm reaching.' She flattened the letter on the desk again.

'It does seem tenuous at best. How are your legs?' Cornelia asked, her voice softer than usual.

Mallory looked down and wiggled one of them experimentally. 'Pretty good, actually. Or as good as they can be.' She swallowed.

'Thank you. It was really kind of you.'

Cornelia smiled. 'It's nothing, honestly. I contain multitudes.'

Mallory opened her mouth to say something else, though she wasn't sure what, when the basement door swung open in a burst of static.

'I'm here, I'm queer, and I'm ready to solve a murd-eer!' Theodore announced.

THIRTEEN

'That has to be one of your worst-ever entrances,' Cornelia said. 'Literally, on a scale of one to dreadful, that ranks an atrocious.'

Theodore pulled his cardigan around him in a huff.

'I thought I'd try something. Mallory liked it, didn't you, Mallory? I might make that my thing from now on.'

Mallory nodded, because it was the kindest thing she could do.

'I do want to reiterate that I am sorry about your friend,' he said softly. 'May he live forever in the Fair Kingdom. I am making myself as available as you need to work on anything you require. Mallory, anything you need me to do, please direct me to do it. And you two—' He turned to Cornelia and Diana '— if you need a warm shoulder to cry on, or a ghost with two sets of ears, I am here.' He settled into his chair.

'We found this on Ben's body.' Mallory handed over the letter and filled Theodore in on where it had been.

'As a Samhain ghost,' Theodore said, 'I would just like to say that the tendency for killers to view Samhain as a free-for-all murder holiday is very, very unsettling.' He turned the paper over. 'The sentence structure is… odd.'

'It is. It took a few minutes to figure out how to crack it, but I can't see any other clues in it. Compared to the riddle, if that's even a clue, this is much more straightforward.'

'And this was addressed to the Undetectables?' Theodore flickered with excitement. Mallory couldn't help but feel it was misplaced.

'No. I found the envelope, it was blank,' Cornelia said, flicking through another tome of spells. 'But we think it's for us.'

'I see. I see.' Theodore scrunched his face and brought the letter closer to his face. 'This part is interesting: "Blair's bell protects none." What does that mean?'

Mallory shook her head. 'No idea, aside from the fact it's a direct reference to a member of the Ternion.'

'Hum,' Theodore said, stroking his whiskers. 'Hum, hum, hum.'

'You can just make the noise, you don't have to vocalise it,' Cornelia said, stretching as she flipped through more of her spellbook.

'I think we should pay a visit to the Observatory,' Mallory said. 'The reference to Blair, and the Ternion carvings in Kuster and Ben's stomachs… Maybe we could ask Observer Johnson to have a chat with us, see if he can shed any light.'

'I can call and see if he's around this afternoon,' Diana said. Mallory nodded her appreciation.

Cornelia slapped the book in front of her. 'Hey, Theodore. Did you know there's a ghost summoning spell? We could potentially call any dead person into ghostly existence. You could have a friend. Who would you want to see? I think I'd like to meet the person who first used forensic entomology in the thirteenth century.'

'I really don't think that's a good idea,' Theodore said firmly. 'No summoning ghosts. Not ever. It's preposterously dangerous.'

'I'd definitely call up Francine Leon,' Diana said, her eyes practically shining at the idea.

Anger flared in Mallory's stomach, quick and hot. 'I'm so glad we have time to banter about irrelevant things when there are murders to solve,' Mallory snapped, wishing she could stuff the words back inside her mouth as soon as they were out.

'Mallory,' Diana said, a little shocked. 'We are taking this seriously.'

'Ben was our friend,' Cornelia said, her voice level, and Mallory's stomach curdled further. She'd been thinking about her friends losing interest in the case, and not about how they were coping with the case being so personal. She squeezed her eyes shut.

'I'm sorry, I was just worried…' Mallory trailed off. There was no way to express what precisely she had been worried about without invalidating them further. 'I'm sorry.'

'I know before we were having a bit of fun, but Ben… this changes everything,' Cornelia added. 'I just don't want to get lost in grief. Not right now, while we have things to be getting on with.'

Diana said nothing.

'We'll give you some space to start up the Magic Magical Machine.' Cornelia pointed to the mass spectrometer. Cornelia and Diana gathered their things in cold silence and moved up to the kitchen.

Shame coursed through Mallory as she pulled her lab coat on.

'Do you want to talk about anything, Mallory?' Theodore asked.

Mallory shook her head. 'I'm just tired. Let's get this done.'

'Are you sure? You didn't name a ghost you'd like to summon. I hope that wasn't for my benefit. Even if the only thing I want you to hear is how bad an idea it is to ever summon anything. We are volatile creatures. Wildly unpredictable. I can barely predict my own actions from one moment to the next. Of course, I was like that in life, too… but humour me. Who, against all advice, would you summon?'

Mallory smiled. 'I only have room in my life for one ghost.'

'And I am quite a handful, I know.' Theodore shoved his hands in his pockets. 'Everyone deals with stress – and grief – differently. Sometimes by senseless babbling. Other times by shouting at their friends. There's no right way, necessarily. Just in case you wanted to know this information.'

Mallory squeezed his arm, a spray of static fizzing against her fingers. 'Okay.' She steered Theodore back, pulling the sheet off the mass spectrometer. 'I need to figure out how to turn this thing on.'

'Luckily I have an extraordinarily retentive memory for machine usage, despite being dead a very long time, and can guide you,' Theodore said. 'That, and I also found an instruction manual and took it to the Offices with me this morning.' He reached into his pocket and handed Mallory a small bag filled with plastic objects. 'And, as per our plan, I got someone at the library to use the 3D printer for me. We're good to go.'

Theodore stood behind his iron screen next to the workbench, containing his static around him. The machine was intimidating, and it had a steep learning curve, but Mallory persevered, using magic as needed to get the machine to accept their 3D pieces and feeling the energy drain rapidly from her body, adrenaline the only thing keeping her standing. After a couple of rounds of testing random objects, she felt ready to begin.

'You're getting the hang of this quite quickly,' Theodore said.

'I didn't spend hours lying down in pain watching videos of scientists talk through the use of various forensic machinery for nothing,' Mallory said.

'Talk me through what you're doing.'

'So my theory is that in looking at magic samples, we can identify the category of magic user, and hopefully see an easily colour-coded pattern emerging. Via these vials.' Mallory held up a handful of small glass tubes.

'Ah, like goths.' Theodore nodded.

'Yes... what?'

'Each Occult subculture has, theoretically, an alternative music subculture equivalent. We are – metaphorically speaking – trying to match the alternative song to the alternative subculture.'

Mallory allowed a few seconds to elapse in bewilderment before continuing. 'Sure. I've been thinking that the historic Occult elemental alignments of vampires with iron, witches with carbon—'

'Ghosts with mercury. It's because we're mercurial. It's very funny.'

'Demons with sulphur, faeries with nitrogen, and trolls with cobalt, it's likely that that—'

'Means something around here. Yes!' Theodore clapped his hands together. 'Let us begin.'

'I suppose we'll start in the easiest place.' Mallory swabbed her own mouth and put the sample through the Machine, checking back on the instructions.

The Magic Magical Machine whirred into life, vacuum pumps humming. Mallory pulled the airlock lever, sealing the sample into the Machine. Every passing second felt like hours. Eventually, the Machine spat out a print-out spectrum chart that she passed over the screen to Theodore.

'Very interesting. Repeated carbon fragments,' he said.

Another chamber whirred and clicked, the 3D-printed attachments forcing a small burst of pearlescent smoke out the side of the Machine into one of the vials. It curled as Mallory picked it up, trying to steady her shaking hands.

'My sample is red.' She held it up as it settled into a ruby swirl.

'And your theory is so far correct,' Theodore said. 'The spectrum charts confirm your magic is primarily carbon-based.'

The basement door opened and Diana popped her head around.

'Hi,' Mallory said. 'I'm sorry.'

Diana held up a hand, descending the stairs. 'Don't, it's okay. I just came to see if you wanted to swab me for anything. And also to offer you some hair.' She stopped. 'Troll hair. It's not mine. And I didn't steal it from a troll, it was a troll hair wig I have that

I was using to make rugs. Goddess, I can't make this sound any less weird. Rugs for the diorama.' Diana sighed. 'Just take it.'

Mallory grinned and passed her a swab. 'Thank you.'

Diana leaned over the Machine after Mallory processed the sample, pressing her face to the display. 'It's so loud!' she shouted. 'Something's happening!'

Mallory held up the resulting smoke-filled bottle: red, again.

'Witch magic, red and carbon-based,' Theodore said. 'I think that's good for phase one. Now me.' He held a hand out and Diana placed a swab into it. He waved it around his face, static flying. Mallory set it into the chamber.

'I got this one,' Diana said, as the smoke emerged. She held up the vial. 'Oh, gross.'

'It's not gross, it's… yeah, it's gross,' Theodore said unhappily, staring at the sickly yellow swirl.

'Yellow for ghost.'

Mallory prepared the peace-offered troll hair.

'Can I do this one? I'm basically your lab assistant,' Diana asked. Mallory reluctantly showed her how to prepare the chamber, feeling a dull wash of pain from the extra, unexpected effort.

This sample returned a swirl of grey-blue smoke, paler than the others.

'Grey-blue for troll magic – though it's weaker, I guess cause it's from hair,' Mallory commented.

'Just like regular DNA!' Theodore said. 'And it's primarily cobalt-based.'

'What else have we got?' Mallory felt a sinking sense of dismay. 'We should've tried to get more samples other than from the victims.'

Diana snapped her fingers. 'The faeries! I haven't washed their cups and I remember who got what mug. I'll be back.'

She returned in moments with labelled sample tubes. In quick succession, the resulting swabs came back green for Felix and Cloud, but different for Langdon.

'Whose is this one?' Mallory held a tube containing a teal swirl. 'Langdon's?'

'Yeah,' Diana said. 'Troll and faerie lineage.'

'Interesting,' Theodore said. 'The spectrum charts for the faeries all have really high nitrogen levels, but Langdon's has much lower nitrogen, and cobalt where the others don't. What's next?'

Mallory took out the beetles that had walked on the bodies from their tiny boxes, still brilliant green. 'Time to see what we got from the victims. Kuster first.'

Mallory held the first beetle in her hand and dithered for a moment with it. As though the beetle knew what to do, it wiggled in her hand, green magic flowing into the testing tube.

'Oh thank you,' she whispered to the beetle, and tucked it back into its box. For the first time, she understood the awestruck reverence Cornelia had for insects.

The Machine rumbled, and Mallory reached forward to pluck the smoke vial. She shook it, and held it up so Theodore and Diana could see the smoke settle.

'Pink,' Mallory said, barely daring to breathe.

She repeated the process for Ben's sample. Mallory felt every second tick down as she waited.

Pink again.

Two victims with pink magic traces.

'Can we call this conclusive?' Mallory asked. 'I know this was the theory, but it feels simultaneously impossible to have achieved, and the easiest thing in the world.'

'Let's look at the spectrum charts again,' Theodore said. He pored over them for several long moments.

'Love that "let's" implies this is a collaborative endeavour,' Diana said.

'They are all distinctly different samples.' Theodore looked up. 'The victims' charts show carbon present in lower amounts than either yours or Diana's, and Ben's doesn't show *any* nitrogen at all, which indicates this is purely the killer's magic; no trace of Ben's faerie magic in the sample. Each sample undeniably supports Mallory's hypothesis of elemental connections to Occult subculture.' Theodore threw the pages down. 'Mallory. You are a genius. You are a modern-day equivalent to Lockyer and Janssen, except you are one person and a girl and not justifying the existence of a noble gas, but asserting a pioneering chemical analysis of magic as yet untested.'

'What a snappy description,' Diana said, but Mallory didn't hear her, for once basking in the idea that she, maybe, wasn't a complete failure.

'We still need demon and vampire samples, just to be sure.'

'I'm sure Cornelia will be thrilled to supply us with a bit of her vampire,' Diana said dryly. 'We need to question him soon anyway.'

'So that leaves demon. I'm thinking, though' – Mallory tipped her finger off Langdon's sample – 'if Langdon's spectrum chart showed that faerie and troll lineage made a unique combination, and we've been right about the elemental alignments so far, this could be combination magic of some kind too. Kuster and Ben's samples showed carbon, right? Just in lower amounts? Pink…'

'Like witch magic mixed with something else?' Diana suggested.

'Yeah. Pretty much,' Mallory said. 'And at present, doesn't help us with our suspects. O'Sullivan and the Night Mayor are witches, but Quinn is a demon and Beckett a vampire, which are all our missing pieces.'

'We're a step closer than we were,' Diana soothed.

Mallory forced herself to take a calming breath.

'Was there anything else we should look at while we're here? The broken glass from the Larix basement?'

'I put that in a bag in that cupboard.' Diana pointed. 'Labelled it TU #003.' Mallory's stomach lurched at the realisation that this was, in fact, the third murder they had investigated.

'I can do this.' Theodore adjusted his cardigan sleeves. 'I would like to contribute.' Mallory switched off the Machine and covered it so Theodore could pass by to his bench.

He placed the glass sample under his ancient microscope and peered at it. The iron hammered into the base of his bench helped him not fill the room with static, but Mallory found it hard to concentrate on what he was doing, her vision dancing.

'I can say with absolute certainty,' Theodore said, straightening, 'that this sample here, without question, is broken glass.'

'Thanks, Theo,' Mallory said, amused.

'But that's all. I would honestly say it's a beer bottle, perhaps. Or a shattered bulb, maybe.' He returned the glass carefully to Mallory.

She stared at the pieces in her hand, bottle green and dark, her mind trying to force it to be significant. 'I'm really aware that because I want this to be some kind of clue, I'm trying to make it be a clue,' Mallory sighed. 'Just put it back in the drawer.' She tipped the pieces into the bag Theodore proffered.

She led them back into the research room, flopping down on the couch.

'I just can't figure out how two crime scenes are so different, but everything else is the same. There was nothing in Kuster's room: a witchlight, books, a laptop, his clothes. It was locked. The second murder was so risky, so public… Ben died in a space where anyone could've walked in and seen something, and he was surrounded by nothing but rubbish.'

'I'm really struggling to see how they're connected, beyond what we know about the Ternion symbol. I'm hoping going to the Observatory will help us. Why would the killer commit murder in such a public place? Why leave us that note?' Mallory said.

'Maybe this was always the plan, to ramp up fear. Or maybe they're devolving and have stopped being able to care about subtlety,' Diana suggested, curling up beside Mallory.

'Unless they're getting more organised?' Theodore said ominously. Criminal psychology was not his forte, but Theodore had watched enough daytime TV when he was alive and worked nights in the lab to know the basics of it. 'We see the Ternion symbol as indicative of the motive, but maybe there's another pattern we aren't seeing. Moon times, stars in the sky, uh… Mercury in retrograde?'

'Could be,' Mallory said pleasantly, but she wasn't really listening as she thought. Two murders didn't make a pattern.

They just made two murders. The Ternion was, somehow, the thing connecting them; it had made an early pattern emerge; those carvings – the letter, the Samhain deadline. They all came together in a panicked jumble, her mind refusing to sort through them, the deadline, six days away, looming over her.

'Theodore, I don't think I can do this.'

Theodore put a hand on her shoulder. 'Yes you can, Mallory. I've known you since you were fourteen years old. You're my best friend. Or as close to appropriately best friend as one can be with the living.'

'That's true, and also makes me a little sad.' Theodore was so wonderful, Mallory wanted him to have as many friends as he desired.

'Are we not friends?' Diana demanded.

'Be quiet, Diana, this isn't about you,' Theodore said, tapping her gently on the head. Some of her hair floated up in the static rush. 'Haven't you heard me talk about my life? I'm tragic. But I'm still proud to have a friend like you. Maybe not a *best* friend – you have plenty of those – but a really good friend, who I would do anything for, even die, despite me being unable to do so again. More's the pity.'

'Theodore,' Mallory reproached, but with gentleness, because she did not understand what it must be like to be alive, then dead, but still existing.

'Sorry. Anyway. I've known you since you were fourteen and you decided your sense of justice was greater than any need to fit in. The first decision you made was to solve my murder. Second was to do experiments to help me remove these.' He threw the cat ears across the room and they instantly rematerialised on his head. 'And we have spent years figuring out scientific advances together, even without formal education for you. You are the most capable person I know.'

'But I am in pain,' Mallory admitted, a lump in her throat. 'I'm in so much pain, I can't think. And only one of those things proved useful. I haven't solved your murder. We didn't get rid of the cat ears. And I don't really know anything about science still.'

'So? You will solve my murder soon. I know you will. It is likely not possible to remove the cat ears. You know lots about lots of things. And despite the pain, you think clearer and better than most folk your age. No, that's not right. You think better and clearer than most qualified scientists I knew.'

Mallory smiled at him. She was lucky to have him as a friend.

'I just can't see what the killer is doing, though it's probably obvious.'

'A third murder, that would help, perhaps?' Theodore said, then clapped a hand over his mouth. 'I don't mean to be so flippant. Just... it would help, factually.'

'For the record I am not offended by that suggestion, even though my friend is dead,' Diana said. 'I think he's right. In a weird, twisted way.'

'Yeah, maybe.' Mallory categorically could not think of anything more horrific than a third murder. 'I just wanted there to be something else. Anything. Anything at all that would help us get justice, for Kuster and Ben.'

Diana's phone buzzed and she pulled it out. 'I think we're about to get that chance. Observer Johnson has said he's got time for us this afternoon.'

FOURTEEN

It had been years since Mallory had been in the Observatory. The taxi pulled up outside, and she marvelled at how beautiful it was. A huge, circular building of white brick and stained glass, culminating in a glass tower at the top where Occult could go to look at the stars and be close to the Ternion.

Diana had passed Mallory a list of potential questions to ask Observer Johnson. One of them was, 'Where do you get your cloaks?' but it was close to the bottom, so she felt confident that she could simply ignore it. There were two murders to solve and too many questions to ask.

Observer Johnson met them at the great glass door, his navy cloak studded with cascading yellow stars trailing the ground. He was short and dark-skinned with a light blue-grey tint, and his face was set with concern, lines crossing his forehead.

'What's this about, then?' he asked, looking between them.

'Thank you for meeting us, Observer Johnson.' Diana beamed

up at him. 'We were talking recently, what with it being so close to Samhain and everything, and we realised, we're Occult, but we know nothing about Occulture!' She raised her hands and let them fall to her sides, her fingers grazing the buckle of her cropped leather jacket. She almost looked like she hadn't been crying most of the night.

He raised an eyebrow, his face still creased with concern. It made for an amusing expression. 'Haven't you been anointed in this Observatory? Bathed in the candle spells and incense as a child, getting the protection of the Ternion? And it's a trick question, because you certainly have. I remember doing it for each of you. I never forget a face.'

'Of course we have. We've just forgotten everything,' Cornelia said.

Observer Johnson sighed. 'I don't forget faces, but I do forget names.'

'I'm Mallory, Diana and—'

'Cornelia Broadwick.' He wagged a finger at her. 'Yes. I was wondering why I felt apprehensive about this meeting. I remember you, from your sisters' anointments.'

Mallory and Diana both glanced at her, but Cornelia remained unabashed.

'I assure you, I am much worse now,' she said cheerfully.

'We really just want to kick-start our knowledge,' Mallory said. 'We figured it's not too late to learn – we are only twenty—'

'Sixty years between us, if you think about it,' Cornelia pointed out. Mallory made a mental note not to let Cornelia lead any interviews in future.

'And we thought, who would know better about the Ternion than you, Observer Johnson?' Mallory fixed a smile on her face.

Observer Johnson looked over his shoulder. He seemed to be under no illusion that they weren't up to something, but Diana's idea to pretend to know nothing was both the best they'd come up with, and also closest to the truth – they knew enough to get by, but not enough to solve a murder.

'All right. Go in the back, there's a place we can talk. I have an appointment with the Faerie Court soon, but I can make time for this.'

Mallory could see Cornelia and Diana working very hard not to react to this reminder of Ben's passing.

He turned and ushered them through the glass door, through another glass door and behind a red curtain, until they were in a red-carpeted circular hall that seemed to branch out into a room for each Occulture.

'Down here.'

He gestured to Cornelia to turn a corner, but she took a sharper turn than expected and collided with some curtains.

'I meant the next entrance, that's the tarot room. Get out of the tarot room, please. *Please,*' he whispered. Cornelia struggled, and Mallory closed her eyes at the sound of fabric ripping and the muffled sound of Cornelia swearing.

'Sorry. The curtain sort of swallowed me up.'

Observer Johnson rubbed a hand over his face. 'Just… in there. Please.' He pointed to another section of curtain, revealing a small greeting room.

'Please, sit. Can I get you anything? Tea?'

He did not look as though he wanted to get them tea.

'We're fine, thank you,' Mallory said.

'So, the Ternion. Elisabella, Hexana and Blair,' Diana said slowly. 'There's like… three of them.'

Mallory made another mental note to ask Diana to refine her level of pretend ignorance for future interviews.

'Yes.' Observer Johnson spoke with the forced pleasantness of a person who fielded many a ridiculous question on a daily basis. 'The clue is in the name. There are three. And I know you know this much. Especially you, Cornelia Broadwick.'

In a reluctant display of competence, Diana outlined what they knew about the Ternion. Laid out in front of an Occulture scholar, it didn't feel like much.

Observer Johnson adjusted his cloak around him, settling back in his seat. 'So you understand that the goddesses helped – and continue to help – bring all the Occultures together in harmony. Elisabella is the carer, Blair offers protection to anyone who may need it, while Hexana gives strength.' He continued, sotto voce, 'Which I am asking for at present.'

'I suppose that brings us to our main question.' Mallory elbowed Diana subtly, who fumbled in her bag and handed her Theodore's book. 'We were reading this book, and were interested in this pattern here.' Resting the book on her lap so she didn't strain her arms, Mallory showed Observer Johnson the picture Theodore had found of the stained-glass window with the interconnecting circles, lines and stars pattern – the same pattern carved into Ben and Kuster's torsos. 'It seems like it's important to the Ternion in some way. I'm quite embarrassed to not know why.' Mallory tried to appear shamefaced.

'From the main wall? Beautiful piece, isn't it?' Observer Johnson said, admiring it through half-closed eyes as though he hadn't been affected by it every single day of his waking life. 'And it most certainly is important. I would say there's no need to be embarrassed, we all start somewhere, but…'

'Do we know where this particular symbol comes from, or what it means?' Mallory asked, resting her finger beside it, avoiding the nausea of looking at it too closely. The last thing she wanted to do was throw up in front of him.

'Of course we do,' he said. 'In the old days, before Occult communities lived together, long before the concept of Apparent witch trials and what have you, it was decided by some community leaders that there should be a place for all belief systems to be observed. Apparents were, in the collective world, starting to become more interested in astronomy. They modelled their astronomers' buildings on our Observatories, but we Observe everything here, from the astral to the astronomical. We needed something to set us apart.'

'Go on,' Cornelia said, unnecessarily.

'I was going— This symbol is an intricate, individual creation made from life and death that is as unique as the lines in a fingerprint. Elisabella alone had this creative power. It is magic at its purest form. The symbol now doesn't play such a big role in teachings, but it is a foundational part of the concept of the Ternion. It *is* them.'

'What would happen if someone tried to replicate her symbols for their own purposes?' Mallory said.

Observer Johnson sat up. 'I can take ignorance feigned for reasons below my capabilities of acknowledging, but I will not take borderline *sacrilege* in my – this, *our*, Observatory. These kinds of questions… they warned me about folk like you, in Observational training. Beware the witches asking questions, they said.'

'Surely it's "beware the witches starting fires"?' Cornelia said.

'I can paraphrase where appropriate.'

'I can assure you, Observer Johnson, there's nothing to fear here. We've told you what we know, and what we'd like to know,' Mallory said, 'and it isn't much bigger than that. Surely asking questions of such a learned scholar is better than us wondering, or seeking answers in more… unsavoury places?'

Mallory had no idea what sort of unsavoury place she would find answers in, but she was willing to bet, if such places existed, that Observer Johnson did.

'We just want to learn,' Diana said in a small voice. 'We yearn for the days of formal education.'

'Flattery will get you nowhere.' Observer Johnson folded his hands, a hint of a flattered smile on his face that disappeared a nanosecond later. 'It would be a most cursed thing. I can't imagine the power that would be needed to do something like that. Most could not, and I don't know what sort of tool you'd need to use to do it. It is beyond powerful magic, hence the Ternion stand alone. Nobody could compare to them, so no more goddesses were added to their number.'

'Have you ever come across any teachings, any writings before about someone attempting it? Could someone use someone else's power? Would the person be using Ternion power, or creating their own?' Mallory pressed.

Observer Johnson cleared his throat uncomfortably. 'To my knowledge, there are original teachings about a death blade –

that's what the straight lines in the symbol are meant to represent. Elisabella created something physical to cut the first symbol. It is said she used the souls of the departed. It is unclear who these souls were, or what happened to them afterwards.'

The hairs on Mallory's arms stood to attention. They had been on the right track with the knife.

'Where did she cut the symbol first?' Cornelia asked.

He hesitated. 'Just into the glass. It was only ever the glass. I have a book, somewhere—'

'Have you seen photographs of the death blade? Does it still exist?' Goosebumps erupted all over Mallory's body, Kuster and Ben torso's flashing before her eyes.

He scowled. 'No. I don't know why anyone would want to see such a thing. I saw it in a dream once. Black, inky, swirling. A horrid, wretched thing that made something wonderful. But that's it. And perhaps that was just my imagination.'

Mallory nodded, her head swirling. 'Could the symbol be used for an alternative purpose? If someone was actually able to replicate this symbol, or make their own blade, for example. Has it ever happened?'

'Goddess.' Observer Johnson blanched. 'Only the Ternion should draw the lines. This piece here, in the Observatory, is said to have been drawn by Elisabella's hand, and I am inclined to believe it. Someone else drawing it would be calling Elisabella forth and that's just… not worth thinking about.'

Mallory's skin crawled at the implications of what Observer Johnson was saying. Their killer could be trying to summon the Ternion.

'But if we did want to think about it? You know, as a thought exercise,' Cornelia said, 'what would happen if someone did call Elisabella?'

'You mean if someone were to summon her?' Observer Johnson's voice shot up an octave. 'Why would anyone want to *summon* the Ternion?'

'Nobody wants to summon the Ternion,' Mallory said loudly. 'I think what Cornelia meant was, has anyone tried to?'

Her heart fluttered in her chest, afraid of what he was going to say next.

Observer Johnson sat forward in his seat. 'I don't believe it has been attempted in history. The consequences are too dire. You believe the Ternion formed towards the end of the Vampire Wars, correct? But I believe the formation of the Ternion *ended* the Vampire Wars. They were directly responsible for facilitating the vampire covenants, the refusal to drink any blood, Apparent or Occult, ever again. The vampires agreed. The Ternion made it binding.'

'Hang on,' Diana said. 'I thought vampires historically synthesised magic from the gifted blood of Apparents. Where do Occult come into this?'

Cornelia shifted uncomfortably.

'This is a separate issue,' Observer Johnson said shortly, 'but some teachings suggest that during the Vampire Wars, there were rumours some vampires requested the blood of any Occult, even other vampires, to expand the range of their powers in an effort to win.'

'Occultures borrow magical concepts from each other all the time, though?' Cornelia said. 'Maybe the mechanisms are different, but the end result is that we can expand the range of our own powers using our own magic. Surely if it was consensual…'

'The problem wasn't the blood itself, or the power, or consent or any of those things, it was *how* the subsequent power was being used, and the scale of it – *if* there is any credence to the legend. Ask almost any vampire and you'll find they're in agreement on this – the Ternion facilitated the implementation of the Do No Harm Charter and its wider implications and conditions for the rest of Occulture, but the vampires made it happen. Most did not want the Wars to begin, did not agree with how destructive things became, and were glad to see them end so definitively, no matter the cost. We owe their ancestors a great deal of thanks.'

Diana nodded. Mallory hadn't known this fact either – like faeries, vampires had their own private customs and beliefs that she had never had the courage to ask about. She tried to formulate a question about the purpose of the Vampire Wars, but the threads kept drifting away from her incoherently. And Observer Johnson had moved on.

'The Ternion restored order, brought Occult communities together, et cetera, et cetera,' he continued. 'The Unified Magical Liaison was born from this union. Every rule, every belief, every practice we hold in Occulture is sewn together at its foundation by the Ternion. It begins and it ends with three.' He exhaled. 'To bring them back would be sacrilege. To ask them to walk this earth again, after all they sacrificed, is unconscionable.'

'But if someone *did* do that. What would happen?' Cornelia pressed. Mallory bit her lip to stop herself trying to smooth it over.

What Observer Johnson said next was measured and firm, a clear indication that the conversation was over.

'The lore says that the return of the Ternion to Earth would cause war and destruction. The Vampire Wars would begin anew. Vampire would fight vampire, who would fight faerie, who would fight demon, who would fight witch, who would fight troll. There would be no order, until a winning Occulture emerged, and then that Occulture would expand to the Apparent world and end the idea of our two worlds existing side by side,' Observer Johnson said, standing. 'It would be as it was: an ugly, tragic fight that could only get worse. We were almost destroyed by the Vampire Wars, and saved by the Ternion, as we continue to be. Even in the unseen everyday of your lives, the Ternion are holding the fabric together, stitch by stitch. Now, about that book.'

He rummaged around behind his chair for a moment and produced a tome that had perhaps looked new and exciting a century or so prior. 'This is what you'll need. It doesn't have all the answers, but it'll save me time.'

Cornelia held out her hand, a grateful smile plastered on her face.

'Rather, you will need to acquire your own copy. I can't give you this one.' It seemed more of a *won't* situation. 'I should think you'd manage that much on your own.'

Mallory was grateful Cornelia managed to simply note the title of the book into her phone instead of responding.

He moved to the curtain, waiting for the Undetectables to stand. 'I can't in good conscience answer any more *theoretical* questions today. There's been a horrible tragedy in the community. Sometimes it feels like the whole world has lost its way.'

'Thank you so much for the recommendation, and your time.' Mallory could see they'd pushed him too hard, but she had to fight to care. He had told them so much, potentially revealed a lot about their killer, and it was all she could think about.

'My time is free to all.'

'Even still, thank you very much.'

'I wasn't finished. My time is free to all… but folk normally choose to leave a small donation. For the upkeep of the premises, of course.'

'Of course,' Cornelia said. 'Do you take card, or is this a strictly cash-only, no-receipts, no-refunds sort of operation?'

He didn't quite manage a smile. 'Please hesitate to ask more questions if you need anything. If you'll excuse me…' He hurried out.

Mallory pulled the curtain back and the Undetectables stepped out into the red corridor.

'So are we all thinking the killer is murdering folk to summon the Ternion?' Cornelia whispered, slipping several bank notes into a decorative bowl as she passed. It would be weeks before Observer Johnson found it.

'That's exactly what I'm thinking,' Diana said.

'And are we thinking that the killer has Elisabella's death blade, or something like it?' Mallory whispered.

The others nodded. Cornelia looked haunted, her eyes ringed with shadows.

'My conclusion is that on Samhain, at the deadline stated in the letter, our killer is going to try to summon the Ternion and unleash chaos on Wrackton, and the world,' Mallory said, her whole body shaking.

'And we have six days to find out who they are, and stop them,' Diana said as they emerged into daylight.

'That's not very many days.' Cornelia raked a hand through her hair. 'At all. But this is it, isn't it? The killer is going big and has no intention of going home.'

Nobody answered, because the reality had just sunk in. It was bigger than what Mallory wanted, bigger than Kuster, bigger than Ben. It was about the world as they knew it, and the solution rested on the shoulders of three twenty-year-olds and one dramatic ghost.

FIFTEEN

'Places, everyone!' Theodore said. 'Quickly, look professional! Do everything you can to distract from the fact I am a cat!'

Detective Inspector O'Sullivan had agreed to meet with them not long after they got back from the Observatory, and this development had shaken them out of their collective shock.

'Theodore, if you could tone it down by like, one single notch, we'd all be able to think and conduct this meeting properly,' Cornelia said, muttering and rubbing her hands together as the research room rearranged itself around her. Diana had put herself in charge of making tea and supplying biscuits and cake. Theodore had put himself in charge of putting them under stress. He happily ignored Cornelia's request.

'Diana, try to keep up the ruse as much as you can,' Mallory said. She swallowed her afternoon meds and choked down a biscuit, trying to keep the crumbs from hitting the now-clean research room floor.

'I am a forensic science student. I am good at learning. I love science. This is a paper on crime scene procedure,' Diana said mechanically. 'I love to science good.'

'Diana.' Mallory raised an eyebrow.

A shot of jealousy ran through her at the thought of Diana taking her place as a forensic science student. The past few days had been the most time Mallory had spent out of bed consecutively in a long time, and it was killing her to do so.

'If all else fails I can monologue about Francine Leon,' Diana shrugged. She had changed, and was now wearing black and red tartan trousers with a blazer.

'Okay. Cornelia, what's our plan?' Mallory asked, pulling her long hair up into a ponytail.

Cornelia bit her lip. 'I don't know, I was thinking it would be an "and we are also here" situation. We'll figure it out.'

'The most important thing is that we get as much information out of her as possible,' Mallory said. Through the basement window, she saw a car pull up at street level. 'Theodore, she's coming! Places, everyone!' Mallory sat at her desk as Detective Inspector O'Sullivan knocked on the door.

Theodore was unsubtly pushed out into the lab where – despite agreeing to not further complicate the Undetectables's lies by speaking to their visitor – he sulked into a microscope.

In a flurry of movement, O'Sullivan shook everyone's hand, a cup of tea was thrust upon her and she was directed into a chair. Younger than any of them had imagined, O'Sullivan surveyed them with dark brown eyes, her lips painted a deep red. Diana eyed her casual but fashionable suit appreciatively.

'I'm DI O'Sullivan.' Her soft brown skin crinkled around her eyes. 'But you can call me Alyssa. Or Sully, like everyone else does.'

'Sully, thanks so much for coming to meet me. My friends have never met a real live detective before, so they asked if they could sit in.' Diana beamed.

Mallory had to admit that her friend got an awful lot with a big, genuine smile and a headful of the most ludicrously fast lies.

Cornelia slid a slice of cake next to Sully in one smooth gesture that made Mallory momentarily hate how ungraceful her own body was. She shoved this down with all the other things she didn't like to think about.

'Your email was very compelling. What's the problem with the assignment?'

'I'm just having a hard time constructing it. Basically, we've to write about crime scene procedure. My classmates were assigned someone to go to, but my student account was hacked, and... well, look, it's a long, boring story,' Diana lied lyingly. 'And I don't want to bother you with it. But safe to say, I'm struggling on the details a bit.'

'Can I see what you've written so far?' Sully held her hand out. A brief flash of fear passed over Diana's eyes.

'Well, it's that I don't really know how to start. I was thinking about where I met you, maybe talking about the procedure of that murder.'

Sully leaned back in her chair, her lips pursed. 'I see. And what did you want to know about that particular murder?'

Diana blinked. 'Just, you know, if it was connected to any other murder.'

Mallory also had to admit to herself that when Diana's lies crashed, they crashed hard.

'I see. And what school did you say you went to?' Sully asked pleasantly.

'I— The… um.' Diana shook her head. 'Goddess, I've forgotten.'

Sully stood.

'This is a waste of my time. What are you, journalists?'

'No,' Cornelia said. 'We aren't journalists.'

'What, then? Did my colleagues put you up to this, is that it?'

'No!' Mallory said. She looked at Diana and Cornelia, and made a decision. 'We… we're private investigators. The Night Mayor hired us. It's all legit, I swear.'

'This is fucking ridiculous.' Sully pulled her coat on and went to leave.

'Detective Inspector O'Sullivan, please,' Diana said. 'Ben DeLacey was our friend.'

She paused, her hand on the door. 'Your friend?'

'Mine and Cornelia's.'

'If you just call the Night Mayor, I'm sure he'll explain,' Mallory said, though her stomach clenched with fear that he'd react how he had in the Larix.

Sully closed her eyes for a second. 'Fine. I'll be right back.'

She opened the door and went to the stairs. Diana whispered a listening spell and they huddled around her hand, listening intently.

'Mr Night Mayor? DI O'Sullivan here, I just—'

There was a pause, presumably as she listened.

'No, no developments, just a query—' Another pause.

'How long does it take to have a one-sided conversation with the Night Mayor?' Cornelia whispered. Mallory put a hand on her arm to shush her, the soft fabric of her jumper pleasant beneath her fingers.

'I asked you to let me know the names of every single party involved in this case, and I would just like to know if you are aware that that unequivocally included any agency purporting to act on your behalf,' Sully said. Another pause.

'How am I supposed to "just know" if it's right or not? Am I to believe *every single* individual who tells me they're someone important?' Sully snapped. Mallory heard an indistinct, tinny rumbling as Van Doren shouted down the phone.

'Of course. Of course. No, obviously nobody else has claimed to be involved, I am asking you to tell me if you've hired—'

There was a sigh.

'Oh, big sigh,' Diana whispered. 'I think he's worn her down.'

'Fine. Fine, thank you.'

She hung up and the Undetectables scrambled to their seats, arranging themselves to not look like they'd been listening as Sully re-entered the lab.

Sully didn't take off her coat this time, just sat in her seat with her legs crossed.

'Okay. I believe you. I think this is frankly insulting' – she circled a finger around the room – 'but the Night Mayor is the Night Mayor, and I think he'd have the heads of anyone who made a show of him like this.'

It was a clear attempt at a mood-lightening joke, but Mallory shivered; this was the second time she'd heard someone suggest Van Doren could kill.

'Don't we know it.' Cornelia grinned, her general anti-police stance outweighed by a genuine opportunity to insult Van Doren.

Sully sighed, clearly deciding to share something. 'This is a temporary new team, and I've just made Detective Inspector. My dad was on the force – Apparent, back in Oughteron, not here. I need to make sure every step of the way that everything's above board. It's not just my reputation here. If I could offer one tiny piece of unsolicited advice, it's this: one of the first skills I had to learn as a detective was learning how to look through bullshit. Mine, and everyone else's. Once you stop fooling yourself that your gut feelings are always right, it lets you tune into your other senses. The truth becomes easier then.'

Her words twisted something in Mallory's stomach, but she pushed it aside. For now, her gut was all she had.

'Anyway. Tell me what you've learned.'

Mallory filled Sully in quickly, leaving out both the letter, and the connection to the Ternion. She might not be as quick as Diana, but she knew not to play all her cards at once.

'That's not bad. You're missing a couple of things,' Sully said. 'Hold on.'

She whispered under her breath and an evidence bag appeared in her hands. 'This was recovered from Kuster's bedroom, under his pillow.' She held it out so they could see a phone. 'It's a recording made on Edward Kuster's phone, from 2 October, which, as you've rightly determined, we believe to be the night of his murder. We also believe this was recorded at or shortly prior to his time of death.'

That cemented a day for their suspects to need an alibi, and gave them something concrete to seek from Van Doren, Beckett, Quinn and O'Sullivan herself. Mallory refused to allow herself to be disarmed by how nice she seemed. Mallory was a person of science, but even she was hard-pressed to ignore how bizarre their interaction with Sully had been so far.

Sully pulled on a pair of gloves, opened the bag and pulled out the phone. She pressed play on an audio file.

Immediately, the room hummed with a discordant whistling sound. It was like nothing Mallory had ever heard before. She clamped her hands over her ears but it kept going, fizzing in and out of the range of the phone's audio capabilities. It was high and inhuman: a horrible, metallic ringing, forcing pressure into her eardrums and threatening to burst them. Shivers erupted over her body, her skin on fire, twitching, burning. It sounded like the beginning and the end all at once and her teeth, against her will, tried to bite down on her tongue.

The recording stopped and Mallory could only hear stillness. Looking to Cornelia and Diana, they had reacted the same way. Diana's hands were in her hair and Cornelia had wrapped the cable from Diana's laptop around her fingers so tightly that her fingers were blue. Sully's face was grim set; she'd evidently heard it before and was prepared.

Maybe too prepared.

'I don't know what it means, if it means anything.' Sully resealed the bag and stripped off her gloves. Her tone was casual, though her eyes flicked between them as she spoke, looking for something in their faces.

'Neither do I,' Theodore whispered loudly. He had crept back up to the research room partition without anyone noticing, leafing innocently through a book.

'I…' Sully looked at him, and then took another sip of tea. Mallory pointed her thumb at him to return to the lab.

'The recording was made at 11:54 p.m., on one of those snore recording apps, so it would only activate if there was a sound. There's nothing recorded before, and that...' Sully searched for the right word, '...silvery sound? Cuts out everything else. No talking, no choking sounds, just... whistle, silence.'

The Undetectables took a moment to absorb this information.

Sully drained her cup. 'This is as far as we've got. I asked all the trolls and faeries I could find who were willing to speak to the police – not many,' she said ruefully, 'if there had been anything similar in the Larix the night of the DeLacey murder, but nobody reported hearing anything.'

'We were there,' Mallory said. 'But it was so loud, I'm not sure anyone would've been able to hear over the sound system.'

'I wasn't on shift when the call came in for both, so it was a while before I got to both of the scenes,' Sully said.

Mallory felt that was an interesting piece of information. A glance at Diana told her that she thought the same thing.

'Were you out somewhere nice?' Diana asked casually.

Sully raised an eyebrow at her, her expression otherwise unchanged. 'I'm sure I was. But that's where we're at. I'm...' she started. 'My team...' She bit her lip. 'That's where we're at.' She said again.

Mallory thought she knew exactly what she meant. Sully definitely seemed as cooperative as Diana had suggested, but she couldn't get what the police had said in the Larix out of her head, or Diana's sense that something was off. A part of Mallory could not bring herself to trust Sully's helpfulness.

'I have beetles,' Cornelia blurted, to Mallory's dismay. It was unnecessary information to share, especially when it was something so unique to the Undetectables. 'Want to see?'

To Sully this must've seemed like an alarming non-sequitur. Mallory wished Cornelia had held onto this particular urge, at least until they were sure she wasn't a suspect.

Before Sully could argue, Cornelia had tipped a *Sonata lutumae* into her hand and was urging her to cast a spell.

'Why am I to do this?'

'It's one cool trick, it'll make doctors hate you,' Cornelia said solemnly. Sully wrinkled her nose, but, despite herself, complied, making vague noises of interest as the beetle reacted.

'This is all very interesting, but I really have to get going.' She tipped the now-green beetle back into Cornelia's hands.

'Thank you for hearing us out,' Diana said.

'I can't promise a third deception will be met with the same patience,' Sully said firmly.

'We won't do it again. I'm a forensic science student, could I simply lie to you if that weren't true?' Diana said.

Mallory fought the urge to kick her in the shins.

Sully frowned. 'Seriously, don't make a habit of it. And, of course, may your friend Ben live forever in the Fair Kingdom.'

She grabbed a final biscuit from the plate. 'I like your outfit,' she said to Diana.

'Thanks, I dressed myself,' Diana chirped, holding the door for her. Sully looked at them all, and strode out. They waited until she was definitely gone to look at each other.

'What do we think?' Mallory asked. She herself was unsure.

'That was weird,' Diana said. 'Even if she has good taste in clothes.'

'I'm sorry I showed her the beetles,' Cornelia said. 'But I had a hunch we needed to seem open to sharing with her, so she'd give us more. We didn't actually offer her anything in return for the recording, and I want her to trust us, just in case we're wrong about her.'

'She's got a lot riding on this,' Mallory said slowly. 'She avoided Diana's slightly obvious alibi question.'

'Be fair, I think it was more semi-obvious,' Diana said indignantly. 'But you're right.'

'Why would someone like Sully want to summon the Ternion?' Mallory said. 'That's got to be our question all along, about all our suspects. Why would our suspect do it?'

'Can I come back in yet?' Theodore shouted from the lab. 'Or must I continue my penance from afar?'

'Sorry, Theodore. Of course,' Mallory shouted. She turned back to the other Undetectables. 'She's in a new role, trying to make her mark. Her colleagues don't respect her and she has familial obligations to carry on a legacy.'

'A semi-reasonable motive,' Cornelia said.

'But isn't that a lot? Like, two murders just to be successful at law enforcement?' Diana said.

'No, I mean if we consider the implications – the potential resurgence of the Vampire Wars if the Ternion comes back, the inter-Occultural fighting and the eventual domination over Apparent society… It's a good motive for someone who clearly feels resentful with where they're at in life. I think we're not really grasping the scale of this; if the Ternion return, there won't be normal jobs any more. She'd be the witch who brought the Ternion back, so she could have a way to protect herself from the consequences,' Mallory said.

'She did help us,' Diana pointed out. 'But who knows? Van Doren hired us, and we still suspect him.'

'Because he's been sensationally weird,' Cornelia said. 'And I hate him anyway.'

'The motive works for him, too, but worse, because we know for a fact he loves power,' Diana said. 'If he found a way to get the Ternion's power, he could move beyond the limits of Night Mayor and become Night President of the Known Planet.'

'Snazzy title, shitty person,' Cornelia said.

'And Grey Quinn… Quinn's scary,' Diana said. 'A beautifully dressed scary individual. He'd stand to gain a lot more power from this too.'

'And if we were still looking at Beckett – sorry, Cornelia – it's come up a lot today. The vampires were mostly in agreement on the covenants, but they can't all have been, or else it wouldn't have happened.'

'Not every vampire wants power,' Cornelia said.

'We still need to consider it,' Diana said. 'He was there that night. And all our suspects have power as a potential motive, which makes sense if we're talking about someone doing something as drastic and destructive as summoning the fucking Ternion.'

'As the saying goes: go big or explode home,' Theodore said.

'Do we think the whistle is a spell?' Mallory asked, closing her eyes. Even her eyelashes hurt. She massaged her temples.

'Definitely.'

'Undeniably,' Cornelia said.

'It sounded horrendous,' Theodore said. 'If anyone cares what I think.'

'I always care what you think, Theo. What else could make us feel so... awful?' Mallory said.

'A deep sense of dread and foreboding,' Theodore supplied.

'Cornelia, can you make trying to find out what that sound was your priority? If you're right and it's adapted magic, maybe the killer used something that makes a metallic, silvery whistling noise, or that you think *could* make that noise,' Mallory said. She pulled her knees to her chest, thoughts slotting together. 'I think the killer likes puzzles. If we take the riddle as the first puzzle – even if we can't solve it, we should take it into overarching consideration – then the cipher from the letter, the locked room, a rapid escape from the Larix unseen by either trolls, who never forget a face, or faeries, who can't lie. The Ternion symbol... They're playing with us, whoever they are. We can't trust anyone we speak to.'

'Not even Van Doren,' Cornelia said.

'Yes. Not even Van Doren. He hired us, but...' Mallory waved a hand. 'Until we can see the bigger picture, we should err on the side of deep distrust.'

Cornelia wrapped her arms around herself. 'That won't be hard. My hunches have always been right. Except when they've been wrong.'

'Cornelia,' Diana said seriously. 'I am not a fan of the man. I too see reason to suspect him. But for the love of Blair, can you just. Very simply. Explain why you hate Van Doren so much.' She held up a hand. 'Very. Simply.'

Cornelia glared at her and held up her hand, ticking things

off on her fingers. 'He has never been consistent. He is obsessed with my parents' influence on the Ghoul Council. Agatha and Ethel,' she said, referring to her older twin sisters, 'told me before I left that he's publicly traded his wife in for a younger model.' She put down a third finger. 'Apparently this is the second time this has happened.' A fourth. 'She's left Wrackton for good now, and he's parading around someone new. The word is that she was his mistress for a while, even though I hate that word, but he's apparently always had at least one.'

'What does that last bit have to do with you hating him?' Diana demanded.

'Nothing, it just supports my hypothesis that he's terrible. The last thing is that Van Doren will never, ever stop looking for power, money and fame. There have always been rumours that he's violent, that he's unpredictable and surrounded by yes-folk who are afraid to challenge him. The only folk he listens to are the UML, and even that seems to be optics. He wants to bring in changes, horrible, anti-folk changes, like the prison – which I don't believe for a second is about policing Occult folk, he'd never spend money on that, this is about using Wrackton space for Apparent money for Apparent prisoners – and I can't support someone like that. Someone like that will always want more. He is dangerous. I know he's dangerous.' Cornelia's hand closed into a fist.

'That's fair,' Diana said. 'I think that's fair.'

Mallory nodded her agreement. 'He's as good a suspect as any, and certainly as good a suspect as Sully.'

'Thank you,' Cornelia said. 'I agree.'

'Can we backtrack on to why the twins told you about the wife thing?' Theodore asked. 'Cause that seems like something they'd say just to wind you up.' He shivered, and Mallory remembered how frightened he had been of them before they'd moved out of the Broadwick mansion. They weren't particularly threatening, but Theodore had never been able to stomach how much they'd enjoyed riling Cornelia.

'For the record, there is nothing more pathetic than a man in his sixties going for twenty-something-year-old women,' Cornelia said. 'She's practically our age! He could literally have a child ten years older than her. Anyway, Ethel and Agatha were all about how *aspirational* this is.' She made a face. 'But aside from this gross display of gender-normative expectations of a male-provisioned lifestyle—'

'Can we come back to this?' Mallory asked. 'Please.'

The others looked at her.

'Sorry,' Cornelia said. 'I got carried away.'

'How unexpected,' Diana said.

'We still need to talk to Beckett, Van Doren and Quinn,' Mallory said, pulling herself to her feet to write *ALIBI?* beside Sully's name.

'As much as I hate to admit it,' Diana said, 'Beckett doesn't seem likely, given what we think is happening. He'd need magic. But we should still talk to him.'

'I can get Beckett over here tonight,' Cornelia said. 'I think he was coming over anyway.'

Diana frowned. 'I can't wait.'

Cornelia glowered at her.

Mallory shot Diana a warning look, though she was feeling equally unenthused by this information. She kept thinking about the conditions that would need to be fulfilled in order for Beckett to be their killer, and how hard it would be to voice them.

Diana ignored them both. 'Back to the Whistler.' She lifted her chin. 'I think that's what we should call the killer, by the way.' She lifted her hands and pulled them apart slowly in the air. 'The Whistler.'

A beat passed as they all digested this.

'I like it,' Mallory said finally.

'Now that that's settled, I have a suggestion,' Theodore said. 'Let's nail this fucker.'

SIXTEEN

The front door opened and Mallory heard laughter in the hall that was at odds with how downbeat Cornelia had seemed before she'd gone out. Beckett's obnoxiously loud voice filled the hallway and Mallory steeled herself for what was undoubtedly going to be a terrible time. She'd remembered to take her afternoon meds, but even the thought of dealing with him had pain shooting down the sides of her jaw and into her neck.

Cornelia and Beckett appeared around the corner, but before Cornelia could say anything, Beckett pressed her up against the wall and kissed her as though they didn't have an audience, and as though she had no need for oxygen.

Mallory and Diana exchanged glances and Diana raised her mug to her mouth, a thousand unsaid words swallowed down in two big gulps. Mallory's cheeks burned.

'Beckett, stop.' Cornelia shoved him away playfully. Mallory was possibly the only one who saw how quickly her features rearranged into the same haunted look she'd worn since the second they'd heard about Ben.

Beckett turned to face Diana and Mallory. Mallory couldn't help but feel there was little difference between Beckett's smile and Beckett's sneer.

'Mallory, old pal.' Beckett reached down to where she was sitting and patted her on the head. Mallory wanted to slap him, but restrained herself. 'Good to see you again, mate. Corn said something about needing to ask me about the other night?'

'Yeah, we just wanted to ask what you saw, if anything.' She forced herself to be composed.

Beckett tilted his head. '*So* sorry about your friend. As the youngest vampire in Wrackton, I've never had to lose anyone – perks of being a vampire,' he said, shooting Mallory a toothy grin. Two years of vampire life was equal to one witch or Apparent year – it was common for vampires to reach 150 years easily, and they rarely died before their time. 'But I've read a bunch of books on grief and the stages of it. Totally happy to help you through it, it's a real mindset thing. Did Corn tell you I've got a psychology degree?'

'No. What a fascinating and helpful thing to know,' Diana said in monotone.

'I just, like… really want to help folk.' Beckett pulled out a chair and spun it around, the legs dragging against the hardwood with a hideous scraping sound that made Mallory want to rip her skin off. Then Beckett's skin off. She took a breath.

'Helping is what I was put on this earth to do, I think,' he said. 'There's a whole philosophy behind it, maybe we can talk about it another time.'

Cornelia had buried herself in the kettle and in finding biscuits, and was studiously not looking at Beckett as he spoke.

'What have you been doing today? I'm really interested in the routines folk amass,' Beckett continued, as though every word he was saying were not the worst collection of words anyone had ever heard. 'Like, I think a routine just says a lot about you, you know?'

Mallory did not know. Mallory did not want to know.

'Working,' Diana said shortly.

'Oh, with the ghost? Corn told me about the ghost.' He nodded knowingly. 'Cat ears.'

'His name is Theodore,' Mallory said, positive Cornelia had told him this already.

'Cool.' He didn't sound like he thought it was cool. 'The fact you have a whole lab in your basement is so weird. You're working on so much nerd stuff down there.'

'Have you seen it?' Diana asked, an edge to her voice.

'No.' He grinned. 'Corn is all about the science stuff, I feel I'm much more of a thinker. Of course, psychology *is* a science, it's just not often appreciated by the "hard" sciences. We encountered that a lot at uni. If you ever want to talk through the mindset of the killer' – he tapped his head – 'I might have some ideas.'

Cornelia smiled at him. 'Thanks, Beck. I'll let you know.'

Mallory wasn't sure who was in more need of restraint, Diana or herself.

The oven timer beeped, and Diana jumped to her feet. 'Pizzas are ready.'

Beckett looked up at the counter, at Cornelia and Diana standing, and back to Mallory. 'Why aren't you helping?' he said after a moment.

Mallory blinked.

'Because she doesn't need to,' Diana said. She was holding a knife in her hand and Mallory wanted very much to de-escalate the situation.

'I just need to sit today,' Mallory said. 'It's not a big deal.'

'Mallory can sit if she wants to,' Cornelia said.

'Yeah but, like… why?' Beckett asked. 'You live here too. Sorry, just trying to understand. I'm the guest, what's your excuse?'

There were few singularly more awkward things in Mallory's life than being asked to explain the absolute core of her functioning, or not functioning, as the case may be.

'I have my reasons,' she managed.

'What reasons? Are you an old lady all of a sudden?' Beckett laughed, looking around him when no one else did. 'Come on, that was a good one. Mallory's being waited on hand and foot like some sort of monarch and you guys are just, like… letting her. I'm not trying to be rude, I just like to try to point out injustices when I see them. And her sitting here for no reason is a pretty big injustice.'

'Cornelia,' Diana said. Her voice was low, dangerous, and she had not let go of the knife. 'Come see me in the basement. For a *boring science thing*.'

The basement door slammed behind them. The shouting started five seconds later.

'Diana seems really volatile,' Beckett said.

'Have some pizza, Beckett,' Mallory said.

She felt flustered and embarrassed. It had taken her a few days to notice how much Diana and Cornelia had been doing for her without her asking, how acutely aware they were of how much of her energy was going into solving cases, and how she hadn't had to say. The idea of being waited on, that anyone could walk into her space and see the situation like that instead of her friends working around Mallory's fear of asking for help, filled her with anger as much as it did with shame.

Beckett leaned over and folded half a pizza into a slice, shoving it in his mouth. He held up a hand while he finished chewing.

'Vampires have to eat a lot, make up for the lack of blood. Did you want some?'

'—*do you think I wanted to leave her alone up there with that FUCKING*—' Mallory heard Diana roar from the basement.

Mallory cleared her throat.

'—*will talk to him AGAIN, I don't know why you think I'm not aware he*—' Cornelia shouted.

'Hope Corn's okay. Seriously, Diana probably needs to talk to someone about her anger.'

'Beckett, in the interest of helping. I'm just wondering if there's anything you can tell me about that night in the Larix? Anything at all, nothing too big or too small,' Mallory said, feeling like her smile was about to crack off her face and into her tea. She got another flash of that bruise on Cornelia's neck and she blinked to push it away. Cornelia wouldn't let him do that, even if Beckett might.

'—*and nor would I want to, for he is but a boy and I have never in my life LIKED BOYS!*' Diana shouted.

'Okay. Does this feel kind of like a job interview to you? You sitting on one side, me on the other.' Beckett draped his arms over the back of the chair and leaned forward. Mallory tried to imagine him killing Kuster, killing Ben, and couldn't. 'Basically, I spent most of it with Corn.'

'Anything else? Did you see anyone, experience anything?'

'Well. There was the incident,' Beckett said. 'And look, your friend is dead, I totally respect that, but that tall one, whatever their name is. Felix? I think they have it in for me.'

'I'm sure Felix just wanted you to respect their customs.'

'See I'd think that, but it's like… that anger, that *rage*, has to come from somewhere. I sometimes find myself moving through crowds of angry folk and I just wonder what their problem is, you know?' Beckett shook his head.

Mallory could've taken a wild stab at what the problem might've been, but she persevered, keeping her own fury clamped down in an effort to get answers.

'Between you and me,' she said conspiratorially. He leaned towards her instinctively. 'Some folk think you did it on purpose. As a distraction from the murder.'

Beckett blanched.

'Goddess, no. I was drunk, and I made a mistake. Just a mistake, but it's that rage I spoke of – folk are ready to jump down the throat of anyone who does anything these days.'

Mallory inhaled slowly through her nose, envisioning the air cooling the rage in her stomach.

'Besides, I think I was just annoyed. I went to the bathroom afterwards, splashed water on my face, calmed down and came back to… to chaos.'

Mallory thought about how studiously nonchalant he'd seemed when he'd re-emerged.

'You didn't seem that panicked about the chaos when I saw you?'

'You did, though, your face was…' He pulled a horror-stricken expression that Mallory tried to not see as an offensive imitation of her. 'But something I learned in one of my lectures is that eyewitnesses to tragic events are terrible because they let their emotions take over.'

Mallory wasn't certain he was recalling that fact correctly.

'So I thought I'd remain calm, see what I could notice.'

'And what did you notice?'

He hesitated. 'Well, nothing really. But if there had been anything to notice, I'd have probably done so because I was keeping a level head.'

Mallory suppressed a sigh.

'But anyway, the whole thing with the faeries. It was a mistake, but I guess with the drinking and the being angry, I wasn't thinking clearly. Crown and Hemlock were throwing blood around on stage and didn't consider who might be in the audience. Everyone respects the faeries, nobody ever cares about vampires. We're an afterthought. We might not share our customs as freely as they do, but it's insensitive.'

The worst individual Mallory knew had just made an excellent point. Occulture ostensibly tried to be inclusive, but anyone who couldn't do magic was left in the dust – vampires and Mallorys alike. It was as good a motive as any, but it made sense to her at the same time.

'That's… I hadn't thought of it that way.'

'Right?'

For a moment, Mallory felt a flicker of potential kinship. He'd shown her a shadow of the version of himself Cornelia must see. Maybe, if he was innocent, this was the version of Beckett that Mallory could get to know.

It vanished a second later when he opened his mouth again.

'Can't believe *anyone* would think it was on purpose. That's so shocking. And hurtful. Ultimately, I think I was just trying to do something nice for the faeries, bolster those inter-Occulture relations, and it was rejected out of hand. Because of a mistake! Shocking.'

'Totally,' Mallory said, desperate to ask her next question. 'Beckett, listen, I'm just doing... doing a survey, I guess. A memory survey!' she continued, an idea forming, 'Basically, I've been wondering how good folks' short-term memory recall is. I'm reading stuff about eyewitness testimony currently—'

'Oh this stuff is *fascinating*. See this is why we're friends, Mallory, I feel you're on the same wavelength as me.'

If Beckett and Mallory were wavelengths, she hoped to be on a completely different frequency.

'So, you know what I'm asking. I'll pick a random date, say... 2 October, and you just say what you remember doing.'

'The second of October...' Beckett said, looking up at the ceiling. 'Oh. I was with my cousin, camping on Mount Hallow. You know, the mountain range where the Vampire Wars started. We go on a sort of sabbatical every year, reconnect with Occulture, so on. I feel really spiritual in that sense,' he said. Mallory had come to realise that every single thing Beckett said was so earnest that he could not hear himself for how loud the earnestness was. 'I actually only got back to Wrackton a few days before Corn did. It's been nice to hang with her.'

Mallory watched him for any indication of discomfort. His demeanour hadn't changed; he hadn't reacted to 2 October as a date.

If his alibi checked out, even with their concerns about his potential to grab for power, Beckett was not the Whistler.

Mallory was just wondering if she should try ask Beckett for more information about the Vampire Wars, noticing that as she tried to formulate a question, the urge to know dissipated, when the basement door slammed open and Cornelia stalked in, Diana following close behind. Diana's hair stood on end.

'Hex war,' she mouthed to Mallory.

Hexing had been a big feature of some of their teenage blow-ups, where they'd ruin each other's hair or outfits or homework. She supposed she should be thankful that it hadn't escalated beyond hair. It was as Theodore had said: grief and stress did strange things to folk.

Diana grabbed her mug and drained it of coffee.

'Anyone want another? No? Great,' she said, not waiting for a response. She slammed her cup down and assembled her coffee, throwing herself into a chair opposite Beckett where she didn't break eye contact, taking scalding sip after scalding sip.

'So, like,' Beckett said, starting a sentence that could only end badly, 'I was thinking earlier, Corn, you still haven't actually given me your thoughts on what went down with the faeries in the Larix. Like yeah, I know your friend is dead – still really sorry about that – but it's just… I feel it needs to be talked about, you know? Babe?' He looked at Cornelia.

Diana choked on a mouthful of coffee and Cornelia had the sense to say, 'I told you you didn't want my thoughts on that, *babe,* and also to please not call me babe in front of my friends because they'd be mean about it.'

'Sorry, b— Sorry.' Beckett picked up his mug, holding it at the top instead of by the handle. Mallory had never wanted to strangle anyone so much before in her life for just existing.

'Has Felix mentioned the sepulture yet?' Mallory asked Diana, tipping her lightly on the arm.

Diana nodded, hostility pouring off her in waves.

'It's in the morning, in the Redwoods.'

'Is that the faerie word for funeral? I've never been to a funeral. Youngest vampire in Wrackton' – he pointed to himself – 'so never needed to.'

'Beckett, has Cornelia mentioned that we're looking at magic DNA at the moment?' Mallory tried, desperate to be out of this conversation. Out of this room.

'Oh yeah, she did. What's in it for me?'

'The knowledge you *helped*,' Diana said.

'I'd still like to think about it. DNA's like, serious,' he said. 'You could clone me.'

'Please just think about it.' Mallory's eyes darted to Cornelia. She had not reacted at all and Mallory wanted to shake her. Ask her why she'd brought this guy into their lives.

Mallory stood to go. 'Let me know if Felix says anything about the sepulture later, I'm going down to do some more work and then heading to bed early.' Her legs and back were stiff and a sickening burn had started in her arms from the stress of talking to Beckett. Even her clothes hurt.

'You know, I was saying to Corn earlier,' Beckett said slowly. 'I don't mind saying that I didn't *love* Ben.'

Cornelia closed her eyes for a second, a very faint flush climbing her cheeks. This was obviously a product of the conversation Cornelia and Beckett had had about him fighting with Felix. 'But that's to be expected; you know what his lot are like about us. They think they're the only Occulture with customs.'

'Why did this seem a pertinent thing to say now?' Cornelia said desperately. 'Beck, now is not the time.'

'His friends were all set to jump me, and everyone seems to have forgotten about that,' he said, holding his hands up.

'That wouldn't have happened if you hadn't refused to apologise to Felix out of respect to the customs you keep mentioning,' Mallory said sharply.

'I know. Look, may he live forever in the Fair Kingdom,' he said, and fell silent.

Mallory had just got her breathing back to normal when he inhaled suddenly. 'I just...'

Diana slammed her mug down on the table.

He continued obliviously. 'I just really think that if they hadn't been so focused on being angry at me, they never would've lost sight of him, and he wouldn't have died. Someone should've gone with him, but they were probably all too busy congratulating themselves for flexing on me just because I made a little mistake.'

'So it's the *faeries*' fault that Ben died?'

'I mean, I didn't *say* that. That's your interpretation.'

'Beckett,' Cornelia said. 'Shut up.'

'Mallory, I'm coming with you.' Diana stood.

'Ouch,' Beckett yelped, clamping a hand to his head. 'Something... that was weird.' He looked around.

Diana turned away and ushered Mallory down the basement stairs.

'What was that?' Mallory asked, her arms shaking. She crossed to the visitor couch and sat on it, sinking into the shapeless cushions left on it. 'This isn't like Cornelia.'

'Did you hear any of our argument?'

'Some,' Mallory said. 'Some choice phrases. Beckett thinks you've got a lot of unresolved anger.'

'We have many unresolved things on our plates, but my anger is not one of them,' Diana said. 'But yeah, I told Cornelia that he was horrible. She insisted he's not like this around her, that his brain falls out around others. I do not understand her fascination with the brainless boy and she has yet to present a compelling argument for keeping him around. She could be dating *anyone* else.'

Mallory nodded in agreement, the energy to be more vehement non-existent. 'Maybe she'll say something to him now we're out of earshot. Especially as she's heard what he has to say.'

'I can't believe how he talked to you.'

Mallory felt the embarrassment return in a fresh flush of shame. 'Don't worry about it. I didn't feel like explaining.'

Diana pushed her hair back, still in disarray from the hex fight. 'What do we do?'

Mallory shrugged. 'Nothing. We can't do anything. We either hope she talks some sense into him, or we end up talking sense into her. But for now we're stuck with him.'

There was another flash of Cornelia's neck bruise in her mind that she pushed away. This was not the time to start doubting each other, nor was Diana in the right headspace for Mallory to introduce something so controversial. Cornelia wouldn't break a covenant. There was still a chance Beckett could use borrowed magic from elsewhere, but that felt like a stretch.

Mallory pointed to the murder board. 'He was in the mountains with his cousin on 2 October and is adamant the fight with the faeries was a mistake, and he had a weak yet compelling excuse for where he was during Ben's murder. I'm not convinced it *was* a mistake, but either way, he's just straight-up not clever enough to be the Whistler. Whoever it is has the power of planning, and he demonstrably doesn't plan anything. If we can get Cornelia to contact the alleged cousin and confirm his alibi, we can take him off the suspect list. We just need some vampire magic DNA to be certain.'

'I can help with that,' Diana said. She held up her thumb and index finger pressed together and Mallory squinted.

'What's that?'

Diana brought it closer. 'A hair. I know hair DNA isn't as good as other DNA, but it was pluck a hair from his head or rip off his skin, so I chose the former. Wisely. Because I am in control of my anger.'

Mallory laughed. 'You're a genius. Put it in an evidence bag, I'll check it.' She looked back up at the murder board, her eyes heavy with fatigue. 'We need to talk to Quinn, and we need to talk to Van Doren, and we need to find a casual opportunity for both. Once I've got a sample of demon DNA, we might get somewhere with the Magic Magical Machine and it might point us towards the right suspect.'

Diana looked at her, and then whispered a summoning

spell. A blanket appeared in her hands and she draped it over Mallory.

'Sorry, no more investigating today. Your eyes are at your chin and you're better off getting an early night. The sepulture is at dawn. I'm not trying to tell you what to do, just… actually I am. Do it,' Diana said. Mallory smiled at that, in spite of the shame coursing through her.

She closed her eyes, and after a moment, allowed her breathing to fall into a regular rhythm and let Diana think she was asleep. She didn't know what to do about how she was feeling. Upstairs, she heard Cornelia's voice rising, and Beckett's in response.

'Sleep well,' Diana whispered, and left the basement through the front door.

When Mallory woke, minutes or hours or days later, the darkness was disorientating and she scrambled around to figure out where she was. She remembered Beckett's behaviour and the rage built instantly. She was sore, she was angry, she was sad.

She wanted to talk to Cornelia. Hear her friend make sense like she used to. Mallory drifted up the stairs, stiffness forcing her to hunch. The kitchen was empty, so she moved up to the corridor where their bedrooms were. The hallway was dark, except for a glow coming from the doorway at the end that led to Cornelia's bug room. Mallory padded down, carefully tiptoeing past Diana's room in case she was asleep. She was about to knock on Cornelia's door, when her ears caught the sound of muffled talking and laughter from inside. She kept walking to the end of the corridor, red light enveloping her as she eased the door to the bug room open.

She crossed the room deep in thought, barely registering the sounds of insects chittering and shuffling over the soft buzz of the ultraviolet witchlights and red heat lamps.

Mallory reached into the terrarium filled with *Sonata lutumae* and lifted out one of the tiny yellow-and-orange beetles, colouring that reminded her of fallen leaves in autumn. Its gold forelegs and the black dot on her back indicated this one was the colony queen, Selene, happily back in her tank now that the magic sample had been fully extracted from her.

Mallory curled on the floor beside the terrarium, the queen crawling across her hand. If she couldn't talk to Cornelia, she'd sit with the next best thing. Mallory smiled and twisted her hand so that it was resting comfortably on her leg. The movement was too fast for the beetle, and her pincers shot out and sliced into the soft flesh of Mallory's thumb.

There was a moment where she simply watched her other hand lift and fall sharply. It felt like a dream, like she was outside her own body. She was a dream, a not-Mallory. A something else.

This other thing Cornelia loved had hurt her. A thing she loved more than Diana. More than Mallory. More than anything.

Mallory was angry, the sting of Selene's bite radiating up her wrist, fury at Cornelia, at Beckett, at everything, rising.

Mallory was sick of grinning and bearing every little thing that came her way. Sick of accepting help and pretending it didn't make her feel like shit, sick of also being afraid to ask, never quite able to smush the feelings down, never quite able to contain her grief, her rage, her loneliness. Sick of having a career on a plate and not being able to grasp it with both hands.

Sick of being sick.

She simply watched as her index finger came down upon the beetle's back and crushed her in an instant. She simply watched when she placed Selene back inside the terrarium and closed the lid.

A single tear tracked down her face.

She could do nothing but watch as the colony immediately frenzied, swarming Selene's body and clambering up the sides of the tank, fighting amongst each other. Every beetle that died disintegrated, until there was only half a colony left, carrying the remains of the fallen as they burrowed beneath the substrate at the bottom of the tank where they'd wait for a new queen to be born.

Frozen horror made its way into her stomach, which churned in revulsion as she realised this was not a dream. She would not wake up, and she could not undo it.

She wiped the tear away and crept back down the hallway to bed.

SEVENTEEN

Five days to Samhain

'Oh good, Mallory's coming.' Diana's voice echoed through the lab as Mallory approached the research room, trying to shake off the stiffness and nausea of waking so early. 'She can settle this. Mallory!'

'What?'

'Cornelia wants to get poison steel silk spiders. But' – she held a hand up to Cornelia's face – 'before she interrupts me, I want you to understand that she not only wants poison steel silk spiders, which, as you can imagine, produce not only steel silk but also poison, she has insisted I keep them *in my room.*'

'*Portia malus ferro* need to be kept separate from other arachnids. If they feel they're in danger, they weave a grille along glass and push it until it cracks. They wouldn't be happy in my bug room, they'd just keep trying to jump to freedom.'

'And you think I want to sleep with that in my room?'

'They're not compatible with six other species in the bug room and they need a natural light cycle! You'd provide that simply by opening and closing the curtains. And carbon dioxide, to keep producing the poison. You talk so much it would be ridiculous to waste all of your, well, waste.'

The anger hadn't faded with sleep, mingled with guilty nausea. Mallory still felt every word Beckett said carved on to her skin, raw and sore. She wore her biggest jumper and her lightest leggings, the pain of the pressure of her clothes a constant reminder of what he had said and how hard she had been working to function every day. The idea of going to any kind of funeral sounded impossible.

Cornelia did not seem to notice; nor did she seem to have noticed that Selene was gone. Her hair was tousled, her eyes tired but still warm. There was no sign of Beckett. Theodore perched on his chair, absorbed in a book and happily ignoring the spirited argument unfolding, largely because it seemed as though Diana and Cornelia were putting on a performance for each other's sake. Cornelia chewed a bite of toast from a cold stack in front of her thoroughly before relaunching into her petition to keep a horrifying-sounding spider in the house.

'Cornelia,' Mallory said, her voice more tense than she wanted it to be. 'We need to talk about last night.'

Cornelia stopped talking.

'I don't... The way Beckett talked to me, what he said about Felix. And Ben.' Mallory struggled to get the sentence out. She wished she'd planned out what she was going to say.

'I'm so sorry, Mallory. Actually I'm more sorry that it wasn't the first thing I said to you this morning, but I was waiting for you to wake before I said anything.'

'Is that why you decided to annoy me with spiders?' Diana asked.

'No. That was unrelated. I'm trying to clear the air, Diana, if you'll let me.' Cornelia sounded sheepish, folding her arms around herself. 'I talked to Beckett about how he talked to you, that you're sick and even if you weren't he was being insensitive and over-familiar. I also talked to him about… well, everything else he said. He's not the best at getting words out in person.'

'Has he tried simply not speaking?' Theodore asked, turning a page primly.

'Theodore,' Cornelia said, warningly.

'Don't shoot the messenger,' Theodore said. 'Shooting me wouldn't work.' He glanced at the table. 'Though you could throw that salt cellar at me and it would *hurt*.'

Mallory pushed the salt cellar further away from him. Salt and ghosts didn't mix.

'Look. He's like… okay, I know what he's like outwardly, but spending time alone with him, he's like…' Cornelia stopped. Mallory had no further information on what 'he's like' could possibly be referring to, but she nodded encouragingly, glad Cornelia was trying to explain.

'I didn't tell either of you this at the time, but uni… wasn't exactly what I thought it would be like. In my defence, while I'd prepared for the practical bits, I didn't consider what it would be like outside of classes. I guess I thought it would be the same as home and it took a while to hit me that I'd have to go out and make friends and stuff. But I didn't want you to think I was having a bad time – especially you, Mallory, it would've felt like complaining about your dream and rubbing your face in it, or something, when it wasn't *that* bad.'

Mallory shook her head, feeling a worried stab in her gut at the idea her friends thought she was incapable of being happy for them.

'So when I got to Sheffield, I thought it would feel like a home away from home in a way, cause their music scene is like ours here, only bigger. And it was fine, I don't know what I was expecting. The Apparents I was in halls with were' – Cornelia searched for a word – 'less than… pleased? To be sharing with a witch, once they realised I was one. I think they thought I had it easy, that I could just magic up essays, so they weren't too bothered about including me.'

'Oh no, you didn't tell them your power is being disgustingly rich?' Diana said, before remembering she was somewhat annoyed at Cornelia and clamping her mouth shut.

'It was a bit lonely at the start,' Cornelia said, for once not fighting back. 'For most of the first two years, actually. It reminded me of being in school again, that absolute apathy towards the concept of Occulture. And then I met Beckett one night in the Leadmill, and… he understood the Occult thing, and the being away from home thing.' Cornelia shrugged. 'The rest, as they say, is too boring and cringey to recount. But he's… he's different.'

'He's like any guy you'd find in any club,' Diana said. 'I do not get what's so special about him.'

'And that's why I tried to tell Mallory first, and not you. Mallory doesn't judge,' Cornelia said.

Mallory swallowed hard.

'I don't expect you to get it. He's wholly different when we're alone. He's attentive, and kind, and wants the best for me. I don't know what the disconnect is between that Beckett and the one you've seen, but I'm going to keep trying to understand.' Cornelia rubbed her arm, her expression almost pained.

'We just want him to… not be like that to us,' Mallory said. 'If at all possible.'

Cornelia sighed. 'Fine. And for what it's worth, he's sorry.'

'Cornelia, you can't be serious,' Diana said. 'You can't be serious that you believe him. He said *horrible* things about our friend.' She looked at Mallory and corrected herself. 'Friends, he said horrible things about two of our friends.'

'I know how he comes across, we're working on it. He's just… like *that* because he's insecure.'

'And you can fix him?' Diana raised her eyebrow so high her eyeliner was in danger of cracking.

'I think I can help him be his best self. He said vampires feel like Apparents as of late, particularly the younger generations without magic. Imagine living without magic in this town?'

Mallory could imagine it quite well.

'He just needs support, is all. To be his best self,' Cornelia said.

'So yes,' Diana snorted.

'Do you accept his apology?' Cornelia asked.

Mallory looked at Diana and tried to communicate what she wanted Diana to hear: that they should trust Cornelia. She had never let them down before. Cornelia had always come through. Mallory owed her now. She had killed a thing she loved.

Mallory also didn't want to be alone again.

'I think Mallory should make the call,' Theodore said from his corner. 'But that's just my opinion.'

Diana nodded her reluctant assent.

The guilt about the beetles rose in her stomach. 'As long as you think he meant it…' Mallory hedged. Diana shot her a glare that she carefully avoided.

'I do. I really do.' Cornelia exhaled. 'Is that the time? We'd better get ready.'

'To be perfectly clear, in case it needs to be said, Beckett is not welcome,' Diana said.

Cornelia stiffened. 'He's obviously not coming. He's said sorry though, you don't need to be so mean about it.'

'I'll show you mean—'

Mallory could see another argument brewing and interjected hurriedly. 'I was thinking last night that we need an opportunity to talk to Van Doren and Grey Quinn. If it's not too inappropriate, maybe I could… do that at the sepulture. He was your friend, I could just… hang back.'

'I don't see an issue with it,' Cornelia said, reaching a reassuring hand out to pat Mallory's arm. 'You're always sensitive, I'm sure you'll handle it great.'

Mallory swallowed her guilt again.

Cornelia would notice the beetles, if she hadn't yet.

Cornelia would know what Mallory had done, and she would hate her for it. Mallory would deserve it.

Mallory held up a hand, her guilt clamped down far enough that she could speak again. 'Just to be sure we're all on the same page, I have doubts Beckett could be the Whistler. Cornelia, could you contact the cousin he was allegedly with on Mount Hallow on 2 October, just to confirm his alibi?'

'I could've told you he wasn't,' Cornelia said. 'And I can try, but from what Beckett said, there's no signal out there, he was radio silent until he was on his way back down and as far as I know, his cousin is still up there.'

'Convenient,' Diana said, but quietly enough that only Mallory could hear.

'I'll try to talk to Van Doren and Quinn today. Once I've got a demon sample, we can move forward,' Mallory said.

Samhain was creeping ever closer.

'I'm just going to keep thinking about where there might be more information about the Ternion. I'm thinking... books.' Cornelia raised an emphatic hand. 'I'll work on getting the musty doorstop Observer Johnson suggested. Why he wouldn't just let us buy his from him, I'll never know.'

As with everything, most problems in Cornelia's world were easily solved by throwing money at them.

'That reminds me, I'll ask Langdon to bring us the Larix CCTV footage.' Diana stood, texting as she walked. 'Taxi's ordered for forty-three minutes from now. I'm so tired.' She yawned. 'I swear if I didn't have magic to get me ready, I would scream.' As soon as the words were out, she whipped her head around to look at Mallory like she'd just insulted her. 'Sorry!'

Mallory stood stiffly, wishing for the millionth time that it didn't have to be like this.

'You don't have to be sorry for using your own magic,' she said lightly, forcing a smile.

'You could always use the Sprinter as intended, and have an endless supply of binding spells and other helpful magic,' Theodore said, suddenly beside her. Mallory loosely draped an arm around his shoulders, holding in his warmth.

'Shush,' Mallory said. 'I can't do that. You know I can't do that, Theo.'

Cornelia had stopped on the stairs, though she didn't turn around. When Mallory held Theodore's arm so tightly that they disappeared into a cloud of static, Cornelia continued on, giving no indication she'd heard.

Like all faerie funerals, it began at dawn, when the sun had barely risen.

In the darkest corner of Redwood Forest, next to the river, the Occult community gathered in a clearing, spilling out into the trees. Used exclusively for sepultures, it was awash with a mix of sombre faerie fabrics and the red non-faerie guests wore out of respect. Ben was so well known and so well loved, the murders had shaken the community hard – practically everyone had turned out to be there. Even the Night Mayor stood in the middle of a crowd of red-clad Office representatives, Jacob by his side. Jacob caught their eyes and waved an enthusiastic gloved hand, before returning his attention to Van Doren, who shook every faerie's hand as they passed. He looked exhausted and stressed, a muscle jumping in his jaw with every interaction.

'Van Doren doesn't look so good,' Cornelia whispered. 'Way more stressed than usual.'

Mallory had to agree that for once, on the subject of Van Doren, Cornelia was not exaggerating.

At the front of the congregation, Felix stood with Ben's family. Dressed in dark green, they had painted a delicate vine pattern up their arms and across their chest, ever the pillar of decadent consistency.

Diana had linked her arm into Mallory's, an action that served to support herself, but also helped Mallory's body, which was so sore she hadn't been able to put on a bra.

'I'll see you afterwards,' Mallory said.

'I'll stay with you. Come on,' Diana said, not giving her a chance to argue, and they slipped to the back of the gathered folk just as the ceremony began.

A lone guitar began to play, mournful, piercing notes stopping the gathered crowd, before a slow, steady drumbeat kicked in and everyone pushed back against the trees at the edge of the clearing as the procession started.

Led by the sepulture master, faeries brought Ben's body in a glass casket to the edge of the clearing. Two faeries with flamethrowers set the outermost trees alight and they burst into pink flames. They burned and burned but did not crumble to ash, and nor did the fire spread.

'We are gathered witnesses to Benedict DeLacey's journey to the Fair Kingdom,' the sepulture master said. Their hands flashed and shallow gashes appeared on the outsides of both of their forearms. They raised them up, allowing blood to splatter on Ben's casket.

'In our blood, Benedict DeLacey will travel across the sea in his casket and be delivered to the Fair Kingdom, where he will rest forevermore.'

The drumbeats grew louder, the guitar joined by another, a steady, humming rhythm plucking goosebumps from Mallory's skin.

Her eyes scanned the crowd, looking for Quinn, for Sully, for anyone who might have graced them with a giant neon sign announcing they were the Whistler.

Felix stood at the front and unfolded a piece of paper. A microphone stand grew from the ground, and as they took their place in front of it, they were a performer with a broken spirit. Felix took the mic in their hands and Mallory could feel their energy settling over the gathered audience.

'Ben was my best friend, my bandmate. If platonic soulmates exist, that was us. Ben was there through every breakup, every argument. Everything I've ever gone through in my life. He was there. We wrote songs and we made art. We'd planned to make history. And now history is all we have left between us. I hope when his bones salt the earth, all of you can feel the strength of him grow within you. Ben is. Was—' They broke off, and swallowed hard. 'The strongest person I know.'

Mallory's eyes filled with tears, but she held them back, afraid if she started she'd never stop.

She looked down to wipe them, and back up, her eyes locking on Grey Quinn mere feet from her, wearing a deep red suit under his cloak, his head bowed. She looked down and saw his hands tucked in close to his hips, thumbs flying over his phone screen.

Mallory shifted closer to Quinn, unwilling to let him leave without a conversation, annoyed he wasn't pretending to care where he was.

At the front, Felix closed their eyes and gripped the mic stand tighter. The remaining members of Crown and Hemlock walked to join them, and a faerie stood at the back with a guitar.

Not replacing Ben, but honouring him. They played a loud, aggressive song, facing Ben and not the audience, and though there were many confused glances among some of the older non-faerie Occult, everyone politely waited till it ended and broke into applause that ranged from rapturous to bemused-but-respectful.

Felix dropped the mic and walked to Cornelia, folding themself into her arms. Mallory wished she hadn't let Diana stand back with her, wished she'd thought it through.

Finally, Van Doren rose to say some words, some that were entirely appropriate, and some that were not, about the fate of the killer being in the hands of all of Occulture and how 'punishment proves to be a deterrent'. The faeries appreciated the honesty, but did not appreciate the deviation from their solemn ritual, nor the obviously desperate bid for re-election votes. Everything in faerie was about ritual and precision, and this was bordering on offensive, if not crossing the line into disrespect, but Van Doren didn't appear to notice the ripples of discontent spreading across the clearing. Mallory could see Jacob watching from the sidelines. Felix's eulogy had made him cry, and his eyes were swollen.

When it was over, they spotted Quinn turning to leave. Mallory and Diana followed slowly, edging between clumps of mourners as he attempted to melt away from the crowd.

'Grey Quinn?' Mallory fixed an appropriate-sized smile on her face.

'Yes?'

No words came out. Mallory stared at him, his eyes boring into hers.

'This has been interesting. Now, leave me alone?' Quinn's nose wrinkled and Mallory could not rescue the not-conversation.

'Oh my goddess. Who is your tailor?' Diana said, and Mallory had never been so relieved to have Diana with her, nor felt so lucky to be Diana's friend.

'That's what I was going to ask,' Mallory stumbled. 'The same question. Tailor.'

Grey Quinn rolled his neck.

'Depends who's asking.'

'Diana Cheung-Merriweather.' She waited a moment. 'Yes. That Cheung.'

'*Designer* Ivy Cheung's daughter. Well, well, well.' He grinned. 'She's been a big name in my household for years.'

'So I ask again: who's your tailor? Love this construction. And the pocket square, such a good touch.' Her fingers brushed the silk fabric lightly.

'Thanks.' He tucked his hands into his waistcoat. Mallory's skin prickled. Quinn was known for being convincing, more so than most demons in Wrackton. 'Was that all you wanted to ask?'

'I maybe have some questions about investment.' Diana flipped her hair back.

'You want to ask me questions, *here*? Didn't you know the deceased? This feels a little gauche, you have to admit,' Quinn said.

Mallory's skin prickled again, but he needn't have bothered to try to convince them; she felt terrible already.

'Just hear me out. So I'm like, an heiress,' Diana said. 'And I guess I just didn't want to pass up an opportunity to talk to someone as well connected as you.'

'I see. Are you an heiress too, then?' Quinn looked Mallory over.

'No, just…'

'My accountant,' Diana said.

Mallory was not, in fact, good with numbers.

'Yes. Give me tax forms, or give me hell,' Mallory said.

Quinn's eyebrow quirked slightly.

'Really, I'm wondering about hotel investment,' Diana said. 'I know there's always big dinners, shoulder rubbing. Heard there was a big investment chat at the last Hotel Quinn launch, and I'm just wondering who I have to compliment around here to be invited to the next one.'

Quinn licked his lips before responding. Demons did not lie, but they did twist reality in a way a faerie couldn't. It was only now that Mallory was really understanding what his notoriety meant.

'Hexana, you have some balls,' Quinn laughed. 'There's another launch in a few weeks. Here's my card, we'll have a drink before then.'

'Thank you so much,' Diana said. 'I just heard about the one back in October, the 2nd, I think, had the Night Mayor and several UML folk at it. I just wonder, like, how difficult it might be to get an audience with the Night Mayor.'

Quinn chuckled. 'I'll tell you, I spent all night in that ballroom and he was barely in his seat. Even with his lovely trophy wife beside him.' He rolled his eyes. 'Not to my taste, of course, but no women are.'

'Unlikewise,' Diana said.

Something unspoken passed between them.

'Call me for that drink,' Quinn said. 'I'm gonna make you so rich. Bye, accountant,' he said to Mallory, and walked away.

Diana blew out a breath.

'You are getting more terrifyingly impressive by the day,' Mallory said. 'Hexana, that was almost frightening.'

'I can't stop shaking,' Diana said.

'What did he say?' Cornelia asked when they caught up with her.

Diana filled her in, complete with uncanny impressions of how he'd licked his lips and the pauses he'd taken, a peculiar sort of expressive talent Diana both possessed and utilised as often as possible.

'Well.' Cornelia pushed her hair back with her fingers. 'We've got to see if we can get hotel CCTV footage from that night, somehow.'

'I know a girl,' Diana said.

'Of course you do,' Cornelia said.

'Fuck,' Mallory said, startling them both. 'I didn't get any DNA from him.'

'Oh,' Diana said. 'If only lying my arse off was my only talent.' She reached into her pocket and unfolded a piece of red patterned fabric.

Quinn's pocket square.

'Did either of you bring evidence bags?'

Cornelia had one in her hands in moments.

'Diana, you just might be the most incredible individual I know.'

'I know.' She blew Mallory a kiss. 'I had to touch it to make sure it wasn't sewn down and I could use a spell to extract it.

There was about a nanosecond where I thought he was going to rip my hand off, but all's well that ends in evidence.'

'Are you both okay?' Mallory asked. 'Cause the next thing we need to do is talk to Van Doren.'

'He just left,' Cornelia said. 'Saw a car pull up.'

Mallory swallowed. 'We'll go to the reception in the Larix, then. Wait for him to head back to the offices. Cornelia, I think you and I will go speak to him.'

'Why not me?' Diana asked.

'You don't stress him out,' Mallory said. 'And I think we need him under stress. We better get going, there'll be no seats left.'

Felix touched her arm and Mallory turned. 'Cornelia said you were here. We're heading to the Larix now.'

Mallory held her arms out and Felix pulled her into a hug. She felt grief radiate off them, realising how sad she was about Ben too, though she'd barely known him.

'This is from Langdon,' they said, pulling back and handing a small package to Mallory, who slipped it into her pocket. The Larix's CCTV footage.

Felix briefly touched their fingers to Mallory's forehead, a faerie blessing of love and honour, and melted into the crowd.

'One last thing,' Mallory said to the Undetectables as they moved towards the trail path to the Larix. 'Let's say for the next hour, we don't talk about murder, or the case, and we just make space to remember Ben.'

EIGHTEEN

Later that morning, Mallory looked up the steps at the entrance to the Mayoral Offices, shivering. The weather had taken an abrupt turn to wintery chill, though Mallory suspected the Redwoods had been glamoured to feel warmer.

'Do you want my gloves?' Cornelia said, her eyes catching the movement. She held up her gloved hands – gloves Mallory realised she'd sent her last Yule.

'No, I'm fine.' Her lips twitched into a grin. 'Let's get this done quickly, though. I'm nearing physical capacity and I've got stuff to do when we get back.'

Her body wanted to be horizontal. She'd pushed herself too hard for days now and it was about to tell her to stop. 'I'm hoping with the pocket square from Quinn, and the hair we got from Beckett—'

'The what?'

Mallory's eyes widened at the realisation that Cornelia didn't know what she and Diana had done. 'We, um… found a hair.'

'Uh huh.' Cornelia narrowed her eyes.

'And it's not because we think he's guilty; it's a control to compare with the victim's samples,' Mallory said quickly. 'Better to rule him out properly than to stand around guessing.'

'It's fine, Mal. We gave our DNA, why wouldn't Beckett?' She shrugged, then threw open the doors to the Mayoral Offices. It was busier than the last time they'd been in, folk rushing around the foyer, everyone trying to finish off the year before Samhain rolled around.

'—last year's Samhain issue of the big dog creature roaming around the Square for days—' a troll said into a headset, jogging past Mallory and Cornelia. Mallory stared after him.

'You'd think with Theodore doing para-anthropology work here for years, they'd have got to the bottom of what keeps causing creatures to escape from the Offices every Samhain,' Cornelia said.

'That would require listening to his findings, which from the sounds of things is a near impossibility.' Mallory took a deep, steeling breath. 'Talking to Van Doren might get us somewhere. We can do this.'

'Heads empty, no thoughts,' Cornelia agreed. 'For Ben.'

'And for Kuster.'

Mallory's head was not empty at all as she moved down the purple-lit corridor; she had a growing sense of guilt and it was Selene-shaped.

She had an opportunity to tell Cornelia the truth about her beetles.

She could fix it easily, and be less of a coward.

But she was a coward.

'Do you want to lead this interview? I won't be angry if you do,' Cornelia said, gently nudging her arm.

Shockwaves of pain radiated from the spot, but Mallory didn't let it show on her face.

'Probably best if I do, though don't feel you can't say anything. I'm hoping your presence will put pressure on him to answer.'

Mallory had all but forgotten how endless the walk to Van Doren's office was. Jacob popped his head out of a side room as they passed. Mallory assumed it was his office, though it seemed to be repurposed from a storage cupboard.

'Hello again, Undetectables!' he said. 'I am very sorry about your friend.'

'Thanks, Jacob,' Mallory said.

A phone rang in the room and Jacob looked back. 'I have to get that. Night Mayors to aide, folk to speak to. I hate phones. I hate anything to do with phones. Give me letters any day. I'll have to let you go. Oh!' He popped his head back out the door, a small smile on his face. 'Please say hi to your friend Theodore, if you happen to see him. And as always, let me know if there's anything I can do for you.'

'Thanks, Jacob,' Mallory said again, feeling like her responses were on a mechanical loop.

It took a long time for Van Doren to bark, 'Come in!' in response to Cornelia's insistent knocking.

'Thanks for seeing us, Mr Night Mayor,' Mallory said.

'Not like I had much of a choice, is it?' Van Doren pulled a pen from his mouth and tossed it on the desk in front of him.

'Even still. Thank you,' Mallory said.

He grunted in response.

'We just wanted to ask some questions.'

'About?'

'We're fact-checking some things,' Mallory said, sliding into a chair after he made a sarcastic "oh please sit" face at her.

'Why?'

'Are you able to ask longer-than-one-word questions?' Cornelia sank into the second chair, crossing her legs. He eyed the way she sat with something akin to disgust. Mallory had noticed Cornelia's habit of making everything look somehow messy just by being in it, but she was so aesthetically pleasing to look at, it never seemed an issue to her.

'Why?' he said again.

'It's just protocol, Mr Night Mayor.' Mallory's plan was largely to disarm him with pleasantries before Cornelia forgot she was meant to be letting Mallory lead the interview.

'Oh.' Van Doren twirled a hand in front of him, like a thought was forming. There were no gaudy rings this time, and Mallory realised that was what she had noticed in the Larix too. She allowed herself to feel pleased at her observational skills before refocusing.

'For an article, then,' he continued.

Mallory glanced at Cornelia. 'Not quite, Mr Night Mayor, if you recall—'

'It's an article all right,' Cornelia said over her. 'An important one, and so I'm sure you understand the need for due diligence here.'

Mallory looked back at Cornelia, wanting to ask what she was doing. She shook her head slightly, her eyes darting around the room like she was expecting someone was listening.

It occurred to Mallory that that may be what Van Doren had been afraid of the whole time: someone listening. A member of the Ghoul Council, someone from the Unified Magical Liaison.

That was perhaps why he'd been so strange all this time.

Mallory smiled serenely, or what she hoped was serenely. Her face hurt. 'So we need… quotes… for this article.'

'Yes?'

She took a breath. 'There was a launch party for Hotel Quinn Indigo on 2 October. Were you in attendance that night?'

'What the fuck line of questioning is this?' He rubbed his face, then forced a pleasant expression. 'Yes. I am delighted to have sourced investors for Hotel Indigo. Quinn is an asset to Wrackton and an asset to our future growth and prosperity.'

'And at this party,' Cornelia said, 'would you say you stayed all night?'

'Yes?'

'Really, we're asking you to walk us through the night of 2 October. At the party. For… the article,' Mallory said.

Van Doren's brow wrinkled, and he scrabbled through his planner on his desk, flipping back pages. 'That night… was the night of the party. Yes.'

'And who were you in attendance with?'

'My partner, Hayley. She's a regional manager for the Quinn Group. Another asset to Wrackton,' he said, though this time his tone was sincere.

Mallory didn't have to look at Cornelia to see her eyes light up. The disarming prong of this two-part attack was over before she'd had a proper chance.

'Can Hayley verify this? And does Hayley have a surname?' Cornelia asked. She had not leaned forward in her seat yet, but that was coming.

Van Doren scratched his jaw. 'Yes. Hayley Eason. We stayed until late. Should've let Quinn comp us a room, really.' He lifted his chin. 'That last bit is off the record.'

It was Mallory's turn to be confused. Van Doren seemed to be treating them as though they were really journalists, and this did not mesh with his fear from just a few days ago of the story getting into the papers.

'That's Quinn as in Grey Quinn?' Mallory prompted, trying not to let this realisation throw her.

'Obviously. What exactly are these questions for?' Van Doren gripped the edge of his desk.

'Did you leave at any point?'

'I am the *Night Mayor*. I work *at night*. I was around as much as I could be.'

'Can anyone verify that?' Mallory asked.

'And how old is Hayley?' Cornelia's back lifted from her chair.

'That's not on my list of questions, perhaps we'll keep that for the end. We really just want to know what your movements were at this party,' Mallory said smoothly.

Van Doren looked at Cornelia, and then addressed Mallory directly.

'I don't recall every individual I speak to at every interval at every event I attend. I'm a busy man.'

'Thank you. Could you tell us where you were the night of Benedict DeLacey's death at the Larix, between 9 and 11:40 p.m.?'

'Easily.' His brow furrowed deeper. 'I was once again with Hayley Eason, in our home, and I went to the Larix after answering a call regarding a murder. Is that all?'

'I just want to know a few more things about Hayley. I had heard you brought her to a party the night before Edward Kuster's body was recovered,' Cornelia said.

'And?'

'A number of people in attendance congratulated you on the youth of your new partner.'

'For goddess's sake. She's twenty-five, I was twenty-five when I first got married! People don't understan—'

'One final thing, Mr Night Mayor.' Mallory kept writing in her notebook, remembering what she'd heard Quinn say in the Larix, thinking of his strange interaction with Van Doren after Ben had been found. 'There are rumours that you have had a hand in the attempted bankrolling of a prison, here in Wrackton.'

Van Doren scratched his beard again.

'That's not a question,' he said finally.

'Let me rephrase what Mallory is so reluctant to ask. Is there any merit to the rumour that if a prison were to be built in Wrackton, you'd want investors to use the site currently occupied by the Larix?'

He huffed.

'The new focus for Wrackton, the entire body of my re-election campaign, will be growth, prosperity and proper punitive measures. Folk care about personal safety, and personal safety comes at a cost. It's time to put Wrackton, and Occulture in general, on the map for something useful as well as lucrative. We're worth more than Apparent tourism. We're worth more than bad publicity from a terrible tragedy involving an Apparent that didn't even *happen* here.'

'A murder definitely happened here,' Cornelia said bluntly. 'Ben was my friend.'

'Semantics, it started elsewhere. I envision things changing for us over the next few years, in a way they haven't before. I can't definitively say exactly what that will entail. You understand, I'm sure.' He bared his teeth in what Mallory read as a threatening smile.

'Can't, or *won't*?' Cornelia asked.

'What are you—'

'What would you do for power, Van Doren?' Cornelia said. Mallory had completely lost control of the interview and she didn't even have it in her to regret asking Cornelia in. She couldn't envision any other way it could've gone.

'If more folk admitted to wanting power, we would not have such a thing as Occult-towns-this versus Apparent-towns-that. Apparents don't care. They think of us as "other" when they think of us, and that is rare. We exist and they exist. We place the distinctions on Occult-versus-Apparent, and with power we would have the opportunity to change that in our favour. There would be cohesion, movement, consideration. Powerful folk exercising that power ultimately helps us, and last time I checked, believing that in itself is not a crime.'

'How much could that power cost these days? One, two bodies?'

He didn't respond, just stared at Cornelia, unreadable emotions flashing across his face in quick succession.

Mallory stood. It was time to leave. Van Doren goggled at her, but didn't respond. It was as much of an answer as they were going to get from him.

'Thank you for your time, Mr Night Mayor, that's all.'

'No, it most certainly is not all.' He threw himself into standing, knocking the table. 'What paper are you from? Are you investigative journalists?'

'We don't need to play this anymore,' Cornelia said, her hand on the door. Mallory gathered herself slowly, bending to pick her bag off the ground.

'Play what? Do you think this' – he gestured angrily – 'is a game?'

'Is that why you hired us then?' Cornelia snapped.

Mallory could sense the second Van Doren's rage boiled over.

'Hired you?' he spat. 'Hired *you*? For what?'

'To investigate the murders,' Mallory said in a small voice.

Van Doren took a deep, steadying breath. He drew himself up to his full gangly height. He looked her directly in the eyes, then Cornelia.

'I. Would. Never. Hire. Amateurs. This is… this is a ridiculous, pompous delusion. If the Ghoul Council heard… or the UML… I'd…' He took another steadying breath. 'Is this a smear campaign? It is, isn't it?' He clenched his jaw as Mallory joined Cornelia at the door, embarrassment lighting her body on fire.

'Mr Night Mayor, you—'

'Enough. This isn't a game. Stay out of the way of the police. Stay out of the way of me. I do not consent to the tearing down of my reputation in this way. I *will* be re-elected. There *will* be changes in Wrackton. We *will* reach heights. Write that in your fucking article.'

He waved a hand and his door flew open. Mallory nudged Cornelia, who somehow took the hint, and left.

'I think we pushed that slightly too far,' Mallory said once they were outside, away from the bustle of Mayoral Office workers. Cornelia had her phone out to order a taxi back home and had sat Mallory down on a bench a few windows down from the main door.

'You think?' Cornelia wiped a shaking arm over her face. 'We didn't even get any DNA from him. Though he almost spat on me a couple of times. That would've been useful. If disgusting and a sensation that no amount of showers would've washed off.'

Mallory raised an eyebrow and reached into her pocket.

'Oh, fuck yes,' Cornelia said. 'You genius. I could kiss you.'

Mallory blushed and looked at the pen in her hand, the one that had been in Van Doren's mouth. She'd managed to manoeuvre it into an evidence bag.

'The opportunity presented itself.' Mallory shrugged, then regretted the movement. 'Though I don't know what we're going to do now. He hired us. He was there. That was real, right?'

Cornelia nodded. 'We got a letter. He sent a car to pick us up. He met with us. He said we wouldn't speak again until after the Kuster murder was solved. B... Ben was killed too, and he refused to speak to us. He told Sully he hired us—'

'But did he?' Mallory said, cold realisation sending shivers up her arms. 'Did he actually? Think back to what we heard Sully say.'

Cornelia closed her eyes, waggling her head from side to side the way she did when she chased a memory.

Her eyes opened, a haunted look in them. 'He just wore her down.'

'I'm not on the Van Doren Is Inherently Evil bandwagon like you, but this doesn't look right. Oh, what about Jacob?' Mallory said hopefully. 'He wrote the letter on Van Doren's behalf, picked us up, took us to Van Doren's door, brought us to the mortuary…'

'He wasn't in the room with us when we spoke to Van Doren. And he was forbidden to help us any further.'

Mallory shook her head. There was only one possible explanation creeping into her mind, and it made her feel sick to say it. 'What if…' Mallory said slowly. 'What if… Van Doren hired us, knowing that he had plausible deniability if anyone asked? He can tell anyone he likes that he has hired outside help, so it would sound like he's trying to take steps to do something about the murders. But at the same time, if we told anyone that we were working this case, he could deny it, and throw our methods and evidence into question. But more than that – if we told anyone we thought *he* was the Whistler, he could spin it that an amateur group of investigators were trying a smear campaign in the lead-up to the elections, and get our evidence thrown out completely. If we discovered this before Samhain, he'd have time to carry out the summoning anyway while folk decided whose side they were on, and by then it wouldn't matter. He could be watching our every move and using our discoveries to make sure he's covering his tracks. It's possible that if it's him, he could be taking opportunities to misdirect us, and we'd have no way of knowing. We'd be the canaries in the coalmine, so to speak, so he'd know if anyone was looking his way, and he'd have time to do something about it.'

'Mallory, no. That's…'

'Entirely plausible?' Mallory frowned. 'You heard him in there. He is completely focused on power. I would not put this sort of tactic past him. We didn't get any information in any sort of legitimate way. Even attending the autopsy… we pretended to be med students. Diana lied to Sully. Twice. We've stolen DNA evidence from our suspects.'

She didn't want to speak it into existence, but it felt impossibly true. Mallory was, ultimately, nothing. Cornelia and Diana could leave at any time and be something. Mallory would still have nothing, her name tarnished forever.

The cold of the bench seeped into her skin and she fought back tears of exhausted pain.

'But the problem still remains: anyone could be the Whistler. And maybe someone was listening in Van Doren's office. Maybe he's just a dick.' She exhaled slowly. 'But Van Doren doesn't *do* puzzles, does he? There are parts of him that fit, and parts that don't. And I don't know what to make of it. Of any of it. The ciphered letter, the lies… that doesn't seem like his style. He's much more heavy-handed. He relies on a planner to function, for the love of Blair. A lot of folk would ignore the idea of him being a criminal mastermind if they knew he had to write down every single thought he has.'

'Mallory, I don't know what to do,' Cornelia said finally. 'I can't think.'

'I know what we do.' Mallory stood, the lights of a taxi pulling into the Square flooding her body with relief, allowing space for hot, determined rage to form. She was going to be something.

'I'm all ears.'

'I need to sleep, first. But when we get back, ask Diana to call Hotel Quinn Indigo and get the CCTV footage. When I wake tomorrow, we go through the Larix footage, and I'll test the remaining samples. We will find evidence of who the Whistler is. Whether it's Van Doren—'

'And I'm really starting to think it is, no joke,' Cornelia said.

'Or someone else. To put it simply, we make like Theodore said, and we nail this fucker,' Mallory said earnestly.

Cornelia barked out a laugh. She held her hand out to Mallory and Mallory stared at it for a moment, before shaking her head and easing herself slowly down the steps to the waiting taxi.

NINETEEN

Mallory had gone for a nap, but found sleep elusive after her body had permitted her the initial wave of desperate, hungry slumber. Every time she closed her eyes she thought about the murders. She thought about how they'd got here and the possibility they were part of the game. She thought about the Whistler, and why they'd left a letter outlining their plan. It seemed so illogical. Kuster died in a locked room, Ben died in a busy bar. The behaviour didn't make any sense. She thought about how her whole body ached from the effort of the sepulture and the trip to the Mayoral Offices. She thought about why Cornelia hadn't mentioned Selene.

She gave up on sleeping.

Mallory still ached all over, but she felt better than she had a few hours previously. The house was dark, except for the kitchen where light seeped under the door. Mallory opened it.

Cornelia and Beckett were at the table. Or rather, Cornelia was *on* the table and Beckett had his arms wrapped around her, both of them breathing heavily. It would've been simply an awkward interruption of yet another uncomfortably intimate kissing moment, except Beckett's teeth were bared, and his fangs were extended, and they were in Cornelia's throat.

Mallory screamed.

She did not mean to, but the sound had left her throat before she'd registered the urge. Beckett snapped back, blood dripping down his chin, and Cornelia jumped up from the table.

'Mallory,' she whispered. Her face was pale and she was sweating slightly, her hair wild. Blood dripped down her neck from the wounds – two nasty, bruising lacerations – soaking into her oversized navy jumper. Mallory's favourite of her jumpers. Cornelia reached for her, but Mallory retreated, running for the door to the lab. She wanted Theodore and safety and she didn't feel safe in this room.

It was indefensible for Beckett to do it, but she couldn't understand why Cornelia would let him. Observer Johnson had said vampires used other Occult blood to obtain magic, so she knew it was possible, but it was only here, faced with it, that Mallory could see that it meant taking Cornelia's magic through her blood and *using* it as his own, not making his own magic with it. Then came the realisation that it wasn't just the wrongness of it; it was entirely horrifying for Mallory to see her friend have her energy drained. Energy Mallory would give anything to have naturally occurring in her own body.

But of course they'd break sacred covenants together so he could have magic too, no matter the consequences. Cornelia had said she could help Beckett be his best self. Mallory had not imagined this was what she meant.

She should've let Diana hex him.

She shouldn't have eliminated him as a suspect.

She crashed through the door to the darkened lab, lit only by the witchlights in the research room partition, but Theo materialised beside her as she slammed the door shut. He didn't get to say anything before Cornelia wrenched the door open.

'It's not what it looked like,' she gabbled, her expression desperate.

'It's exactly what it looked like, surely?' Fury rose in Mallory's throat and she fought to push it back down. It would spill over if she said a single word more. This was illegal. Not only that, it was *wrong*.

'What is what *what* looked like?' Theodore asked.

Beckett was right behind Cornelia. Blood streaked his chin, but his fangs were gone. His arms snaked around Cornelia as he looked at Mallory, a sneer more than a smile on his face.

'What was that about? I thought Diana was the dramatic one, but that was fifty shades of fucked up, running out here to cry to dead-Other-Daddy,' he hissed, his words quick, pressured, his pupils overblown. He had Cornelia's magic, his own body metabolising it into something wildly out of control. 'What we do between us is none of your business, Mallory.'

'We're trying to solve a murder to stop the Vampire Wars restarting and destroying all of Occulture, and what's the fucking point if you're just going to break the covenants anyway?' Mallory shouted.

'Beckett,' Cornelia said, almost reproachfully. She was shaking.

'What you do between you *what* is none of Mallory's business?' Theodore asked. He flickered and Mallory could feel his energy, feel her own energy, feel everything going wrong in her body and she couldn't get it under control. Not when it felt like something was ripping through her.

'DO NOT HURT HER,' Theodore screamed, before Mallory could say anything else. Beckett dropped one of his hands, but the arm looped around Cornelia's waist pulled her in tighter. His eyes were still wild. Cornelia's magic was coursing through his veins, raised on his skin. For every bit as pallid Cornelia looked, Beckett was flushed and full of life. Full of magic.

'NEVER, EVER DO THAT AGAIN, OR SO HELP ME.'

Beckett recovered suddenly, the sneer back in his voice.

'So help you what, Cat Man? Are you going to purr at me? Smother me with your cardigan? You can't do anything to me. You're attacking me simply for existing and I won't stand for it. Corn and I decided on this together. This is *our* business.'

Pressure built up around Mallory, Theodore's static building. It was as though Beckett was feeding off all their rage. There was a pulse. Mallory staggered, but nobody was free to catch her and she hit a bench before half falling to the ground. She caught herself, but pain burned up her arms and her hip where she'd struck the iron edge. Cornelia moved to grab her, but Beckett still had a hold on her. Theodore crackled with energy and rage.

'You have no idea what I'm capable of, you jumped up little *shit*,' Theodore hissed. There were no theatrics in him now, just pure, absolute fury. 'No idea at all. If I had a life to protect all three of them with, I would use it. I don't trust you, and I don't trust your judgement, and I don't believe you know when to stop. There's a reason vampires stopped using magic a long time ago.

You don't know what you're doing. I will not let you use her as a means to power. I WON'T!'

A witchlight blew in the window, pieces of crystal glass shattering and spraying across the research room floor. It dimly reminded Mallory of something, but she didn't know what.

Beckett released Cornelia, the contempt still on his face, his eyes still wild. He was intoxicated by magic. Mallory crawled back to the research room partition. Her body shook but she couldn't tell exactly how much damage she had caused or how much pain she was in; that would come later, when she was lying down and she wasn't terrified. She had never been afraid of Theodore before, but now she couldn't shake the fear rattling through her bones. With one hand she got her phone out to call Diana and set it down, loudspeaker on. Most of what Theodore was saying would come out as static hissing, but she'd get the context, and would hopefully come running.

Mallory hugged her legs to her chest and watched as the others raged above her. She was as powerless as Beckett was powerful.

As Theodore and Beckett screamed at each other, Mallory caught Cornelia's eye and motioned for her to come to her. Cornelia was grey now, but her neck had stopped bleeding, small scabs forming over the bite marks already. Mallory was angry at her for doing it, angry at her for giving away her energy like that, but she looked so unwell and Mallory couldn't leave her like that. Cornelia made her way over on shaking legs and sank down beside her. Without speaking, Mallory gently guided Cornelia's head on to her lap and got her to put her legs up on her chair. Her fingers worked their way through her curls, brushing them back off her sticky forehead, stroking the stubbly sides of her head. Though clammy, Cornelia's skin felt hot. Her eye were closed and Mallory looked down at her eyelashes grazing the tops of her cheeks, at her tiny dusting of freckles across her nose, barely visible thanks to her current pallor, the bites in her neck and the navy jumper Mallory loved. Her friend.

'The Do No Harm Charter exists to protect EVERYONE!' Theodore screamed at Beckett. 'I have to follow RIDICULOUS rules that get amended *constantly* and you think you can come in here, to my house and *bite* one of my *friends?*'

'YOU'RE A FUCKING GHOST, YOU DON'T KNOW ANYTHING,' Beckett shouted, circling Theodore like he was going to attack.

'I AM LITERALLY COMPOSED OF ENERGY, BUCKO. EVER HEARD OF THE LAW OF THERMODYNAMICS?' Theodore got right in his face, drawing himself up to his full, not very impressive, height.

'My name is *BECKETT*,' he screamed, then kept screaming in frustration.

Theodore didn't back down. Beckett wiped the blood from his chin with the back of his hand. He stared at it for a second, then licked the blood away and Mallory's stomach lurched.

Cornelia's other hand rested back against Mallory's lap, and without thinking Mallory's own hand drifted to it.

'Are you okay?' she whispered.

Cornelia's fingers wrapped around hers. 'I'm a little weak. You?'

'Same.'

'Sorry I didn't catch you.'

'Sorry I *did* catch you,' Mallory said.

Cornelia squeezed her fingers and let them go slack. She

dropped her legs down from the chair and twisted her body into a more comfortable position, but left her head where it was, her eyes still closed.

That's when Mallory realised everything had gone silent.

She looked up at the same time as Cornelia's eyes snapped open, her head turned slightly to see what had happened. There was nothing, only static where Theodore and Beckett had been.

The lab door opened and Diana was still speaking into her phone even as she ran to the research room. '…and nobody ever tells me anything, I sleep alone for five minutes and this is the shit we have to deal with—'

'Diana,' Mallory whispered, and Diana stopped speaking. 'How much of that did you hear?'

'I heard static and Beckett screaming about magic. Please tell me he didn't—'

'He did.'

'What the *fuck*, Cornelia?' Diana's face froze in horror.

'Yeah. Theodore is furious. I'm not too pleased myself, but he's next-level fuming.'

'Oh,' Diana said again. 'Are you okay?'

'Yeah. I'm just tired. We probably need to go back upstairs.'

'I am furious at you,' Diana announced to Cornelia. 'Just so you know.'

'You can be furious upstairs,' Mallory said. 'Let's *go*.'

'No,' Cornelia said, looking up at Mallory from under her eyelashes. The colour had somewhat returned to her cheeks, but she still looked ill.

'No what?' Mallory asked gently, like she was afraid to be too loud in the silence.

'No, we need to wait until he's back. Both of them.'

'Back from where?' Diana asked.

'I'm not sure, but it shouldn't have been possible, wherever they've gone.' Mallory sighed. She was angry at Cornelia, but Cornelia did not look like Cornelia right at this moment. She looked frightened, and regretful, and small. It pushed out any capacity Mallory might've had for analysis of the situation.

'I think we shouldn't be here when they get back,' Diana said firmly. 'Especially as I've no idea what the fuck is going on.'

'Can we just agree to go upstairs for now? I really need to go back to sleep.' Mallory rubbed a hand over her face.

'We all probably need to sleep.' Cornelia begrudgingly let go of Mallory's hand and pointed to where the static was, over the door. 'I'm just afraid of what Theodore is doing.'

'Me too,' Diana and Mallory said in unison.

'Especially me, as I have no context for what happened in the first place,' Diana added.

Theodore snapped back into the lab just then, a witchlight flaring as he did, but there was no Beckett.

'Theo?' Mallory asked.

He smiled as though nothing was wrong. This was alarming, because everything was wrong.

'I forgot you were here. Are you okay?' His face furrowed with worry. 'Why are you on the ground? Mallory?'

'Where's Beckett?' Cornelia asked. Theodore looked around him, seemingly disorientated.

'We went to a cemetery. *The* cemetery. Theirs. And I left him there.'

'You did what?' There was a chill in Cornelia's voice.

'He... I don't really understand, to be honest. We were both in the witchlight, I think.'

'You took him in there?' Mallory stared at him. She hadn't thought Theodore could bring anyone with him, though, admittedly, they'd never tried. 'What did you do?'

'He's not hurt! I can't... I don't...' He looked at the witchlight and back at the room in wonder. 'I was in the witchlight, and I thought about the cemetery, and then we were there. I showed him what biting can do. Why he's not permitted to drain anyone of their energy. Why his people stopped.'

'Theodore, how did you get him there?' Diana said.

'I don't know!' He clutched his head, cat ears slipping momentarily. 'I didn't know I could bring him through, it just happened. Samhain ghost powers strike again. But he's fine! Goddess, he's just a boy. A stupid, stupid boy. But I wanted him to see what he could do to you, to everyone in Wrackton, if he went too far. That was all.' Theodore waved his hands to demonstrate his innocence.

Cornelia visibly relaxed, but there was something akin to shock settling into her face that made Mallory want to take her hand.

'I'll talk to him later. Theodore, I appreciate your concern, but he's done research,' Cornelia said, her voice tight, her body rigid. 'I know what I'm doing with him, and I really need you to not interfere.'

'Cornelia, please.' His voice was soft, pleading. 'We're friends, right? This was something unsafe that happened to you. And if something unsafe happens to you again, I have to go to the

Council. Even if that damages our friendship in future. I'm…
I'm your mentor, as much as I am your friend. I have to do the
right thing by you.'

'Theo,' Cornelia said.

'Cornelia.'

He was at Mallory's side now, and extended a hand to her. She
took it and he hauled her up, then enveloped her in his cardigan.
It smelled like ghost, like always, and she was grateful for the
hug. She needed to shake off the electric feeling in her hand from
where Cornelia touched her.

Mallory was much taller than Theodore, but she still felt safe
in his arms. He was home, a second family, and this was where
she was meant to be. She had his protection, always. Theodore
leaned back to look at her seriously.

'I'm sorry for being so taxing.'

'Which time?' Mallory asked faintly.

Theodore grinned at her. 'All the times. But especially this
time. I let rage get the better of me.'

'It's okay. I promise,' Mallory said.

'Just… keep an eye on Cornelia, please,' Theodore whispered.
'This isn't right. I'm still angry. But I think she needs friendship
first, anger later.'

Mallory nodded.

'Are you sure you're okay?' Theodore asked loudly, peering
as close to Mallory's face as he could. 'You're a little ghostly pale,
and that's sort of my thing.'

'*Theodore.*'

'She's okay, Theodore.' Cornelia rested her hand on Theodore's
and the three of them disappeared into static.

'What I don't understand is, why did you let it happen?' Diana asked Cornelia. She was, by all accounts, behaving herself. She had ordered food so Cornelia could start replenishing her blood supply, which was the biggest peace offering Diana could offer a situation.

Mallory twisted her chopsticks in her hands, thinking about Diana's initial question. They sat on cushions on the floor in Mallory's room in a triangle, like they used to when they were younger.

'I don't want to talk about this if you're going to be judgemental,' Cornelia said around a mouthful of rice noodles.

'I am offended,' Diana said. 'I mean, you're right, I'm judging you, but now I'm offended too. I'm only judging the situation because I literally can't understand what you get out of the arrangement.'

Cornelia sighed. 'I really hoped you wouldn't find out. We talked about this, extensively. I was trying to help him.'

'*Help* him?' Mallory said, sharper than intended.

'Yeah. We have so much power, we aren't even aware of the privilege that comes with that. I know you don't always agree with Beckett, but he did point out how many vampires felt like Apparents, especially of late. We, and faeries and demons and trolls et cetera are able to do whatever we want; vampires often feel as though they exist on the fringes of society. It's hard for some of them to reconcile belonging to the Occult community when there is so much stigma attached to vampire magic.'

Cornelia stuffed another dumpling in her mouth, managing, somehow, to be very neat about it.

'The stigma is there *because* of the Vampire Wars. They destroyed Occulture. Cornelia, did it occur to you at *any* point how dangerous it would be investigating a case where someone is trying to summon the Ternion, when the Ternion were directly responsible for the end of the Vampire Wars, and to simultaneously break a very fucking old and very fucking important covenant?' Diana said around a mouthful.

Cornelia blinked.

'Did you understand at *any* point that this was a really dangerous time to be messing around with the Charter? Or even think about what could go wrong?'

'I understand all that,' Cornelia said, with the air of someone who had not considered it until four seconds ago. 'But Beckett's probably not all that wrong, either. I don't expect either of you to understand.'

'You're not giving us much of a chance,' Diana said.

'I want to understand how you could give him your energy like that,' Mallory said quietly.

Cornelia looked at her then, clearly exasperated.

'Just because you don't have as much energy as I usually do doesn't mean you can police how I act and what I do with my body.'

This was the first time Cornelia had ever had anything remotely bad to say about her illness, and Mallory didn't like it.

'Don't say that to her,' Diana said.

'Please don't fight my battles for me, Diana,' Mallory said, anger spiking.

They looked at each other. It had historically only ever been

Diana and Cornelia who fought. Mallory never used to get involved, always trying to keep the peace.

'Why don't we just forget the whole thing?' Cornelia opened another food container. It was even more unusual for her to be the first to back down. 'Beckett's cousin has been studying vampire magic for years. He had a theory about how it could work so Beckett, and the other vampires, could move from surviving on food to thriving with blood, with magic, without any negative repercussions. He'd just been away with him recently – this is the one still on Mount Hallow – and thought he'd give it a go. A small amount of blood, just to start.' Cornelia paused. 'Except there were negative repercussions. He said he'd go slowly, and he didn't. I don't… I didn't…'

Diana scooted closer to her, though her eyes were still hardened. 'Like I said to Mallory, I'm going to hex him the moment we lay eyes on him again. Cornelia, you're the smartest person I know. How did he get you to agree to this?'

'I… I don't know. I don't think he *did* "get me" to do anything, I was… he made sense, it…'

Mallory closed her eyes, thinking about what she thought she saw on Cornelia's neck earlier in the week, the flash of angry purple nothing like the marks on her neck now. 'Was this the first time?'

'Of course it was – and the last, I guess. Wait,' Cornelia said suddenly. 'You've been talking to Mallory about him behind my back?'

'Cornelia, you're basically a whole other witch around him. He's obnoxious and awful and he's convinced you to break a *literal sacred covenant*.' Diana clenched a fist. 'Find me a single other vampire – who is not an allegedly studious relative – who would be okay with this.' Mallory could see her trying to be measured. 'You hate anyone else who acts like him. What were you going to do if someone found out you'd given him some of your blood? You don't do things like this. You don't break old covenants. You break rules, sure, but not *covenants*, and certainly not for any boy, objectively pretty or not. This is not okay and we're worried about you.'

'Mallory, is this true? You don't like him?'

It felt like a betrayal for Mallory to nod her head. 'I... thought that was really clear from our last conversation about him. He's...' She hesitated. 'I just feel like he maybe doesn't really think before he speaks. Or acts. He said some shitty things to me, even before we were introduced.'

'When?'

'Doesn't matter now. The point is, he's shown us who he is and we have to believe him. You keep saying that's not what he's like, but when is he like anything else?' The words left Mallory in an anxious rush, afraid Cornelia would turn on her. 'And the whole thing with Theodore...'

'Theodore was out of line,' Cornelia said firmly. 'Everything else aside.' She chewed the inside of her cheek, then dropped her chopsticks on to her lap. 'Why didn't you say you thought it was this bad?'

Diana said nothing.

'Mallory?' Cornelia prompted.

'We tried. Not very hard, clearly. We knew you couldn't hear it, even if we did try harder. But Cornelia, he sucks. Literally and figuratively.'

Mallory braced herself for the explosion.

'Fuck.' Cornelia ran her hands through her hair, comprehension dawning in her eyes. 'I… don't know what to say. I guess I just couldn't see it.'

Diana said, 'A, you had your tongue down his throat too often to notice, and B, telling you this this baldly would've resulted in an even bigger argument than we've had. As it stands, I am amazed we aren't fighting all over again.'

Cornelia laughed, but it was hollow.

'I just… I don't know what to do.'

'I know what you could do.' Diana picked her own chopsticks up again and mimed throwing them away. Cornelia rolled her eyes and reached over to spear another dumpling with her chopstick.

'Very funny. I mean it though, I don't know what to do. You're my best friends, I love you both. I just thought maybe I was…' Cornelia took a bite, and they waited while she chewed and swallowed. 'Maybe I loved him too.'

Mallory did not think that she believed in whatever love Cornelia was talking about. Maybe this was just a thing people went through; losing yourself to someone completely unsuitable in the hope that person could change, that they could behave better, be better, be all the things you imagined them to be just because you wanted them to. It was a painful thought; the idea of loving the idea of someone, and not who they actually were.

'We love you. And we want the best for you. But the only thing we've actually properly fought over since we've been back together has been Beckett, or Beckett-adjacent things. That's not coincidental,' Diana said pointedly.

Cornelia exhaled. 'I hate this.'

'Me too,' Mallory said.

'I love him. But if the two friends you care about most in the world are telling you they hate your boyfriend...' Cornelia trailed off again, her expression rueful.

Mallory reasoned through what she wanted to say. 'We just don't want him to hurt you, that's all.' She felt a pang of guilt, knowing she was a hypocrite. 'And it's not from a place of being overly protective, either; we have seen what he's like. He has been unsympathetic since Ben died. Has he even asked how you are? Checked in on you? Done anything to support you?'

Cornelia stared at her in disbelief, as though this had never occurred to her before.

'It's not much to ask that he would make you feel better, be there for you, bring you food, do something for you. But you're grieving, Cornelia, and he chose that time of extreme vulnerability to get you to... to...' Mallory gestured at her neck. 'Instead of supporting you, or waiting till a time when you were definitely sure this was something you wanted to do.'

A small tear tracked down her cheek; Cornelia never cried.

'Hey.' Mallory took Cornelia's hand, lacing her fingers through her own without a second thought. It felt natural. Their rule of three, alone in a room, felt natural. This was what she was supposed to be, underneath the illness and the ambition and the science and the magic.

'Hey yourself.' Cornelia wiped the tear away. Diana looked at their hands pointedly, but said nothing. Mallory hastily withdrew her hand, embarrassed.

'I need to figure it out. Thank you for being honest with me,' Cornelia said.

'Any time. Well, not any time. We picked a specific moment

for this honesty,' Diana said. 'But in general, any opportunity we have to be fully honest with you, we will.'

That stung Mallory's conscience and she shivered. There had been a perfect opportunity to be honest about the beetles. She was not honest.

Cornelia's thumbs jabbed out a text, presumably to Beckett. She threw her phone on the bed angrily. 'I don't know why I'm bothering to text him now, anyway. He's high as shit, I'll have to wait for him to come down.'

Tiredness swam in Mallory's head. She turned slowly to Diana, feeling as though she was underwater.

Cornelia's phone buzzed and she startled. 'It's not him,' she said after a second. 'Some books I ordered about the Ternion are out for delivery. So I get books delivered to me, and I get to deliver a crushing blow to my soon-to-be-ex.'

Even Diana didn't touch that one.

'I'm mostly joking. Except I'm not.' Cornelia dabbed at her throat. Mallory's gaze zeroed in on the tiny scabbing marks again and shuddered.

'I need to sleep now,' she whispered.

Cornelia took the food containers from around Mallory and helped her stand. Diana pulled back the covers.

'My meds.' Mallory could feel her brain powering down even as she tried to pull off her jeans.

Cornelia had already got them from Mallory's bag. 'Do you need anything else?'

Mallory shook her head, too tired, too sore and too full of guilt to speak.

Diana switched off the light.

PERIMORTEM III

Beckett Kingston was a prince among folk.

Or so he'd have you believe.

He was all-powerful, all-mighty, and had just survived a fight with a ghost.

His girlfriend's blood raged through his veins, and as he lay on the site where his ancestors had fought, staring up at mausoleums and crypts, he stroked the grass beside him and opened his mouth to scream. It was a whoop of joy, of terror, of delight.

He had been warned by an older cousin, who had spoken to someone else, who had heard from someone else, what drinking blood for the first time felt like. He was prepared, and yet he wasn't. There was fury burning through him and his teeth longed to bite into the soft flesh of his own elbow crease, tear out a blue vein and let it rush out over the grass. His cousin had warned him of this too. The power felt destructive. Ripping open a vein wouldn't do anything to him; he'd feel tired for a few days, but he'd be okay again.

The fight with the ghost had been short-lived. Beckett was angry at him, and he thought about how he'd make sure something was done, the next day, or perhaps the next, whenever his power wore off and he felt like himself again. The Ghoul Council would want to hear about how a ghost had transported him, against his will, to a remote location. It didn't seem right.

Beckett thought about Cornelia as he ripped up clumps of grass and burned them with the white lighter he carried everywhere. He let the ashes fall down on his jacket, the leather growing damp as he stared up at the stars, wondering what now. What could he do now?

He'd tell you the answer was anything.

He felt magic coursing through him and the grass around his head began to sprout upwards, weeds tangling and blades shooting up towards the sky. He whooped again, louder, happier, prouder, and then he heard music coming from one of the crypts.

His family crypt.

He could try to raise the dead. He could try to do *anything*.

He threw himself to his feet and walked towards the crypt. Were he still alive, Beckett would tell you that the noise coming from it quickly stopped sounding like music. Had he bothered to find the words, he would've said it was orchestral, but not. It grew into a whistling sound, and Beckett wondered if this was the hallucinations someone via someone via his cousin had warned him could happen his first time.

And then he felt that urge to rip out his vein again, except it was in his throat and he reached up his own hand to touch the soft skin there. Something else was tearing at his veins, but from the inside, and he felt a bloom of blood in his mouth again and he thought of Cornelia, how willingly she'd given her power to him, how much Beckett wished he was able to love her properly.

Or at all.

He'd have told you a similar story to the first two victims.

Tongue severed.

Stomach carved.

Dead.

TWENTY

Four days to Samhain

Mallory sat up, pulled into waking by the sounds of sobbing coming from down the hall. Her eyes would not obey her command to open, crusted with sleep and the desire to never function as intended again. She fumbled with the covers and got out of her room just as Diana also stumbled out into the bright light of the hallway.

'Cornelia?' Mallory croaked.

Diana pushed the door open. Cornelia sat in a crumpled heap on her bed, one hand pressed to her still-pallid face, the other hand holding her phone. Mallory pried her fingers off it.

'Hello?'

'Is that Mallory? This is Detective Inspector O'Sullivan here,' Sully said. Her tone was gentle, but the use of her full title made something in Mallory's stomach drop. 'I'm afraid there's been another murder.'

'Oh no.'

Why Sully would call them to tell them didn't make sense. Cornelia crying didn't make sense.

'Yes. Found this morning. A young vampire, Beckett Kingston,' Sully said.

Mallory's blood went cold. The world felt strangely tilted, a sense of foolishness at having suspected him descending into her stomach.

'Beckett?' Mallory whispered.

'What's happening?' Diana asked, her arms around Cornelia, rocking her side to side. 'Mallory?'

'I'm sorry,' Sully said.

Mallory took in a shaky breath.

'Is it like the others?'

Sully paused.

'I can't talk about active cases, Mallory.'

'Is it like the others?' Mallory demanded. 'Did he die like the others?'

Diana gasped. A small wail escaped Cornelia.

'Mallory…' She hesitated. 'Yes. All the same. We found him in Vampire Cemetery. I need Cornelia to come down to the station soon to give a statement. It's better if she comes voluntarily; if she doesn't come in by this evening we'll have to bring her in.'

'Why?'

Mallory's brain spun. They'd told Cornelia to break up with him and she'd presumably sent him angry texts; she couldn't fathom how that could be reason enough for the police to suspect her.

'Someone needs to answer for what's happening here, and it's not going to be me,' Sully said. Mallory shivered, the phrase landing strangely.

'But can't you interview her at home? I don't understand why you want her to come in,' Mallory insisted.

'Just get her here, please. I— I have to go. I'm sorry.'

The call dropped.

'No. No.' Cornelia wailed again, louder this time. She sank down onto the floor beside the bed, lying like a discarded puppet. Diana sat her up just as she started hyperventilating. Mallory watched this from above, feeling as though she had been released from her body. This couldn't be happening.

'I need to see him. We have to go. We have to make sure.' Cornelia grabbed her phone and dialled Beckett's number, but it rang out six times before Diana managed to get it off her.

'Cornelia. Cornelia. Sully said it was the same as the others. Beckett's been killed by the Whistler. I'm so sorry. I am so, so sorry,' Mallory said, her mouth moving so slowly she could barely get the words out.

Cornelia screamed. She screamed so loud that Theodore must have heard from the basement, for he leapt through the closed door in a spray of static.

'What's going on?' Theodore said, his hand raised as though he was going to strike down whatever intruder had arrived.

'Beckett,' she sobbed.

'What has that boy done now?' Theodore dropped his arm, irritated.

'He... he...' Mallory swallowed. 'He has been murdered. By the Whistler.'

Theodore stared at her for a split second before he reached for Cornelia, who crawled to the end of her bed and into his arms. Mallory and Diana stood too, rumpled from sleep, dazed, sickened.

'I'm so sorry. I'm so sorry,' Theodore kept saying over and over, stroking Cornelia's hair. 'What happened?'

'We don't know any details, we just found out.'

'I was going to end… He didn't…' Cornelia sobbed.

'How about I make you some tea?' Diana said.

Mallory couldn't do this. Not after last night. Cornelia had been about to end things. They'd told her they hated him.

'I called him a cretin. A treacherous incubus. I called him so many things.' Theodore's face scrunched in pain, dawning comprehension continuing to cross his features in waves. 'I'm so sorry. I am so, so sorry.'

'Theodore,' Cornelia said weakly.

'What is it?' he asked.

Cornelia wrenched her head away from him, her eyes bright with new terror.

'They want me to go in for questioning. I have to give a statement. It's voluntary, but I… I did…' She gestured at her neck. 'This is really bad.'

It was bad. Mallory could see how bad it was, Cornelia having to go and admit she'd broken a sacred covenant just before Beckett died.

Theodore pulled at his cardigan, static flying. 'You're not going alone. I can explain what happened, how Beckett got to Vampire Cemetery. Calmly.' He held up a hand. 'There is a method to speaking to the police. Above all else, be calm. Next, don't say anything.'

'How—'

'It's not like it is on TV shows. A thing I haven't been able to watch in a very long time. Do they still make shows, Mallory?'

Mallory nodded, the cold shock still in her veins. Cornelia looked as though she was barely standing, propped up by clouds of static as Theodore occasionally reached out a hand to steady a tilt.

'In the shows of my yore, asking for a lawyer was seen as an admission of guilt, but it isn't. If you get into a situation where you feel you need one, ask for one. Do not say anything. Do not elaborate on anything. If they ask a question and it could be a yes or no answer, give that.'

'I know all this,' Cornelia said, wiping her arm across her eyes. 'I know.'

'I'm still telling you the rules,' Theodore said firmly. 'Don't say anything; if you must speak, speak little; ask for a lawyer; above all else, remain calm. Got it?'

Cornelia nodded, then burst into tears again. Mallory and Diana reached for her and let her sob into their shoulders. Mallory rubbed soothing circles on her back, fighting the urge to tell her it was okay.

It wasn't okay. It would never be okay again.

'As soon as you're ready, Cornelia, come down and get me. We will go together. We'll be back here before you know it. But take your time. I truly have all the time in the world.' Theodore nodded at them and stepped through the wall, leaving the Undetectables to hold Cornelia in her grief.

It took a while before her tears stopped. Diana made tea and she and Mallory forced toast into Cornelia, who eventually accepted her friends were going to keep trying until she agreed to ingest something solid.

Cornelia tried to pull herself together, and Mallory felt her body pulling apart.

'Cornelia, you couldn't...' Mallory hesitated, not looking at Diana. 'I know this is probably the worst timing ever, but could you bind my legs?'

'Of course.' She wiped her face. 'You can literally ask me for that any time.'

'This seems like the worst time to ask you for anything.'

'I get that, but this isn't a big deal to me.' Cornelia smiled for the briefest second. 'Besides, it's not a spell I can teach you to do on yourself. You need my energy to make it work, and I have enough to give you.'

She made Mallory lie down and whispered, 'Bind.' Mallory immediately felt some relief.

'I heard what you and Theodore said about the Sprinter being a database.' Cornelia moved to her dresser as Mallory sat upright, her heart leaping. 'I was going to try it there and then, but I wanted time to test it, and I thought of it last night when I... couldn't sleep.' She touched her neck. 'I was going to give it to you today.' She pulled out a crystal pendant on a soft black cord and held it out to Mallory.

Diana made a *hmm* noise in her throat.

'This has a binding spell in it. I thought about the Sprinter as a store when I was testing spells on it and wondered how I'd isolate it, and I think I did it. So here. Take it. For whenever you feel ready to use it. There's one in the Sprinter too, but I thought knowing you had the option whenever you needed it...' Cornelia dropped it into Mallory's hands.

Mallory didn't know what to say. She wished Diana would stop staring at them.

'Thank you.'

Cornelia waved dismissively 'It's nothing to me to do magic. Never has been.' She sniffled and resumed crying.

Mallory had never seen Cornelia be so vulnerable as she had in the past few days and it was jarring. Cornelia was always so *together*, and Mallory knew it wasn't fair to judge someone's togetherness on their response to grief, but she couldn't help but think that Cornelia was, perhaps, not as complexly composed as she seemed.

Mallory slipped the necklace over her head and held the crystal to her chest. 'Thank you.' She held out her arms and Cornelia folded herself into them gratefully. Mallory tried to stem the sudden feeling of apprehension at the idea of Theodore and Cornelia going to the police station together. Despite how in control Theodore seemed of his ghostliness, folk never fully trusted him, and Mallory worried about how he would be received, even with Cornelia there.

'Keep working, while we're out. Theodore and I won't be long,' Cornelia said into Mallory's shoulder. Diana looked at them both strangely, and Mallory peeled herself away.

'I called Hotel Quinn Indigo about the CCTV as requested,' Diana said when she and Mallory were situated in the basement, Mallory already feeling steadier thanks to the binding spell. 'While I was making tea. I multitask like that.'

'What did they say?'

'I knew the receptionist.' Diana batted her eyelashes. 'You remember Lina?'

Mallory bit back a grin. 'You said something about no dating for a month, and I said something about holding you to it.'

'I was very persuasive. You'd be proud.' Diana tossed her hair back. 'She can't give us a copy, but has promised to go and watch it herself and tell us the movements of Quinn and Van Doren on the night of Kuster's murder. She'll call back as soon as she's done it.'

'Brilliant. Okay. There's the Larix CCTV footage too, but maybe we'll wait until Cornelia is back to go through that. She'll want to watch it with us, and I'm not sure I'll be able to watch it a second time.' Mallory smoothed her hair back. 'We'll wait for her return to also really think about why it's another victim we know, and focus on the practical evidence instead.'

'The Whistler is watching, whoever they are.'

'As of yesterday, I'm more on the Van Doren train than I have been, but…' Mallory said. 'Something doesn't quite fit. It's like all of our suspects – Quinn, Van Doren, Sully. They all kind of fit in their own ways, but not quite.' She shook her head. 'We've a heap of other evidence to go through, and I'm not brilliant at interpreting the Machine charts alone.'

'Would a simplified bar chart help?' Diana asked excitedly. 'Bitches love bar charts. It's me, I'm bitches. I could be your lab assistant for the day.'

'Are you sure?' Mallory said.

'That's not even a question. Where do you want me?' Diana said, grabbing her blue lab coat.

The hum of the Magic Magical Machine filled the basement and Mallory carefully lined up their items: Beckett's hair, Van Doren's pen, Grey Quinn's pocket square.

'Let's start with Beckett, then,' Mallory said. 'We're looking for a pink magic sample. Obviously… obviously Beckett didn't do it. But maybe another vampire did, and this will help narrow down who it isn't, at least. Theodore and I think the vampire spectrum will be iron, so we're hopefully going to see something silver-grey or sooty.'

Mallory silently, begrudgingly, thanked him, though he hadn't given the hair freely. He really was helping folk, even in death.

'Poor Beckett,' Diana said. 'Like, don't get me wrong, he was a fucking dick and I take back none of what I said about him.' She paused. 'And also none of what I thought about him. But I don't think he deserved to be murdered by the Whistler.'

'Nobody deserves to be murdered,' Mallory said, preparing the sample and inserting it into the chamber. She pulled the lever to close it. 'But yeah. Me too. I feel sorry for him. Sorry for the whole situation.'

The Magic Magical Machine hummed and Diana readied herself to pull the sample from the Machine. She held it up as Mallory took the chart and examined it. She still didn't really know what she was looking for, still didn't fully know the language of the Machine and hoped Theodore would be back soon to go through it with her.

Diana shook the vial. 'It's soot-coloured! Vampire magic is silver-grey *and* sooty!'

Mallory recorded this and put the vial with the others. 'The killer's magic can't be a combination of vampire magic, then. Not a vampire. Grey Quinn next.'

She held her breath as she prepared the sample.

'Can I put this one in?' Diana whispered, already taking it

from her in her enthusiasm. Mallory stepped back and winced as Diana enthusiastically slammed the chamber closed.

Mallory took this vial out herself, shaking it.

The smoke in the vial curled and darkened until it was a brilliant, sapphire blue.

'It's not Grey Quinn. We can wait to hear what Lina says about the CCTV, but… I think he can be eliminated.'

She took a breath. The moment of truth. Mallory prepared the Van Doren sample.

'I'd like to do this one myself.'

'He's a witch, though, isn't he?' Diana pointed out. 'Witch magic could potentially make pink.'

'I don't think we can discount it being any witch,' Mallory said, 'but I still want to be sure there isn't anyone whose magic would produce a pink signature.'

The Machine groaned and juddered, almost hesitating before the puff of smoke appeared. Mallory lifted it with shaking fingers.

It curled around itself slowly, slowly. Mallory felt every nanosecond pass until Diana said, 'Oh *shit*.'

The sample was pink.

Van Doren's magic was pink.

'Oh shit,' Diana said again, her face suddenly draining of colour. 'Oh shit, he's really a suspect. Oh shit, we are really on the right track. Oh goddess, Mallory. We're working a murder case. We've been working a real life serial killer case. I think it's just hit me. I need to sit down.'

Diana dragged over a stool and perched herself precariously on it, grumbling that the seat wasn't wide enough to support her having a mini breakdown.

'Witch,' Mallory said mechanically.

'I know Van Doren is a witch.'

'No, *you're* a witch. One with magic who can make the seat bigger,' Mallory said impatiently, her brain flitting through what she knew, what they still didn't know.

Van Doren was a real suspect. He could really be trying to summon the Ternion. The Machine had given her an answer.

Diana rolled her eyes at herself and muttered a spell so that the seat of the stool was more comfortable to sit on.

'I suffer discomfort all the time as a fat person and *for what*,' Diana grumbled, but Mallory wasn't listening.

They had eliminated Grey Quinn as a suspect, that much she was certain of. Van Doren had a pink sample. It could be him. He could be the Whistler. This could all be over.

'Wait,' Mallory said, slamming her hand down on the bench with force she already regretted. 'We need a Sully sample to eliminate her too. I can't… I can't get excited about this until we're sure.' She closed her eyes. 'I don't know where we're going to get one. She— BEETLES,' Mallory shouted.

'Where?' Diana almost fell off her stool.

A stab of fear pierced Mallory's stomach as the guilt at what she'd done resurged, but she pushed it down. 'When Sully was here. She held one in her hand, Cornelia got her to do a spell.'

'You're a genius, and Cornelia's delightful nerdery has helped us once again.' Diana hurried into the research room to rummage around Cornelia's desk and lifted a beetle out of the beetle box. It gave up the green magic sample quickly.

'Thank you,' Mallory whispered to it. 'Thank you so much.'

She reset the Machine and stood there with her arms and legs vibrating with anticipation, when Diana said, 'Oh, Cornelia's back,' just as the basement door crashed open and Cornelia ran in, breathless and panicked. Mallory's stomach dropped. Something was wrong.

'They've taken Theodore into custody.'

Mallory turned and took in Cornelia as she rounded the research room divider. She was panting, sweat sticking her hair to her head, her eyes wild and red-rimmed. A fresh set of tears fell and Mallory went to her. She took her hand, Diana took her other one, and she felt the familiar pulse of energy flow through them. This seemed to calm Cornelia enough to get her to shake off Diana's hand and rub her fingers together, a teapot materialising on the table next to the visitor sofa.

'Need... a drink.' Cornelia threw herself into the chair, looking drawn and shaken as she raked her hair back from her face.

'What happened? Where is he?' Mallory asked urgently, sitting on the sofa. She should've said something earlier, should've stopped him going, and this fresh guilt curled itself around all the other pieces of guilt she was carrying.

'What happened to the rules?' Diana raised her arms, exasperated. 'He had rules!'

'I gave my statement to Sully and another police officer and it was fine,' Cornelia started.

'What did you say?' Mallory said.

'I told the truth. Mostly.'

'What does that mean?' Diana asked.

'It means I handled it well.'

'No. I know when you're being evasive,' Diana said. 'Start from the beginning.'

Cornelia poured a cup of tea and drank it in two gulps, steadying her breath. She wiped her tears away.

'So first they brought me into a room. Theodore said he'd like to give a witness statement, as he was with me and Beckett last night.' She swallowed. 'I told them that we'd been together, that Theodore and Beckett got into a fight, that they went to Vampire Cemetery together, that Theodore came back alone.'

'Did they ask what the fight was about?' Mallory asked.

Cornelia nodded.

'Did you tell them?' Diana pressed. 'By all means, drip feed us this story like a filter coffee.'

'Shut up, I'm trying,' Cornelia snapped. She ran her fingers through her hair again. 'I told them that Beckett had bitten me, yes.'

'And?'

'And what?' Cornelia shrugged angrily. 'I got out of it.'

'How?'

'I listened to Theodore's rules.'

Diana shook her head. 'No, that's not it. You broke a sacred covenant and admitted it to the Wrackton police. Bullshit you're here and just didn't say anything.'

Cornelia scrunched her nose. 'The interviewing officer who wasn't Sully knew my family. I promised a preferential ticket to the next ball, whenever that may be.'

Even Mallory had to snort at that.

'What? I used my disgusting levels of privilege to get myself out of a situation,' Cornelia said defensively. 'I *hate* the police. How I was treated versus Theodore…'

'Yeah, now's the time to get annoyed about this.' Diana rolled her eyes. 'Just explain about Theodore!'

'I got out, and asked where he was. He'd been taken into another room. I pretended I needed a drink and hung outside his room and did a listening spell.' She took a deep breath. 'You know his rules? You know the way he told me to follow them to the letter?'

Mallory nodded.

'He did not follow a single one. I heard them ask about Samhain ghosts and he told the police about all the rules for Samhain ghosts. The following is an accurate impression of the moment I heard him implicate himself.' She cleared her throat, and stood, drawing her arms in to herself.

'"If you were *really* going to ask yourself who the Whist— I mean, the murderer was, you would do well to consider every single avenue and not just Cornelia – who can't possibly have done it, as I say,"' Cornelia-as-Theodore said.

Diana snorted and Mallory bit back a smile. It was an extremely accurate impression.

Cornelia widened her eyes at them, before continuing: '"Cornelia wasn't even the last one with Beckett."'

Mallory felt her stomach drop, seeing where this was going.

'"If you were to properly consider it, why, even *I* could be a suspect in that case. No, no, really! I was alone on 2 October. My friends were at the Larix the night of Ben DeLacey's murder,

and then I was the last one to see Beckett Kingston alive."'
Corneleodore said.

'Oh for fucksake,' Diana said.

Mallory closed her eyes. 'What happened then?'

Cornelia took a deep breath. 'The police said, "You're a
Samhain ghost, aren't you?" and Theodore said, "Why, yes I am,
thank you for noticing!" Then they asked him if he could walk
through walls. He gave a demonstration of how he could do so –
walked right out into the corridor where I was sitting and waved
at me. Fucking *waved at me* and then popped back through the
door. I could practically hear the cogs turning in their heads as
they watched him do this.'

Mallory swallowed hard. He'd implicated himself so easily.
She knew he hadn't murdered anyone, but proving it was a whole
other issue, and they should've known this would happen.
Mallory should've known, and stopped him going. 'He really
doesn't have an alibi for any of the murders that I can think
of right now. And he really can walk through walls. But what
possible motive could he have?'

'The police have that one covered too.' Cornelia sniffed. 'He
landed back in and babbled some more about his ghostly abilities,
and they said, "What would you give to be alive again?" And
Theodore said, "Oh, anything!" And they said – yes, you can see
where this is going – "Would you consider yourself jealous of the
living?" And Theodore said, "I suppose that's fair. I really miss
sandwiches and watching TV shows, I often envy those who
can partake in both."' Cornelia sat down and wrapped her arms
around her knees, hugging them to herself. 'Next thing, they'd
broken out a ghostlight and had contacted the Ghoul Council.'

'No.' Mallory's arms shook. 'His biggest fear.'

'By the time they got to putting him into it, he was talking himself around in circles. He literally wouldn't stop talking.'

It was not hard to believe.

'And he kept saying, "No you don't understand, I didn't do it," and then asking himself under his breath, "But what if I did do it, though?"' Cornelia bit her lip to stop herself laughing, though it was not funny.

'So the police think Theodore is so jealous of the living,' Diana said slowly, 'that he killed an undead vampire.'

It was almost funny.

'We have to get him out of there,' Mallory said. 'Now. We're going to prove his innocence.'

The Undetectables assembled in the research room. Cornelia had showered and had been force-fed biscuits and tea, and Mallory was surging with adrenaline. Diana paced anxiously.

'So, motive. He does envy the living, but not like that. And we seem to know more than the police in this regard – this is a ritual killing about summoning the Ternion. So let's forget their supposition and look at our own. Why would Theodore want to summon the Ternion?'

'He wants to solve his own murder,' Cornelia said.

'He wants *us* to solve his murder,' Mallory amended. 'When we got that first letter from Jacob, I thought he'd written it himself to get me to call you two so we could get together and try to solve his murder again. He was upset about the anniversary.'

Diana and Cornelia exchanged glances.

'He has also helped all the way along. He's helped with the Ternion, by pointing out the glass, he's helped me with the—' Mallory cut off, whipping her head around to stare at the Magic Magical Machine. She'd forgotten the last test was interrupted. She held up a hand and crossed into the lab, lifting the vial and hurrying back in.

'Sully's sample is pink too,' Mallory said breathlessly.

'*Too?*' Cornelia said. Mallory filled her in quickly.

'Where would we be without my beetles?' Cornelia said, somewhat smugly.

'A little less creeped out at all times,' Diana said.

'Focus, please!' Mallory remembered Selene again and pushed another stab of guilt down, promising herself she would confess to Cornelia, she would face the consequences, just not now. 'Theodore's sample is yellow. Sully and Van Doren are both pink. That's enough evidence for me that Theodore didn't do it, but it won't be enough for the police.' She paused. 'Think!' she shouted, and Diana and Cornelia both jumped.

'Erm, okay. If we start with… with Beckett,' Cornelia said hesitantly. 'Theodore had opportunity, as he was alone with him. We've no idea what happened there, and no way to check.' She welled up again.

'Then with Ben. We can disprove he killed Ben.' Mallory rubbed her hands together anxiously. The answers were there, she just needed her brain to move faster than slow-pouring porridge. 'Come on, Theodore, prove your innocence. Come on, Theodore… CCTV!' Mallory exclaimed. 'Diana, get a laptop!'

'It's here.' Diana sifted through a pile and grabbed Mallory's laptop, shoving the USB stick into it roughly.

'Careful!'

'Sorry, I'm just feeling exuberant.'

Cornelia had resumed crying, quiet tears tracking down her face.

They sat and scanned through all the footage from 8 p.m. until just after 11:30 p.m. on the night Ben died. 'We're looking for any crackle of static, anything that would indicate Theodore was in the place.' Mallory held up a page that accompanied the USB. 'Langdon said there was a camera pointed close to the doorway of the basement area where Ben died, so if Theodore was there we'd see something cross the screen. He can walk through walls, but he also breaks cameras.'

They watched until they saw themselves, shaken but determined, push everyone out of the space and slip in to investigate. Diana pressed her fingers into the back of Mallory's hand and Cornelia stiffened, but the Undetectables stayed otherwise stoic. As they'd known in the Larix back then, this was a time for cold scientific analysis, not feelings.

'No evidence of Theodore in the Larix. And there's no way he could have got in there without affecting the camera,' Mallory said. 'He can't have done that either.' She took a deep breath. 'Last, but not least, Kuster.'

'His apartment is on the edge of Oughteron Forest,' Diana said. 'Literally right on the Wrackton-Oughteron border.'

'Think,' Mallory commanded herself. 'Think.' She pressed her thumbs into the edges of her eye sockets, trying to make the pain dull down long enough to form a thought.

'Theodore has a radius,' Diana said suddenly. 'His haunting radius.' She jumped out of her chair and went to the map of

Wrackton. She peered close at the boundary lines. 'The east side of the Redwoods is all faerie-owned, and belongs to Wrackton, so Theodore can go there without getting thrown back. And yes, Kuster was last seen in the Mayoral Offices, but Kuster was found in his bed in a locked room. And his locked room is on the west side of the Redwoods, right on the edge where it becomes Oughteron Forest, beyond where Theodore can go. He didn't do it! He can't have! If he tried, he'd get thrown straight back to the place he died. That is, here.' Diana gestured to a spot a bit to her right.

'So he didn't do it,' Mallory said, not liking the relief in her own voice. She hadn't thought him capable of it because he was her friend, but she should've trusted her gut on this one. Sully had been wrong about gut feelings; they often came in handy. 'He can't have. It's completely, provably implausible. And we knew this. Even when I doubted the letter was real, no part of me thought Theodore capable of murder, just of making one up, and I was right. Theodore is officially eliminated as a suspect.'

Cornelia stood and grabbed her coat. 'Stay here. I'm going to get him back.'

TWENTY-ONE

Things seldom work out quickly when you want them to, and Theodore being freed upon Cornelia's insistence did not fall into 'seldom' territory.

'The Ghoul Council still want to follow up at a later stage,' Cornelia said when she got back. 'But I think there's a good chance he's cleared. I told them about the limits of his haunting radius, and informed them that if they wanted confirmation that he would've messed up the electronics in the Larix on the night of Ben's murder, they should look at their own CCTV footage from the time he was in holding and make their own deductions. They didn't say I was right, but I saw them realise. This is red-tape bullshit I couldn't make them drop any quicker.' She rubbed the bridge of her nose.

'So he'll be back soon, right?' Mallory said. Part of her still feared the police weren't going to let him go. 'And they'll get him out of the ghostlight?'

'All they said was, "The Ghoul Council will need to follow up first," which I'm taking as a win. They have no grounds to hold him, and I think they know it, even if they were pretending otherwise.' Cornelia looked exhausted and fragile, all the fight gone out of her in a rush. 'I'm going to go and be on my own for a little while. Think those books were delivered, so I'll take them upstairs.'

Mallory squeezed her arm lightly as she passed. 'Let us know if you need anything.'

Cornelia nodded. Diana grabbed her into a hug before letting her go into the house, sitting quietly with Mallory while they continued looking through the evidence, a sickening feeling in Mallory's stomach telling her they couldn't be sure Theodore would be allowed to come back until the moment he walked through the door, either properly or spectrally.

'I know I said I was going to go and be on my own, but you need to see this.' Cornelia opened the basement door less than an hour later, a book under her arm.

'I sincerely hope this isn't fresh hell,' Diana said. 'I've had enough hell for today.'

'Here.' Cornelia threw the book on the table. It made a heavy, dull thud. She flipped through a section of pages where she'd stuck colourful tabs. 'It's the book Observer Johnson told us to get. It's so dull-looking I actually didn't realise it was meant to be a book of folk tales, but there's an extensive chapter on the Ternion that clarifies a lot of what he was saying. Interestingly, it's pre-formation, before they were goddesses.'

'I'm sort of terrified of becoming famous. Like, imagine folk writing about shit you did before you were in the public eye,' Diana said. 'Horrifying.'

'For you, maybe,' Cornelia said dryly.

'For you, there would be multiple chapters titled 'PRIVILEGE', and it would range from parts one to… how old are you now?' Diana shoved her gently, but there was no malice in it. She was treating Cornelia like she was a raw nerve, but of a sort that needed to not become sentient until this was all over.

'You were saying, Cornelia?' Mallory prompted, though Diana was absolutely right and they all knew it, Cornelia most of all.

'Yes. Sorry. So Elisabella is daughter of Hecate and stepdaughter of Morrigan, and formed a blade to honour her mothers. She got Hexana and Blair to find a way to link their magic together – but this is academically understood as "linking beliefs", as in linking all the Occultures together, apparently,' Cornelia squinted at the page, her glasses sliding down her nose. 'Which I think we can take to mean the death blade Observer Johnson told us about. My main research sticking point is that there just aren't many books on Murderous Spells For Killing Folk, but I think this here is a reference to the ritual and Elisabella's knives specifically. And it's written in an affectation of English, so shut up in advance.' She cleared her throat. Her face was drawn and puffy, grief hanging over her, but it did not stop her putting on a silly voice to read, '"Useth a stiletto of darkest desire, a stiletto sev'nth more, f'r pow'r and proximity of t'rnion."'

'It doesn't say that,' Diana said.

'It absolutely does.' She flipped the book around to show them. 'I think this was a revised edition from the middle of the last century, though. Later, it mentions the phrase "seven souls for seven blades", and makes repeated references to "Blair's ring", whatever that means.'

Mallory looked back at the murder board, at the letter and the line that said, 'Blair's bell protects none,' her mind sifting through associations. 'What if "Blair's bell" is something to do with Blair's ring? Like the ringing of a bell? It's tenuous, and a very literal interpretation, but if we assume the first poem we found is also from the Whistler, and take the murders at hand themselves, we can probably assume the Whistler likes puzzles. This could be a direct reference to Blair's ring.'

Cornelia frowned. 'That would be horrendously constructed if that was the case.'

'Maybe there's a clue in the symbol itself,' Diana suggested. 'Observer Johnson confirmed that the lines represented Elisabella's death blade, whatever the hell it actually is. It's not beyond the realms of possibility that the circles are rings, and the rings mean something.'

'Like a summoning circle?' Cornelia said.

'It's possible,' Mallory said. 'Seven souls for seven blades... are there multiple knives? Are there going to be seven deaths?'

She shivered. Three down, four to go. It was too many already.

'The penultimate, most interesting thing to me – and this is something I will be leaving in Observer Johnson's suggestion box because I feel he could've saved us time by telling us about this instead of making me read a fox-riddled opus' – Cornelia pushed her glasses into place – 'is that this story is under an event called the Shrouding. It doesn't explain what that means – of course it doesn't, that would be far too much to ask of a book or indeed of a literal scholar of Occulture – but it alludes to Blair's participation in the Shrouding being the first act that eventually led to the formation of the Ternion.'

'What does that mean?' Diana asked.

'No idea. Feels important, though, like some sort of ritual that may or may not hold the key to this whole thing.' Cornelia stood back from the desk and stretched.

'What's most interesting to me,' Mallory said slowly, 'is how all of Occulture – us included – observe the Ternion in their own way, but when you think about it, the Ternion are sort of terrifying? Nobody can clearly explain the truth of how they came to be, there's multiple different interpretations – are they sisters, were they friends, were they really Morrigan and Hecate's children or were they chosen? Even here, we're saying there was something called a death blade, some linking of magic, and boom, Ternion. This is just a beautiful mystery that doesn't seem to be recorded in any history we can lay our hands on. We've no idea of the truth of how they came to be. And look.' Mallory pressed her hand onto the book. '"Seven souls for seven blades?" It sounds like folk were killed to make it happen. And we just… think that's fine?'

'When you put it like that, Mallory, yeah, it's a little bit fucking weird.' Diana rubbed her eyes. 'Cornelia, you said "penultimate thing," and my desire to mock you for your word choice is being outweighed by my need to know the final thing.'

'Ah yes. Finally, it mentions Hexana took the final step – presumably to the Ternion formation – at the first hour of Samhain, and brought "their seven souls to ground".'

'What does that mean?' Diana frowned. 'It sounds violent. Is it violent?'

'I think it's just a kind euphemism for "murdered the shit out of seven folk and used them to become the Ternion", but it doesn't actually say, funnily enough,' Cornelia said, earning a scowl from Diana.

'That's what the Whistler is trying to do, then. Repeat this, to bring the Ternion back. At Samhain's hour, when the veil is thinnest,' Mallory said. She looked at Sully and Van Doren's vials. 'Cornelia, are you ready to talk about why the Whistler might have chosen Beckett?'

Cornelia bit her lip, nodding.

'Okay.' Mallory looked at the ceiling. 'Who is Beckett Kingston, and why would someone kill him?'

'Vampire,' Diana said. It was the nicest thing she could've said about him.

'Vampire... who suddenly had a lot of power,' Cornelia said, chewing the edge of her nail. 'It doesn't say in the book how the souls were chosen or how the blade comes into it, just says "carefully selected" to "enhance the best chance of harnessing power".'

'These are not just sacrificed souls. These are your carefully selected, goddess-summoning sacrificed souls,' Diana said in a saccharine voice.

'The specificity of *why* doesn't necessarily include the state he was in at time of his death. We shouldn't discount it out of hand, but it also maybe shouldn't be our main focus,' Mallory said quickly. 'We've so far had an Apparent, a faerie, a vampire. If there's to be seven, maybe the Whistler will go for troll, demon and witch too, then maybe double up on one Occulture. Could be a planned one-of-each scenario.'

'There's the fact it was a stranger, then a friend, then a… well, a boyfriend, in terms of proximity to us.' Mallory massaged her temples. 'I hate to point it out, but Samhain is creeping in just as the murders are creeping closer to us. I think we're right in saying the Whistler likes puzzles. There is a puzzle here to solve. Maybe it's about attention?'

'Why out in the open?' Cornelia asked. 'We've had locked room, busy club, open outdoor space. And why Beckett? He liked attention, but it's not like attention he got could transfer to the Whistler.'

'Wait, that could be it, Cornelia.' Mallory snapped her fingers. 'If this is about power, and harnessing, maybe the Whistler is somehow storing the power of each of these folk to use in the summoning.'

'But Kuster didn't have power.' Cornelia's phone buzzed and she sighed when she saw what was on the screen. 'Beckett's funeral is tonight.'

'Tonight? That's quick,' Diana said. 'How do you know?'

'Vampires have specific rituals around daybreak after death, I don't… I don't fully understand. I'm not invited.' She wiped her eyes. 'Langdon just texted. The Larix are catering.'

'That's bullshit,' Diana said. 'He was your boyfriend.'

'Kin only. And he was only newly my boyfriend,' Cornelia said.

Mallory looked at her vials again, thinking about how they only had two victim samples. Not enough evidence to prove it was Sully or Van Doren. She needed a way to get a sample from Beckett's body, to compare to his hair, to compare to the magic traces found on the other victims. To be sure she was doing it right.

'Would it be majorly disrespectful if we, say... snuck you in?' Mallory asked. 'Because I have an idea.'

The taxi left them at the long driveway to the Kingston house, though 'house' was a distinctly ungenerous description.

'This is a fuck-off vampire castle.' Diana gazed up at it. She held an umbrella as high as she could, trying to shield both herself and Mallory from the relentless drizzle.

Mallory gazed at what was certainly a fuck-off vampire castle.

The Kingston household was bigger than the Broadwick mansion, a sprawling building in grey and black with gable roofs and a turret, lit in every window with golden lights, the driveway dotted with witchlights and lined with LED strip lights along the edge of the path.

'That's a fucking turret!' Diana exclaimed quietly. 'If Cornelia wasn't already a Broadwick, I'd say she was with him for the money.'

'I can literally hear you, Diana,' Cornelia said, 'and I am not impressed. Let's go.'

They crept on to the lawn and around the side of the castle, searching for a way in that wouldn't be populated by vampires.

'If we can just slot you in the back of the room, you can be there and leave before anyone notices,' Mallory reassured her, not entirely convinced by the whole idea now that they were here trying to carry it out. Vampires took their rituals very seriously, and kept them largely separate from the rest of Occulture. She didn't think they'd take kindly to being gate-crashed, and she was afraid of what they'd do if they found out.

'Get down!' Cornelia hissed, and they ducked back behind a shrub. Mallory peered around the side cautiously as Cornelia cast a listening spell. A big, multi-paned window showed Mallory a roomful of vampires.

Mallory had been expecting a funeral set-up, maybe pews, or a view of Beckett's coffin. She was not expecting a long table laden with black candlesticks and black plates, hundreds of high-backed chairs and black place cards with guests names' written in silver ink. The view of the other side of the table was obscured by a long, raised area in the middle, veils and candles covering the entirety of it. Every seat held a vampire, and every vampire ate in absolute silence, small course after small course.

Mallory felt like she was watching for hours.

'What is happening?' Diana whispered. Mallory shushed her.

'We can't get you in there,' Mallory said, distraught. 'Maybe when they leave, or move on to the next part, we can try.'

Cornelia watched in silence.

The guests were handed a candle each and the vampires moved their chairs back as one, the screaming scrape of wooden chairs on stone floor cacophonous.

A vampire stood and pressed one of the wall tiles and a brass hand crank unfolded from it. She turned it slowly, carefully, a clicking sound filling the room. The ceiling opened along the length of the table, the sky dark and heavy with the anticipation of sunrise.

'Is that…' Diana asked, but didn't finish the sentence.

The box rose from the centre of the table, the veil sliding off and lifting to the edges of table, forming a barrier between the guests and the box that Mallory now understood to be Beckett's coffin. It lifted high above the table and they looked up as it rose to meet the sky.

A second veil fell and a light as bright as sunrise burst from the open skylight. Cornelia, Mallory and Diana watched as the box was enveloped, obscured from view, a smokeless fire.

No body, no sample. Mallory swore silently.

Next to her, Cornelia cried soundlessly.

Beckett burned for a long time, a raging ball of fire that glowed on and on until, finally, the flames receded and all that was left were ashes.

'We're going to get caught if we don't move,' Cornelia said flatly, pulling Diana to her feet. Mallory tried to unfurl from her position and staggered, her thigh muscles screaming in pain.

'Someone's coming. Move. MOVE!' Diana hissed, rushing them back around the way they came. They heard low voices ahead. 'Shit. Shit.' Diana hesitated, wild panic on her face. Mallory wished she wasn't so tall and so sore and could crouch right down in the flowerbeds. 'In here!' Diana wrenched open a door into what appeared to be a mudroom, piled high with coats.

Mallory moved to the door into the castle and peered through a crack. Regular footfall outside told her they'd be hiding in here for a few minutes; all they had to do was not get caught.

'This probably wasn't my wisest idea,' Diana said sagely, 'but it was the best option I could think of in the moment. And you two froze, so if we get caught I am only one-third responsible.'

'Dr Ray is here,' Mallory whispered, ignoring Diana even though she agreed with her. 'And so is Van Doren, and Jacob.'

'Seriously?' Cornelia said angrily. 'They said kin only.'

Mallory turned back, an idea forming at the sight of Dr Ray. 'Diana. How well did you end things with Izna?' she said, referring to Dr Ray's mortuary technician.

'Medium-well, I'd say.' Diana smirked.

'Well enough to ask her for a favour?'

'Go on.'

'Could you ask her to bring us a victim sample from Beckett's autopsy?'

'Why the balls not, I suppose.'

'Great, I just—'

The door opened and Mallory came face to face with Jacob, who squeaked in surprise.

'Mallory! Diana, Cornelia! What are you doing in here?'

Cornelia grabbed his arm before Mallory could react and pulled him into the mudroom.

'You didn't see us here,' she said firmly. 'You tell nobody you saw us here.'

'I didn't see you here,' Jacob repeated. 'Of course. Like I said, anything you need from me!' He glanced back at the door. 'I just came in to get our coats. Did you... did you know the, ah, the deceased?'

Cornelia nodded.

'Well?'

'He was her boyfriend,' Mallory said.

'Goddess. I'm sorry.' He glanced back at the door again. 'I... I've never been to anything like this, I didn't grow up around Occult folk. You wouldn't find anything like this in the orchestra, let me tell you.' He laughed nervously.

'Trust us, absolutely nobody who isn't a vampire knew what to expect today.'

'Oh, did you see—'

A buzzing emanated from his blazer and he patted his pockets, pulling phones out and replacing them until he found the right one. Mallory wondered if Van Doren did anything for himself, and if that meant he had ample time for murder.

'This is Mr Night Mayor's. I need his coat.' He grabbed for the pile closest to him and grabbed two coats. 'And to get the phone to him. I'll see you around again, I'm sure. Tell Theodore I said hi.'

When he was gone, the Undetectables slipped back out the door and away into the dawn with no further incident.

After a short nap and a big breakfast, there was a tentative knock on the basement door. Diana opened it and Izna stood there nervously, glancing around her as if Dr Ray would emerge from the very walls.

'I could get in so much shit for this. You owe me a coffee.' She passed over a small packet and Diana threw it over her shoulder to Mallory, who just about caught it.

'I can get you a coffee right now,' Diana said. 'Two, if you also say you brought a copy of the police file.'

Izna sighed and handed over the file.

'You are a goddess, thank you so much,' Diana beamed, bopping Izna gently on the head with it. 'Two coffees, coming right up.'

'No,' Izna shifted to her other foot. 'Like, owe me a coffee… with me.'

'Oh. Well, can we see where we are in three weeks? My Mallory won't let me go on a date. If you mean date, which I think you probably do.'

'It's… you… your mum?'

'No,' Diana said patiently. 'My Mallory.' She pointed and Mallory waved awkwardly.

Cornelia snorted, leafing through the Ternion book.

'Um…' Izna said, and shook her head. 'Just… text me in three weeks, then.' She shoved her hands in her pockets and jogged up the stairs.

Mallory was already on her feet and heading for the Machine. 'It's nice she still wants to go on a date even though that was the weirdest exchange I've ever participated in.'

'It's just so hard to be so in demand,' Diana sighed. Her phone buzzed and she answered, turning away from them.

Cornelia followed Mallory into the lab as Mallory switched on the Machine again, preparing the sample. Cornelia's fingers lingered on the evidence bag.

'I know you hated him. I know I was going to break up with him.' Her voice cracked. 'But I really fucking miss him.'

Mallory closed her eyes. 'Oh, Cornelia.'

'Don't,' Cornelia said. 'I don't want to start crying again. It's fine. It's done. We would've been done.'

'Missing him isn't a flaw. His ashes will be interred in Vampire Cemetery, right?'

Cornelia nodded.

'You can visit him whenever you want. Nobody can stop you. You can go in the middle of the night if you want to. Any time you like.'

The Machine juddered and Mallory held up the vial. Pink again, different from Beckett's pre-death sample.

Mallory took it back into the research room just as Diana hung up the phone.

'That was Lina, from Hotel Quinn Indigo. I have another future coffee date lined up' – she grinned – 'but that's not the important part. She said she got a visual on the table Van Doren was at the event on the night of Kuster's murder – it was him, Grey Quinn and Hayley, Van Doren's partner. Quinn stayed seated all night – that's definitive – and so did Hayley, but Van Doren left the room alone a number of times. There are bathrooms to the back of the room they were in, but she said footage shows him actually leaving the hotel for a forty-minute stretch, right across the time window Kuster was killed in.'

'Okay. Okay. So Van Doren, no alibi, pink sample. Sully, no way to verify alibi, pink sample,' Mallory said. Hope stirred in her chest. 'There's just the small issue of needing to find out what pink actually means.'

TWENTY-TWO

Three days to Samhain

'Theodore is here,' Theodore said in the third person, holding his arms aloft in triumphant return. Mallory sobbed in relief as he stepped through the basement door and enveloped her in static. 'Theodore is cleared. Theodore wishes for the first time in a long time that he could drink some beer.'

'I can get you a cup of tea to hold?' Diana offered.

Theodore nodded happily. Mallory couldn't stop the tears rolling, unsure what she'd been so scared of.

He only let go to accept the cup from Diana, savouring the warmth in his hands.

'Police stations are awful, even when you're dead. Once the Ghoul Council was contacted, they let me out of the ghostlight. And yes, it was as bad as I feared. I shall never recover.' He closed his eyes. 'There was hardly anyone in the station, just some old demon ladies. One of them kept clanking her walking stick against the iron bars and shouting, "DEAD! DEAD MAN!" at me, as if I couldn't possibly have known this about myself. I did make the lights flicker a bit, but she wasn't deterred. They left me there for so long, I thought that I was actually going to have to stay there forever.'

'Couldn't you just have walked through the wall beside the bars?' Diana stood on tiptoe to ruffle his hair.

'That's not really the point, is it, Diana?' he huffed.

'Theodore, I have discovered something potentially brilliant while you were gone,' Mallory said. 'And I really, really need you to tell me I'm on the right track.'

She showed him her results.

'Sully *and* Van Doren with the pink samples,' Theodore said. 'This is extremely interesting.'

Mallory's heart beat faster and faster as he poured over the charts, his expression unreadable.

'I think, Mallory…' His face broke into a grin that was so full of pride she thought she was going to cry again. 'I think that you are more brilliant than you give yourself credit for. Your theory was right. Every individual Occulture has its own distinct magical signature. And that's what makes you brilliant. This is going to help a lot of cases in future. Hopefully mine. And it is certainly going to help you now.'

Mallory did cry. There weren't many tears, but it was enough for Theodore to pat her arm in a soothing spray of static.

'Now. We have a slew of murders to solve,' Theodore said. 'And we have reassuring evidence that I did not do any of them. So let me get this straight. Or, I should say, gay. Van Doren and Sully are both potential matches. Of all the folk, in all of Wrackton, they happen to be matches.'

'That's what we're hoping to prove, yes. It's a good indication that we're on the right track, we just need to… know what car we're in,' Mallory said hopefully.

'Is nobody going to acknowledge Theodore's terrible joke?' Diana asked.

Theodore beamed. 'I am so proud of you, Mallory. I am not a ghost-for-hire, but seeing as the Offices are now closed, and I am no longer Wrackton's most wanted, I am available to aid you on your quest to solve these, and any other murders you might want to solve. We will find your metaphorical car.'

Mallory felt a stab of anxiety; she hadn't thought about Theodore's murder in days.

'Thank you.' She gave him a hug, trying not to show how she felt, the warmth of him serving as a literally painful reminder of how badly she was holding up. Mallory needed caffeine, she needed more meds, she needed more sleep. She was so tired of always needing more sleep.

'Wait, aren't the Offices closed a bit early?'

'I checked in upon my release from my inequitable exile – they're apparently closing not only the Offices, but the streets around the Offices too, because of the Office creatures that breached containment last year.' Theodore shuddered, sparking gently. 'I wish the worst thing Samhain brought out of the Offices was other ghosts, but alas.'

Mallory went up to the kitchen and grabbed a drink out of the fridge, swallowing it in three mouthfuls, along with her afternoon medication and four cookies from the jar on the counter before retreating back down to the lab. She returned in time to hear Theodore talking to someone.

'Theodore, there's… oh!'

Mallory stopped short when she realised that Theodore was standing with Jacob, who looked remarkably enthusiastic about the impromptu basement tour-slash-date he suddenly found himself on.

'So this is our lab, if you want to see it,' Theodore said. 'Diana is busy at work in the research room, we shouldn't disturb her – oh don't look at the wall, it has murder photos on it, that's it, just slink past, no looking. This is the lab! It just has Mallory in it, at the moment, but it also has other… lab…stuff…'

She smoothed her ponytail back from her face and tried to appear less like she needed to be in bed. Jacob was a little static-y due to Theodore's proximity, but he smiled when he saw Mallory and gestured at the box he'd brought.

'Doughnuts!' he said. 'Sorry to just drop in like this, but I… after last night. Or this morning, I should say. I wanted to bring some… comfort? So here. Comfort, in doughnut shape. They're ring doughnuts, the superior kind. And they're gluten and nut free, just in case.' He handed the box over to Mallory, who held it thoughtfully for a second before setting it down on the bench.

'I remember when I could eat doughnuts,' Theodore said wistfully.

'How is Cornelia doing?' Jacob asked. 'I really couldn't think what else would be helpful at this time.'

'About as well as expected, honestly.' Mallory slid onto a stool.

'Yes. I imagine she is a little worse for wear right now. Please give her my condolences,' Jacob said. His looked so genuinely full of empathy he was close to tears. 'I really wish there was a way I could help you figure all this out.'

'Us too,' Mallory said. 'But we're doing our best.'

Jacob adjusted his hat, then took a breath. 'I think I should probably tell you, DI O'Sullivan was asking me about you three. She seemed... concerned about you.'

'Concerned how?'

Jacob shook his head. 'She was asking all sorts of questions. Just if I knew you, if I'd say you were friendly. She said it was routine, but she didn't ask me about anyone else. I don't know... maybe I shouldn't have said anything about her.' He waved a dismissive hand.

Mallory frowned slightly, unsure what that meant.

'Oh that reminds me,' Theodore started, then met Mallory's gaze and changed his mind. 'That I will ask you to remind me to tell you what I was reminded of at a later, more appropriate time.'

'This lab is nice,' Jacob said, after a beat.

Theodore jumped on the subject change.

'Yes! It's a nice lab. Great lab. Full of equipment. Would you like to see the fume hood cupboard? It's over here. And these are test tubes! I'm sure you know that.'

Theodore spoke as though he had never before spoken to anyone at all, babbling and pointing at things and getting impossibly flustered while Jacob politely responded as though everything he was being shown was as fascinating as Theodore was acting. It was a borderline uncomfortable exchange to watch.

'Do you do forensic science down here?' His eyes lit up. 'Can you do a DNA test on me?'

Theodore opened his mouth to start what Mallory knew would be a very protracted explanation of what sort of information you could get from DNA, and she intervened.

'We haven't got the facilities to do that at the moment,' Mallory said easily.

She needed Jacob to leave, needed to find out who the Whistler was. She was so close she could taste the answer on the tip of her tongue, metallic and tangible.

'DNA tells you a lot about who you are,' Theodore said seriously.

'I watched a documentary the other night about it, how it's used in paternity tests. It's a big feature of Apparent daytime television, if you didn't know,' Jacob said earnestly, then caught himself. 'Sorry, I tried to talk to Mr Night Mayor about this but he said if he wanted to talk Apparent shop, he'd talk to his father.' He looked at his watch. 'I should really get going. The Offices are closing for Samhain but I have to be on call in case of creatures or... further murders.' He laughed awkwardly.

'Can I interest you in the test tubes again? Look, they're so round-bottomed,' Theodore said quickly, evidently afraid Jacob would leave. He talked and gesticulated, dragging Jacob around the lab to tour different, not-very-interesting things.

'So, Jacob,' Theodore tried to catch Mallory's eye as he spoke, and she realised he was not picking up on her *oh please leave* vibes. 'Did I hear you say you had a girlfriend before?'

Jacob's face fell. 'You... did, yes. I wondered what she was doing with a fool like me, and...' He pulled his hat off and raked a hand through his mess of curls before jamming it back on his head. 'She... ah. This is so embarrassing. She ended things, a few days ago. I just...' He swallowed hard, as if he was trying to stop tears coming. 'I mean, it was for the best. For both of us.

It was more mutual than you'd think, just… instigated by her.' He lifted his shoulders, embarrassed.

'I doubt you're a fool. You don't seem foolish. I mean, you seem good at things. At life. Your job, you seem good at your job! You got your, ah, doughnuts here safely. That's good work.'

'No need to mock, Theodore,' Jacob said playfully, pronouncing his name so carefully that Mallory felt she was grossly imposing on something intimate.

'Oh, hi, Cornelia,' Jacob said.

Mallory turned to see Cornelia standing with two giant mugs of tea in her hands, a book tucked under her arm. She looked exhausted, hollowed out by the events of the past few days.

Mallory stood and winced as her legs throbbed.

'Are you okay?' Jacob immediately reached out a hand to help her, but she waved him away.

'I'm fine, seriously. Nothing I can't handle.' She smiled at him. 'Cornelia, Jacob brought you doughnuts.' Mallory slid the box to her as she reached the end of the stairs.

'How are you doing?' Jacob's mouth was drawn in concern.

'I could definitely be better. I tried reading.' Cornelia dropped a book on Occult prisons on the counter. 'But it didn't work. I'm on a chapter about decommissioning the Empathy Cage Prisons. Allegedly decommissioning in this case just means someone locked the door behind them. If you wanted to know more, no you didn't, because that's all I've read.'

'I see. I heard there was one in Wrackton, wasn't there? Mr Night Mayor was talking about it at one stage. Apparently, it's still somewhere in the bowels of the Mayoral Offices. Or the Orifices.' Jacob grinned, presumably at his semi-successful callback, and looked at his watch again. 'Goddess, I'd really better get going.' He patted Theodore on the arm as he passed.

Diana got up from her desk as he left. When the door closed, Theodore stood with his head in his hands.

'What's wrong?' Mallory approached his other side.

'It's just that… I was just thinking,' A tear appeared on Theodore's face. 'This isn't about me. Of course it's not. But I was just thinking, I wished he didn't have a girlfriend, and now…'

'Theodore. Before you start down this awful, winding path of self-flagellation, please be aware that you did not cause a breakup, and this is not your fault. You had a thought, but thoughts contain no power,' Diana said.

'Even ghosts' thoughts?'

'Even ghosts' thoughts,' Diana said firmly. 'Now, stop pushing me into the role of calm negotiator when I am ready to furiously solve this case. We need to figure out what a pink magic sample means. Now.'

Theodore laughed at that. Cornelia stared off into space, not appearing to hear.

'Wait,' Mallory said, something Jacob said coming back to her. 'Remember when we were testing samples first and I suggested it was combined magic?'

'That was after you looked at Langdon's sample.' Diana nodded. 'The teal faerie-and-troll concoction. Which now I say it out loud, sounds a little gross.'

'Jacob said Van Doren said if he wanted to talk about Apparents, he'd go to his father. We also know *Sully* has an Apparent father, because she told us he was in the Apparent police,' Mallory said slowly. 'What if that's the link? Pink means witch with an Apparent parent.'

'And given that we've never got to test an Apparent, aside from Kuster's postmortem sample, it's wholly possible you were just missing a component,' Cornelia remarked, running her hands through her hair.

'Is that enough to go on, Theodore?' Mallory chewed her lip.

'I think so. I don't know any Apparents anymore who would consent to testing, but it seems a solid enough assumption! Oh, speaking of suspects,' Theodore announced, 'Detective Cat-stable Wyatt would like to add some information to the case. On my way back here, I sighted a suspect.'

'Van Doren? Where?' Cornelia jerked into alertness as if she was going to run after him.

'Cornelia, your one-track focus when you've got multiple suspects will be your downfall,' Theodore said. 'Not him. Detective Inspector O'Sullivan. I led with that, by asking you to call me Detective Cat-stable Wyatt...' He planted his hands on his hips. 'You know, sometimes it feels as though nobody understands a single thing I say.' He frowned.

'Sometimes you just say things slightly out of range for us to understand, that's all,' Mallory soothed.

'My audience is out there,' he said. 'But, on the first matter of business: I saw DI O'Sullivan, just out on the street a few moments ago. She saw me. I looked at her. She looked at me. I looked at her. She climbed into her car and drove away. It is not a crime to stand on a street – I have checked, it is not a crime – but she was just standing there, and it would seem my very presence unnerved her.'

'Interesting,' Mallory said, her skin crawling. 'And Jacob said she asked him about us.'

'The first thing is suspicious as fuck, but why would she be asking about us?' Diana demanded.

'You know,' Theodore said thoughtfully. 'It's possible there's another individu—'

There was a flash, followed by a sharp crack, and Theodore froze in place.

Mallory stood in horror and reached for him, but static fuzz flew from him and her hands stung as she tried to touch him.

'Theodore?' Mallory shouted. 'THEODORE!'

TWENTY-THREE

Diana and Cornelia tried to touch Theodore too, muttering spells, but his face was frozen in place, his skin fizzing with energy.

'What do we do? Theodore!' Mallory shrieked.

'I… I don't know,' Cornelia said.

Mallory pressed her hands to her head, trying to make her heavy brain think. It was always too hard to think. 'Iron! Grab the iron screens, let's completely cut out any spatial interference. Now!'

The Undetectables moved quickly to pen Theodore in, his newly aggressive static hitting the iron like sharp raindrops. His body juddered and glitched, like he was splitting apart. Cold, sinking horror landed in Mallory's stomach. Something was very wrong.

'Maybe it was too much interference in the room?' Mallory looked at the Magic Magical Machine in alarm. 'We know he can break things, but maybe too many things can break him?'

'Why don't we look online?' Cornelia said, her eyes frantic with worry. 'Or maybe there's a spell somewhere.'

'Yeah, okay. There's definitely going to be a Dr Internet result for "how to corporealise your fracturing ghost",' Diana snapped, her phone already in her hand. She threw it on to a bench in frustration after a moment. 'And as expected, it's not a thing. There's barely anything on Samhain ghosts at all.'

They stood around him for an achingly long time, not knowing what to do. Mallory wanted him to come back. Wanted him to finish his sentence, whatever it was.

'Why don't we leave for a bit? Check in on him in a while,' Mallory said finally. She didn't want to leave Theodore, but wondered if stepping away for a bit would give him a chance to regroup.

Mallory curled in a ball on the floor in Cornelia's room next to the fire. Cornelia had slid her a cushion and a blanket, and she stared into the flames, wishing they'd tell her what she needed to know.

Diana threw herself back into the room, returning from her third hourly check after Theodore had fractured.

'Any change?' Mallory asked. Diana shook her head, settling down beside Mallory.

'I hate this.' Cornelia punched the cushion beneath her lightly.

Mallory nodded helplessly. 'It feels too much. We just got him back. Maybe being in the ghostlight messed him up?'

'If that's the case, he'll be okay,' Cornelia said firmly. 'Ghosts come out of ghostlights intact all the time.'

'How can we know that? What ghosts do we know who we can check with?' Mallory dropped her face into her hands.

'I guess we can only wait and see,' Diana said, but Mallory knew that none of them would be able to sleep properly until he was back to normal.

Cornelia blew out a breath. She was wrapped up in a dressing gown over a big jumper.

'I'm going to change. I'll be right back.' Diana darted out of the room.

Cornelia laid all their evidence out, and when Diana returned, she had another diorama in her hands.

'I made another one last night, when I couldn't sleep and was puzzling over Beckett's murder. When in doubt, I find Francine Leon very soothing.' She hesitated in the doorway. 'Cornelia, if you're not able to look at it, don't.' She set it down and Mallory could see a tiny paper Beckett lying in an overgrown patch of grass in the centre of Vampire Cemetery. She shivered.

Cornelia swallowed. 'It's fine.'

Diana scooted down next to Mallory.

'So. An Apparent, a faerie, a vampire. Three of seven souls. Two days to Samhain and certain destruction of Occulture as we know it,' Mallory said. 'Two suspects that we can't ask further questions of because of their positions of power – Sully and Van Doren. They're equally viable killers. I've been feeling it since Sully's comment about someone needing to answer for the murders. I can't explain it, but it felt… wrong.'

'But one more likely than the other,' Cornelia said immediately. Mallory laughed, despite herself.

'Van Doren's motive is clear: he loves power, so he would benefit hugely from summoning the Ternion. And even though he hired us to investigate, he's been inconsistent and, frankly, behaving very weirdly ever since we took the case,' Mallory said. 'As I said after that interview Cornelia and I did, I wouldn't put it past him waiting to see if we'd say something publicly, especially with how back-and-forth he's been on whether we're legitimately hired.'

'But as you've pointed out multiple times, he doesn't seem likely to make it a game.' Diana folded her arms, staring into the flames. 'Thinking back to that first meeting, he was like a whole different person.'

'He's always had sledgehammer subtlety in everything I've ever seen him do. Even the way he hired us, it was messy, but there was no coyness to it. He's confusing, yet ultimately direct,' Cornelia said. 'Something we didn't consider is that Jacob brought us to him. Maybe sending us away when they'd been desperate to find a PI agency to take it on would look suspicious, and he just… assumed nobody would want to touch this with a bargepole.'

'And instead we brought him the whole barge,' Diana said.

'He has no alibi for 2 October, and his alibi for the night of Ben's murder is only his partner, Hayley.' Mallory closed her eyes. 'And it's not like partners never lie.'

'Especially partners of very powerful, much older Night Mayors,' Cornelia added.

'Then Sully. She helped us with the whistling spell, and she's been reasonably nice, but it seems to jar terribly with what we've heard others say about her,' Mallory said. 'She's much smarter than Van Doren, so the letter and the cipher are more her speed. Perhaps we weren't meant to find that letter on Ben's body – maybe it was a calling card for her team. That could be why she didn't comment on the weird riddle when she saw it, or mention it to Diana – it wasn't for us in the first place. Although, just because it was in an evidence bag doesn't mean it was picked up at the scene. The only other individual who had hands on that file that we know of was Van Doren, so it's just as plausible he slipped it in there, though again, I think that's too subtle for him. On the other hand, we know two of the three victims, and that is starting to feel deliberate, and a bit frightening, if I'm honest.'

Cornelia shook her head. 'None of this makes sense. It's like we're being laughed at at every turn, or like the Whistler knows we're looking. Which, if the Whistler is either Van Doren or Sully, is entirely the case – they've known since the start.'

'Let's look at the scenes again,' Diana said firmly. 'I read the police file. Seriously, Cornelia, if this is too much for you…'

'I get to decide that. But thank you.' She put her hand over Diana's.

'Okay. Well, the theory is that Beckett died not long after Cornelia sent that text to him. There was evidence of magic all around him – witch magic. If you'd believe it, Cornelia, your name is redacted in the police file under the part where they discuss where he got the magic from in the first place.'

'I'd believe it. Hexana, I literally can't do anything actually wrong around here, can I?'

'And your diamond shoes are too tight, too.' Diana grinned, earning her a shove.

'I just… for once, I just want to believe that the whole system isn't corrupt, but it is. I BROKE A SACRED COVENANT,' she shouted.

'We know.' Diana pulled back from her, wincing. 'We know you did. Anyway.' She animated the diorama. It was just Beckett, lying on the grass and cackling, shoots growing up around his head. Tiny, glinting witchlights hung all over the mausoleum in the background as Beckett choked, carvings appearing in his stomach as with Kuster and Ben.

Cornelia didn't look away, though Mallory wanted to.

'Did the file mention whistling?'

'No. Beckett was found quickly. A vampire who'd gone for a walk – in the cemetery of all places, classic morbid vampires – found him and called the police. Apparently he checks out fine, he was at work on both nights of the first two murders.'

'I've been thinking about the recording more, and I think the problem is just that – it's a recording. There's no magic in it, so my beetles can react, but can't do anything with it. The whistling itself is probably still the key, so the recording is proof it has something to do with the... the murder,' Cornelia said, her eyes still on the model of Beckett. 'But it's not anything else, and I think I've exhausted all avenues on identifying what it actually is.'

'It does seem like another dead end. And there's just nothing here in the diorama that gives a clue to how the Whistler is doing this.' Mallory peered closely at everything behind Beckett, but all she saw were witchlights. 'There's no indication of how the Whistler got in and out of Vampire Cemetery without that vampire who called it in noticing something, or how they managed to do the same thing at Kuster's place and the Larix. Or any clue to how the Whistler got a spell in that would target three different individuals in exactly the same way, or where the death blade comes into it at all, if we're even right about that part.'

A splash of water hit the floor and Mallory looked up to see Cornelia was sobbing.

'Maybe we should stop,' Mallory said. 'And check on Theodore again.'

Mallory loved her friends very much, but this was too much. Theodore missing was too much. She needed him. She had just got him back.

'One last thing. I wanted to point this out, because it occurred to me last night.' Cornelia wiped her face angrily. 'Look.'

She whispered and a map of Wrackton and the Redwoods appeared. She stuck a pin in Kuster's apartment, a pin in the Larix, and a pin in Vampire Cemetery.

'I may be bad at maths, but what does the exact middle of that look like to you?' She moved back so Mallory and Diana could see.

'The Mayoral Offices,' Mallory said.

'My money is on Van Doren,' Cornelia said, like it was the first time she'd ever brought it up.

'We know,' Diana and Mallory groaned in unison.

Cornelia half-smiled. 'I'm just saying. If we go through our clues, we have many, but they're not adding up to a bigger picture. Maybe it's time for some hunches.'

Cornelia shuffled around the pages in her file and went through them in rapid succession.

'We have: carvings that indicate an impending Samhain summoning of the Ternion; possible understanding that the killer is using Elisabella's death blade or a derivative thereof; riddle that may or may not be from the killer, but is indecipherable; decoded, vaguely threatening letter promising more will die; whistle recording of doom; magic trace confirmation that the Whistler is someone with witch and Apparent family, pointing to Van Doren and Sully. We have three definite victims. A tongue-severing signature. Possibly four victims to go.' She looked up. 'And a big old map arrow pointing to Van Doren.'

'Maybe.' Mallory lay back on the floor. Her muscles protested at the movement, feeling every single bone and ligament touch the hard wooden floor as she closed her eyes, her thoughts emerging like sludge as she tried to see the bigger picture.

'I need Theodore here to help. This is so unclear. I feel like I'm missing something really obvious, but I just can't get it. And I'm really worried about him.'

They were all in agreement.

'That's how I feel about the dioramas. Like they're mocking me, showing me what I'm just not seeing,' Diana said.

'We should go check on Theo again,' Mallory said, just as a low buzzing sound filled her ears.

She looked at Cornelia and Diana for confirmation that they could hear it too.

'What is that?' Diana was on her feet first, opening Cornelia's bedroom door. 'Ugh it's horrible, it's…' Her eyes widened in horror. She took off down the hall as Mallory staggered to her feet, her stomach twisting in dread.

'Whistling.'

PERIMORTEM IV

Theodore Wyatt had died once before, and so was familiar with its mechanisms.

He had been in the middle of a thought that he'd been excited to share with Mallory when he'd disappeared.

He had not just fractured in the room, he would say, were he not dead. He had fractured within himself. One moment he had been there, the next he was nothing. Surrounded by darkness pressing in from all sides – sharp, crystal-cool, nothingness. His arms and hands and face and body expanding and contracting as he felt what remained of himself contort into something new, something full of a sound he could almost identify, even in its distortion, but not quite. It reminded him of a theatre, or an auditorium. Had his thoughts not been fracturing into nothingness he would've recalled the dim memory his brain was struggling to process, and he would've delightedly discussed it with his friends, had he not been dying, had they not been slipping away from him forever.

It was hard to kill a ghost, but not impossible.

TWENTY-FOUR

Mallory threw off the blanket from around her shoulders, stumbling over it as she pulled herself down the stairs, pausing to shove her feet into slippers. Cornelia's slippers skittered as she wrenched the kitchen door open. The whistling grew louder as they approached and Cornelia threw herself at the basement door, trying to open it. It was locked.

'I didn't leave it like that. Theodore? Theo?' Diana banged her fist against the door. Mallory's head was about to explode from the volume of the whistling in her head. In reality it was much higher, more nuanced; metallic screeching at levels that could burst an eardrum.

No response. The buzzing whistle grew louder still, and Mallory's teeth kept involuntarily pressing on her tongue, trying to gain traction as Diana fumbled with the lock, slapping her palms against the door as she tried to get the door to give in with magic.

'Move,' Cornelia said. They complied. She kicked next to the lock and the door crashed open, but even as they moved Mallory realised the whistling had stopped.

'Theodore?' Mallory shouted. 'THEODORE!'

They ran in, tumbling over each other to get down, Diana almost falling down the stairs.

'Forget me, get him,' Diana panted as they raced down to him.

Not even Theodore's cat ears were visible above the iron screens. Mallory and Cornelia pulled them back.

Theodore lay on the ground in the spot where he'd died, his eyes closed. He was the least static she thought she'd ever seen him. The most corporeal. The most human.

They stepped forward together, Diana gripping Cornelia's arm like they had the first time they'd ever met Theodore.

There was no ghost standing over his body this time.

Mallory took another tentative step forward, kneeling carefully beside him.

'Theodore?' she whispered. She wasn't able to make a louder sound. She reached out to hold his hand, but he did not move. Her hand went through him, like he was not quite there and she pulled back with a gasp.

He looked human, but he wasn't. She noticed slackening in his jaw.

'Can we lift his shirt?' Cornelia asked quietly. 'To check?'

'I can't,' Mallory said. 'I can't do it.'

Diana stepped in front of her, pushing her back gently. In a swift movement, she flipped the hem of his shirt up just enough to show that there were carvings.

Theodore seemed to swirl before Mallory's eyes, and then he vaporised, disappearing into the air.

Mallory opened her mouth, but no sound came out. They were frozen in a moment that seemed to take a year to pass, a lifetime to breathe through, the foreboding in Mallory's stomach travelling down, down, through the floor, through the earth, into the ground.

They stood in the basement for an endless time, until there was no haze left at all. Theodore was gone.

'He's dead.'

'He was already dead,' Cornelia said sharply.

'But he's gone, Cornelia. He's gone. Theodore's gone.'

This was worse than not solving his murder. Worse than him being a suspect. Mallory had never felt pain like this before. Her body was always hurting, but this pain, this guilt, was so big, so intense, she had no space for it.

'We need to call it in,' Diana said eventually. 'We have to tell Sully. If we don't and she's the Whistler, she'll know we suspect her.'

'Okay. Okay. Can we...' Mallory trailed off.

'We can leave here first.'

Diana and Cornelia stood either side of Mallory, helping her up the stairs. Mallory didn't speak again until they were back in Cornelia's room. She was shaking and cold, shivers wracking her body.

'This... he's dead, but the Whistler still killed him, somehow,' Mallory said. 'It means the seven souls for seven blades part means something more literal than just... than just kill. Right? Cause Theodore wasn't alive. As a ghost, as a Samhain ghost especially, he can't be created or destroyed, but he's gone somewhere. So maybe that's where the death blade comes in: the Whistler is using it to harvest souls. It has to be magical, or Theodore wouldn't be affected, and it has to do more than just kill; it has to sever the connection Theodore had with Wrackton.'

'I think that's a pretty good deduction, Mallory,' Cornelia said. 'It's not the killing, it's the what's happening afterwards. Which I guess confirms why Samhain is so important – if souls can cross over when the veil is thinnest, the Whistler is possibly planning an exchange. Seven literal souls in exchange for raising the Ternion?'

It was a horrible thought, and one Mallory didn't have the bandwidth for.

'I'll make the call,' Mallory said, already lifting her phone to her ear. If she didn't do it now, she never would.

Theodore was gone.

'Sully, it's Mallory.'

'What's wrong?' Sully asked.

'There's another victim. We just discovered him. Our friend, Theodore…'

'The ghost?' Sully asked.

'Yes.'

Mallory stumbled over her explanation of what happened. Sully remained silent while she spoke.

'Is there a body?'

'No, he's… we saw the carvings, we heard the whistling, he… He evaporated. But we witnessed it happening.'

'Mallory,' she exhaled, 'this is clearly very upsetting to you, and I am terribly sorry for your loss. But your friend was already dead, and I'm afraid that without any evidence, we can't count him as a victim.'

'What do you mean?' Cornelia practically roared in Mallory's ear.

'Is that Cornelia? Let me speak to her.'

Mallory duly handed over the phone while Cornelia argued with Sully on loudspeaker, insisting they'd witnessed enough, insisted he was gone, insisted he was a victim.

'I really don't think counting Theodore is a wise decision. He's legally dead already, to my understanding.'

'But there was whistling,' Diana said. 'Like all the others. It's the *same*.'

'I'm so sorry. I really, really am. But ghosts officially cannot be classified as victims of any crime. That's the Ghoul Council directive.'

There were no conscious thoughts in Mallory's head. Everything felt empty. The past few days had been nothing but horrors. It was almost Samhain. They were failing over and over to get any answers. And now Theodore...

Theodore.

Mallory's friend.

The only person who had not abandoned her.

Who believed in her, who was not in the slightest bit bothered by how prickly being in pain made her.

'He's a victim,' Cornelia said. 'A real victim.'

'There is nobody else to corroborate that.'

'We can! This is the second time he's been murdered.'

'I'm aware of Mr Wyatt's beliefs that his death was not accidental, just as I am aware you were very young when you found his body. It's understandable you would want to believe—'

'—not *believe*. We *know* he was murdered, both times,' Cornelia insisted.

'Without physical evidence, we can't really consider it. He was already dead. He wouldn't have even been regarded as missing had you called me earlier. It would be impossible to convince a ju— the Unified Magical Liaison that a crime had been committed here. I am sorry. I have to go.'

She hung up, and Mallory, Diana and Cornelia exchanged glances. Mallory had not truly understood how her friends had felt when Ben had died, or how Cornelia had felt when Beckett had died. This was numb. This was cold. This was painful and nothing all at once. Mallory felt as though she might float away.

'This moves Sully up the suspect list,' Mallory said. 'But that's it. That's all I can think of. She's discounting evidence, trying to discredit us. It's suspicious.'

Diana nodded. Cornelia's jaw was clenched and Mallory could see a muscle twitching. Diana was expressionless, like every emotion had drained out of her. Mallory did not know what she looked like, but she was dimly aware her mouth was drawn into a tight line. If she let go of the tension, she would let go altogether. She would come back into her body and she would be forced to feel.

'I can't do this,' Cornelia said.

'Me neither,' Mallory agreed, relieved at finally being able to admit it. It was too much. She couldn't do it. 'I'm terrified if we don't stop, someone else we love is going to die.'

'Are you both completely out of your minds?' Diana said, suddenly snapping back to herself. 'What happens if we stop now? It'll be Samhain and we will be out of time. The Whistler is going to try to summon the Ternion and if we don't do something about it, we're guaranteeing it'll happen. We'll have *let* it happen. Stopping isn't going to do shit, it won't fix shit. And you know this!'

Mallory thought about reaching up a hand to try to soothe Diana with a pat on her arm, a pat on her hand, but it was not her hand and not her body. She was not there.

'I need to rest,' Mallory said, but it was not Mallory speaking, it was the deadened, nothing-Mallory. Neither Cornelia nor Diana reacted as she left.

She went to her room and climbed into bed, gladly letting the lights go off in her head.

TWENTY-FIVE

Two days to Samhain

Mallory woke from a very strange dream. In the dream, she and her friends had lost Ben, Cornelia had lost Beckett, and Mallory had lost her best friend. She had also failed to solve the murders of any of the three – *four* victims. Every day of this dream, Mallory tried and tried to piece together clues from a string of undetectable murders. She was in a constant pain flare, and every day it crawled closer to Samhain, a deadline that would see the Ternion summoned if they didn't discover the killer before midnight. A killer who whistled, or who made something whistle horribly in order to choke their victims to death in order to steal their souls. Mallory's nightmare continued, where she had no real leads, apart from a suspicion that it was their revered Night Mayor, or maybe the police detective in charge of the case. She was running out of time. She was nothing, and she was in pain. It was a strange dream that seemed to envelop her in its impossibility, adding suffocating heat to the air, making every breath difficult, making every moment long, drawn-out, impossible.

The reality sank in a beat too late; it was a twisted reality and Mallory didn't want to be part of it any more. She wanted to mourn a ghost and she wanted to run away. Theodore might have been dead before, but his being truly dead, really dead, felt unfathomable. It felt empty. It felt like nothing at all, yet blanketed over every painful thing Mallory was afraid to feel. Worse than before Cornelia and Diana had come back. Worse than getting sick, worse than failing to solve Theodore's murder – his first one. That there were now two was unbearable.

She turned over and realised she was not alone.

Cornelia lay on her back, hands folded behind her head, staring at the ceiling. She had earbuds in, but was not listening to anything. Her body was on Mallory's soft pink sheets, her chest rising and falling in a slow, gentle rhythm.

Mallory nudged her, and Cornelia took the earbuds out.

'You slept for a long time.'

'Okay,' Mallory said. They looked at each other.

'I noticed you were almost out of meds, so I called the dispensary,' Cornelia said softly. 'Just to make sure you had a refill soon. They said they'll have them ready this evening.'

'Thanks.'

Mallory felt flat. Not just emotionally, but physically like her world was lacking in depth and dimension.

'Do you want to talk about it?'

'About what.' It wasn't a question, just a dull statement.

'Theo—'

'DON'T say his name.' The snarl was involuntary, Mallory's anger more alert than she was.

Cornelia, to her credit, did not flinch.

'*Theodore*' – she stressed the syllables of his name – 'was my friend too.'

'I know, but I can't… I just can't…'

'Ben was my friend. Beckett was my boyfriend. A shit one, and a relatively new one, but my boyfriend, nonetheless.'

'I'm sorry. I am. But… And I don't mean this dismissively. But just because your relationship with Beckett had a… a physical element, doesn't mean you loved him more than I loved Theodore. I'm sorry, I know how that probably sounds.' The words burned as they left Mallory's throat, the wrongness of admitting her true feelings a new kind of agony.

'Oh, a "physical element". Great, here we go.'

'"Here we go" nothing, I'm not Diana, this isn't an attack. I'm just saying.'

Cornelia closed her eyes for a moment, like she was weighing something up. It was uncharacteristic for Cornelia to think before she spoke, and the pause made Mallory's stomach drop. 'I'm saying it doesn't have anything to do with anything. It just doesn't. It doesn't have any relevance to this conversation, it doesn't make anything matter more or matter less. What I do with my body is absolutely none of your concern, unless I ask for your opinion, and even then it'll be just that – your opinion.' She paused. 'As hard as this will be to hear… it feels like you're holding me to standards you never would have, had you not got sick.'

Tears sprang into Mallory's eyes before she had even a second to register what Cornelia had said. 'Don't. Please don't bring that into this.'

'You started it.'

'Not everything has to be a fight, Cornelia!'

Cornelia looked away. 'I'm sorry. I'm being horrible. Just forget I said anything.'

'Why bother starting it if you're not going to continue?' Mallory wanted her to argue, the guilt over killing Selene rising and mixing with the annoyance. Cornelia didn't reply, her eyes on the ceiling. Mallory swallowed down the anger. 'Fine. Let's stop talking about it.'

Cornelia twisted her whole body around to face her. Mallory could feel her breath on her cheeks, see every freckle. Cornelia's glasses dug into the pillow and were askew. Mallory wanted to stare at her forever, even in her fury and her nothingness. Cornelia was Cornelia. Cornelia was unreachable, but Mallory knew that she wanted nothing more than to try. And she knew that if she prodded at that feeling, made it speak to her, she would open the floodgates and that could only ever lead to more pain. So she did not think about it. She pulled her eyes away from Cornelia's and turned away.

Cornelia waited a few moments before scooting closer, her breath warm, tickling the back of Mallory's neck. She draped a hand gently over Mallory's side in a peace offering hug, the pressure so slight Mallory would have been barely able to tell it was there if not for the warmth of Cornelia's skin through the thin cotton of her T-shirt.

'I won't talk about it. I'm sorry, Mallory. I'm really sorry.'

Mallory didn't respond, but didn't move and Cornelia left her hand where it was. Mallory wanted to pull her gently closer so Cornelia's arm encircled her body, closing the distance between them. The urge to do so was so sudden, so intense, it made her fingers tremble, her heart hammering so loud she was sure

Cornelia could hear it. They lay in silence for as long as Mallory could stand it before she gently shrugged off Cornelia's hand and sat up as slowly as she could.

'Let's go down to the kitchen. Get some food. Talk,' Cornelia said. 'It'll benefit both of us. I'm still a little weak since… before. Have to make sure I replace those red blood cells.'

'Don't want to.'

'There were three things in that sentence. You have the option of not doing one of them. Which is it?'

'Talk.'

'Let's go.'

She helped Mallory up and they went down to the kitchen together.

'There are blueberry muffins?' Cornelia said, trying to lighten the mood.

Mallory shrugged. She liked food, but just then everything seemed dull and pointless.

'What about toast?'

She shrugged again.

'We don't have to talk. We just have to be here. Eat food. Go back to bed.'

'Thanks.'

'I hate seeing you like this,' Cornelia said.

'Didn't say anything about the state you were in over… you know.'

'No, you didn't. But this isn't a comment on the state you're in, it's just… Your light's gone out, and you're Mallory. There's always a light on, no matter what, so this is a horrible way to see you.'

Mallory's heart stuttered, just for a moment, but it was enough to make her press her hand to her chest, giving guilt over Selene a chance to seep in. She didn't deserve Cornelia.

'Are you okay?'

'Yeah.' She didn't elaborate. The toaster popped and Cornelia liberally buttered the slices before adding jam. She slid this and tea across the table. Mallory picked at the crust and eventually managed to nibble all of one slice. Cornelia made her another two cups of tea. Mallory drank these, but they tasted of nothing even though she knew they had about four cubes of sugar in them each, because Cornelia had no respect for tea and Mallory did not want to tell her she was ruining it. She never had, not in all their years of knowing each other or in all the cups of tea Cornelia had poured for her.

Cornelia appeared concerned while she sipped the tea. 'This is okay, you know. That you feel like this.'

'It's not.'

'It is. Really. I feel it too.'

Mallory smoothed back her hair, deep breaths hurting her lungs as she forced herself to feel normal, act normal, be normal, even for a second. Cornelia was talking about grief, she had to be, and Mallory wanted her to be talking about something else. She wanted her to say she had felt all the things for Mallory that Mallory had been feeling for her for the last while, the last forever, probably for as long as she'd known her.

'Mallory,' Diana said from the doorway, breaking the moment. She was holding the dollhouse diorama in her arms and a box of miniaturised lab items was balanced on top. 'I just came down to work on another diorama. It's probably pointless, but it's making me feel useful.' She looked between her and Cornelia, brow wrinkling. 'Sorry if I'm interrupting. I think I'm doing a lot of that these days.'

Cornelia shook her head, smiling slightly. 'Want help?' She reached for the clear box as Diana ducked back, and it slid out of her hands. She caught it, but a tiny witchlight fell out and hit the table. It shattered.

'Shit, sorry.' Diana put the dollhouse down just as Mallory reached to scoop up the pieces. She stared at them, a distant thought coming into focus, feeling like she'd seen splinters of glass like this before, just as Diana shrieked.

Mallory's heart jumped into her throat.

'Witchlight!' Diana said. 'Diorama!'

'Please! Be more coherent than this!' Cornelia said, looking between them.

'I told you there was something I was missing. I TOLD you.' Diana pulled the diorama towards her. There was a new room above Beckett's scene, a shell of the basement.

'Kuster's locked room? Laptop, clothes... witchlight.' Diana pointed. 'The Larix basement with Ben? Bottle, plastic, broken glass. But what if it wasn't broken glass, but *shattered witchlight*?'

A shiver erupted up Mallory's arms.

'Oh my goddess,' Cornelia said.

'Vampire Cemetery has so many witchlights in it that it's basically visible from space,' Mallory said.

'I've been *asking* over and over how the killer got in. Theodore could walk through walls but he could also *travel by witchlight* and Beckett managed to too!' Diana spoke rapidly, the words practically falling out of her mouth. 'In the basement, the whole fucking thing is basically witchlights.' She pointed excitedly at Cornelia. 'Theodore and Beckett got through a witchlight together, and we just thought it was just a Samhain ghost power, but maybe folk can travel through alone. And even if they individually can't... maybe a *spell* could. The Whistler has been using witchlights! And if they didn't put a spell through, well... they could've entered and left the Larix via witchlight, and it broke behind them because it fell. That would explain how Langdon didn't see anything – the Whistler was already gone.' Diana folded her arms triumphantly.

'Hexana,' Cornelia said.

'An object almost every single person who has set foot in an Occult town would have in their home or on their person. It's been staring us in the face,' Mallory said, feeling at once relieved to have more information, and devastated it had taken them so long.

'If we assume the spell has been getting into the locked bedrooms, rather than an individual...' Diana touched the witchlights in each of the scenes and whispered a spell. A murky haze lifted from each of the lights, circling, until it landed on the victims.

'This is just a guess of how it might work, but... it's possible.'

'The Whistler has been using witchlights,' Mallory said again. 'And we can't tell anyone. There's no one left to tell.'

'Theodore saw Sully outside yesterday, didn't he? And she stared at him for a long time,' Diana said.

'Which isn't a crime. Lots of folk stare,' Mallory said fairly. 'But her dismissal of his death...' She exhaled. 'On the other side, we can't tell Van Doren either, as he's just as likely the culprit.'

'This is why power is bullshit,' Cornelia said. 'We have decent reason to suspect two of the most powerful folk in Wrackton, and if that's not totally fucked up, I don't know what is.'

Mallory jiggled her leg in frustration, an ache burning through her calf with every bounce. An uncomfortable truth had settled in. 'We believe it's seven souls for seven blades. It could be that there is a pattern – the victims so far are an Apparent and three from different Occultures, but that wasn't necessarily the Whistler's intention. We've no idea how they're choosing their victims, but we do know one thing for certain: the Whistler knows who we are. All the deaths, with the exception of Kuster, have been folk we know. Folk we love. They have three victims left. There are three of us. What if we're next?'

Cornelia and Diana's expressions fell.

'Why?' Diana frowned.

'Rule of three.' Mallory gestured weakly at them. 'Ternion, also rule of three. We don't know the specifics of what the spell requires beyond possibly needing seven souls. It's as plausible as anything. Even if it's one from each Occulture, it could be one of us. There hasn't been a witch soul yet. I don't think we're safe.'

'What do we do?' Cornelia chewed her lip, thinking. 'They – or their spells – are coming through witchlights. We can hardly just take every light out.'

'Can't we?' Diana gestured around her. 'Use regular Apparent lamps and candles for a couple of days? If the Whistler can't get in, they can't get to us.'

'We can't do that in the basement; the witchlights are built in down here,' Cornelia protested.

'Then we stay in the main house. Goddess knows there's enough rooms, Cornelia. We just stay up here tonight, get some sleep, and tomorrow we make a decision on who the Whistler is. We stop them,' Diana said.

Mallory held up a hand. 'We need to promise, right here and now. We don't leave the house without saying something. We stay where we can see and hear each other.'

Cornelia and Diana moved to gather up everything they needed. 'I'll move the murder board into the kitchen and we can just make that the new research room,' Diana said. 'We can pull out the witchlights and I'll find a lamp. We can also try locking some entryway doors and windows, which is something I notice you're particularly awful at doing, Cornelia.'

'Do I seem like someone who can find keys at a moment's notice?' Cornelia demanded.

'Promise me,' Mallory said again, the fear of anything happening to either of them too much. The beetle flashed before her eyes, guilt writhing in her stomach at how much she needed them here, with her, alive, safe, almost as big as her need to unmask the Whistler.

'Of course I'll stay here, Mallory,' Diana said seriously. 'Of course I will.'

'I would never do something so idiotic, it's not even a question.' Cornelia smiled encouragingly at Mallory. 'I'm going to sit up there and read my silly little book and mull over this case until it's solved. I swear.'

Mallory believed them both.

Mallory jolted out of sleep, her arms reaching for Theodore as he spoke to her, asked her for help, but he wasn't there. It took a while for the dream to clear. He would never be there again, and no amount of chanting his name in her head was going to fix that.

He was gone. Theodore was gone.

'I wish you'd come back,' she whispered into the dark, her heart breaking. 'I wish I could ask you for help. I wish there was a way to get you back.'

Mallory sat up.

There was a way to get him back, and she couldn't believe it had taken her this long to think of it.

She slipped out of bed and padded into the hall. There was no light on under Cornelia's door as she passed, and Diana's snores followed her down to the kitchen.

The spellbooks they'd been using for research were stacked neatly on the table, and Mallory sat in the still quiet of the night flipping through them, searching.

There it was.

The spell she'd snapped at Cornelia and Diana for joking about, the one that led her to tell Theodore there was only space for one ghost in her life. A ghost summoning spell, that might bring him back. All it asked was for her to make a sacrifice of the heart.

'Now's the time when you'd make many suggestions of what that is, only some of them useful,' Mallory mumbled to the idea of Theodore.

She thought for a second. A sacrifice of the heart was probably something meaningful to her. She was tired of losing things, but she closed her eyes and whispered under her breath, her chest catching with the exertion as a photograph appeared in her hands. It was her, Diana and Cornelia at Mallory's last birthday before she got sick. They were standing on a bench with their arms in the air, Cornelia and Diana holding her hands on either side, and they were shouting the lyrics to some song. Their faces young, happy, unaware of what was to come. It was one of her favourite memories.

Mallory pulled a grey plate from the cupboard and found some matches. She read the spell passage quietly, asking for Theodore to return at dawn, and set the photograph alight. Pain exploded up the back of her skull as she did, into her face, across her shoulders, her legs and feet and hands and torso burning, throbbing, fatigue bearing down on her like an avalanche.

The photograph curled, the flames high, green and smokeless, until there was nothing but ashes. Mallory gritted her teeth as she unlocked the basement door and sprinkled the ashes over the banister, locking the door again.

She staggered back into her room, and had just reached her bed when she heard a thump in the hall. Barely daring to breathe, she dragged herself to the door.

'Theodore?' she whispered.

Silence greeted her and she waited, disappointment setting in. It had been worth a try. She'd owed herself that, at least.

She lay down again.

TWENTY-SIX

Samhain Eve

Mallory should not have believed both her friends would stay where she'd left them.

'This is not how I envisioned spending the day we were meant to be trying to take down the Whistler,' Diana said. 'I would like to remind you that I said, "Let's wake Cornelia," and you said, "Let her sleep a bit!", and I'm not saying it's your fault we can't find her, but I am not *not* saying that.'

Despite the pain and how her body felt like it was entering rigor mortis, Mallory had been awake to watch the clock slide over to midnight, and had barely slept since. One day until Samhain. It did not feel as momentous as she'd thought it would. It was factual. It was happening. She had less than one day, and this was an unnecessary complication.

'I know, I'm sorry!' Mallory buried her face in her hands. She and Diana had got up early to work, but knocking on Cornelia's door had only elicited silence.

Mallory had thought it best to let her rest. She'd lost her boyfriend and hadn't slept in days. Mallory and Diana could come up with the plan alone, and wake her then.

It had been too many hours before they'd realised she wasn't in her room, that it was empty, sheets mussed and her coat gone. They'd searched the whole house, Mallory hoping Theodore would emerge. They called her phone over and over, and it kept ringing out. Mallory insisted they continue trying to work, but her attention kept being dragged away by Diana's dwindling patience.

'What was the point in promising not to go out if she was just going to do it anyway?' Diana snapped. 'This is just like her. The literal day we planned to confront a fucking murderer, she pulls an absolute Cornelia and does her own thing.'

'I bet there's a perfectly reasonable explanation. She slipped out the back door to get food, or something,' Mallory reasoned. 'We took all the witchlights out; the Whistler couldn't have got in here.'

Diana stomped up the stairs again swearing under her breath, as though she was hoping Cornelia had reappeared since she last looked. Mallory heard thumping as Diana ran back down.

'Hey, so, terrible news you're going to hate.'

'Excuse me?' It was a polite question that belied the fact a tendril of dread had curled through her so fast, Mallory thought she would collapse.

'Her phone was in her bed.' Diana held it up, all traces of anger gone. 'I think something's wrong.'

Time brought itself to a standstill and there was nothing Mallory could do. She couldn't move. Her hands were not hers. Everything was cold, prickly fear. Cornelia was missing.

Seven souls. Mallory swallowed.

'Shit,' Diana said, which seemed like the most appropriate response she could give in the situation.

'I'll call Felix, in case she's with them.' Mallory pressed the screen on her phone as quickly as her shaking fingers would allow.

Felix picked up immediately. 'Mallory! It's really nice to hear from you.'

'This isn't a social call, sorry. Have you seen Cornelia?' Mallory could barely contain her panic.

'I haven't,' they said. 'Why?'

'She's missing. We're just checking if she's with anyone.'

'Shit.' There was the sound of muffled talking. 'Langdon and Cloud are here too, they haven't seen her either. Is there anyone else? This is kind of all her friends accounted for.'

'There's no one, is there?' Mallory shook her head at Diana, who started pacing the room.

'No. I will look, though. Keep me posted.'

'Thanks, Felix.' Mallory hung up. 'What if she went to confront Van Doren or Sully without us?'

'She wouldn't.'

'It's *Cornelia*. Who would she go to?' Mallory pressed her palms into her eyes until yellow-blue spots exploded in her vision. 'I don't know what to do.'

'We can't panic,' Diana said sensibly.

'I am panicking,' Mallory said. 'I am panicking, very much.'

'Excuse me for one second,' Diana said, and shrieked at the top of her lungs. Mallory blanched, but regained her composure. Diana took a deep breath.

'We are no longer panicking. Come on, we're private investigators. This is our skill set. If you were Cornelia, where would you go?'

'Without my phone? Nowhere.'

'Okay if you were Cornelia, and you were thinking too hard and forgot how to perform basic functions, and also were a rude little shit who lied to your friends' faces about staying in the house... where would you go?'

Mallory pushed her chair back and stood, stretching carefully. 'Food, maybe, but it's Samhain Eve. Nowhere is open that wouldn't deliver.'

'So not that. Where else? What would Cornelia do?'

'She'd contain multitudes,' Mallory said, 'and unfortunately that makes it impossible to predict her next move.' She groaned into her hands. 'What about her notes? Did you look at her notes? Maybe she figured something out and went... somewhere.'

'I'll get her notes.' Diana summoned them, pawing through the pages. 'Last page, last thing she was working on. She's... just written "Sully" and "Van Doren" out on the page over and over.' Diana threw her hands up. 'That could honestly mean anything. She could've done anything in the night. She keeps telling us she contains multitudes!'

'In the night,' Mallory repeated, a memory floating back. A hunch forming. Hunches that had no place in scientific investigation, but that Cornelia believed in wholeheartedly.

'In the night?'

'I told her, after Beckett died, that nobody could stop her going to visit his grave at any time,' Mallory said, twisting her mouth. 'I literally. To her face. Told her to go. Anytime.'

'FuckSAKE,' Diana shrieked. 'Why wouldn't she wake one of us?'

'Diana, have you seen us lately? We don't look great. Me especially.'

'I didn't like to say. But also, offence taken, I look amazing.'

'Also,' Mallory said, ignoring her, 'we hated Beckett. She knows this. Her feelings about him are complicated. She is totally alone in her grief for him. So yes, she'd probably go alone without waking either of us.'

Mallory thought back to the noise she heard in the night and cursed herself for not going out into the hall, down the stairs.

'Without her phone?' Diana demanded.

'If I was Cornelia and I contained multitudes,' Mallory handed Diana her coat. 'I would not want anyone to bear witness in a vulnerable moment.'

Diana was already ordering a taxi, dialling a number after poking at the app for a few seconds.

'I need a taxi to Vampire Cemetery. Yes, in Wrackton. What? It's not a blast radius zone, it's just a bit of, I don't know, spectral activity— Yeah great, happy Samhain to you too.' She clenched her hand around her phone, hanging up. 'I forgot the bullshit fucking ARGGGHHH. By which I mean, there are no taxis in Wrackton today, because of the creature incident last year, until after midnight tomorrow night. We need a car. You can't walk, can you? Stupid question. Can I carry you? No, that'll be too slow. Who has a car? Why don't I have one? I can drive, for fucksake. What am I doing with my LIFE?'

Mallory pulled her own phone out, determined to retain some control over the situation, and over her agency.

'Felix, it's me again. No, we haven't found her. Listen, can the Undetectables borrow your car? We think we know where Cornelia is.'

'Hexana, it's freezing.' The cold immediately settled into Mallory's already-sore body from the brief moment it took her to get inside Felix's car. She pulled her scarf up over her nose.

'Why does Felix have to be so tall?' Diana sat as far forward as she could, her short legs still straining to reach the pedals. Soft music played over the car stereo that couldn't be turned off, and Mallory realised it was one of Ben's solos. Her heart ached.

Someone waved as they drove past, and Mallory nudged Diana to slow down. She unrolled her window as Jacob caught up to them, panting a little.

'You haven't seen Cornelia around anywhere, have you?' Diana said from her window.

'I'm sorry. Is she missing?' He frowned. 'Can I help?'

'We've got it covered, thanks, Jacob.' Mallory smiled at him.

'I won't keep you. I imagine she's struggling a bit, after losing...' He trailed off. 'I hope you find her soon. Perhaps I can send over some puzzles later, if you find her? Don't know a single person who can't be occupied by some brain-bending puzzles!' he said cheerfully.

Evidently, Jacob had never seen Cornelia throw a particularly frustrating jigsaw in the bin.

'Thanks, Jacob, don't go to any trouble,' Mallory said. 'But let us know if you see her anywhere.' She rolled the window up and they continued on.

They picked a careful path down to the Kingston crypt, Diana leading the way. The cemetery felt empty, crows cawing in the echoing silence. Mallory looked around for signs of Cornelia, her brain already trying to prepare her for finding her friend dead.

That was a sentence she would never have said two weeks ago.

Mallory hoped Cornelia was just crouched in front of where Beckett had been interred, but there was no sign of her. Wilted flowers lined the walls. The bouquets were mostly for him, Mallory realised. He was the youngest vampire to be interred in fifty years, and he would be the most remembered for years to come.

They walked up and down between ancient family crypts and ornate mausoleums, Mallory's body stiffening as wind whipped over them.

'We can't even call her,' Diana grumbled.

'I don't think she's here. She – oh.' Mallory broke off as they stumbled upon a flickering piece of crime scene tape, and realised where they were. At the far end of the cemetery, surrounded by statutes and sculptures, ornate fonts and gold-foiled arches Mallory recognised from their miniatures in Diana's diorama, they stood at the Vampire Wars memorial.

Where Beckett had been killed.

There was nothing here but candles, some still burning down in semi-liquid puddles, witchlights and a bunch of black roses. Nestled among the flowers was a card with Beckett's name on it in block capitals. Mallory lifted the card and flipped it over, revealing a ciphered, flickering note on the other side. The same flickering, moving cipher as on the letter from the Whistler.

She broke the code and it rearranged itself before her eyes, not into another note from the Whistler, but a note from Cornelia. Diana read it over her shoulder.

> *There are no words in the English language momentous enough. I miss everything about you, about us, and it is particularly painful.*
>
> *C x*

Mallory felt wrong for having read it.

'It's from Cornelia.' She replaced the card carefully.

There was something tugging at her attention. Something wrong with the code being there at all. It wasn't like Beckett was able to decipher it, and unlikely that many folk did what Mallory just had, reading cards in bouquets for the deceased. While it was possible Cornelia had wanted her words to go unread, it being the same cipher as the Whistler used was strange. There was also the fact that the words didn't sound especially Cornelia-like, but then, nobody knew how Cornelia and Beckett had communicated in private, least of all Mallory.

'Goddess.' Diana took a step back, dodging a puddle of candle wax starting to migrate towards the memorial wall. 'She's definitely not here. Why hasn't anyone invented a proper folk-finding spell?' Diana demanded.

'Because personal safety,' Mallory said, even though it hadn't warranted a genuine response. Her eyes were drawn to the puddle. 'These candles were recently lit.'

'Those have like at least ten hours of burn in them, but that's still not too long ago.' Diana crouched down. 'Someone has been here, though, there's a footprint here.'

Mallory couldn't shake the hunch. 'Just wait a minute. Just a minute. Look, Diana. Look around. That cipher card doesn't read much like Cornelia. Why was it coded? This entire time the Whistler has been playing a weird game with us. Either it's really a note from Cornelia, or...'

'Or it's a clue in itself,' Diana said thoughtfully.

'Help me look for a second. The card is about Beckett, there might be something here.'

They scoured the walls, running their hands over each memorial plaque. Mallory felt around the edges of Beckett's brand-new plaque, her fingers catching on something.

'Here, there's something here! I can't get it out.'

Diana reached into her pocket and pulled out a pair of tweezers, carefully extracting a folded piece of paper.

It too was ciphered, the letters dancing. Mallory muttered the decoding spell again, the pain intensifying in her arms.

Bravo you little cunning things
you know how the canary sings
Not just a poet that's my luck
come and seek that which I took
danger lies within our wake
the spirits dance until night breaks
cages hold and so do souls
you have until midnight tolls

'First of all, Mallory, that is the worst poem I've ever read. Like, oh my goddess, that's horrific. The Whistler needs to do a poetry class or like, read a book or something. "That which I took," just dreadful.'

'Diana.'

'I know what you're going to say, but I insist upon this. There is never going to be an appropriate time to critique a murderer's poetry skills!'

She was right, but Mallory couldn't hear it.

'"You know how the canary sings… Cages hold and so do souls… spirits dance until night breaks…"' Mallory repeated to herself. 'Diana? We need to go get ready. I know where Cornelia is. The Whistler has her. And I know who they are.'

TWENTY-SEVEN

Five hours to Samhain

'Mallory, you know this is likely a trap.'

Mallory surged ahead of Diana, hobbling down the stairs to their research room door and throwing it open. She didn't even bother taking her coat off.

'Where're our kit bags? And get us some salt, please, for the spectral disturbances. Can you draw protection sigils? There should be some in the *Witch Compendium*.'

'Of course I can, but Mallory just... slow down.'

'Van Doren has Cornelia,' Mallory said, allowing it to be true. 'He's the Whistler, Diana.'

'Are you sure?'

'I said those exact words outside the Offices when Cornelia and I went to visit him. I said the Undetectables would act as the canaries in the coalmine. He's been watching all along, listening, seeing how close we got.' She looked at her phone screen. 19:02. 'There's no time. We've five hours. Less than, now.'

Diana sighed, but gathered up the things Mallory said while Mallory gathered up her strength.

She touched her crystal necklace and could not stop the thought that if she used the spell inside it, it might be the last thing Cornelia ever did for her. The last token she had of their friendship. She tucked it inside her jumper.

Diana reappeared and tossed her a bottle of salt and some packets left over from a recent takeaway. Mallory filled test tubes with the salt and put them in her and Diana's bags, the salt packets into her jeans pockets. Salt and ghosts didn't mix, and they'd need whatever help they could get to protect themselves from the spectral disturbance in the Offices.

'Can you do a binding spell? The one Cornelia does for me,' Mallory asked.

'I can try. Hold still.' Diana muttered the spell and Mallory felt the sweet, vague relief of compression travel up her legs.

'Mallory, you're shaking. Are you okay? Let me get you some tea, something before we go so you can take your meds.'

'There's no time. We need to go now.'

'We don't know when she left here,' Diana said. 'We don't know when he took her.'

'But the Whistler probably knows we found the note, and we've got four hours and forty-three minutes left.'

She could feel wild, frenetic energy coursing through her. The answers that had evaded her for weeks were staring her in the face. Cornelia's hunch had been right.

'She was so insistent that it was Van Doren.' Mallory pulled her coat off and started sketching sigils inside with a fabric marker Diana tossed to her, her hands shaking so much she had to re-ring the circles over and over. 'And there's no way Sully would know to use the cage, the prison, as a clue. We never spoke to her about prisons, but we asked Van Doren about his plans.'

Mallory's mind raced. Pieces were slotting together to form a messy picture of what had been happening all along.

'It's been staring us in the face for weeks, I just didn't want to jump to conclusions. Cornelia was right. He hired us to muddy the waters. He could go anywhere in town and not raise suspicion because he thought he had some incompetent detectives looking in the other direction.' Mallory pulled herself to her feet.

'But Mallory...'

'It's a trap, I know. Seven souls, seven blades. Four dead, one missing... two walking into a trap. Feels like enough, doesn't it? But we have to try. What else do we need to get into the building?'

'Uh... willpower. And an energy drink of your choice.'

'Fine. Meet back here in ten. We're going to the Mayoral Offices. And we're going to get her back.'

Diana finished packing a small backpack full of objects Mallory didn't pay much attention to, but that Diana swore were essentials. Mallory got changed, swallowed her meds and took a caffeine pill, trying to steel herself. Diana wore entirely inappropriate shoes for the situation, but when asked, she said, 'I can use the heels to stab someone in the neck. I don't see what the problem is.'

Mallory could not fault her logic.

The neon sign with the Mayor's face on it flickered, the only light on in the Offices. Mallory didn't know if they'd even be able to find Cornelia in time to stop her being killed, or if she was marching the Undetectables to their collective death.

Diana flicked the hazard lights on and climbed out of the car, locking it.

'Are you leaving those on?'

'They're park-anywhere lights, so… yeah. Not like anyone is going to try move us tonight of all nights, but I'd rather us still have a getaway car. Come on.'

'Diana, I don't know if now is the best time for you to learn that they are not *actually* called "park-anywhere" lights.'

It had started to drizzle, daylight well and truly faded, and Mallory felt time and space shifting her back to the beginning, when they had stood on these steps not knowing anything of what was to come. Before Theodore.

Before Cornelia.

Wind howled through the empty square.

'Let's go.' Diana, all but dragged Mallory up the stairs. 'One at a time. We can do this. The building will likely fight us, and the spirits will be angry that we're bringing in sigils and salt. But if we move slowly, carefully, and deliberately at all times, we will maybe certainly be okay. And failing that, we run like hell.'

'Are you sure?' For one brief moment Mallory felt as though she couldn't go on.

'Well I believe in myself a lot. I've been blessed by the goddesses with good self-esteem. And I believe in you, too, so yes. I'm sure.' Diana looked up at Mallory's face, the neon glow lighting her eyes. They were as wild and frightened as Mallory's must be.

Together, they pushed the wooden front doors open.

Nothing happened for a moment. Wind picked up from the square and hit Mallory in the chest. They staggered back and grunted, then forged forward, trying to enter the building. Mallory could feel something pressing at her sides, her mind, her eyes, and she whispered spells of protection to herself, asking the Ternion to shield her. The spells sapped strength from her limbs immediately, strength she didn't have to give. Diana grabbed her hand and they stepped through into the darkened reception area of the Mayoral Offices for the last time.

It was dark inside, devoid of the bustle Mallory had seen the last few times they'd been in.

The halls were cavernous, echoing, marble bouncing their footsteps back at them, Diana's loud and striking, Mallory's soft and meek and apologetic, as they moved towards the corridor containing Van Doren's office.

'We can't be fully sure this is it. That this is where he's got her.'

'But we're as sure as we can be. The poem may be bad, but it's telling us she's here.'

'Seeing as we are possibly walking to our death, is there anything you want to get off your chest?' Diana asked.

Mallory hesitated, something she'd been fighting against saying out loud rising to the surface of her tongue like she couldn't hold it down anymore. She had just decided to say it when Diana held up a hand.

'Actually I retract that statement. It's probably better if you tell *her* what I think you're going to say, when we find her. Cause we will find her. You don't need to tell me, because I already know. I know everything. This is, like, my top skill. But not now.' Diana grinned at her, and pulled her phone out of her pocket.

'Just in case there's significant disruption further in and my phone doesn't work, someone should know where we are.' She texted Felix, presumably letting them know they were marching to aforementioned possible doom. Her phone buzzed immediately, but Diana ignored the call, sending Felix a string of hearts before turning it on silent.

'If we survive this, they'll forgive us.'

They stepped forward in unison and Mallory placed her hand on the door of Van Doren's office. She turned the handle and Mallory took in a sharp breath.

TWENTY-EIGHT

Four hours and two minutes to Samhain

Vincent Van Doren had had a short life, all things considered. He was around sixty, claimed to be around forty, and looked about fifty. He was angry and short-tempered and blustering. He was impulsive and unconventional. He insisted upon there being neon signs of his face all over town. He threw parties and mismanaged money and wrangled more from other places, somehow, always wheedling something out of someone. He fought every rule the UML created, and was nothing like his mother or his mother's father, who had been Night Mayors before him. He had too many important contacts and too many opinions. He sought out too many favours and was too well known for his ability to hold a grudge. He barely had respect from his contemporaries, and had convinced them to give him chance after chance after chance. He had made mistakes. He had tried to change. He had stopped hiding his private life by bringing Hayley out in public. He had underestimated the sheer scale of the problem Occulture were facing, and that was the tip of the iceberg in terms of underestimations. He was a wholly unsuitable candidate for Night Mayor, all things considered.

But, as it turned out, he was not a serial killer.

Diana's heels clicked as they approached the grey rug.

A sheet had been thrown over Van Doren's desk, hiding it from view, but there was someone sitting in the chair, shrouded and unmoving. Mallory did not have to ask Diana to hand her a pair of gloves. Diana snapped a photo of the room and the desk before Mallory took a deep breath and peeled the sheet back.

Van Doren looked peaceful now, or as peaceful as someone could be with their heart carved out and set on the desk in front of them. There was a black-handled knife inserted into his vena cava like it was some sort of delicacy waiting to be served, an oily sheen to the blade that was mostly hidden by a dried coating of blood. Some had trickled off the edge of the wood and stained the floor a dark, rusty brown. His eyes were closed, his face relaxed, and Mallory sensed that he did not know he was dead. It was a blessing. Perhaps Elisabella was watching over him. His killer had left him with his shirt unbuttoned, his vest slashed open, his black tie askew, his hair tousled. The Ternion symbol stretched across his chest, but Van Doren wasn't bloodlessly marked like the other victims; vivid, scarlet, scabbing slashes had torn through his skin. He still could've been sleeping, if sleeping was an activity so disturbingly gruesome that it would stick with whoever stumbled upon him forever.

'Someone did this with a real knife, I think.' Mallory crept closer. 'There's actual blood, and hesitation marks – some of those cuts are deeper than others.'

'Now what?' Diana whispered, turning her head away.

They had seen so many bodies since the case began, but this felt different. This was a king sitting at his throne, slain where he ruled, and it felt like they were encroaching on what should've been a restful place.

'His planner is here, look. Observation of Newly Interred Ashes, 4 p.m.' Diana leaned closer, and then snorted. 'He's written, "Beckington?" beside it.'

This guy had never been capable of being the Whistler.

Mallory felt sick. She had been so sure it was Van Doren. They were still in the Whistler's game. And if it wasn't him and it wasn't Sully, they were back to square one, only now Cornelia was missing and the clock was ticking down until three vengeful goddesses were summoned.

'Should we cover him up again?'

Diana helped her shake out the blanket, leaving him to his eternal slumber.

'There's no blood anywhere else, only here at the desk,' Mallory noted. 'No mess. There's no trail.'

Diana combed the carpet and the floor with a sharp eye, looking for anything that would tell them where they should look next.

The building rumbled and shuddered. Mallory closed her eyes as the grey walls seemed to ripple.

'Okay, so, we were wrong. Think, think, think, think.' Mallory tapped her forehead, flipping through the planner again. 'The whole thing has been a game. It's hard not to think this ending was inevitable, on the face of it. A cipher leading us here to Van Doren's body. It's just one big puzzle.'

Mallory closed her eyes. She looked down in front of her.

A name, written on the planner. An instruction, reminding Van Doren to remind someone to do something for him. To help.

Puzzle.

Several memories shot into her mind at once, like the word had been a key. 'Who has said something about puzzles to us recently?'

Diana's mouth opened. Mallory's legs shook and her stomach cramped painfully, nausea threatening to overtake her completely. She swallowed.

'Who has had every single opportunity Van Doren has had? Who has tried to be nothing but completely and utterly helpful the entire time? Who *came to get us* to bring us here, to start this whole thing off?'

'Who is going to let me answer a single question, because it's not you!' Diana shrieked. 'Mallory, it can't be. It can't be—'

'Cast a screening spell against him, please, so he can't hear us. Now.'

Diana did, squeezing her eyes shut. Mallory felt something soft yet invisible touch her skin, like she and Diana were covered in a blanket, a thin shield against anyone trying to listen in.

'We can't say his name,' Diana said. 'And as long as we don't, he won't be able to hear us until or unless I lift the spell. Maybe that'll give us enough time to think.'

It felt like scant protection in the Offices.

'We don't know what he's got working for him here tonight. Maybe he's got a bunch of spirits on his side, or something else in the building. He could have control over the Ternion for all we know.'

'And we're just two girls with a glorified blanket spell and a dream,' Diana said. 'Are you sure it's him?'

Mallory shook her head, another thought occurring to her. 'Of course I'm not sure. But think about the spell. The whistle. What if it wasn't whistling, per se, but *a whistle*, like an instrument? When we heard it, when Theodore...' Her throat constricted and she swallowed. 'When Theodore died, I heard cadence to it. I couldn't hear it at the time, but I think they were *notes*. It wasn't just one continuous sound.'

Diana's eyes deadened. 'And what if we knew someone who was a musician, but specifically a musician in an orchestra. Who told us this, over and over. I'm not asking it as a question, because I hate the concept of rhetorical questions.'

'Cornelia figured it out when she repurposed the binding spell for my legs,' Mallory said, her nails digging into the palms of her hands, frustration and exhaustion washing over her. 'Ages ago. That the whistling was magic, but magic twisted into a new purpose and not an existing spell. It comes back to what Theodore always said: magic is only as effective as the knowledge you have. If he knew music, if he knew how to manipulate it...' She looked around. 'Where is he?'

'Is he even still here?' Diana sank to the ground, her eyes flicking back over the sheet, over Van Doren, who was not getting any less dead as the seconds passed.

'Yes,' Mallory said. 'Yes. If the bad poem told us anything, it's that he's here, and so is Cornelia. The Whistler wanted us to come here, but I think he would make it a game. It won't be as straightforward as keeping her in an office or a meeting room. If she's still alive – and she is, I know she is.' Mallory's tone challenged Diana to disagree. 'I think our magic has been linked for so long that we'd feel it if she was gone. But if she's still alive, it'll be a puzzle that leads us to her.'

'And we were meant to find Van Doren here. If there are more clues, then maybe this is the room we'll find them in.' Diana pulled herself to her feet.

They looked around, Cornelia's name thumping around Mallory's chest like a drumbeat. Her brain had frozen over, and it would only whisper how worthless she truly was. How undeserving of her friends she was. How this, all of this, was her fault.

She shoved it down.

Cornelia needed her. She was not losing another friend to the Whistler. There were many things Mallory could not do, would perhaps never be able to do again, but there was a part of her that would always, always, take over and do the right thing when it came to forensics. She had practised her whole life for this moment, and stepping up was barely a conscious choice.

'Quick as you can. Crime scene procedure.' Mallory snapped on her gloves. They took a side each and carefully lifted objects, moving quickly but methodically around the room until they got back to the desk. The minutes ticked by in agonising self-awareness as they tapped the walls and pried up the edge of the rug, looking for a trapdoor, a trick door, anything. Mallory whispered revealing spells as she went along, focusing her attention on what kinds of magic could possibly exist in the Night Mayor's office, ignoring how it made her body ache more, how it demanded she sit down. There was no time. She was adrenaline and pain and fury and determination, and she was almost proud of herself.

She gave Van Doren's body a wide berth. Every time she looked at him, she remembered that Cornelia was in the hands of the person who had done *that*.

'Ah-ha.' Diana opened a cupboard at the back of the room.

'If you make a closet joke, Diana, I swear on Hexana—' Mallory swung around.

Diana smirked. 'If I'd known that Cornelia in peril was going to make you express your indignation I would've tried this years ago.'

Mallory shot her a withering look, feeling a jolt of freedom as she did. Diana liked her. She liked Mallory in all forms of Mallory, and there wasn't any time to feel it.

'What about the cupboard?'

'If you were someone who wanted to make a game out of serial killing, would you go for a trapdoor, or would you' – Diana tapped the back wall – 'go for the false back? This has a false back in it. You know, I literally spent years as a little kid knocking on panels and the backs of wardrobes, hoping for a secret passageway?'

'Push it open.'

Diana's nails scrabbled along the wall and she found a pressure point. The back of the cupboard clicked open slowly.

'Ah-ha,' Diana said again, and Mallory wished that she would not make a habit of exclamatory discoveries.

The panel swung back fully and a corridor came into view.

'Good work!' Mallory whispered. They had been talking quietly since they'd got into the building, but now Mallory was on high alert.

'Are we sure about this?' Diana peered into the corridor. It was too dark to see anything. 'What if this is a maze?'

'I think this is it. We've only a few hours to go, we can't waste time second-guessing ourselves.' Mallory's body shook from exertion. She regretted ever wanting to solve a murder, but she was determined to see this through to the end.

'This is the grand finale the Whistler has wanted all along, isn't it? A showdown,' Diana said, something Mallory had thought over and over and over on the drive here, when they walked into this office thinking it was Van Doren, and right now as she stared into the corridor.

Mallory's stomach twisted, the dawning clarity of who the Whistler was a knife of shame and guilt. She adjusted her bag. 'No matter what, we're walking into something unknown.'

Diana nodded, the answer hitting her as hard as it had Mallory. 'Then let's keep going.'

Mallory checked her phone. It was 21:14. She looked at Diana, who reached over and took her hand.

'I love you. I'm proud of you. I'm proud of *us*.' She squeezed Mallory's hand lightly, her navy-blue nail polish stark against Mallory's pale pink. 'And no matter what happens, we tried our best.'

'That's my line. I'm meant to give the speech.'

Diana laughed. 'Sometimes the nicest people in the world need someone else to do the speech for them. I know what you'd say to me, so I'm saying it back to you, in case you need to hear it.'

Mallory could've cried.

'Promise me something,' Diana said.

'Is it a quick promise?'

'Mallory.'

'Anything.'

'If we survive this, can you stop trying to swallow yourself?'

Mallory looked at her in surprise. Diana rolled her eyes.

'You think we didn't both see this happening? You cannot make yourself small to make other people happy, Mallory. I've seen you swallow rage and anger and frustration and sadness, and I for one am sick of it. You went from someone very smart and very driven to someone who second-guessed every single thing that came out of your mouth for reasons that were not your fault. You're so focused on being *reasonable* you've forgotten kind honesty is the best thing you can do for someone. Even if it hurts.'

Mallory swallowed. Her unfamiliar pride mixed with Diana's words had unlocked something inside of her, but she didn't have time to explore it. 'I'll try. Promise.'

'I'll go first.' Diana climbed through the cupboard without a backward glance. Her heels clicked on what sounded like tile as she righted herself and felt along the walls, mumbling revealing spells.

Mallory scurried back to check one more time that the office door was unlocked. She wanted to give them every chance to escape the inner depths of the Offices, if needs be. They couldn't know what, if anything, they would be escaping from. The Whistler and the Ternion, or spirits, or both. And that's if they got out alive. The veil was thinnest, the Mayoral Offices had their own defences, and nothing liked to be disturbed. She hesitated, wrapped her fingers around a salt packet in her pocket, then stepped through after Diana.

TWENTY-NINE

Three hours and thirty-seven minutes to Samhain

The false back swung shut, sealing them into the corridor. Mallory checked anxiously to see if she could still open it. A hidden notch responded to her touch and the hatch sprang open again for a second, giving Mallory a flash of Van Doren's office, before slamming closed.

Satisfied they had an escape route, she straightened up to find herself in a perfect replica of the main lobby of the Offices, with a few unsubtle differences. The first was that instead of the hideous blue mosaic tiling, this floor was tiled green and had an unnatural glow about it. The second was that rather than the witchlight sconces lining the walls and ceiling in the Offices' main lobby, this replica was lit by torches in strategically placed holders.

The final difference emerged slowly from what would've been the corridor to Van Doren's office, forelegs clattering on the tiles, lumbering movements swishing its body side to side. Its antennae twitched and it paused for a moment.

It being a giant, armoured mantis.

'I know I brought stab shoes for this exact sort of situation, but I really, really was hoping I wouldn't have to use them.' Diana crouched, as though that would hide her from its view.

The mantis hissed. Giant mantises were not unheard of, and they often hissed. What made this particular mantis interesting was that it was not the size of a regular giant mantis, but taller and longer than Mallory. It had glowing red eyes, black scales, and did not much behave like a mantis at all. Its head turned towards them with interest, eyes flashing.

'Here be dragons,' Diana whispered.

Mallory did not dignify this with a reply.

'Okay. Okay. Hold on, I'm thinking.'

The only things she could think of were basic spells, spells she'd long since allowed herself to forget because they were no longer accessible to her. Mallory whispered the simplest life detection spell she knew, and a doorway at the end of the hall lit up with a subtle glow. She had to believe it was Cornelia.

The mantis hissed again, one armoured leg clacking against the tile, then another, and another, as it inched forward, closing the space between them.

'She's here.' Mallory gestured to the door, which was unnecessary, given the circumstances. 'We're going to get her, and this is going to be okay.'

Cages hold and so do souls.

'And I know exactly *what* she's in,' Mallory said, the pieces continuing to fall into place. 'She's been talking about it all week. The Empathy Cage. It's the only explanation for why she hasn't blasted her way out of here by herself already. The Whistler even mentioned it being here, decommissioned in the bowels of the

Mayoral Offices, and if this doesn't count as the "bowels"...' She gestured uncertainly.

'Then call me IBS, because I am having trouble digesting all of this information, Mallory.' Diana's eyes hadn't left the mantis. 'What do we do?'

'You distract, I'll run.' In truth, Mallory did not want to be either the one trying to run past the mantis or the one fighting it off, because its spines looked razor-sharp, its armour tough and its entire posture suggested it was very, very pissed off.

'Fine.' Diana clicked her heels together and knives slid out of the toes.

Mallory stared, only breaking the stare to check if the mantis was coming closer. It had settled in the middle of the corridor, putting itself directly between them and Cornelia, so she returned to staring at the knife-shoes.

'I told you these shoes would be useful for hitting an assailant. Ready?'

Mallory was not ready, but she did her best to be.

'When I say, go.'

Mallory tensed to run, her body hurting, but adrenaline dulling it to a point of being bearable.

'*Fue-GO*,' Diana shouted. Mallory propelled herself along the corridor, her muscles already screaming at her, the fire Diana had summoned a burning inferno that rose above them, roiling along the ceiling. It burned and burned, ready to drop on the mantis which had started skittering down the corridor towards Mallory, claws clacking and terrible armour bouncing off the floor as it jumped towards the fire and was instantly consumed in flames. Mallory's shoulder slammed into the wall and she cried out, knowing it would bruise and ache for weeks, but continued on, skirting around the flaming mantis and running for the door which would not open when she tried the handle. Instead, a small bowl slid out next to it, and Mallory knew what it wanted. Some kind of sacrifice.

Everything about the sacrifice bowl was already such a cliché that she wished Cornelia was there to be scathing about it and point out the injustices of vampire treatment versus semi-sentient buildings asking for blood.

'Diana!'

Diana had a knife-shoe held to the mantis's head as it thrashed and writhed beneath the stream of flames she'd summoned, a burning rope of enchanted fire that wrapped around the mantis's limbs and held it down. Sparks flicked harmlessly against Diana's skin as the oxygen was slowly sucked out of the hallway.

'I can't get in!' Mallory shouted.

'If you hadn't noticed, I'm kind of busy!'

Mallory's heart pounded. Her head pounded. Her skin pulsated with the effort of standing. This was not the time for her body to crash. She couldn't afford a blood sacrifice; it would tip her over the edge.

Mallory reached into her pocket and pulled out her lock picks.

A thing that is important to note about lock-picking is that it is a highly practised skill, especially when trying to do it in a life-or-death situation. It was one Mallory had thankfully mastered. She inserted the anchor piece into the lock with shaking fingers, pulling down when she felt tension in the pins. She wiggled the second pick in, pulling the anchor around, hoping against hope that this would work, every passing second a jackhammering beat of her heart. Diana and the mantis skated up and down the hall, always too close. Mallory was sure the picks would break and jam the mechanism when the lock clicked open.

'Diana!' Mallory shouted again, but Diana waved her on.

'I'll stay here, keep watch!' Her face contorted in a mixture of terror and grim determination. Mallory thought Diana was enjoying fighting the mantis a little too much.

She emerged into another corridor, this one the same as the last, minus the angry mantis and determined woman.

Light flared again, and she saw a form at the end of the hallway, huddled with their face pressed into their knees. They were wearing a coat, and they had short hair.

'Cornelia! Hey, it's me!' She jogged towards the figure. They unfurled and Mallory came to a staggering stop, her shoes sliding on the tiles.

The figure lifted their head and a burst of static stuttered around them.

'Oh, goddess,' Mallory whispered, a sickening tremor shuddering down her back. They were too late. They were too late. *They were too late.*

THIRTY

Three hours and twenty minutes to Samhain

She crept closer as the figure moved into the light. They'd failed her.

The ghost stood and Mallory saw their face.

It was not Cornelia.

'I'm so sorry. I thought you were my friend.' Mallory moved closer, her hands up, trying to soothe the flickering form as she approached. Her heart hammered hard as she came face to face with a girl around Cornelia's height, with shorn hair and a mournful expression.

'Are you okay?' Mallory felt the pulse of a ghost trying to reach into her head and she shrank back. With one hand still raised, she deftly opened and emptied a salt packet into her jeans pocket. She'd never needed salt around Theodore. 'Please don't do that, I'm trying to help.'

The ghost pulled back, static spluttering.

'Are you real?' she asked, her hands reaching for Mallory.

'I think so. Hard to know in here, but yes.'

'I was real once. I was able to leave here before. Please don't leave me here. DON'T LEAVE ME!' she screamed, the force of it pressing against Mallory's skin and Mallory fought the urge to back against the wall.

'I have to find my friend.'

The ghost screamed again.

'I have to find my friend, but I can stay for a moment. What happened to you?'

'I was real. I was real! I was real!' She flickered in and out of Mallory's eyeline. Mallory hoped the tiny salt packet was enough to protect her.

'What's your name?'

'Katherine.'

'How did you get here, Katherine?'

Katherine's face sagged.

'I don't remember. I was real, and then I was elsewhere. And one day I was here in this corridor. This shameful hallway will not let me go. When the wind blows, the cradle rocks.' She drooped further, her arms at awkward, unnatural angles from her shoulders. 'I have not been real in a very long time.'

'How old are you?' Mallory asked.

'Older than time. Older than the earth beneath this sullied room, this hallowed eve, this life, all lives. I am old, I am old, I am old.'

Katherine's voice dropped in volume, but still she flickered.

Mallory closed her eyes for a moment and whispered the life detection spell again. The doorway behind Katherine lit up, more brightly this time. Cornelia was still here, she was sure of it. Still alive.

'Do you remember how old you were when you died?'

'No. He said he'd help me remember.'

'Who is he?'

'The man.'

For a moment Mallory thought she meant him. The Whistler. 'What man, Katherine?'

Katherine took a deep, shuddering breath. 'The man who is a cat.'

It took a split second for Mallory to register what she'd said. 'Theodore. Theodore was here? When?'

'I DON'T KNOW!' Katherine screamed. 'I don't remember!'

'It's okay. It's okay! Theodore was here. Theodore... Theodore is gone, now. But if he wanted to help you, and couldn't, I can try.' Mallory's brain reeled.

Theodore had told her he wasn't allowed to speak to another ghost. Had never been allowed to. Not without permission. If he'd spoken to Katherine, he would've said, she was sure of it, though Katherine seemed so certain she knew him.

'He said he wouldn't leave,' Katherine whispered. 'He promised.'

This stung Mallory deeper than she'd care to admit. He hadn't come back. She hadn't wanted him to leave.

'Can you remember what Theodore said to you?'

'He said he wouldn't leave. He said he'd help me.'

'When did he say it?'

'I don't know. Forever. A long time ago. He was not a cat first, and then he was.'

She heard Theodore's voice in her head then, clear as if he was right in front of her. *Forever is a long time, Mallory.*

Mallory knew she didn't have time to process this information. Katherine had met Theodore before he'd died. For at least six years, Theodore had known there was a ghost, possibly a Samhain ghost, in the halls of the Offices, and said nothing. And he had spoken to her since his first death.

Her brain twisted around itself trying to make sense of it, seeing a possible context for his first murder for the first time ever but unable to examine it.

'He left me. He left me behind, after he promised.'

Mallory snapped back to the room.

'He didn't leave, Katherine. He was taken.'

'Taken by who?'

'Someone else. Someone who has my friend.'

Katherine looked at her, her eyes glassy.

'You mean the person in the bad cage. He took her. The *other* man.'

Cages hold and so do souls.

'I need to get to her. And if you let me go, I promise I will work to figure out why you're here.' This was a very big promise, but Theodore had been trying to do something for Katherine. If he wasn't here to help any more, someone needed to finish his work.

'Please come back. Please come back, witch girl.' Katherine reached out and stroked a finger down Mallory's face. Mallory shuddered, but did not divert her gaze from Katherine's.

'I will. Would you mind moving? I think she's in here.'

Katherine drifted down the hall, curling into a ball again. Confident that she wasn't going to get in her way, Mallory moved towards the doorway cautiously, her fingers still gripped tightly around the lock picks. This one was not locked, so she slid them into her pocket. The room was brightly lit inside, the same eerie green flooring almost an illusion underfoot. The door slammed shut behind her and she heard a click. She lifted her foot to take a step forward, and paused, wobbling on already weakened legs.

The ground moved.

Teemed with bugs.

Beetles.

There were hundreds of them, and they duplicated themselves over and over, more springing up in terrible clusters. Mallory recognised the genus immediately: they looked just like Cornelia's sound beetles.

Worse. They *were* Cornelia's sound beetle.

The one she'd squished – the queen.

Hundreds, maybe thousands of duplicating beetles ran up walls and were magically squished over and over. Squished beetles climbed up Mallory's legs and spawned more beetles, covering her in crawling, skittering, angry little creatures. Her skin crawled and her hands shook as she tried to push them off her, magic failing her, unable to see because the floor was alive with the ghost of her biggest guilt and she had to feel glad that she had never murdered anyone because there would be bodies everywhere and she could not handle this, not even for a second.

She was trapped in this horror that repeated itself on a loop, more beetles, more beetles, grow squish dead grow squish dead.

This was how she would to die. Mere hours until Samhain. Mere hours to save Cornelia. Mallory would to die in this room with these beetles, under the weight of her guilt.

She wished she had told Cornelia the truth, days before, minutes before she went missing.

Tiny arms crawled across her skin and inside her clothes, and she felt hopeless.

There was nothing for it but to let herself sink down, down, into this death that would come. It would be painless. She would simply fold under their weight. Maybe even sleep, choke, die. That would be a relief.

Just as she was about to succumb and slide down into the tsunami of arthropods, she saw it ahead of her, almost hidden in the fabric of the hallway.

A heavy stone door slotted into the wall. In that room, Mallory knew, deep in her heart, would be an Empathy Cage. And inside the cage, Cornelia.

Pulling herself to her senses, Mallory refused to let terror take over and she swam to the top of the beetle pile. They continued to grow, squish, die as she rested on top of them, and somehow this renewed focus made them forget about her, continuing their short, sad, life cycle just long enough that Mallory shoved herself toward the door, vague triumph invisible among the terror that shook through her, not quite in her own body, her arms and legs moving independently of her thoughts.

The lights went out and Mallory screamed, stifling the noise with her hands in case several mutant beetles decided to take a trip inside her mouth, but she kept pushing, one hand reaching for the wall, realising it was, literally, fabric. It rippled underneath her fingers and fell, the outline of the doorway distinct as she waded knee-deep through beetles, lips clamped shut and afraid.

She reached the door, feeling for a catch, a lock, but there wasn't one she could sense. Mallory pushed away handfuls of beetles and pressed both hands on the door. It started to swing towards her, sweeping against the tide of dead insects, and Mallory pulled it just wide enough to climb inside.

She felt a tickle in her arms, spreading up into her chest as she scrambled into the room, dragging herself on her hands and knees. The stone door slammed shut behind her, a smattering of beetles still climbing over her legs, which had started to burn.

There was no cage she could see.

There was a sense she'd lost something small, mired in the pain and fatigue and desire to lie on her face for a week, but she didn't take the time to investigate it, distracted as she was by a voice that said, 'Please tell me you're joking.'

THIRTY-ONE

Two hours and fifty-seven minutes to Samhain

'Cornelia?'

It was so dark, Mallory could barely see her lying on the stone floor. Witchlights were embedded high up in the arching roof. She did not know why she'd been expecting a literal cage; it was a prison cell, covered over with silver mesh. She scrambled forward the final few feet until Cornelia was in front of her, her face unclear but there.

'Are you really here?' Cornelia touched her leg to check she was real, then pulled her into a hug. 'You came for me. You absolute idiot. Or idiots, plural.' Cornelia dipped her head into Mallory's shoulder and held her there.

'In defence of Diana's honour, I insisted. She's outside fighting off a giant mantis with one of her shoes and a handful of fire spells. I had no choice but to carry on alone,' Mallory said, but some of it was muffled in Cornelia's hair. She could smell her, through the layers of dust and fury coating her since she had gone missing, and Mallory's stomach flipped in a way that wasn't entirely unpleasant.

'You shouldn't have come. You're stuck in here now with no magic. I know you didn't have much to use before, but it's gone.'

That explained the sense of loss, and the burning in her legs. The binding spell Diana cast had been stripped from her, and the screening spell with it.

Mallory pulled out of the hug. She was not ready to, but it felt like the right thing to do. Instead, she scooted her body close to Cornelia, their legs almost touching, feeling her warmth. Feeling glad she was alive. But she did not touch her. She did not breathe in her scent again. She could not. Beckett was not even dead a week. Cornelia would not, could not, *should not* like the way Mallory was thinking and Mallory didn't like it herself. She could think of nothing else. Her eyes were unfocused, even by in-the-dark standards, and she fought to stop her heart from hammering in her chest.

'Not having magic doesn't bother me, I barely felt it,' Mallory said.

'It was like having my lungs cut out,' Cornelia groaned. 'Still feels like it.'

Mallory tried the door experimentally. Nothing happened, which was expected. She wasn't strong enough to force the door, and she knew Cornelia had to have tried hundreds of times in hundreds of ways.

'Shit,' Mallory said.

'I tried that,' Cornelia said, lying down again with her arms behind her head. 'Used even more severe words. Called it a fucking arsebadger at one point. Door was having none of it. Didn't make me feel better, either.'

'But Diana—'

'Is the most capable person I know.' Cornelia's voice had softened a little. 'And she'll be okay.'

'I agree. She's wonderful.'

'That she is. So she'll fight whoever is out there.' Cornelia rolled herself up into a sitting position and scooted over beside Mallory. Their legs touched at the ankle.

'Do you know who the Whistler is?' Mallory asked after a minute.

Cornelia made a small *hmm*ing noise at the back of her throat.

'Whenever I say his name he comes in here, and he's so fucking ANNOYING,' she shouted, 'that nobody wants that.'

'Diana cast a screening spell so we could strategise. We couldn't say his name either,' Mallory said, the thought of facing him down now that they knew what he'd done causing every muscle in her body to tense in terror.

Cornelia settled back on her forearms.

'So, confession. I promised you I would stay in the house. I lied. It got dark.' She paused. 'I missed Beckett. We were going to break up, we weren't good together, I know all of this, but I feel... I feel bad, Mal. It was the middle of the night, I'd been working on a hunch – you know my hunches.'

'I know them well,' Mallory said fondly.

'"Why didn't you wake us," I hear you ask? Well. This is where I broke the promise. I looked in on Diana and she was curled in this tiny ball, her hand was still clamped on a book she had been reading and I couldn't wake her. I wasn't even going to try to wake you,' Cornelia said pointedly. 'And alone in my pointless panic, I thought... I can risk going to see Beckett. I'll be back before anyone knows. I thought – erroneously, it must be said – that if the Whistler had struck at the cemetery once…'

'Why would he return to the scene of the crime?'

'Bingo, baby.'

Mallory blushed in the dark.

'I didn't see it coming. I was standing outside the mausoleum, trying to work up the courage to go in, and then I just… wasn't any more. I was here.'

They sat in silence for a few moments. Mallory listened to the clicking of hundreds or thousands of beetles climbing over each other outside the cage.

'You know what we could try, though?'

Mallory's mind skipped through a string of unrealistic scenarios that she tried to stop at hand-holding, but carried on to mouths touching. Cornelia was her friend and she was ruining it with every stupid, impossible, pointless, yearning thought, thoughts that had no sense of appropriate timing.

'What?'

'You know what. The only thing that's going to get us out of here. Besides, I am extremely thirsty and I have had no choice but to sleep in the clothes I came here in, and you know how I feel about that. I think this is a trap. I think we're going to die.'

'If I ask what, it's because I don't know what you mean.' Mallory tried to pick Cornelia's eyes out of the rufescent gloom, but couldn't be sure she was staring into the right part of her face. Cornelia laid her hand carefully down beside Mallory's, leaving just enough distance that she knew it was there, but just far enough away that it could've been accidental.

'Who are you and what have you done with Mallory?'
Cornelia laughed. 'Okay. There are three of us. Three victims
left. The only option, the only one I can see, is that you kill
me. Without a third victim, the Ternion can't be summoned
before the deadline. Save yourself. Save Diana. You get out of
here alive.'

'Cornelia.' Mallory leaned towards her. 'You contain multitudes.
Are you telling me that of all the multitudes in all of the world,
this is your solution? Zero out of ten.'

She said the words lightly, but she was shaking. Had she not
got here, had they not come to rescue her...

'I knew it would be a big ask. But it's the only way.'

Mallory shook her head.

'Aside from the fact that I can't, it's not. Van Doren is dead,
Cornelia. He's in his office. He's got the carvings. Killing you
won't stop this. We find a different way out.'

'Fucking *Hexana*, can I not have *any* fun these days?
That's... actually a bit upsetting. I hated him, but... damn.'
She slapped a palm on the floor. 'I like that you clearly thought
the two of us in here would figure something out, but no. The
only way out of the cage is to unlock it, and for that you need
the key, picks won't work.'

Mallory exhaled.

'I didn't think I'd actually be in here with you. I thought I'd
be breaking you out from the outside, somehow.'

'Mallory. I've been so ridiculous. I put us in danger. *I* put us
here. I made you come here. You came for nothing. If I'm dead,
Diana can escape, and he won't be able to use you. You're clever.
You'll get out. This is an inevitability.'

The idea of Cornelia trying to sacrifice herself, trying to make Mallory complicit, all to stop the Whistler, made Mallory want to be sick.

'I can't.' She touched her fingertips to Cornelia's. Allowed herself the barest of touches. A pit of desire grew in her stomach, hot and angry and confusing. Her skin burned and she forced herself not to think about taking Cornelia's fingers in her own, no matter how natural the gesture felt as though it might be. She swallowed. Cornelia did not move.

'There's no guarantee it'll even stop him if we do it.'

'But isn't it better than waiting to find out?'

It sounded ludicrous coming out of her mouth, but Mallory knew Cornelia was being serious and it scared her.

'You could live. You could publish research. Diana could take over the world. She's going to anyway, this would just accelerate that.'

'But we'd lose *you*. I'd lose you,' Mallory said. There was more she wanted to say, so much more, but she wasn't able to verbalise it and it was killing her.

'And I you.'

Mallory wanted to scream. She wanted to let it all go, let it come bubbling to the surface and let weeks, months, years of pent-up rage leave her body in one exhausted rant. She wanted to tell Cornelia why she was stupid, selfish, silly to think this was an answer. That losing her was going to bring them anything but more grief, more pain, pain they couldn't come back from, because their lives would be shaped by the loss of Cornelia. Every second Mallory spent too long in bed, every time she stopped trying, had to stop because of the pain, didn't start a degree, didn't finish something, she would be guilty of wasting the life Cornelia gave for her.

She wouldn't do that.

Instead, she forced herself to talk about something else equally difficult.

'Hey?'

'Yeah?'

'I did it.'

'Did what?'

'I killed Selene. The beetle queen. When you and Diana had that fight over Beckett. I got up in the night, and… I killed her.'

Cornelia was silent for one long, ever-stretching beat.

'I know.'

'I'm really sorry…' Mallory started, before her brain caught up to what Cornelia had actually said. 'Wait. What?'

'It didn't make any sense, at first, though I thought it must have been you. Because you're *you*. But maybe I don't see you the way you see you?'

It was the most shrewd Cornelia had ever been about Mallory.

'And even if I did see you the way you saw you,' she continued, 'it probably wouldn't be the truth. It probably wouldn't be real.'

'Maybe,' Mallory said. 'How did you know?'

Cornelia laughed.

'Every time the beetles were mentioned in front of you, you looked more haunted than Theodore. Shit, sorry,' Cornelia said quickly, 'I didn't mean to bring him up.'

'Why didn't you say anything?'

Mallory felt all the guilt, the shame, evaporate, rising up into the vaulted ceiling of the prison.

'I won't lie, I was mad at you. I understood exactly why you did it. I even understood why you felt bad. I was just mad that you thought I didn't love you enough to forgive you.'

Mallory's heart jolted.

'I…'

'You're going to dispute it, so don't. I've known you since we were small and idiotic. You've changed in lots of ways, but you're still you.' Cornelia tipped her gently on the hand.

'I…'

'Please stop trying to interrupt me during vulnerability hour,' Cornelia said. 'I know Diana and I fucked up. We didn't invite you places. Didn't give you a chance to say no. We thought we were being kind, not asking you to get yourself to London to see Crown and Hemlock that time, but we weren't. We took your choice, your agency away.' Cornelia shook her head, a blurred shape in the darkness. 'That's unforgivable. And in contrast, the worst thing you did in retaliation was kill a beetle. A beetle I loved, but that's all you did. And I don't know for sure, but whatever the fuck is going on with these beetles tells me that you've carried the guilt since you did it. Enough,' Cornelia said firmly. 'Enough, now.'

'Cornelia…'

'I know, I'm wonderful. You deserve my friendship, but I am awesome.'

'Let me finish a fucking sentence!' Mallory said forcefully.

Cornelia laughed, loud, hearty. Alive.

'I got us into this mess,' Mallory said.

'No, I did.'

'No. I made us take the case. Now we are here, facing death,' Mallory said firmly. 'My fault.'

'What part of "enough" isn't computing? We're here because…
some bastard decided it. That's it. *Some dickbag* planned this out.
I can't say I accept this fate, because this fucking sucks and I
believed life had more to offer me, but it is the truth. I can't
blame me, you, Theodore, Beckett, Ben, Kuster… I can only
blame *some wanker.*'

Mallory blinked back a tear.

'Okay,' she said. It came out wobbling and unsure. She cleared
her throat and tried again. 'Okay.'

'Good,' Cornelia said, as if that settled things.

'Sometimes I think I don't know you very well because of how
often you surprise me.' Maybe not being able to see Cornelia's
face was emboldening, but Mallory couldn't have stopped herself
saying it if she'd tried.

'I'm very wise thanks to being alone in the dark, no magic for
company and not a damn shower or biscuit in sight.' Cornelia
sighed. 'But to be honest, I think I spend a lot of time hiding
myself. Just in case.'

'In case of what?'

'This wasn't the topic at hand, just in case you've forgotten.'

'I know.'

'But I will answer,' Cornelia said after a pause. 'In case people
see and don't like the real me. I can be confident, and sometimes
act worthy of the Broadwick name and all that's expected of me.
I can move through life like it has all been handed to me – and
don't get me wrong, I know it has. But if I let people in, and that
doesn't work out… I don't really know what the fear is. Maybe
I'm just afraid of ever having to confront the idea that people don't
like me. Because they don't. Not the way everyone likes you.'

'That—'

'I'm not finished. Don't interrupt Death Row Confession Time. It's disrespectful,' Cornelia said. 'I wish more than anything I could channel whatever Diana has going on. She's fearless.'

'She is.' Mallory ignored everything else Cornelia had said because she simply didn't have the words to respond in a way she felt justified the weight of the confession.

Cornelia paused. 'Although, if we get out of here alive, that doesn't actually excuse you from course-correcting. You had better find me a new colony. Or a new insect.'

Mallory exhaled.

'Thank you.'

'For what?'

'Understanding me.'

A pause passed between them.

'I found something else out too. Did you meet the ghost outside?'

'Yeah, she screams at the Whistler any time she sees him. I heard her shouting at you too.'

'She said she knows Theodore. That she met him before he ghosted. He's never mentioned her before, but apparently he's promised to help her? He... I think there's more to his first murder than he's ever told us.'

She had failed him. Failed to find out what happened to him, failed to look hard enough. 'We just should've done more.'

'We solved his second murder,' Cornelia said firmly. 'He would appreciate that.'

The floor rumbled, rattling the cage, and the beetles peeped frantically.

'How long do we have?'

Mallory pulled her phone out. 'Just over two hours.'

'We're running out of time. You need to decide, Mallory. Can you do it?' Cornelia leaned close to her, breathed the words on her skin, and Mallory shivered.

'I—'

Something moved in front of her face and she flinched, scrambling backwards even though it hurt her hands to do so, realising that it was the prison door gliding open, light from the hallway flooding in.

'Mallory,' the Whistler said, not sounding surprised in the slightest. 'How nice of you to join us.'

THIRTY-TWO

Two hours and thirteen minutes to Samhain

A witchlight flared and Jacob stood before them, still dressed in the overcoat and beanie Mallory had seen him in that afternoon, still smiling like he hadn't a care in the world. He looked at Mallory as though she were an old friend who had finally accepted an invitation to meet for dinner but had lacked the foresight to let him know.

'I'm so pleased. The whole gang is here,' he continued. 'Or close enough.' He pocketed a key, catching Mallory staring at him.

'Oh this? A combination of the key and a spell stops the Empathy Cage from working on me. It's a whole thing, I won't bore you with it.' He winked at her, then looked down at Cornelia. 'Can I get you anything? Some water? I realise I have been a terrible host.'

'You can get the fuck out of my face,' Cornelia said pleasantly.

'Such vitriol from such an otherwise lovely person. You know, Diana really hurt my mantis. That's not a euphemism. But that's also not your fault. You can't be responsible for the actions of your friends. Which is why I am sure you understand that I hold you in no way responsible for my actions.' Jacob smiled, the witchlight casting shadows over his face.

'What?' The brightness forced Cornelia to squint up at him, but it didn't stop her twisted glare.

'You. My friends.' Jacob faltered a little.

'Oh, buddy. We aren't friends. And, actually, we aren't buddies either.'

Jacob shrugged.

'Friendship is in the eye of the beholder and all that. Mallory, I need to ask you to move over just a smidgeon.'

'Jacob. Why?' Mallory found her voice.

'It's just a little bit, so I've got a more room to see you both better.'

'No, I mean *why*?'

'Why what?'

'That first day, when you came to see us, and then in the mortuary. You were so...'

'Repulsed? I don't like death.' He shivered. 'I don't know about you, but I know plenty of other artists who don't like looking at their work.'

Mallory recoiled, pulling a muscle in her neck as she did so. Every bit of her body hurt and she tried so hard to not acknowledge it. Not now. She clamped a hand over her neck and bit down, clenching her jaw as she waited for the spasm to pass.

'What's the problem?' Jacob frowned.

'Her problem is that you are an absolutely reprehensible, sock-like excuse for a person,' Cornelia snarled, with just enough venom that she got away with the insult being one of the least insulting things she could've said about him.

'It *is* art. I don't know what else you would call it. Surely you're impressed? You spent days chasing me, trying to figure out who I was. Days of research. Days of work. Days of death. Every single one was an art form. A puzzle piece. I tried to show you all along, I tried to keep you involved.'

'You killed Kuster. You killed Ben. You killed Beckett. You killed *Theodore*.'

'Theodore, in my defence, was already dead.'

'It doesn't matter,' Mallory snapped, fury throbbing in time with the pain in her neck. 'You still removed him from this life without asking if he wanted to go. That isn't art. You're a monster.'

Jacob adjusted his hat, a strange expression on his face. 'They always make monsters of the mavericks. I did something new. Something interesting, something nobody else would dare to even dream of.'

'Why?'

'Oh, Mallory. Do you think I'm going to sit here and tell you why?' He slapped his thigh lightly. 'Time is fading. The opening in the veil will disappear soon. I need to reach beyond whatever is here now and get this finished. You're all here now, so we can get going. Cornelia, it has been a pleasure to know you and observe you, but I fear you are all the final pieces in this puzzle, and this has been a long time coming.'

He moved to the cage door. 'But wait. First, tell me, Mallory. Did you solve it? When did you know?'

Mallory didn't answer, because she was embarrassed. Embarrassed he had been right in front of them this whole time. All she'd had to do was look, *really* look. She'd let her own principles be clouded by perception. She hadn't really thought, in all her times speaking to him, that he was capable of murder.

'Van Doren.' When it was almost too late to do anything.

'Ah!' He grinned. 'That was so late! I'm genuinely surprised. I gave you so many clues, Mallory. So many. I tried so hard to get you to stop me, in a way.'

'Stop you?'

'Oh no. No, no, no.' He waggled a finger in the air. 'We can't get into this now. It's showtime. I will say, though – you and I, we could've been such great friends. You're so… clever.' Jacob bit his lip, excitement bubbling over. 'I could've been friends with any of you, really. Goddess, you've been calling me the Whistler. You know, whenever I heard anyone say that name I got all these goosebumps.' He held up his arms.

'Theodore could've been your friend. Or more. He trusted you,' Mallory spat. 'He trusted you. He *liked* you.'

'I know. I will admit, it killed me a little to make him into art.'

'You made him suffer. And the thing about Theodore is, he's actually easily pleased. All he wanted was to love you.' Cornelia had pulled herself to her feet and planted herself opposite Jacob.

'Really?' He scratched his chin thoughtfully, mawkish in the face of what Cornelia had just said. 'I could've gone for a guy like him, easily. Apart from, you know, the whole dead thing.' He wiggled his head side to side, like he had made a brilliant point, but when neither of them responded, the mawkish expression returned. 'I suppose it doesn't matter now. Had we got involved, I'd have had no choice but to tell Theodore what I was up to, and he likes to talk *so much*. And as they say about wagging tongues…'

'Force the person who owns said wagging tongue to asphyxiate on it and then become part of a ghoulish ritual?' Cornelia said.

'Precisely. You get me. It makes me sad that I had to choose you. I wasn't sure, when I started, who would be the end. But then I heard all about you, from Theodore. He would tell anyone who'd listen in the Offices all about your little agency, and it wasn't hard to overhear. He would talk endlessly to anyone who'd listen about how brilliant his wonderful friend Mallory Hawthorne was, how clever she was, how she was unmatched and could fix any problem she faced down.' He smiled fondly. 'I found an Undetectables card among Van Doren's things – thank the last aide he had for keeping *that* safe. I found you… I didn't intend to choose you like this, you just posed a very opportune moment for me. It felt like a sign.' He pointed to the ceiling, pressing his finger to his lips. His tone lacked urgency, but there was something so intense about this entire situation it sent cold shivers down Mallory's spine in waves. Theodore would've had no idea about any of this, wouldn't have known who was listening, had never seen Jacob before he came to them.

'I really do have to go now, time's marching onward. The Ternion can't wait for little old me.'

'Do you really think the Ternion are going to be happy about the murders, Jacob? Happy about what you've done to our community, to the Do No Harm Charter, to everyone who has ever loved Kuster and Ben and Beckett and Theodore?' Cornelia moved closer to him. Mallory wanted to pull her away.

'And Mr Night Mayor. Though I'm not sure he was capable of loving anyone back,' Jacob said thoughtfully.

'How is this going to work out for you?'

'I've just realised you've figured out what this has all been about! That's wonderful. Wonderful.' He checked his watch. 'Fine, I've got a minute. Naturally, you've established part of my art was to draw on the limited writings that spoke of Elisabella's seven souls for seven blades in the establishment of the Ternion. You understood, of course, that that was a mistranslation and meant seven *cuts* with one single blade, right? That each soul was collected and harnessed within one single death blade?'

'Of course we knew that. A baby could figure that out,' Cornelia lied.

'Oh this is so exciting. Anyway, I picked someone different each time, just let the Ternion guide me on each. Kuster was an easy target, an easy first try. I saw you with your faerie friend in an alleyway after we'd first met. I was going for the tall one, actually, but their friend walked into the basement, so that was... unfortunate.' He smiled. 'I thought this method was a nice little play on the virgin sacrifice thing, it's often taken so *literally*. We live in a purity culture with no room for nuance, I often feel. I bet you've strong feelings about that, Cornelia.' He grabbed Cornelia's arm and she slapped his hand away. 'Ha. I always had a feeling, of the three of you, that you were the dangerous one.'

'She's not, you know,' Mallory said.

'She is. Look at her, she's practically feral with rage. There's your danger.'

'I think that would actually be me.' Diana dropped a witchlight on the cage floor, a flare of light bursting in the space between them. In one swift movement, she swung a length of pipe. It connected with Jacob's head and he went down.

THIRTY-THREE

One hour and fifty-seven minutes to Samhain

'Anything he can do, I can figure out and do better.' Diana dropped the pipe and reached out to help Mallory up, and then grabbed Cornelia into a deep hug. 'Goddess, I hope that pipe wasn't structurally essential. And fuck, I can't believe that worked.'

'Diana, how did you…?' Mallory couldn't properly formulate the thought.

'I just… did. I was panicking outside trying to find a way in that wasn't going to alert him. Once I'd finished with the mantis I started hunting around looking for air vents, because like hell was I walking through those beetles.'

It had not occurred to Mallory that the beetles would continue existing once she wasn't in the space to make them materialise with her guilt.

'I called the police, just so you know. I don't know if who I spoke to could hear, there was a lot of spectral interference. And they're definitely not coming in here until Samhain has passed, so we've probably got to get ourselves out. For the record, I was going to actually crawl through an air vent for you two. But I didn't fit. One of the most pressing issues of our time is actually how the makers of air vents are exclusionary in their consideration of size accommodation of the average air vent crawler, given that anyone might need to undertake a daring rescue mission.'

'But you digress,' Cornelia said.

'Yes, all of this to say, I found my way back to Van Doren's office and there was a witchlight on the table, and like any scientific experiment, I followed a hunch, figured out how to put myself in it, visualised myself standing with Mallory, and here I am, travelling through space to save your arses.'

'Diana, what if you'd got stuck in the witchlight?'

'But I didn't. Please honour my genius, it is so often overlooked. Especially as it was genius unknown to me, too.'

'You are a genius and I love you, but you shouldn't have got yourself stuck in here. We need to get out; there's no time.' Mallory ran her hands over the door.

'I knew, literally *knew* you two would probably decide that killing each other would stop him, and I wasn't about to live in a world where I had to live longer than you. We've started a newer, riskier chapter of everything with this job. But it's not a job I'd want to continue without you.'

'Are we really worth dying for?' Cornelia asked.

'Well, no. Also, thanks for confirming you were actually going to try un-aliving yourselves, you horrifying little beasts. The whole point of all of this was to stop anyone else dying. I think we've lost enough already, so on balance I was happy to try. Ergo, we all die in a horrible blazing inferno of some pick-me guy's vanity project, or none of us dies. And I offer that seriously, while hoping we don't have to do it. No matter where I go, no matter what I do, no matter who I meet, you will both always mean the world to me. Simple.'

Days ago, Mallory had thought she didn't matter to Diana at all. She had thought she didn't matter to anyone.

'Diana, the only thing that could make me love you more is if you happened to have a carton of juice on your person right now,' Cornelia croaked.

Diana laughed and shrugged off her mini backpack. 'As it so happens, I came prepared.' She tossed it at Cornelia, who caught it and laid it on the floor.

'Magic doesn't work in here.'

'I also know this. But slap the front of the bag.'

'What?'

'Trick magic, barely counts, an Apparent could activate it. Slap the bag.'

Cornelia laughed, a short, dry bark as the bag expanded revealing drinks, painkillers, three knives, a knuckleduster, plasters, and a packet of tissues.

'Diana. I love you.' Cornelia downed one of the bottles of water in two gulps, grimacing as she swallowed. She opened the second and drank it slowly, finishing half of it before passing it to Mallory with a packet of painkillers.

'Drink.'

'Thanks,' Mallory mumbled. They weren't her usual ones and weren't likely to even take the edge off, but she took two.

Diana stood over Jacob, frowning.

'How long do you think he'll stay out?' Cornelia asked.

'I'm not sure. Mallory, any thoughts?'

'He could come around any minute. We need to get out of here.' She looked down at the knives. 'Can we use these?'

'We could try.' Diana stooped to pick them up. She flicked two of the blades out and jiggled them in the lock as a makeshift lock pick, but she couldn't get it to budge. Mallory crawled over and tried too, barely daring to believe this could work again, but the door remained locked.

'Blood,' Cornelia said.

'Don't you start,' Diana snapped, rounding on her. 'We know what happened the last time.'

'Shut up,' Cornelia said in her most reasonable voice. 'I meant if we make a blood sacrifice right now. Maybe it'll let us go.'

'We could try. Can Mallory—' Diana started to ask, but Mallory struggled to her feet.

'Sometimes I worry that we spend so much time looking for complex solutions to complex problems, that we forget to listen to what folk tell us very plainly.' Mallory staggered to where Jacob lay and searched through his pockets. 'He told us how he got in here.' She held up a small bunch of keys triumphantly, one glinting silver in the light.

She unlocked the door and Diana stumbled towards it, catching it in her hands. Mallory followed right after, grabbing Cornelia's arm to drag her out with her.

Jacob stirred.

'What's going on?'

They did not answer, as they were instantly surrounded by thousands of clacking, angry beetles, no longer squishing themselves, thanks to the dissolution of Mallory's guilt but still multiplying at alarming rates, rising up to create a barrier between the corridor and the Undetectables. Mallory wondered what the Offices would've put here in their place if she had not been so consumed by self-reproach.

'Diana,' Cornelia shouted. 'Fire spell!'

'I don't have any magic yet!' Diana rummaged in her bag and pulled out a lighter. 'Sorry. So sorry.' She dropped the lighter and Mallory waited for the beetles to scatter, unsure what fire was going to do.

The wall of beetles burst into flames.

'Shit. I see your wall of beetles and I raise you a wall of beetles, but on fire.' Diana danced back out of reach as a tongue of burning, angry insects swiped at her face.

'They do that,' Cornelia said, as though this was a normal observation to make. Mallory made a brief mental note to ask what the goddess Cornelia had actually studied at university.

Jacob crawled towards the door of the cage and dodged around the beetles as he rubbed his head. 'I just need you to come with me so I can finish this. We have a secondary location to get to. I've spent ages making it right because this is the end. I thought we were reaching a point of agreement. Two of you have to die, and I have to finish what I started. Please don't make me use force, it makes me feel bad. Girls. Ladies. Women?'

'I prefer persons. People. Anything but that. I am *not* a lady. Or a woman. I simply contain multitudes. And you aren't finishing shit.' Cornelia's foot snapped out and kicked the door so it swung in violently.

His fingers caught the underside, probably crushing them, but he pulled himself upright with a groan.

'I just want to know what you're doing.' Jacob moved and the burning beetles surged. Mallory, Diana and Cornelia staggered back, closing ranks so they huddled together. 'Your magic won't be back for hours yet, there's no use fighting.'

Mallory's eyes darted around, looking for anything that would save them this deep in the Offices, but her panic did nothing to lessen the towering horror of burning beetles.

'We just need to wait!' Mallory gasped, not caring how much it hurt to be pressed so tightly against her friends. 'They're insects, they'll either burn up quickly or try to escape the smoke!'

She coughed.

'She learned that from me!' Cornelia pressed back against the wall, her arm crushed in behind the small of Mallory's back, Diana tucked in tightly below her elbow.

As Mallory had hoped, beetles at the top of the wall began to crumble, crisp, blackened shells dropping from the wall in a rapid cascade. The flames dimmed as the beetles attempted to extinguish themselves until they were just a smaller towering horror of smoke-damaged and very angry beetles.

'GO!' Cornelia shouted, and they ran for the exit. Mallory shouldered the door open, screaming as she did, and they were in the corridor. She couldn't run as fast as her friends, so Diana and Cornelia grabbed her by an arm each, and rocketed down the hallway and towards the exit.

'DON'T LEAVE ME!' Katherine shrieked as they passed her.

'I forgot about her too! Shit,' Diana said, her hands inside her bag. She tossed a vial of salt behind her, where it exploded open. Katherine screamed in fury.

'Please stop him, I promise I'll be back!' Mallory shouted over her shoulder. 'I'll finish helping you like Theodore said! Diana didn't mean the salt!'

Mallory tried to look back. Katherine stood and contemplated her for a long, long second, before nodding.

A burst of static, followed by muffled sounds of a struggle sounded behind her. Mallory kept her focus on the door ahead of them. Her palms slammed against it as she and Diana both fumbled for the door handle, but it was stuck shut.

She turned back. Jacob and Katherine were a haze hanging in the centre of the hall.

'Unlock it, Diana.'

Diana held her hand out for the keys that Mallory smashed into her palm, but none of them matched.

'Wait, wait, this was the sacrifice door!' Mallory said. 'We don't need our own magic to get out.'

'This place is full of surprising horrors.' Cornelia kept watch over their shoulders.

Mallory took a deep breath. 'I will do anything that is going to get us out of here. But I am not cutting my palm.'

'Yeah, I think we can agree the old cut-the-palm-for-a-sacrifice routine is tired. I'm all about cut-the-shit. Featured in this month's Vogue: Occult,' Diana said, but the despair in her tone was not honest, and the ghost of a smile flickered across her face. She was covered in scrapes and dirt, and Mallory noticed that she was barefoot.

'We have to do it now,' Cornelia said. 'Before the ghost lets him go.'

'What if I try saying a spell instead to like, help the magic along? Even if it's not our magic? This is what Apparents do in their belief systems, allegedly.' Diana cleared her throat, because Diana was the best at making up spells on the fly. 'We call upon Blair. Hear our plea, our request for safety. Hear us as we ask you to deliver us from this evil gobshite, and return us to whence we came.' She cringed, but continued. 'In return we will grant you a day of honour. A day of silence. Both the same day, to clarify. But all of three of us offer a day, which I guess is three days. Please hear us, goddess, or whoever is listening. We want out. Thanks.'

It was not her best work.

Even still, there was a rumble, and the door opened. Whether it was Blair, another goddess, or the Offices wishing to be rid of them, they were out.

The building was angry now, the walls rippling and rumbling as they skittered along the tiles. Samhain was close and they had engaged with its defences. It demanded more. An explosion blew behind them and they ducked, but kept running. Mallory tried to see where it was coming from, but they were moving too fast and the explosion had thrown up smoke and something else she couldn't identify.

'Where are you going?' Jacob called, sounding for all the world like his friends had decided to sit at a different table, and not at all like he had just tried to kill them. 'I need you! Mallory, I need you!'

They didn't answer and kept running, arm in arm.

They were back in the first corridor, and Mallory could feel her body begging her to sit down. The panel was within her sights and she reached for it, the safety of the main Mayoral Office building calling to them. Felix's car was outside and they were almost free, almost safe. They could call Sully, they could call the Ghoul Council. They could worry about what to do with Jacob later, because they'd be outside and away from this.

The floor tiles began to bend under Mallory's feet and she moved faster, dragging Cornelia with her. The walls shook, a sconce crashing to the ground.

Another explosion erupted in front of them this time. The last thing Mallory saw as she was thrown backwards were the twisted remains of the armoured mantis, belly-up and disembowelled.

THIRTY-FOUR

One hour and twenty minutes to Samhain

Mallory's eyes opened to a stretch of purple. It took her a moment to realise that she was in Van Doren's office, staring at the ceiling. She couldn't move, only blink. Slowly. Painfully.

This could be death.

She thought it was. Some kind of cold, terrible death where she would be forced to look at horrible things for the rest of eternity. The ceiling was really very offensive. Van Doren had no taste.

She remembered Van Doren was dead, and everything else flooded in.

She twisted her head frantically, trying to see where Cornelia and Diana were. If Mallory was alive, maybe they were too.

'Mallory.'

She had not noticed Jacob, but now she could feel the energy coming off him in waves. His voice was low, unthreatening, and yet it made every nerve in her body come alive with fright. He walked towards her, that same bounce in his step, slower now, clutching his side, injured in the explosion. Everything he did was wrong. Everything she thought she knew had evaporated.

She couldn't believe she had ever doubted his capability. She couldn't believe she hadn't simply known it was him.

'You're awake! This is very good.'

'Where are they?'

She stared at his feet as he approached, those floppy lace loops that had seemed so unthreatening. He crouched beside her and looked at his phone screen.

'Don't worry about that. We've still got a bit of time. Do you want to know the plan now? Everything's in place, nothing can go wrong. I can tell you why I chose you.'

She shook her head, pain radiating down her neck as she did so.

'Why you're summoning the Ternion is of no interest to me. I don't want any part of it. None of us do. You're the Whistler.'

'Summoning the Te—?' He broke off and clutched his head. 'No, no, no. I thought we were on the same page. I hate to be so misunderstood. I'm not summoning the Ternion.'

'But the death blade, the murders, the symbol…' Mallory trailed off. Thinking hurt too much. Talking hurt worse.

'Goddess, I cannot believe this. I'm not summoning the Ternion. I'm *becoming* one of them. A fourth. And before you say there are three Ternion and the clue is in the name, I know this. But summon?' Jacob pulled his hat off and adjusted his hair. 'That would be a life of indentured servitude. I'd be a lackey. A butler. A glorified house plant. No, what I want is what nobody else has dared to dream about, nobody has dared to commit to writing. Nobody has dared to admit to wanting. Why worship a goddess if you could simply become one? And it really is so simple, if you think about it as I have.'

He sat down beside her, his legs crossed, leaning forward like they were having a pleasant chat.

'Simple? How could it be simple?' Mallory clenched her jaw.

'Maybe tonight you'll understand how useful lateral thinking can be, the doors it can unlock, the chances it can give you to be something, someone else.'

'Why?'

'Why not? I really thought you had this all figured out. My motivation was so clear. So obvious. I even told you a few times. Okay, fine.' He smiled at her. 'You've twisted my arm. Early on, right when I'd chosen Edward Kuster, I met Theodore.'

'Theodore didn't know you when we first met,' Mallory said, hating this new image of Theodore as a liar that was building in her mind, wanting to refute it. Theodore would've said if he knew Jacob. He would've.

'Of course he didn't.' Jacob frowned.

Mallory closed her eyes.

'Mallory, I thought you were smarter than this.' She opened her eyes again to see him frowning at her, a line of disdain across his forehead. 'I told you, so long ago, what the answer was.'

'I got the letter. I got the cipher, I cracked all the codes, but we just couldn't…' A wave of nausea hit Mallory's stomach and she swallowed hard, her throat raw and sore.

'You missed the first clue. The Kuster clue.'

'We found that. After the letter we figured it was hinting at Samhain, it just didn't…'

'It was my first riddle, and I was sad to see you didn't realise the key to unravelling it was right there. Lateral thinking, Mallory. The six lines were written on top of a sudoku puzzle.

Six squares empty, six numbers ranging from one to six. The order the numbers fit into the squares was the correct order to read the riddle in. Then of course you would realise that each puzzle grid was made up of three by three squares. There were three words in each line – also scrambled – leading you, or your contemporaries, to the conclusion that this was about the Ternion, Elisabella's ritual repeated anew, and my plans to be a fourth. It was my first test. I had to test my worthiness and give myself a chance to be caught. Then I realised that perhaps I was cheating, as only someone practised in thinking as I do could've followed that logic. Besides, that guy already exists, I needed a better USP. So I tried again, with you specifically in mind, and this time I gave you more clues.'

'What?' Mallory wanted to ask more, but she was so confused, so dismayed that the first puzzle was unbelievably unsolvable, she was reduced to single-word squeaks of confusion.

'Doughnuts.' Jacob clapped his hands once. 'It was genius, I am so disappointed you didn't figure it out with the doughnuts. It was a three-fold key. I was so, so sure you'd come get me. I could barely sleep, lying awake every night waiting for sirens.'

'I don't—'

'Let me start from the beginning, then.' He rubbed his hands together. 'Once upon a time there was a harmless boy named Jacob Gabbott. Except' – Jacob made a noise like a buzzer – 'no, there wasn't.'

'But then…'

'He's me, yes. Mallory! Please! Jacob Gabbott *exists*, all right, just not harmlessly. He walked, talked, bumbled about in the bowels of the Mayoral Offices. Learned how powerful Theodore was, heard him talk about you. All three of you – the rule of three, your private investigator agency. He talked about you *constantly*. You were so loved.' Jacob smiled at her. 'Part of me thought nobody would bat an eyelid at Kuster dying and I'd be two or three souls in before things really ramped up unless I intervened on my own behalf, but the whole locked room thing made folk latch on, and the Apparent police were more competent than I thought – obviously not *that* competent, or we wouldn't be here. So you see, Mallory, the answer was doughnuts.'

Mallory wanted to scream.

'I thought, doughnuts. What are circular doughnuts, but rings?' He moved his hands side to side as though he was cupping a doughnut in the air. 'Rings, Blair's ring. That's the first key. It was obvious, I felt.'

When Mallory didn't respond, he tutted.

'Anyway, when Mr Night Mayor got all worked up about the first murder, I thought there was a better opportunity than the poem to test fate. And it was fate, wasn't it? I met you and I was sure it had to be you, if I was to go through with it.' His voice dropped. 'I saw how much you wanted recognition. How easy it would be to make that happen for you, while also ensuring the Ternion really wanted this for me – if they wanted me stopped, you would be so powerful, and if they didn't, you'd be the perfect sacrifice. The Ternion did the impossible, all those years ago. It was only right to recreate the impossibility of the situation. If you figured out it was me, it would be the Ternion speaking through the three of you – rule of three, Ternion. Simple, really, if you give it the proper amount of thought.'

'Are you saying you wanted us to catch you, just so you could know if the bad thing you were doing was definitely bad?' Mallory could barely make sense of it.

'Yes? It was the simplest way to ensure things were going as planned. I fear this is why this has never happened before – those who fail to plan, fail to prepare. I chose to operate with near-complete transparency.'

The simultaneous truth and lie of his words made her swallow hard. Mallory tried to speak, but he held up a hand and she felt her throat close up. She choked, willing her brain to be rational, to breathe through her nose, but panic rose up through her body and overwhelmed her. He rested his face on his hands.

'Please don't interrupt. I just need you to understand. Seven souls for seven blades was such a simple way of me making that recognition happen. I got to know folk in the community quite quickly. People liked me very much, I think. And I did everything I could to let the Ternion stop me.'

Mallory wanted to ask how, but couldn't, so just thought the words strongly in his direction, narrowing her eyes through her panic.

'And you probably want to know how.' Jacob sighed. 'So, first of all, I wrote the letter asking for help. And – please stop trying to speak, I'm talking – I played that part well, I felt. The anxious aide coming to request your services for a horrible, horrible murder. And I knew exactly how horrible it was. And then… I was nervous, in front of Cornelia. I knew the Broadwicks knew him, and I wasn't sure how much you and Diana were aware of his usual mannerisms – nobody steered Theodore down that path, so it was impossible to find out.'

Mallory wanted to ask who he was talking about, but her throat tightened.

Jacob shook his head. 'So if it has to be spelled out...' He pulled a ring out of his pocket, identical to Van Doren's giant, gaudy emerald one, and slipped it on. Jacob twisted it and Van Doren appeared in his place.

Mallory's breath caught in her chest. This was impossible, but the answers were all there, incomprehensible as they were.

'Every bit of Blair's involvement in the formation of the Ternion was about concealment of identity. This is faerie magic. The cost is a tiny bit of pain – just a little blood – but it's so worth it,' Jacob-Van Doren said. 'I can be anyone, any time.' He winked, pulling the ring off. Jacob's form returned as blood beaded at the base of his finger. He wiped it on his jacket.

'If Elisabella, Blair or Hexana had willed it that I not join their ranks, I would've been found out before now. It's just basic logic. So much of it was basic logic. You figured out the ciphered letter from the Larix, I assume? Oh.'

He released the hold on Mallory's throat so she could croak out a sentence.

'That this whole thing was about the Ternion, and the Samhain deadline.'

'Yes, yes, but that's not the only bit. This is somewhat affirming, I think? Perhaps the Ternion didn't wish for you to figure it out and obstructed my efforts at clarity...' Jacob held up a finger. 'Do you have the letter on you? Course you don't, I have one here. Hold on.'

He reached beyond Mallory's line of vision and shuffled through what sounded like papers. He shook the letter out delicately. 'This is the other part where doughnuts came in – an instruction. The second fold, if you will. I think I've got a pen here. No, charcoal will have to do.' He leaned the paper on his knee and ringed letters, humming under his breath.

'Do you see?'

He held it in front of Mallory's face. Her eyes scanned the words, nausea plummeting into her stomach.

'That's not…' But it was. It was the wording on the letter. The same one offering a Samhain deadline. The first letter of every fourth word had been circled, spelling out…

'*My name is Jacob,*' Mallory read. It felt like a disgustingly simple trick, something she should've seen.

'I know it's not exactly world-class ciphering, but I was really trying to get you to see me. I wanted the Ternion to have every opportunity to intervene to stop me, whatever the cost. Prove my worth. I told you who I was. Wait, then in the cemetery, I left another…'

'Poem.'

'You found the poem! Great. That's one of my best ones. I've become really confident in my writing recently. I'm something of a polymath,' he said, with genuine humility that felt at odds with the urgency of the moment. 'Music, rituals, and poetry. I wish I could talk more about my skillset, but we must press on. Though there was another note, supposed to be from Cornelia.' He jerked his head to the other side of the room. 'And that one said TIME UP in the same silly little code. I thought that would be a big hint to help you see the first clues, as you'd clearly veered off track majorly by missing my biggest hint, but no matter. You got here in the end, the way it was meant to be.'

Jacob lifted his hand again and her throat closed up once more.

'We've still got time. Let me tell you a story. A short one. Imagine being a little boy, living in Oughteron, hidden away with your Apparent mother. Imagine your father was very powerful in Occulture. Imagine he had never, ever bothered to tell anyone about your existence. He was ashamed of you and your mother, afraid it would threaten what he already had. His power, his lineage. Imagine he had a lot of control over other people, and imagine he had a lot to lose, so he pretended to himself that hiding you and your mother away was the best thing, even though nobody would care that this powerful man had an Apparent mistress. Oh, imagine that too. Imagine your father had a wife and a mistress, and you arrived and he hid his shame.'

Jacob placed a candle in front of him, his fingers absently trailing through the flame.

'Imagine this father, this worthless, worthless man, sends you away forever. You don't get to take his name. He sends money, sometimes, to your mother. Imagine you lived among Apparents for most of your life, not understanding much of magic. That they tried to raise you as one, though you're a witch to your core. Then that worthless man wanders back into your life twenty-nine years later, upon realising that any heir of his with his new partner, or possibly the one after that, might not be old enough to take over what he affectionately calls "the family business" by the time he dies. He's suddenly aware of mortality, you see. He promises your mother all sorts of things if she agrees, not that it's her business, because that boy is an adult now, has been for years, has his own life, his own dreams, his own hopes. But he asks for a year. Just a year. One that takes you away from the career you had before, away from the musical talents you've had, the two decades of practising every day to be the best.

'You'd gladly do it for her, for just a year, but in that year he continues to pretend you don't exist. He doesn't call you son. He orders you around like you're nothing. Snaps at you, doesn't introduce you to his new girlfriend who is ten years younger than you, give or take, as anything other than a *colleague*. He doesn't ever say your name with care. Your mother is frightened she'll lose the house he bought her, because if he doesn't help it'll need to be sold to pay for her care. You don't want to believe he'd be that callous. Imagine how angry you'd become. How much more you'd want. How much you'd think about ways to dilute his power, make some of it yours, or find power he could not access. Just a few pies he had not put his fingers into. He'd taken all our power away from us before to keep his hold, he could do it again in a heartbeat.'

Mallory forced herself to take slow, shallow breaths.

'I wanted so badly for you to figure this all out, Mallory. All the pieces were there. "I was an orchestral flautist before all this!"' He affected a high, earnest tone, almost mocking himself. 'I said this to you twice. I told Theodore that first day when I came to the Undetectables for help that witchlights could be used for spells, and for people, though that part was implied. Said it in front of you. Brought you in to see a body, let you see me in the room where Theodore died again. Gave you hints. I just get the sense you never really believed in me as a viable suspect, and that hurts. But I know you believe me now, and that's what matters.'

It was simultaneously so earnest and intense, Mallory had no idea what about it scared her. His words barely registered. She only wanted the power to speak. Almost as though he heard her, he fluttered his fingers and the chokehold released.

'Where are they?' Mallory rasped. He had held her attention for long enough.

'Cornelia is over there.' He pointed to a corner and Mallory tried to twist her body around. The explosion had made it impossible to pretend she wasn't in pain, though she wasn't sure where the aftermath pain started and fibromyalgia pain ended as every nerve in her body made itself known.

Cornelia groaned. She was, for the time being, alive.

'Where's Diana?'

'She's by the door. Don't bother, I've locked them all. I thought what she did with the pipe was quite rude, so I've left her out of our little circle for now. She seems to like me the least. And honestly, I only needed two of you. One of you is an extra free offering to Elisabella, just in case cutting out the esteemed Mr Night Mayor's heart did something… janky.' His lip curled. 'I like to have backup plans, just in case. You often see killers – and I'm not really one, not in a way that matters – be overconfident. I put in all the fail-safes. I actually would've taken Diana and you over Cornelia – too messy to have the Broadwicks wrong-footed by losing a child, but she was just in the right place at the right time. I was always going to lure one of you away with something. I knew the rest would follow.'

Mallory wanted to scream.

'You can go to her, if you like.' He gestured at Cornelia again and Mallory dragged her body into a crawl, but her movements were slow and it took her an excruciatingly long time to get to her, her necklace slapping against her collarbones as she moved. Cornelia lay in front of Van Doren's desk, his body still there under the sheet. Jacob had surrounded her with candles and it was so horrifying to look at, Mallory cried. Jacob waited until she had crawled into the circle and arranged herself around Cornelia's body so that she was cradling her head. Cornelia's eyes were glassy, but she was conscious, or just about.

'It's me,' Mallory whispered. 'I'm here.'

Cornelia blinked slowly at her.

'This is so cute.' Jacob crouched in front of them.

He whistled.

Cornelia clapped her hands over her ears. Mallory's body lanced with pain. Everything seemed like it was ending, like she was falling off the side of the world over and over in the space of a heartbeat.

'STOP!' she screamed.

He did.

'Orchestral flautist, my own specially created magic. You can do that, you know. Make magic do whatever you want, so long as you understand what it's doing. I spent years not knowing my own magic and not knowing what was possible. It is quite likely Elisabella did something similar, to be honest, but I just took frequencies uncomfortable for human ears and pushed them to the limit. The spell did most of the work for me, I just set the traps. Delegation. My father...' Jacob pushed Van Doren's body with his fingers and it slid slowly off the chair, a tangle of limbs and blankets. Rigor mortis had not yet set in, perhaps never would. 'Would have approved, had he not been such a fucking dick.'

'He's your father?'

Jacob coughed out a laugh.

'Mallory, please. I told you myself days ago! My father made me leave my position as orchestral flautist for a life of meaningless politics. I told you again, minutes ago, the story of my life. Vincent enjoyed trading good things for worse things. He'd betrayed his first wife for my mother, and then traded them both again, and again. Is there anything more pathetic than a middle-aged man with a girl younger than his own son?'

Mallory remembered Cornelia's words, which had been essentially to that same effect.

'I have something I'm proud of. Real talent. I made folk choke on their own tongues, asphyxiate on their own power, their own voices, sacrificed them for the greater good. And my piece-of-shit father didn't know. He didn't even leave me with the Van Doren name. That was stripped from me. TAKEN!' He screamed the last word.

Mallory could not think what to say next. She felt as though the earth was crashing down around her. She was looking down at someone else cradling Cornelia in their arms, in this room, at Samhain's hour.

'All those times I came around, checking up on you, all those times I was so conveniently in the places you were, at crime scenes or just *happening* to be wandering by. You were so convinced it had to be someone suspicious. Someone overtly powerful,' he said. Mallory's skin felt clammy as shame swept through her.

'We did think that. And we were wrong. We know we were wrong. We thought it was…'

'My father, if this is what passes for "father" these days, and if not my father, the *lovely* Alyssa O'Sullivan.'

'Yes.'

'And it wasn't.'

'Clearly not,' Cornelia croaked. Mallory ran her fingers over her hand in reassurance. Her eyes did not open.

'Because it wasn't. It was me,' Jacob said. 'Just in case you weren't sure. Now you are. It was me.' His voice was uncertain, like he had expected the revelation to be something more. Something bigger.

'Okay. Well. Time to die.' He pointed at Cornelia. He whistled again and Mallory screamed. Cornelia convulsed and Mallory tried to hold on to her, but she was choking and there was nothing she could do.

They were going to die here. This was the end.

'Wait!' Mallory yelled, and Jacob abruptly stopped whistling. 'Why him?'

'Why?' Jacob paused Cornelia's murder, releasing her from the hold, crouching beside Mallory so they were practically eye to eye. He held a black-handled knife, the one that had been in Van Doren's heart on the desk, spinning it between his fingers. Now that it had been wiped clean of blood, Mallory could see it for what it was, oily with shadows that flitted close to the surface of the blade. She hadn't recognised it then, but knew now exactly what she was looking at. Each shadow was a soul, fighting for escape against the surface of the death blade.

416

'He was never going to let me go. Don't you see? He'd bargained for a year, then he would ask for another, and another, until I was swept up in his life, in his rules, in his town. I wanted more for myself. You'd think ambition would've spoken to him, but he just never *saw*.'

'What made you want to become one of the Ternion? Why not something else? A smaller, more achievable goal.' Mallory watched the blade, the glass black and oily and wickedly sharp. It looked fragile, like it would shatter if he gripped it too tightly, or if any pressure was put on it.

'Oh come on, Mallory. Blair. Elisabella. Hexana. *Jacob*.' He said each name with commanding relish, like he had practised this moment. It was possible that he had. 'Why would I settle for less than I deserve? Nobody should.' He twirled the knife. 'I spent a long time wanting to burn this whole town to the ground and start over, even before I came here. Burn the bones of everyone that ever enabled him. Choke the life out of the rot, the arrogance of folk here. Make them understand a powerful mayor can still be a shitty person and a shitty father and that this shit matters. I could do it with my own power.' He swung his arms and rolled his neck.

Cornelia choked again and Mallory tried to get her to open her mouth, her brain telling her to catch hold of Cornelia's jaw and stop her biting her tongue off, even though it was pointless; magic could not be stopped like that. If Jacob's whistle was going to hurt her, kill her, it would happen.

There was nothing she could do. She was powerless, and he was about to become powerful. Mallory was out of options.

Except for one thing.

The only thing he could not control and could not have planned for, even with the cage stripping their magic away, preventing them from casting new spells.

Mallory had known her place in Occulture for years, had learned how to survive on scraps of magic here and there, and had learned how to think outside the box when the moment called for it. She'd show him lateral thinking.

She cleared her throat, squeezed Cornelia's hand in hers, and placed her hand on her chest. Her fingers caught in the necklace Cornelia had given her. The necklace she had kept wearing out of stubborn refusal to use the spell for fear there would be a real emergency and she would not be equipped for it.

She opened her mouth and said one word, clear as anything. 'BIND.'

THIRTY-FIVE

Fifty-eight minutes to Samhain,
not that it matters any more

The death blade, under the pressure of the binding spell, shattered in the ringing echo of Mallory's shout, pieces ricocheting off the desk and back up into Jacob's hat. A black cloud floated out and rose above his head, roiling against the ceiling.

Cornelia stopped choking.

The whistling died away abruptly, and all the candles went out.

Cornelia remained still and unmoving and Mallory was defiant in her agony. Jacob stared at her, his hands limp at his sides. He did not seem to notice the angry cloud above him, and so could not appreciate the perfect reflection of his mood happening in the room.

'What did you just do?'

But he knew. They all knew. The room shook and smoke billowed from the walls, red and angry. The candles flared back into life, burning high and licking the purple ceiling. Paint dripped down, hitting Mallory's face in the horrific light.

'I can't believe you've done this.' He sounded more surprised than anything. 'What am I supposed to do now?' He pulled his hat off his head and threw it on to the ground in a childish gesture. 'I planned for *everything*. Cornelia made it so easy for me to get you here.' He raked his hands through his hair, curling in on himself for a moment. 'She literally returned to the scene of a crime and *let* me take her, and you, Mallory, you, I cannot believe *you*. You know how precious life is. I'm useless outside of the Ternion. All my life, not accepted, not treated properly. Overlooked. I worked so hard for this. You broke it with… with a nothing spell.'

He was ranting now, distracted. Mallory shook Cornelia, tried to get her to stand. Mallory couldn't see if she was injured so badly that she couldn't move. There was blood all over her jacket, still tacky to the touch. She didn't know for sure if it was Cornelia's, but there was enough of it that it scared her.

'I thought you were like me. I saw you swallowing down your feelings every day, resenting yourself. Your friends lost and spinning and you running around after them, trying to be brilliant, trying to be something. Pretending to be in charge when you wanted to curl up into a ball and cry. We are the same.'

Mallory had to force herself to tune back in to him.

'We aren't,' she croaked.

'Oh, that's right. You're *nice*. I forgot. I'm terribly sorry.' But he did not sound sorry at all.

'We are leaving now. I am getting out of here, and I don't want to see you again.'

She no longer cared what he did to her. Die now or die later, it didn't matter.

Jacob threw his hands up, pulling at his hair. 'I don't care! Why did you do it, Mallory?'

The cloud transformed above him, indistinct shapes but clear colours forming in it, yellows and reds and greens and charcoals. It was the freed souls, Mallory realised, and they were organising.

'You're not taking any more of my friends. I did it for Cornelia. And for Theodore.'

He was up there with the others, she knew. She hoped his spirit was free now. She couldn't take the time to process how she felt about the idea of Theodore likely never coming back, but she also knew Ben was free, and Beckett, and everyone else she hadn't been able to save in time.

'Yeah, you dick,' Cornelia said. Mallory got the distinct sense that Cornelia was far more injured than she'd thought if that was the best she could come up with.

Jacob screamed in frustration as Cornelia managed to scramble to her feet, pulling Mallory with her.

'It took me MONTHS to make that blade. MONTHS,' he shouted.

'And lo, here are the consequences of your actions,' Mallory said, earning a tiny snort from Cornelia as the freed souls formed into something huge, angry and ineffable.

Mallory backed away and Jacob roared thunderously, the floor beneath their feet rumbling as the mess of souls surrounded him, circling. He dropped to his knees and the souls forced their way into his ears and nose and mouth. He howled until his voice was cut off abruptly, a split second of loud silence as he was completely hidden from view, surrounded by an angry, flashing mass that seemed intent on consuming him.

The mass thinned. For a moment that stretched into infinity, Mallory saw Jacob's face clearly as trickles of something dark and bilious leaked from the corners of his mouth, his eyes widening, his skin turning red, then blue, his throat working. Deep, guttural sounds were the only thing she could hear until his mouth opened, blood pouring in rivulets, and a piece of flesh thudded to the floor, louder than it should've sounded. Jacob slumped forward, the flashing mass became opaque again, and he was hidden from view.

Mallory didn't have to look closely to know the piece of flesh was his tongue.

She also didn't have time to panic that the Offices had just been fed an organ.

The building responded violently, screaming, rumbling, dust falling from the ceiling as the very foundations of the Mayoral Offices were threatened by the influx of spirits. The bell jar from Van Doren's desk shot across the room to hit the door next to Diana.

Arm in arm, Mallory and Cornelia stumbled to the door, forcing it open with the last of Mallory's strength. Cornelia bent to try wake Diana, and sat on the floor, gasping.

Diana lay in a heap on the ground. Her head was pressed up against the door, her legs bent at awkward angles. Mallory checked her pulse. She was still alive, her skin clammy and her breathing shallow.

'Diana. Diana!' Mallory shook her. She reached for Diana's hand and saw her fingers were wrapped around something small, clutched tightly to her chest.

'Help me,' Mallory said, and she and Cornelia took one of Diana's arms each, dragging her out of the door. She didn't stir, even as her head bumped over the threshold. The building growled in fury as they crossed back into the hall.

The building did not want them to leave. Mallory heard hissing and the walls rippled, the lights long extinguished.

'This way,' Mallory croaked. She adjusted her hold on Diana and she and Cornelia took slow, painful steps towards the front door. Towards freedom. Behind her, something growled sharp and deep, and the wooden door of Van Doren's office splintered. Mallory ducked. There was pressure on her skull, pressure on her torso, the building demanding she relinquish her hold on her own body.

A door exploded as they passed and rocked them sideways. Mallory tripped and landed hard on her knees next to Diana. It seemed impossible to ask her body to carry her to the front door, still so far away down the corridor. She felt her eyes closing and couldn't stop them. She was out of fight, her body seized and aching, her arms unable to lift, her mouth incapable of speech.

A clock tolled a warning somewhere in the distance.

She thought she could hear sirens.

THIRTY-SIX

Two days after Samhain

Mallory woke in a hospital. She knew this because she woke to the sound of someone screeching, 'This is a *hospital!*' in the corridor outside her room, and then Felix was in her line of sight. They had a massive bunch of flowers in one arm and a cuddly bee toy in the other. She tried to raise her arms but found she couldn't, suddenly aware of the blue waffle blanket over her, wires connecting to every part of her body, a drip, and the low beep of a heart monitor.

Felix put the bee down at the end of her bed, where it looked up at her with plaintive eyes, and placed the flowers on her windowsill. Finally, they sat on the edge of the bed, carefully keeping away from both her wires and from her body.

'Hey,' Felix said.

'Hey.' She realised her throat was drier than anything. Mallory looked around her for something to drink, and Felix grabbed the cup on her bedside table, bending the straw so she could drink without having to lift her head. She drank until she

424

slurped the dregs, noticing Felix was dressed in pink leopard-print leather trousers.

'Heard you lost a fight with a building.'

'I heard that too.'

'I'm so sorry.' They gently stroked her fingers. 'Not just for this. But for everything. I thought of all three of you, you were the most likely to solve Ben's murder. I didn't realise… Until the night he died, I didn't realise how absent I'd been from your life. You were a good friend, doing everything you could for Ben, but also for me. It's hit me hard how much I've let you down by drifting away in the last few years.'

Mallory shook her head, regretting the movement. She didn't need to hear this. Not now. 'Don't. We caught the Whistler in the end. Cornelia—' She suddenly realised what this meant. 'Diana. Where are they? Where's Jacob? What happened?'

'I feel I now understand what the nurse meant when I asked to see you and she said that this is a hospital and I need to be respectful and not overexcite you.'

'Felix, please tell me.'

'They're okay.' Felix patted her hand again. 'Diana's had a few brain scans. She had a concussion, but more importantly, her hearing… I'll let her explain. They said it might heal, but… Cornelia needed some surgery, she broke an arm. Some smashed ribs, too. She's furious about being on bedrest. She has some burns from the explosion and a bunch of gnarly-looking stitches on her arms. Is that enough detail? Do you need more? An interpretive dance re-enactment of what it was like trying to get in contact with you and calling the hospital?'

'No, that was great, thank you.'

'You also have gnarly stitches, but I haven't seen them so I have no idea how bad they are. Except for that cut on your face. That's pretty bad. No—' They stopped Mallory's hand as she automatically touched her face. 'You're covered in bandages. I don't know the details.'

'Thanks, Felix. Do you know what happened?'

'I spoke to that detective... Sully? They had to find witches capable of coming in to get you from the hallway after the last explosion. The building wasn't letting anyone in. She pulled you out, actually.'

Mallory curled her fingers around Felix's. They kissed their own fingers and pressed them to her forehead.

'You solved Ben's murder. I would be eternally thankful for this.'

'Would be?'

'If you hadn't completely fucked my car in the process. There are pieces of it all over Mayoral Square, fluttering in the breeze. I'm still thankful, but you and Diana owe me a car.' Felix smiled. 'I'm just glad you're okay. I said this to Diana and Cornelia too and they told me to be quiet, but I really mean it. I can't lose anything else, Mallory. I cannot lose any of you.'

'You...' But Mallory couldn't finish the sentence. Her heart lifted at the idea of being missed by anyone other than Diana and Cornelia. That anyone cared enough to miss her, much less many folk caring.

'What about Jacob?' she said instead.

'Oh, he's gone, they think. Sully wants statements when you're ready to talk, and the interim Night Mayor is here. For now, you rest, you heal. I'm here for support, and to talk about your wounds in extensive detail.'

Mallory's heart lurched. She didn't want to talk to an interim Night Mayor, who would not understand the intricacies of the case.

'Here, now?'

'Yeah. I'll get out of your face. Langdon and Cloud are outside, but I decided I was the most special of your friends not involved in the incident. Plus, I wanted to see for myself that you were okay.'

'Thank you for my bee friend.' Mallory gestured at the soft toy with her fingers. The movement was a mistake; even her fingers hurt.

'The shop was out of bears, and I liked the bee's face.' Felix winked. In a few long strides, they were out of view.

All her energy leeched out of her and she fell back asleep. She woke a few times to be subjected to rounds of blood pressure checks, more medication and a dressing change. Her head pounded, both from general fibromyalgia and because that was, apparently, normal after a series of explosions and a near-death experience.

The next time she opened her eyes, the sun was setting. She found a call button near her head. Moments later, a harried-looking nurse bustled in.

'Sorry to bother you, but do you happen to know where my friends are? We were probably all admitted together. The Mayoral Offices explosion.' She described them. He directed her down the corridor and, after some minor negotiations about how far she could walk, he agreed to push her down the hall in a borrowed wheelchair, trailing a drip beside her.

'You're one of the famous investigators, I presume?' he said.

'What?'

He laughed.

'There has been nothing but reporters and journalists and even a TV crew standing outside the hospital for the past two days trying to get an interview with one of you. There's an inquest going on about who killed the Night Mayor; some people are saying it's a long-lost son back for revenge or something absolutely bonkers like that. And everyone wants to know what the Mayoral Offices are really like on Samhain or if the creatures are a hoax. Some hoax, given the state of you all.'

'Strange,' Mallory said. 'I'm sure the truth will come out eventually.'

The nurse wheeled Mallory into a room that was, to her surprise, densely populated with folk. Cornelia was sitting upright in her hospital bed. Diana perched next to her, practically curled around her, a hospital blanket around her shoulders. Her hair, piled on top of her head, revealed a giant bandage covering one of her ears. Confusingly, Sully and Dr Ray were both there, standing as close to the window as they could, but the room was tiny and the addition of Mallory, a wheelchair, and a nurse made it feel overwhelmingly cramped.

'Mallory,' Cornelia said, breaking into a smile. Diana turned and her expression held such relief, Mallory thought she might cry.

Dr Ray shifted out from behind the bed, approaching her. 'I'm about to do something that is an absolute break in propriety,' she said. Bracing herself for some kind of admonishment, Mallory was surprised Dr Ray bent down and stiffly pulled her into a hug.

Every single second of the five-second hug made her skin

burn, but Mallory did not know how to extricate herself from this particularly awkward, and unexpected, embrace.

'And now we shall never speak of this again. You poor, idiotic child. If I'd known that day in the mortuary...'

Mallory exchanged glances with Diana and Cornelia, which told her that she had done the same to them. Dr Ray appeared to be experiencing a range of emotion that Mallory had not previously thought possible. The nurse helped park her beside the bed, turning her so she was mostly facing everyone.

'Oh my fucking goddess.' Diana stared at Mallory's face in horror. A swoop of self-consciousness descended into her stomach.

'Nice to see you too, Diana,' Mallory laughed. 'I'm so happy you're both okay. Hi, everyone.' She waved and realised moving at all was a bad idea. It would be some time before the pain from her injuries and her fibromyalgia flare lessened. Sully smiled at her.

'So I bet you're all wondering why I've gathered you here,' Cornelia started.

'Mallory came of her own volition,' Diana pointed out. 'You were, actually, going to do this without her.'

'I was letting her rest!'

'I am here to witness the statement,' Sully said. 'And it may be used as evidence when presented to the Unified Magical Liaison.'

'Fine.' Cornelia adjusted her sling. 'I have gathered you to explain what happened two nights ago. Three weeks ago, Wrackton fell afoul of a serial killer, who started with an Apparent victim out in Oughteron.'

'Cornelia.' Mallory forced herself to speak. This wasn't about anger, or revenge. This was just about her. Despite the fact she was both not fully sure the story was straight in her head, and not yet certain it had actually happened.

'What is it?'

'Pass the mic.'

Cornelia frowned, then sat back, another unreadable expression on her face. 'And now Mallory is going to explain what happened.'

Mallory took a deep breath. 'Three weeks ago, the first of five ritualistic killings occurred. Though the killer started with a victim from Oughteron, it was believed to be someone living within the Occult community. Night Mayor Vincent Van Doren hired the Undetectables, private investigators, to solve the case. Except, he didn't. The real murderer used a magical ring to masquerade as the Night Mayor.'

'He did what?' Cornelia spluttered.

'Shush. Until the end, we believed we were in the employ of the Night Mayor. Using a combination of pioneering scientific methods developed in collaboration with one of the future victims, we set out to identify the magic the killer used. Only, it wasn't initially detectable. It wasn't anything we had seen before, even when we found a way to identify magical involvement. We turned to reconstruction. Diana developed something unique,' Mallory said, nodding her head encouragingly at Diana to continue.

'A series of dioramas based on Francine Leon's nutshell dioramas,' Diana said quietly. 'Helping you solve crime, anytime.'

'Yes, that. We had a swathe of possible suspects. A locked room, then a busy bar, then a public space, then another locked room.

It looked, for a time, like our main suspects were Van Doren and... you, Sully.'

'I told you that would happen,' Dr Ray said mildly. Sully pursed her lips.

Mallory kept going. 'We developed a theory around the potential motivations of the killer we came to call the Whistler. Once we'd established the murders involved the Ternion, and specifically the summoning of the Ternion, we focused on power and looked to those in Wrackton who had it, or wanted it. With the initial help of Cornelia's *Sonata lutumae*, I managed to isolate magical DNA and narrow down the killer as a witch in Wrackton with an Apparent parent. Then, Sully, you dismissed our report that Theodore was a victim. We could not inform Van Doren of this, because he was still a suspect. Then Diana figured out how the Whistler was getting in and out of the crime scenes: witchlight. Truth be told, we were misdirected at the end. Jacob Gabbott, aide to the Night Mayor, captured Cornelia and set a trap so we'd think Van Doren was the one behind it. The problem is, we repeatedly discounted Jacob because we believed it was someone power-hungry. And he was, there's no doubt about that. But the power he craved was righting a familial wrong. He had tried to give us a series of increasingly senseless clues that we were unable to solve, though there was an area of oversight: we had ignored the witch lineage of our two suspects. And therein lay the answer, or part of it. Van Doren was his father, and Jacob Gabbott was angry. But bitterly, twistedly frustrated. He didn't want to summon the Ternion, he wanted to become a fourth member.'

'Like the world's shittest pop group,' Cornelia said.

'We'd spoken to Observer Johnson about the Ternion, and eventually learned of the foundation of the Observatory, and of the Ternion. Seven souls for seven blades, where Elisabella apparently sacrificed Occult in order to ascend as a goddess. There's little written about it, but what little there was, Jacob figured out. We had missed a number of clues until it was almost too late. Subtle, strange clues. Jacob, the orchestral flautist, had created the whistling spell. It was not really a whistle, but a combination of badly played notes at disturbing frequencies. The fact of the letters he sent us, puzzles he wanted us to solve.' Mallory swallowed. 'A very important consideration in the undetectable nature of this case was that he wanted us to stop him. In his mind he gave us every opportunity. But it wasn't about the Undetectables, or about the community – though he resented that too. Jacob Gabbott thought of Wrackton as an extension of his father's neglect of him, and he was looking for himself in anyone he could find. We were meant to challenge him, to his mind. If we challenged him, it would've been the Ternion speaking through us. The rule of three through the rule of three, so to speak.' Mallory swallowed again. Diana inched over and handed her a cup of water, which she downed in two gulps.

'There was the issue, Sully, of you calling Van Doren and him asserting that we were a legitimate agency. I recall now seeing Jacob demonstrate that he had Mr Night Mayor's phone on him at all times. He tried to be ambiguous and not let you speak, I think, so if you brought it to the real Van Doren's attention again and he denied it ever happening, you would assume he was too stressed and busy to remember talking to you. He used a number of deceptions, with the ring and proximity to Van Doren, to achieve his goal, and tried to make these deceptions transparent.'

Sully's face moved through a smile and a frown and some other emotion Mallory didn't catch.

'Up until Cornelia went missing, it was all to play. A letter we found in Vampire Cemetery directed us to the Mayoral Offices to find Cornelia,' Mallory continued.

'By the medium of a crime upon Occulture: the worst poem I have ever read. Decades from now, children will study this poem in schools as a What Not To Do guide.' Diana crossed her arms.

'Members of the Undetectables had suspected the Night Mayor wished to reopen the old prison said to be in the Mayoral Offices, hidden within the building somewhere. It was here where Cornelia was held overnight, and where Diana and I found ourselves temporarily imprisoned.'

'How did you get out?' Sully shifted against the wall.

Mallory quickly explained the events of that night, up until the point where Cornelia was almost killed.

'We couldn't enter the building,' Sully explained. 'We got the call from Diana, and it took a while to understand where she was, and by then the Offices were alive with Samhain energy.'

'I don't know what happened to Jacob. Did you find him?'

Despite all the death, all the bodies, Mallory was seized by a desire to see him on the slab, just to make sure he was gone.

'We think he's dead, but his body hasn't been recovered,' Sully said. 'There are still teams searching for his remains. But we understand he confessed in full and that the killer was, unequivocally, Jacob Gabbott.'

'And I insisted it was Van Doren, but it was *a* Van Doren in everything but name, so I wasn't totally wrong,' Cornelia added.

'Thank you for that, Mallory. I can't quite write the statement with some of those details in it, but we can figure something appropriate out,' Sully said, ignoring Cornelia. She rubbed her fingers together. 'I'm sorry you ever thought I was a suspect.'

'I told you they might,' Dr Ray said again. Sully elbowed her gently.

'Can you tell us why you were standing around outside our house, and why you asked Jacob about us? Seeing as we're sharing,' Mallory tried. She had nothing to lose by asking.

'I was resistant to the idea of you investigating at first, because it was an insult to my profession for Van Doren to hire what I considered amateurs to do my job – or so I thought. The case got more and more complex and I had no answers, much like you. I had my own set of suspects, but I didn't even look at Jacob. Not once.' Sully sighed. 'I kept away from the Undetectables as much as possible because I thought, and genuinely still do, that there was a conflict of interest there. Folk around you kept dying. You may have been looking at a big, geographic picture of Wrackton, but I was looking at an interpersonal map. You were in the centre of it all. I was worried the killer was someone close to you, or even, goddess forgive me, that it could've been one of you. It was all too close, you were too involved.'

'I may contain multitudes, but not that many,' Cornelia said.

'Then when Theodore died, I didn't believe you. I thought it was a trap of some kind. I'm sorry. I really am.'

'We thought you were attempting to cover up the murder,' Mallory said.

'And here's where I told her that she was going about this wrong. I was her alibi for, I'd say, effectively every single night she wasn't working,' Dr Ray said. 'She didn't want to share that, given how this town likes to talk, and I understood that insofar as not wanting gossip, but look at the mess it made.'

'Thanks for that, Pri,' Sully said.

'This story can't leave this room. Not in this iteration,' Diana said, quieter than normal, and Mallory finally realised she wasn't able to hear her own voice to modulate it. 'I have got no fewer than seventy-eight media requests in the agency inbox, and there have been untold numbers of online posts about this case in the last two days, and they're growing constantly. If we tell this story, it's on our terms.' Diana looked to Sully. 'And it'll be with you. Jacob wants notoriety. Someone, somewhere, is already planning on writing a biography. Imagine the biography. Imagine the straight white Apparent man with no prior knowledge of crime or Occultures writing this biography.'

This made the room laugh, but Mallory got the distinct impression Diana wasn't joking.

'I'll have more questions about everything. We need your account of how you found Van Doren's body, as that evidence was also destroyed, and the location of the cage in question. We need to make sure that what happened is properly recorded,' Sully said.

'What will Wrackton do without a Night Mayor?' Mallory asked, realising the full extent of what Van Doren's death meant. 'Felix mentioned an interim Night Mayor. Will we have to speak to them?'

'That's why I'm here.' Dr Ray stepped forward. 'Well, no. I am here because I wanted to know how the two of you' – she pointed at Cornelia and Mallory – 'got into the mess you did. But I'm also here as interim Night Mayor. The UML agreed, until the by-elections next year.'

This felt like solid, reassuring news to Mallory.

'My first act as Night Mayor will be instating a proper police force.'

Mallory felt her face fall. This was not what they wanted. She looked to Cornelia, whose face hadn't changed.

'This force will be small and headed up by Alyssa. It will be under strict instructions to use only a pre-approved, trusted forensics lab in solving any future cases. It'll be an *actually* collaborative effort. No more of this, what do you call it, "no headline, no help" bullshit that the current police force seem to operate on, and absolutely no having only one point of contact should anyone suspect anyone on the force. Actual case solving. Actual community efforts. Actual, useful regulations. Actual work to make sure nothing like this ever happens again. I will still be the pathologist for the town, but I hope to Elisabella that there are no more murders in Wrackton.'

'I transfer in officially to Wrackton next week,' Sully said. 'I can come and talk to you afterwards, make sure that there's an official contract between us and the Undetectables.'

'Wait.' Mallory felt she'd missed something. 'Dr Ray just said—'

'That's Mayor Doctor, to you,' Dr Ray interrupted, but she was smiling.

'Mayor Doctor said—'

'I said a pre-approved, trusted forensics lab. I only know of one in Wrackton. Well, there was another, but it was set up mostly for anthropology and it was destroyed in the explosion. I will come inspect the premises myself before I sign off on anything. Miss Hawthorne, please keep up. I'm offering you a job.'

'But...' Mallory said. She tried to think how to word what she wanted to say.

'Thank you very much, Doctor Mayor, but my colleagues and I are going to have to respectfully decline. We have one rule, and it's no police,' Cornelia said.

'Rules can be changed.'

'What Cornelia means is...' Mallory said, then shook her head. 'No, actually. She said what she meant. What *I* want to say is that we said no police, because the Undetectables started as a means to help someone who wasn't being helped. The police didn't help this person. We wanted justice for Kuster, to find out who had killed him and how. We wanted to help. I think I can speak for us all when I say we still want that. We will of course cooperate with Sully's team whenever we are required to, and if you have work for us on a case-by-case basis, we will give it consideration. But we respectfully decline this offer of a job. I have a job. I want to do it by my principles.'

She waited for backlash.

'That's quite all right,' Dr Ray said. 'Thank you for your impassioned rejection. There'll be an inquest by the Unified Magical Liaison that you'll be required to give statements for, but it's just a formality. Jacob was playing with old, traditional magic. There's a possibility the option to collaborate will re-emerge after the inquest.'

'And as they say, tradition is just peer pressure from dead people,' Diana shifted. 'I don't know, though. I've got at least three genuine offers of future work to the Undetectables inbox. They were almost buried underneath the press requests.'

'What sort of work?' Mallory asked.

'Missing persons, and a suspected jewellery thief.'

'Excellent.'

'Perhaps things can be excellent when you've rested. We'll leave you for now, check in in a few days. Oh, the funeral for Van Doren is on Saturday, should you wish to be there. It would be understandable if you weren't feeling up to it,' Sully said.

'I am happy to represent you,' Dr Ray added.

Mallory glanced at Cornelia and Diana.

'I don't think we can take another funeral.' Cornelia took a deep breath and winced, clutching her side. Mallory was relieved. She couldn't do it either; she wanted rest. No more death. Just relaxation and back to a life without murders, even for a while.

The room emptied and the Undetectables were alone for the first time in days.

'I think you saved my life, Mallory,' Diana said.

'I did what you would've done.' Mallory shrugged, regretting it when it hurt immensely.

'You saved us a death by a serial killer without any magic. I literally couldn't do that.'

'And we won't even begin on what you did for me,' Cornelia said.

She smiled at Mallory then, holding her gaze for just a moment, an acknowledgement of the intensity of their time in the Empathy

Cage wordlessly passing between them before Mallory broke the stare, fiddling with the ID bracelet on her wrist.

'We are all equally wonderful. I really need to go lie down. Can you call a nurse?' Mallory's body sank deep into the wheelchair seat, aching, searing, begging for rest. Cornelia pressed a call button next to her bed. 'I need rest, and I need help getting to the rest place.'

'Who are you and what have you done with Mallory?' Cornelia asked.

'I realised, somewhere in the Offices, that I don't need to second-guess myself. I thought I needed to be all nice all the time, because that's how everyone perceived me before I got sick.'

'Nobody is always nice. Kind is better. Honest is better. And you're already that,' Diana said.

'I couldn't see it. All the things I choked down were just things I was telling myself I *should* do, as if I had to somehow make up for the fact I have a chronic illness.'

'I was hoping someday you'd realise that you were wonderfully inspirational.'

'There's a pervasive problem in how non-disabled folk see chronically ill folk,' Mallory started, but Cornelia laughed.

'No, I'm not talking about like "wow, this woman puts herself through hell so people without disabilities can feel better about themselves!" kind of inspiration. I just mean…'

'You're a badass. A badass who happens to be sick. But mostly just a badass,' Diana finished.

Mallory's heart lifted slightly. Things had the potential to be okay again. Here in this room, anything felt possible.

THIRTY-SEVEN

*Two weeks after Samhain, but who's
even counting any more*

Mallory knew that Theodore Wyatt had not enjoyed dying the first time while wearing a cat costume, so it was hard for her to comprehend that he would have endured it a second time. But the veil was no longer thin; it was two weeks past Samhain. Mallory had to face a terrible, awful truth about Theodore: he was gone.

It was a hard reality to process, but she was grateful that she had tried to bring him back. He had been miserable as a ghost. He had never wanted it. It was selfish of her to want him in her life longer than he wanted to be, even if she felt like she might break without him there. Nobody ever wanted her to be happy the way Theodore did. He was a friend, and a mentor, and the purest example of a connection she couldn't imagine herself ever having in her life again. There was a hole in her heart where Theodore resided, and she didn't believe she'd ever think of him again and not feel overwhelmed by the magnitude of the loss.

It was raining again, as it often did in Wrackton and had done continuously since Samhain. Mallory slid the curtains in the research room open a crack. She finally had enough energy to take down their murder board, folding all the pieces of TU cases #002–005 carefully into fresh folders with SOLVED stamps on the front, filing them away. This was just another day, despite how few of the Undetectables's close circle remained.

Her fingers closed on a different folder, and then she was pulling out all the files associated with TU case #001, laying them out in front of her.

Mallory turned on the Magic Magical Machine. The room filled with a humming and she had to stop herself from grabbing the iron screens and pulling them around her out of habit.

She pulled out the lightbulb, the one Theodore had first died holding, from its crumpled evidence bag and swabbed it, preparing a sample. The Undetectables, and then Mallory alone, had handled it carefully over the years, and then not at all.

If there was an answer to be found here, she'd find it.

The Machine beeped and produced a new vial, one Mallory held up to the light.

A red swirl curled in the bottom and she clutched it to her chest.

Theodore had been murdered by a witch.

It was not enough for Mallory, but it was something.

Something it had taken her six years to learn. He had been murdered. A ghost knew him, from before.

He was gone, and he was not coming back.

'We got a lead,' Mallory whispered. 'I got you a lead.'

She closed up the Machine and stood to leave, surveying the lab and the research room. It would never feel right without

Theodore, she decided then. No amount of cases, no amount of anything, would make this feel right, but she'd have to make it work.

She turned to go.

Then Mallory felt it, creeping up her legs, stealing its way into her sleeves and into her cheeks.

The warmth.

She felt as though her heart had been wrapped in a hug, and she knew.

She knew as she turned what she would see, and there he was. Standing in front of her, on the spot where he had first died. Cat ears on, whiskers still standing to attention. Tears painted his cheeks in permanent sadness, and his cardigan was somehow bigger on him than ever before, but aside from that, he was him. He was exactly who he was supposed to be.

'Hello, Mallory.' Theodore smiled and opened his arms.

AUTHOR'S NOTE

This book is very much a work of fiction, but as with all fiction, it contains some truth.

The true love of Diana's life, Francine Leon, is loosely inspired by the fascinating historical figure Frances Glessner Lee, who I first came across in a video on the Smithsonian American Art Museum's YouTube channel, 'Murder is her Hobby: Frances Glessner Lee and The Nutshell Studies of Unexplained Death'. Like all people who succumb to information rabbit holes, I found a documentary – *Of Dolls and Murder* – and then Bruce Goldfarb's book, *18 Tiny Deaths*. Like all writers who are people who succumb to information rabbit holes, I was seized with a need to write something about what I'd found.

In the mid-twentieth century, Glessner Lee utilised a lifetime of fascination with murder to become what can be considered the inventor of modern forensic science. Her work not only revolutionised the way a crime scene is treated by investigators, but also inspired the first-ever true crime documentary.

Though she did not obtain a formal education in medicine, Glessner Lee established a long-term relationship with the Harvard Medical School faculty, where she helped design a department of legal medicine in an effort to reduce the annual number of unsolved murders. The department was dedicated to teaching doctors how to identify signs of murder, which was not universally taught at the time.

In the 1940s, over the course of two years, Frances Glessner Lee designed and built what became known as the Nutshell Studies of Unexplained Death. These were a set of scaled dollhouse dioramas of meticulously constructed crime scenes, complete with tiny victims, tiny weapons, and tiny clues. They were to act as training tools for officers at Harvard to learn how to treat a crime scene from the moment it was discovered. The Nutshell Studies were unsolvable – she created solutions as to how each of the tiny victims died, but not the why, nor did she give any clues as to the identity of the perpetrator. At the time of writing, these dioramas are still in use in police training.

In establishing Francine Leon's story, I wanted to honour the genius of Glessner Lee without fictionalising the actions of a real person, particularly one who went out of her way to not become the face of her work while she was alive. And so, in the same way Wrackton is not a real place – sorry, or perhaps not sorry, depending how you feel about it – Francine Leon is not a real person. To my knowledge, the only piece of personal history Leon and Glessner Lee share is the creation of the crime scene dioramas Diana brings to life.

ACKNOWLEDGEMENTS

If you're reading this, please know that I am still alive, and that consequently these acknowledgements made it into the book you have in your hands. Unless you've stolen my laptop, in which case: please stop reading my files, you're going to find out weird things about murder you can never unlearn. I know authors say this all the time, but it really is true – books are not written in a vacuum, and I have so many people to thank for getting me here.

First and most effusive thanks goes to my brilliant (almost certainly magical) agent, Zoë Plant – team precious ghost child Theodore forever! Thank you for making an actual dream come true. Have I mentioned that you are brilliant? Thanks also to everyone at The Bent Agency who has supported me thus far – I feel incredibly lucky every day that I'm supported by such an excellent bunch.

An equally effusive thank you to my wonderful editor George Sandison, for understanding what I was trying to do with the book (and for finding it funny) and really getting the world I built, plot holes and all. (Sorry again about the plot holes.) Thanks also to the fabulous Katie Dent for your careful editorial eye, Julia Lloyd for designing the perfect cover (it's the perfect amount of whimsical and the exact shade of purple I was imagining!) and everyone at Titan Books who has helped make baby's first publishing journey so enjoyable.

A further thank you to the amazing sales teams in the UK, the US and beyond who have championed me so far. At Gill Hess, a major thank you to Jacq and the rest of the team for building the hype and ensuring the book will make it into the hands of readers. To the booksellers who got excited about this book early – thank you a million times over, your support genuinely means the world.

Maybe the next thanks was for the friends who helped along the way – Amy Clarkin and (a second thanks, you're that good) Jacq Murphy, for your invaluable feedback, enthusiasm, and for being wonderful; Robin Stevens, for generally being a genius and giving me time you didn't have to write notes on an early draft; Fran Quinn, for listening to every single garbled plot point and read-out sentence, for your suggestions, daily writing calls, laughing at my awful jokes and your unwavering support – I quite literally couldn't have done it without you. To Deirdre Sullivan and Meg Grehan, for cheerleading and chats, and to the Marybeths, for helping shape my writing habits when I was still figuring out what kind of writer I wanted to be. Thank you to everyone who has been enthusiastic and kind and generally brilliant over the last few years – if I have somehow not thanked you by name, know that I am thanking you in my heart.

To Words Ireland, the National Mentoring Programme, and Dave Rudden – this isn't the book we were working on back in

2020, but it gave me the confidence to see this one through to the end. Achievement unlocked!

To Michael, for being my home, my family, my soulmate, and for remembering I need sustenance to live more often than I do. To circle back to the beginning: you were right. Thank you for believing in me when I don't, and for continuing to believe in me regardless.

And finally, to Alecksyy – who didn't do anything, but just likes to be thanked.

ABOUT THE AUTHOR

Courtney Smyth is a caffeine fiend, one web search away from their newest fixation, and, most relevantly, a writer of stories. Their work has also appeared in anthologies *Into Chaos* and *The Last Five Minutes of a Storm*, and in Paper Lanterns Literary Journal. They have been writing about ghosts, demons and murders since they were ten and have no plans to stop. They are from Dublin, currently living and writing in the West of Ireland with their partner and their pet corn snake, Steve.

@cswritesbooks
courtneysmythwrites.com